TICKET TO RIDE

SHEILA NORTON

Copyright 2014 Sheila Norton

Image: Anneka/Shutterstock (www.shutterstock.com)

Sheila Norton

TICKET TO RIDE is Sheila's thirteenth novel. She has been published by Little Brown/Piatkus (as Sheila Norton and as Olivia Ryan) and also enjoys a successful self-publishing career.

She has also written short stories for magazines including Woman's Weekly, Yours, The People's Friend, etc.

She worked for most of her life as a medical secretary, until retiring early to concentrate on her writing.

Sheila enjoys hearing from readers and can be contacted through her website: www.sheilanorton.com

Books by Sheila Norton:

<u>Romantic comedies:</u>
The Trouble with Ally
Other People's Lives
Body & Soul
The Travel Bug
Sweet Nothings

<u>'The Tales From' series (written as Olivia Ryan):</u>
Tales from a Hen Weekend
Tales from a Wedding Day
Tales from a Honeymoon Hotel

<u>'The Sisters' Series</u>:
Debra Being Divorced
Millie Being Married

<u>Short story anthologies:</u>
Travellers' Tales
Let's Get the Kettle On!

<u>Novels set in the 1960s:</u>
Yesterday
Ticket To Ride

<u>A novel with grandparents at its heart:</u>
A Grand Thing

To find out more about the author and her books, or to apply for email updates, visit : <u>*www.sheilanorton.com*</u>

PROLOGUE

March 1954 : Fremantle, Western Australia

He held her hand as they stumbled together down the gangplank: a sturdy boy with neatly combed brown hair and a small, skinny girl whose bright blonde curls were pulled sharply off her pale little face and plaited into pigtails tied with blue ribbons. The other children they'd been travelling with for so long on the ship, whose cheerful voices and shouts of laughter had buoyed their spirits throughout the voyage, had now fallen as anxiously silent as themselves. There was no pushing and shoving, no hurry or excitement in the disembarkation – just a subdued, orderly shuffling forward into the unknown.

'Don't worry, Susie,' he said, gripping her hand tighter as they neared the end of the gangplank – neared the solid ground of the dock that represented their immediate future. 'Stay close to me. You'll be all right.'

Christopher had said it so often during the past six weeks, it had become a kind of mantra, to calm himself as well as her. *Don't worry, Susie*, when they were called away from their friends at the children's home and told they'd been specially chosen to be sent on this trip, this holiday to a far-off land where it would be warm and sunny. *Don't worry, Susie,* when they were packed off together on the train to join the huge crowd of children boarding the *SS Melbourne* at Southampton – some crying, some quietly frightened, others treating the whole thing as a big lark, singing and joking with their pals. Some had come from such unimaginably distant places as Liverpool, Hull, even Scotland and Wales – places Christopher had only heard of in geography lessons at school. He and Susie were the only two being sent from their own home, and she wasn't exactly his pal: she was two years younger than him for a start, and a bit of a cry-baby. But he felt sorry for her and knew it was his duty to look after her. She was only little, not quite nine yet and she looked like a gust of wind might blow her clean off the ship; whereas he was eleven, almost grown up by comparison, and expecting to go to the grammar school later this year, when they went back home. He swallowed hard. *If* they went back home.

He had no idea why they'd been sent all this long way away, if it was just for a holiday. Nobody seemed to be able to tell them what was going on – but a horrible, sick feeling had been growing in his stomach over the last couple of weeks of the voyage, a feeling that they were all being punished. He didn't know what for, but it must have been something bad, something that meant their various homes and orphanages wanted to get rid of them, and he was afraid it was for good.

He couldn't tell Susie about these fears, of course. Couldn't even voice them to any of the other boys on the ship. Most of them were acting with the same cocky bravado as himself – pretending that sailing halfway round the world with dozens of other kids was nothing more than a super adventure, like something out of a Boys' Own annual. He knew Susie needed him to be big and brave, to keep telling her it was going to be all right, so that's what he'd been doing, and what he'd keep on doing. He squared his shoulders, forced a smile onto his face as he jumped down from the end of the gangplank and helped her down after him.

'Here we are, then!' he said brightly, although in fact he had no idea where they actually were. 'Hang onto my hand, and don't let go, or you'll get lost in the crowd.'

'This way, children – this way, hurry up.' Someone was shouting and blowing a whistle to summon them all together. 'Come on, don't dawdle or you'll be left behind. OK – boys to the left, girls to the right. What's the matter, kid? Don't you know your left from your right?'

Christopher was standing in the middle of the two hastily formed groups, still clutching Susie's hand.

'Yes, of course I know!' he retorted, stung. He wasn't stupid! 'But I've got to stay with Susie.'

'What is she? Your sister?' The man with the whistle stepped closer to them, looking at them both without much interest. 'Tough luck, kid – she goes with the girls, you go with the boys. Unless you're not sure which you are,' he added with a nasty laugh.

'No! She has to stay with me!' Christopher's voice was shaking. He was scared of this man, scared of his loud voice, his huge bulk, the smell of him, the air of menace about him. But Susie was clinging so hard to his hand that her nails were digging into his flesh. He could feel her trembling, hear the sobs she was trying to stifle. He'd promised to look after her. He wasn't going to let her down now, the very minute they'd arrived!

'Troublemaker, are you, boy?' the man snarled – and before Christopher could reply, he was being hauled off his feet by the back of his collar and dragged towards the other boys, who all fell silent and watched with big frightened eyes as he was dropped on the ground in front of them. He scrambled up, searching desperately for Susie, just in time to see her being shoved with only slightly less force into the girls' group.

'Susie!' he shouted as the boys were pushed roughly into a crocodile formation and marched towards some waiting trucks. She looked up, holding out her little skinny arms, crying out to him. Twice, he tried to break away from the crocodile and run back to her – the first time he was shoved back again by the big man; the second time he was smacked so hard across the back of the head that he fell to the ground and had to be helped up by a couple of the other boys.

'Don't be an idiot,' one of them whispered, tugging him along towards the lorries. 'You've got to do what they say.'

He was crying as he finally climbed into the second truck, wiping the tears away crossly with the back of his sleeve, determined not to let the other boys see him reduced to being a big baby. As the truck reversed and turned back past the girls, he saw her for the last time. She was standing alone at the front of the group, staring up at the lorry, looking for him.

'Christopher!' she cried out. 'Come back!'

He scrabbled across other boys' legs to get to the back of the truck, to watch her for as long as he could before they turned out of the docks, out onto the road, leaving her behind.

'I'm sorry!' he tried to yell above the noise of the lorry. 'Don't cry! Don't be scared! I'll come back for you!'

He kept shouting, long after she was out of sight; until his voice gave way to tears again and one of the other lads, a Liverpool boy of about his own age called Adrian who'd been one of his friends on the ship, put his arm round his shoulders and said,

'She can't hear you any more, Chris. You'd better leave off. She'll be all right.'

'I'm going back for her,' he insisted fiercely. 'I'm gonna go back and find her – I will, I swear it! I don't care what they say!'

'All right, whack. Yeah, all right,' the other boy agreed.

The truck chugged on, and on, for hour after hour in a sweltering heat such as none of them had ever experienced, and the boys stared in silence at the unending miles of dry and uninhabited countryside, wondering if this was really the beautiful new land, the sunshine holiday they'd been promised.

And as some of his companions finally dozed off to sleep, Christopher rubbed the sore place on his hand where Susie's nails had gouged him as he was dragged away from her, and repeated his vow to himself, over and over, like a prayer.

I'm going back for her. I'm going to find her. I'm going back for her. I'm going to find her. I will. I will. I will!

Chapter 1

December 1968 : Shanklin, Isle of Wight

Jack Hunter had disappeared. Not that anybody had been looking for him up till now, because nobody had realised he was missing. His girlfriend, Frankie, thought he was at home with his mother on the Isle of Wight. His mates in the band thought he was with Frankie in Essex. It wasn't until he'd missed dates with both, that the truth became apparent – he'd either been abducted by aliens, or he'd done a runner.

Rob couldn't make it out. Why the hell would anyone *do* that – just bugger off, without a word to any of his mates, without even leaving a message or having the decency to at least phone one of them? He'd thought he and Jack were good mates. They started the band together. If he'd been in trouble, Rob would have helped him, for crying out loud – Jack should have talked to him

Of course, Jack hadn't been his usual self since he'd been going out with Frankie. He'd been going on, and on, to anyone who'd listen, about how special she was, how different from all the other girls. They'd all taken the Mickey out of him – he'd got it bad, all right. Well, that was OK, as long as it didn't interfere with what had always been the most important thing in their lives – the band, the music, the gigs, the rehearsals.

When he hadn't turned up for a rehearsal on a Tuesday night halfway through December, the boys assumed he'd stayed over in Essex with Frankie. He'd been there for the weekend – he'd taken to doing that whenever the band didn't have a booking on a Saturday night. But they always got together on Tuesdays and it was annoying that he just hadn't turned up. He could have phoned.

'Give him a call,' Bernie said.

'What's the point? He won't be at home – he'll be over there with her, and she's not on the phone.'

Rob didn't even feel like trying to call him, anyway. When all was said and done, if he was starting to put his new girlfriend before his mates, his band, what did that say about him? About them, and their future – just as they were beginning to get more bookings, more popularity, as a result of appearing at the new pop Festival on the Island in August.

'It's gonna be a problem,' Pete said, voicing what they were all thinking. 'It was never gonna work – him going out with a bird who lives so far away. He's gonna start wanting to spend more and more time over there.'

'Yeah.' Rob stubbed out his cigarette, crossly. 'What the hell is he playing at?'

'Let's give him a break,' Bernie said, shrugging. 'He might be sick, or anything. I still say one of us should give him a call, or go round and see him, maybe tomorrow, and find out what's going on. Instead of just thinking the worst.'

It was true – Rob *had* been thinking the worst of him – and thinking the worst of Frankie too – imagining she was trying to get him under her thumb and keep him away from his mates. He had to admit, he'd been feeling vaguely annoyed with Jack ever since he'd been going out with Frankie, and he knew it had more to do with his own feelings than anything Jack had done wrong – and that was hardly fair. So the next day after work, rather than phoning him, he went round Jack's place himself. Better to front up and have it out with him – if he was there, of course.

It was dark and raining when he walked up to Jack's house, but there weren't any lights on inside. Rob had to knock about three times before Jack's mother eventually peered through the window at him, looking like she was scared he might be the bogeyman calling. When she saw who it was, she opened the door just a crack but seemed determined not to let him in.

'Is Jack there?' he asked. He'd known Betty for years, so he couldn't understand why she seemed so nervous, like he was a stranger.

'No. He's gone,' she said.

If he hadn't been holding onto the door, because he'd been expecting to go inside, he got the impression she would have shut the door straight away.

'What do you mean, *gone*? Gone where?'

'Just gone.' She wouldn't even look Rob in the eye. 'Packed his bags and left.'

'Packed his bags? What – gone for, like, a holiday, or what? Gone over to the mainland, has he, to see his bird ... I mean, his young lady?'

Still she wouldn't look at him. She pushed at the door a bit, trying to get him to go. What was the matter with her? Maybe they'd had a row – that would explain why she was acting so odd. It wasn't like Jack, he'd always been so good to his mum. Betty wasn't a very well woman. She was probably only the same age as Rob's own mother, about fiftyish, but she had bad arthritis and couldn't get around very well. Jack said that was why he still lived with her. He'd always looked after her, ever since they moved over here to the Island from London when his father died. Rob couldn't believe, even if he'd argued with her about something, that he'd just walk out on her, unless ...

'He hasn't gone to live with her, has he?' he said. 'Is that it?' No wonder she didn't want to talk about it, if that was the case.

But she just shook her head. 'I don't know where he's gone. He didn't say. But he's gone, all right?'

All *right*? Rob stared at her. No, it wasn't bloody all right! It was all wrong! He couldn't believe Jack hadn't told his mum where he'd gone, and he couldn't believe she was acting so funny about it, either. Rob was even more convinced now that Jack had gone over to Dagenham to be with Frankie, and that Betty was naturally upset about it.

'Are you OK?' he asked, feeling concerned for her. 'I mean – he *is* coming back, isn't he?'

But she just pushed the door a bit harder, so he had to step back out of the doorway.

'Goodbye, Robert,' she said – and there was something so final in the way she said it, it made him actually shiver. And then the door was shut.

'He's buggered off to be with *her,*' Pete agreed when Rob reported back to him on the phone later. 'The bastard! He might at least have told us he was going!'

'I know. I can't believe it. We're gonna have to cancel Saturday night if he doesn't come back soon.'

They had a booking at a function in Sandown – a big one. And another one the following Friday. They wouldn't be able to perform without a lead vocalist, even if Pete or Rob were to take over lead guitar. It would involve so much extra rehearsal, it would be ridiculous.

'And if he's not back by the twenty-second ...' Rob began slowly, the reality of the situation beginning to really hit home.

'Oh, flippin' heck! The Up Beat Club!' Pete said, groaning. 'We can't cancel that!'

The Up Beat was a club in Stratford, in east London, where all the big bands had played. There was a rumour that it was owned by some big shot in the East End gangland – but whether or not that was true, it had given some of the bands their best breaks. It was well known for featuring 'undiscovered' bands on Sunday evenings, with tickets only seven and sixpence (six shillings for ladies) – and those bands often went on to have hit records. The boys had managed to get a booking there, for the twenty-second of December. It was by far the most exciting thing that had happened to them since they'd started the band, and it was all because someone had seen them, and liked them, at the festival in August. He was a manager from London who was there to pick up new talent. He'd got the band this slot at the Up Beat Club and was going to come and watch them there. If he liked them, he was going to try and get them a recording contract.

'There's no way he's gonna miss *that*,' Pete said after they'd both calmed down somewhat. 'He'll be back in time for that, for sure.'

'Well, if he isn't,' Rob said, 'then he needn't bother coming back at all, as far as I'm concerned.'

Nobody could forgive someone who let their mates down as badly as that.

A couple of nights later, with still no word from Jack, Rob had a phone call from Frankie.

'Hello,' he said, without bothering to ask how she was. 'What the hell's going on?'

'What do you mean?' she said. 'I was phoning to ask if you knew where Jack was. His mum wouldn't tell me, and now it seems like she's had the phone number changed, or something.'

'Oh.' Rob took a deep breath. 'He's not with you, then?'

'No. He was supposed to come last night, but he didn't turn up. I tried to call him, but his mum was funny with me. She just kept saying he wasn't there, he'd gone. What's happened?'

'I don't know, Frankie. We haven't seen or heard from him since the weekend, so we just assumed – me and the lads – we assumed he'd stayed over there with you. We're really pissed off – sorry, pretty annoyed with him. He didn't show up for rehearsals on Tuesday night and no-one can get hold of him.'

'He hasn't been at home at all?'

'No. I went round there Tuesday night, but his mum was really odd with me too. I thought they might've had a row.'

'Why? He thinks the world of his mum! What would he row with her about?'

'How would I know?' he said irritably. 'Jack's been so different since he's been going out with you.' He paused and sighed. 'Look, to tell you the truth we all wondered if he'd abandoned us – his mates, the band – to be with you. Just as we'd got what we've all been working for all this time – the manager, the booking at the Up Beat Club, the chance of a recording contract – he's buggered off, turned his back on it all without even having the guts to tell us.'

'No, he wouldn't do that! You know how excited he is about it all! The band's the most important thing to him!'

'It *was*,' Rob said pointedly. 'Till he met you. Now, that seems to have changed, if you ask me. He's never missed rehearsals before, and we've got a big gig on Saturday night. We're gonna have to cancel. We're bloody furious with him, if you want to know the truth, Frankie. We all reckoned he must have run away with you or something.'

'Well, he hasn't!' she retorted. 'I've just told you – I phoned his mum, and I tried again last night but there was no reply.'

'Didn't you keep trying?'

'Yes, I did!' she snapped. 'There's no need to get funny with *me,* Rob, I'm just as worried as you are! I ran out of change in the end. I had to walk through the pouring rain to the phone box, and there was a queue of people waiting to use the phone by the time I'd hung up and tried again three times. In fact there are two people waiting outside now, looking like they're getting cross – and my money's going to run out any minute.'

'All right, I'm sorry. Look, if your money runs out ...'

'I'll call you again, all right? Tomorrow, about the same time? Can you go back round to his mum's again? Please? Try and get her to tell you – I bet she does know where he's gone. He *wouldn't* just walk out on her like that. Or you. Or me,' she added, sounding like she was going to start crying. 'I know he wouldn't.'

'Yeah, OK,' he agreed. 'You're right, it doesn't make sense. If he's not with you ...'

'He must be staying with one of his mates.'

'I've tried them all. Everyone we could think of. Nobody's seen him. He hasn't been to work – his boss said he'll give him his cards if he turns up now.' There was a silence. 'I don't know what to think, now, Frankie,' he added. 'It's ... very weird. I don't know what the bloody hell he's playing at.'

'Me neither,' she said quietly – and then there was a long beep as her money ran out. For a few minutes Rob sat there holding the receiver, staring into space, then he jumped up and got his shoes and coat on. He needed to get to the bottom of this, and Frankie was right – the only way was to go and see Betty again. If necessary, he'd insist on going inside this time, and stay there till she told him what was going on.

The house was in darkness again. He knocked, twice, then tried peering through the front window, but the curtains were closely drawn. So he knocked again – so hard, so many times, that eventually a woman came out of the house next door.

'There's nobody there, love,' she said, folding her arms across her chest.

'Are you sure?' It was hard to believe. Betty had a lot of difficulty getting out and about without help. If Jack wasn't around, she'd be stuck indoors. He glanced at the front window again. No sign of movement. 'Have you got a key?' he asked the neighbour. 'Only – look, I'm a friend, and I'm worried about them. About Betty. I ... don't know if she might have had a fall, or something.'

The neighbour shook her head. 'I told you. She's not there. They've gone.'

'How d'you mean, gone?'

'Well, when I looked out the window this morning, early like, there was a van out here. And all Betty's things were being loaded into it. I came out to ask Betty if she was moving, because she hadn't said anything – and I got told to mind my own business. Betty went off in the front of the van, looking straight ahead – no goodbye, not even a wave or a nod of the head, nothing. I couldn't believe it. We've always been friends. I've made her a Christmas pudding! I always do, every year, but she's not going to get it now, is she? I don't even know where she's gone!'

'You mean ... they've *moved*?' Rob said, stunned.

'Well, that's what it looks like, don't it, dear? And never a word! Not a goodbye, or ...'

'And was Jack with her? Her son?' he interrupted before she could start off about the Christmas pudding again.

'Not a sign of him. I haven't seen him since ... oh, I don't know, since Sunday probably. I think Betty said he was over the mainland at the weekend to see his girlfriend again, but he was definitely back on Sunday night. Heard him on his flipping guitar, and haven't heard the damn thing since. That's a blessing, if nothing else!' She sniffed. 'Still, they were good neighbours, when all's said and done. I reckon they've got behind with the rent and done a runner. She might've said goodbye, though – telling me to mind me own business like that! Huh!' She turned to go back into her own house, calling over her shoulder: 'If you find her, you can tell her Gladys says she'll have to go without her Christmas pudding this year!' And she slammed the door, leaving Rob standing on the path, feeling the sleet on his face and a cold fear stealing into his heart.

Something was wrong. There wasn't any logical explanation for this. If they'd had to move house, whatever the reason, Jack would have *told* him. He'd have told his girlfriend! Perhaps he and his mum were in some sort of trouble, and Rob just hoped that in a day or two, he'd contact his mates, and they'd find out what it was all about.

But the weeks went by, and nobody heard a thing. They tried to find a new vocalist but there wasn't time, before the Up Beat Club gig, and they had to cancel that, as well as everything else. They were upset, needless to say, but they were worried too. Frankie kept calling, crying down the phone to Rob, and he felt helpless with pity for her. He wished she'd give up and find someone else. Eventually they found someone else for the band, too. Luckily Dave, the manager, still wanted to give them another chance, and he'd got them another booking at the Up Beat Club, so they were rehearsing like mad with Andy, the new bloke. He seemed to have fitted in well.

Jack Hunter? If it wasn't for Frankie, and the fact that she kept phoning, hoping he could help, Rob would have given up by now and tried to forget about him. Like he seemed to have forgotten about everyone else.

Chapter 2

Dagenham, Essex

'Let's face it, people don't just suddenly vanish off the face of the earth, do they,' Frankie's friend Lou said, looking kind of satisfied about it, as if she'd been proved right. 'There has to be an explanation.'

'What sort of explanation?' Frankie said, not that she really wanted to hear the answer.

Lou was a year or so older than Frankie and a bit of a hippie. When Frankie had started at the bank as a typist straight from school at sixteen, she'd looked up to Lou, and tried to copy her hair and clothes, but she only ended up getting into trouble when her beads dangled over the Gestetner machine and the supervisor said they might strangle her. But since Frankie had been going out with Jack, there'd been a different, slightly cooler feeling to their friendship.

'Well – all that stuff about being in love with you!' Lou snorted, and Frankie wanted to hit her. 'It was a load of rubbish. He obviously *didn't* really care about you at all, did he. He's finished with you.'

'If he has, he's finished with everyone else too!' Frankie said crossly, trying not to cry. Crying wasn't going to help, especially not in front of Lou. 'His mates, his job – even the band!'

That was the most incredible part, the part that there was no explanation for. Jack would *never* have deserted the band! Even if ... Frankie swallowed hard. Even if he had deserted her!

Lou shrugged. 'Well, at least you didn't give in and sleep with him,' Lou said. And then, because Frankie didn't answer, she stared at her and added in a whisper: 'You *didn't*, did you?'

'So what if I did?' Frankie was so narked with her, she pretended to feel braver about it than she really did. Inside, she was desperately scared. She knew what a risk she'd taken.

'What – you went all the way?' Lou said, sounding horrified. 'He did use something, though, didn't he?'

'No. I told him it'd be all right.' Even though she was annoyed, she was hoping Lou would reassure her. 'Just once won't hurt, will it?'

'Are you mad? Are you joking?' Lou dropped her voice as the supervisor turned to look at them. 'What – is this because of being Catholic – all that stuff about not using contraception?'

'Course not! I don't care about all that! I had enough of it from the nuns at my school!'

'Well, I hope for your sake you're not pregnant. You must be mad!' Lou said again. 'And now he's left you – what did you expect? That was obviously all he was after, and once he got what he wanted ...'

'Oh, shut up!' Frankie got up and went out to the toilet, ignoring the look the supervisor gave her. She didn't want anyone to see she'd finally lost the battle against the tears that had been threatening all morning. She washed her face and looked at herself in the sink. What the *hell* had happened to Jack?

Lou had been with her, back in August, when she'd first met Jack. In fact if it hadn't been for Lou, and her boyfriend Terry, she probably never would have met him. They'd got tickets for the first ever Isle of Wight Festival, and Lou wanted Frankie to go with them. Apparently her mother wouldn't let her go anywhere overnight with Terry on their own until she was twenty-one.

'You have *no idea* how lucky you are, living with your sister,' she said.

Frankie did know, perfectly well, and never forgot it. Until she'd moved in with Marianne, her life had been so constrained by her own mother, she'd hardly gone anywhere or done anything. But living with her sister hadn't suddenly given her access to a trust fund. The festival tickets, according to Lou, were twenty-five shillings each.

'I can't afford it,' she'd told her. 'I have to give Marianne most of my money, for my keep, and I don't have much over.'

'That's OK,' Lou said. 'Terry's treating us both. He earns a lot more than we do.'

So of course, Frankie had accepted. Who wouldn't, for the chance of a trip to a rock festival! That first year, it wasn't even called the Isle of Wight Festival – it was rather more grandly billed as *The Great South Coast Bank Holiday Pop Festivity*.

'It's been advertised as *the greatest pop festival ever held in this country*,' Lou said, proudly, as if she'd organised the whole thing herself.

Lou always took on this air of superiority whenever she was talking about music – on account of the fact that Terry was the drummer of a pop group. They were a local group from Dagenham, called *Butterfly Wings*. Terry sometimes picked her up from work in his Morris Minor, which had butterflies painted on the doors in psychedelic colours. Some of the girls were madly jealous of her but Frankie wasn't, because Terry might have been a drummer with a pop group, but he was a drip. He was tall and gangly, with a high-pitched whiny voice and a silly giggle like a girl's. Frankie was sure that if she ever got to go out with someone in a group – and she wanted to, desperately – he'd need to be a lot more of a man than drippy Terry. But now, as things had turned out, she was thinking perhaps she should have been careful what she wished for.

The festival had been amazing. It was held in a field, and the stage looked like it was an old lorry trailer, but some of the biggest bands of the time were performing there: The Move, The Pretty Things, Tyrannosaurus Rex, and even Jefferson Airplane, who'd come over from America for it.

It all kicked off at six o'clock, with a local group from the Isle of Wight playing first. They were called the Crazy Snakes, and they were nothing like any of the bands that normally appeared in the dance-halls back home in Essex, or anything like all the flowery hippie people at the festival.

'Look at *them*!' Frankie shouted in Lou's ear, trying to make herself heard above the noise. They were all dressed in black – black shirts, black leather trousers, wild hair, wild black looks. They prowled up and down the stage looking like they wanted to hiss and spit at the audience rather than smile at them. And they *belted* out their numbers. Stuff like the Rolling Stones' *Jumpin' Jack Flash* and Manfred Mann's *Mighty Quinn*.

'They're good,' Lou shouted back.

'Not bad,' Terry said, pulling a face, 'if you like that sort of thing.'

His own group liked playing nice gentle songs like *San Francisco*, with lyrics about wearing flowers in your hair, or pretty romantic songs like *Everlasting Love*.

'They're fantastic,' Frankie said, staring at the lead singer of the Snakes as they launched into *Mony Mony*. She could have sworn he was looking straight back at her – but obviously, that was ridiculous, when the field was packed with so many people.

'You ain't seen nothing yet,' Terry yelled in his whiny voice. 'All the big bands will be on later.'

The atmosphere of the crowd was like nothing Frankie had experienced before. Everyone was singing along, swaying to the music, jigging around to keep warm. After it got dark it was unbelievably cold – considering it was only the end of August. Frankie and Lou had got sleeping bags, though, and ended up getting zipped up in them soon after midnight. They huddled together for warmth and drank cider while they sang along with the music.

Lou fell asleep eventually, leaning against Terry's shoulder. After a while Frankie felt cramped and told Terry she was going to stretch her legs. It was when she was pushing her way back through the crowds that someone shouted out at her from the middle of a noisy group sitting close to the stage.

'Hello, Blondie!'

He was standing up, staring straight at her, and she realised with a shock of excitement that it was him: the lead singer of the Crazy Snakes. And close up, he was even more electrifying than on the stage. He was *gorgeous*.

'That's not my name,' she said, trying to be cool. He was pushing his way through his mates and coming closer.

'Didn't mean anything by it. It's just – I saw you, in the crowd. When we were on stage. It was your hair I noticed,' he said. 'It's beautiful.'

She gulped with surprise. Blimey! Nobody had ever said anything like that to her before. Sometimes other girls said they wished they had long blonde hair like hers – mainly since Marianne Faithfull had been so popular – but ... *beautiful*? She didn't know how to respond.

'So what is it, then?' he went on.

'What?'

'Your name. What is it, or is it a secret?'

'Oh – Frankie. It's short for Francesca.'

'Nice,' he said. 'Did you like our act, Frankie?'

'Yes. You were fantastic.'

She wasn't normally shy, but she was overcome by the fact that he was bothering to speak to her at all. He was so good-looking – dark and really tall, much taller than her – not that this was difficult as she was only five foot two. And he must have been at least twenty, probably even older.

Frankie hadn't really had a proper boyfriend – her mother had hardly let her out of her sight when she was living at home. Recently she'd been out a few times with a boy who worked in the post room, who'd kissed her experimentally in the back row of the Odeon, and dumped her when she didn't want to go any further. She didn't care. She wasn't too bothered about getting another boyfriend unless he was in a rock band. Music was all she cared about – she was crazy about it. To Frankie there was a big difference between going out with someone in a rock band and going out with just any old body. So it was unbelievable to be standing there with the lead singer of the Crazy Snakes staring into her eyes. She had the strangest feeling her life was never going to be the same again.

'You haven't told me *your* name,' she pointed out.

'Sorry – I'm Jack. Jack Hunter. Listen – Fairport Convention are coming on now. Stay and watch them with us. We've got the best view of the stage from here.'

'But my friends will be wondering …'

'I'll help you find them afterwards.'

He found a spare corner of one of the groundsheets where he'd been sitting with his mates from the band, and he introduced her to the others as they sat down together. There wasn't much space, and they were really close together. She could hardly breathe.

'You're frozen,' he whispered.

'I've got a sleeping bag. But I left it back there, where my friends are.'

'Here.' He took off his leather jacket and put it round her shoulders. On top of her light summer coat, it felt really heavy and snug. 'Let me warm you up a bit,' he added, putting his arm round her and pulling her even closer. She couldn't help thinking her mum would have a fit if she'd known what she was doing – after all, she didn't know him at all. But she leaned against him, closed her eyes, and they sat together like that, listening to one of the best bands of the night. She didn't want it to end!

It was a shout from Lou that finally broke the spell. She and Terry were heading towards them from across the field.

'Frankie! Where the hell have you been? We've been looking for you everywhere!'

'Sorry!' she said. 'You were asleep. I told Terry I was going for a walk.'

Lou stared at her. So did Terry.

'Oh! This is Jack,' she said quickly. 'He's the lead singer of the Crazy Snakes – you know, the first band that played.' She was so proud to have met him, especially introducing him to soppy Terry whose own band wasn't a patch on Jack's, that it didn't occur to her how it must have looked. She still had Jack's leather jacket on, and he still had his arm round her. 'Jack, these are my friends Lou and Terry.'

'Hello,' Terry said. He didn't sound too charmed.

'Hi, Jack,' said Lou. She gave Frankie a look, and she felt herself blush.

'We need to get going, Frankie,' Terry said.

'Yes. Sorry.' She took off the leather jacket and handed it back. 'Thank you.' She glanced up at Jack. She liked him so much already, she knew she was blushing bright red. Even though it was dark and drizzly, she felt sure he must have noticed. He could probably feel the heat coming off her cheeks.

'You're welcome, Frankie.' He put his arms round her again and, in full view of Lou and Terry, he bent down and kissed her. It was a proper long, slow kiss and it certainly knocked spots off her previous experiences in the back row of the Odeon with the boy from the post room.

Terry cleared his throat loudly, and Lou squawked 'Flippin' *heck*!', and she surfaced slowly from the kiss, smiling into Jack's amazing deep brown eyes.

'Do you really have to go?' he asked.

'Yeah. Unfortunately.'

'Can I call you?'

'I'm not on the phone.' Her lips were still stinging and quivering from his kiss, so it was difficult to even talk.

'Well, here's my number.' He got his cigarettes out of his pocket, tore the flap off the packet and borrowed Frankie's lipstick to write the number for her. 'Give me a call, right?'

As they walked out of the field she kept looking back at him until she couldn't see him anymore. She felt like she was in a dream.

'Well, that was a fabulous night,' Lou said as they got settled in Terry's car. Neither she nor Terry had spoken up till then – it was like they didn't know what to say about Jack so they were just pretending it hadn't happened. She yawned and stretched. 'The best night of my life.'

'Yeah, mine too,' Frankie said. She closed her eyes, still thinking about that kiss, and after a while she fell asleep. But she knew she was going to call him; she knew, even then, that it was going to lead to something – something exciting.

She wasn't to know, of course, that before long she'd be wishing she'd never met bloody Jack Hunter, never sat there with his leather jacket on, and definitely never let him kiss her. But how was she supposed to know that only a few months later, he was going to disappear off the face of the earth like some kind of magic act, but without the puff of smoke?

Chapter 3

Dagenham

While December drifted on, freezing cold and miserable, Frankie continued to call Rob almost every night to see if there was any news, any change, any sign of life at Betty's house in Shanklin. It was frustrating living so far away, and talking to Rob was the only way she could feel involved in the search for Jack. Apparently he and the other boys from the band had contacted everyone they could think of, but nobody seemed to have a clue where he was. There weren't any old school friends to call, as Jack had only moved to the Island seven or eight years previously, and it was only now he'd gone missing that his band mates realised how little they knew about his previous life. He'd never even told them exactly whereabouts in London he used to live or where he went to school.

At first, Frankie had wanted to call the police. She'd been terrified that Jack might be hurt, or that someone could have taken him somewhere against his will. But Rob reminded her that his mother had gone too, apparently voluntarily, snubbing her neighbour in the process.

'For some reason best known to the two of them, they've chosen to disappear off the radar,' he said.

'So you don't think the police ought to ...'

'Frankie, I seriously wonder if this is something to *do* with the police. Maybe he was in some kind of trouble. Did he ever mention anything like that to you?'

'What – you think he was involved in something dodgy? No, of course not!' she retorted. 'Anyway – you've all known him much longer than I have. If he had some sort of dark secret in his past, he'd have told *you*, not me!'

'I guess so. Well – you're welcome to keep calling, but to be honest, I don't know what else we can do.'

And then, eventually, one evening Rob told her:
'There's a new tenant in the house. They can't be coming back.'
'Did you talk to them? The new tenants? Do they know anything?'
'Of course I did. But they haven't got a clue. The landlord just told them the property was unexpectedly vacant.'
They were both silent for a moment. Frankie felt like they'd finally reached a dead end.
'I suspect one day he'll just bounce back into our lives,' Rob said, trying desperately to sound optimistic, to cheer her up.
'Oh, will he!'
Suddenly, she felt furious. Furious with Rob, for trying to jolly her along by making this whole thing sound like little more than a game of hide-and-seek. Furious with herself for what she'd done – for *doing it* with Jack, despite all the warnings she'd heard all her life, particularly from Marianne who had taken her to one side when she'd realised how serious Frankie was getting with Jack and quietly begged her to be careful. But mostly, she was furious with *him*. And she was sick of pretending, even to herself, that she wasn't.
'Well, he needn't think he's going to bounce right back to *me*, Rob, because I tell you what – he's got another think coming! He can bugger off, that's what he can do! He needn't think I'm sitting around every night crying over him, because I'm not – right? I'm going to get on with my life, and I don't care if Jack *never* comes *bouncing back*. And if he does, you can bloody well tell him I said so!'
'All right, Frankie,' Rob said gently. 'Don't cry.'
'I'm not crying!' she yelled, and put down the phone. She wouldn't bother to phone him anymore. There wasn't really any point now, was there?

She walked three times round the park before she went home. By then, she'd dried her tears. She looked up at the front room window of her sister's house and saw that while she'd been out, they'd put up the Christmas tree. The lights were sparkling red, blue, green and yellow, and there were paper chains hanging inside the windows. *Christmas*. She'd forgotten about it, and it was only a couple of days off.

She let herself in, and stood for a while in the lounge doorway staring at the tree. She could imagine her little nephew Joel's excitement in the morning when he was brought downstairs. She was aware, now she started to think about it, that Marianne had been working hard over the last couple of weeks – making the Christmas pudding and the cake, so that they had time to mature, going out shopping and returning with her basket full of Christmas presents. Wrapping them up at night after Joel was asleep. Writing cards, buying special treats like biscuits, dates and nuts and squirreling them away so that nobody started on them before Christmas Day. All this had been going on while Frankie hid away in her room, moping and crying over Jack. Well, she was done with that. If he cared so little about her that he couldn't even tell her where he'd gone, then he didn't deserve her love any more, however hard it was to believe or understand. She'd have to grow up, and shape up, and get over it.

She found Marianne in the kitchen, washing up – and went straight up to her and put her arms round her.

'I'm sorry. I've been awful lately. I haven't helped you, not with Joel, or Christmas, or anything.'

'Don't be daft.' Marianne hugged her back. 'I know what you've been going through. I just wish I knew what to say, to make it better.'

'Nothing. You don't have to say anything. From now on, Mari, I'm going to stop being so stupid.'

'It's not ...'

'It is!' she said crossly. 'It's stupid to waste my time over him, isn't it, because he obviously doesn't care about me, whatever he said. So I'm just going to get on with Christmas, and get on with ... everything.'

'Good for you, little sis.'

Frankie swallowed hard. *Stay strong*, she told myself.

'Now, are there any clean tea-towels? Let's get this lot dried and put away. The Christmas tree looks gorgeous. Shall I make some more paper chains?'

And her sister hugged her again and looked like she was going to cry herself.

Marianne was three years older than Frankie, and had rescued Frankie from their mother's stifling clutches the previous year.

Things had really come to a head back then, with Frankie becoming more and more resentful about being treated like a child, never allowed to go anywhere or do anything, and she'd finally told her sister she couldn't stand living at home any more. Marianne understood exactly how she felt, because she'd been pregnant with Joel when she and Grant got married, and their mother, Hilda, had never got over it. She'd had a face like a prune right through the wedding and she'd never left off about it since.

Marianne had tried her best to stick up for her little sister.

'She's seventeen, Mum! If you carry on treating her like a kid, she'll end up rebelling.'

'So you think I should let her go out gallivanting with the boys, do you?' Hilda had shot back at her. 'Getting herself into trouble like you did, and bringing disgrace on the family? One wayward daughter was bad enough.'

Marianne was livid. 'I'm hardly wayward! I'm a perfectly respectable wife and mother – married according to the rituals of your precious Catholic church!'

'Don't you go defiling the name of the Holy Mother Church, young lady! I don't suppose you've set foot inside St

Teresa's since your wedding day! Not even to have your poor child baptised, God bless his poor little soul!'

Marianne looked at her sister, shaking her head, but Frankie just shrugged. She reckoned it was a waste of time to argue.

'We got married at St Teresa's for your sake, Mum,' Marianne said quietly. 'You know perfectly well we have had Joel baptised. You refused to come to the christening.'

'Christening! Is that really what you call a pathetic ten-minute blessing at that take-it-or-leave-it Anglican church? All the non-believers have their children baptised there, just so they can have a big party afterwards.'

'OK, that's it.' Marianne stood up, bright pink with annoyance. 'I came round to try to talk to you about Frankie. I might have known it was just going to provoke another string of insults about me and my marriage.'

'I don't need you interfering, and nor does Francesca,' Hilda said. 'As long as she's living under my roof she'll abide by my rules, and the less influence you have over her, the better.'

'In that case, Mum – I'm not living under your roof for another single day!' Frankie had joined her sister at the door. 'Marianne says I can go and live with her, and that's what I'm going to do, whether you like it or not.'

'Over my dead body! You're underage, young lady, and you'll do as I say! Go to your room now until you're ready to apologise for that outburst.'

'She might be underage, but she's allowed to leave home if she wants,' Marianne said. 'I'll wait for you, Frankie, if you want to pack your bag now.'

Their mother looked like she was going to pass out. Frankie went upstairs to pack, and when she came back down with her bag, her mother and sister both looked like they'd been crying. She never found out what else had been said between them, but it felt like it was her fault. It wasn't a nice feeling. But the benefits of living with Marianne had soon helped her to get over it.

All over Christmas time, Frankie managed to keep up the bravado. She bought last minute presents, helped Marianne with the dinner, played with Joel, kept up the happy family chatter over the turkey and the pudding. But by New Year, she knew she was going to have to talk to her sister. She was almost a month late, and she'd been feeling sick and imagining she was getting fatter. She'd heard all these things whispered about by other girls, but had no idea how long you were supposed to leave it before you went to the doctor to find out whether you were actually having a baby. *A baby!* She felt hot with shame and panic as she remembered that time – that one time, late at night after everyone in the house had been asleep, when she'd got so carried away with Jack she hadn't been able to say no. *Surely* she couldn't be that unlucky – after just one mistake?

Marianne didn't even need to be told, though. She'd seen the pinched look of anxiety on Frankie's face, noticed the unused packets of sanitary protection in her drawer, and felt like her own heart was going to break for her. A week or so into the new year, she found Frankie lying on her bed, looking pale and ill. She sighed and sat down next to her.

'Is there something you need to talk to me about?' she asked her sister gently.

Frankie shook her head. 'I'm OK,' she said, giving Marianne a smile. 'Just ... really bad period pains.'

'Oh. Poor you – I'll get you some aspirin and a hot water bottle.' She stroked Frankie's hair back off her face and swallowed back her feelings of relief. Relief mixed with something a little harder to define. Before her marriage, Marianne had been training to be a nurse, and she'd learned something very few people talked about: that a late, heavy period was often, in fact, an early miscarriage. She was never going to know whether she'd guessed right. But she was sure as hell never going to tell Frankie that she realised it was a possibility.

As far as Frankie was concerned, everything was OK now; everything could go back to normal and she could *really* forget all about bloody Jack Hunter. Wherever the hell he was.

Chapter 4

January 1969 : At sea

There was no going back now; they'd soon be there. Jack was up on deck, leaning over the rail staring at the miles, and miles, and miles of bloody endless ocean, and wondering how the hell it had ever came to this. Although the need to leave had always been a possibility – he'd even prepared for it, some time ago, just in case, going through the whole procedure and having his application accepted, without actually booking his passage – he'd never really believed it was going to happen – that he'd actually have to go, ever, let alone so suddenly.

Obviously, the hardest part was leaving everyone behind. It had almost broken his heart to abandon the Snakes, especially as they were so close to getting a manager and a recording contract. He'd lain awake every night in his bunk, trying to stop the agony of thinking about Frankie by wondering about the band instead. Had they found another lead singer? Did they get to do the gig at the Up Beat Club? Had they gone on to make their first record, without him? They must hate him for the way he'd deserted them, letting them down at the most crucial time possible, and without a word of explanation. But probably not as much as Frankie must hate him.

Frankie. How was he ever going to get over it – leaving her behind, probably never seeing her again? He knew he had to face it, she'd find someone else, and how could he blame her? It was eating him up, wondering how she reacted to him disappearing the way he did. Did she cry? Did he break her heart? Or was she just plain livid? That was what he preferred to think – that she'd ranted and raved, called him all the names under the sun and sworn to forget him. He could imagine her now – her face red with anger, her eyes flashing, tossing her beautiful hair and saying what a bastard he was. *That's my girl!* he thought. He didn't want to imagine her crying. Thinking about that could tear him up inside. They hadn't been going out for all that long – but oh boy, she sure had got to him. She was something special. He was never going to forget her.

When he met her, it had actually felt like an electric shock. She was like a little bit of dynamite, with her bright blonde hair and her energy and excitement about life. Jack's mother had even warned him about getting involved with her – and she'd been right, in a way. Frankie was only eighteen, educated at a convent school and kept cloistered away from men by her mother till she left home a year or so before. Whereas he, at twenty-seven, sometimes felt like he was old before his time. He'd seen life – a bit too much of it – and he'd sometimes felt jaded by it. It was only when he was performing with the band that he got back his zest and enthusiasm.

His life should have turned out differently. He was the cleverest kid in the class at his primary school back in east London, and the only one who passed the Eleven-Plus to go to grammar school. He was a wartime baby and they were poor – like every other family in the area – but he was the only child and his father had wanted him to do well. He used to take the young Jack to the library at weekends, and to museums and art galleries, and when he started taking an interest in music, his parents had scraped together the money for him to have guitar lessons. They couldn't afford a guitar – he'd had to borrow one from the teacher – but eventually when he was old enough to have a paper round he'd saved up till he could buy his own. He still remembered the thrill of that day – holding his very own acoustic guitar. He was fourteen years old, it was 1955 and Bill Haley and His Comets were belting out *Rock Around the Clock*, and he was pretty sure that he was going to be a rock star some day.

He'd done well at the grammar school, went on to do A-levels in maths, physics and music – that was always his best subject – and he ended up with good enough grades to get offered a place at university. His parents were over the moon – nobody else in their family, nobody they even knew, had ever been to university before. His ambition had been quite modest – to become a schoolteacher, probably teaching maths and music. But that was always only going to be the bread and butter job, because by then he was already getting together with other students to form rock bands, their names and line-ups changing term by term as the various members lost interest, left university and moved away, or formed different bands of their own. It didn't matter. One day, Jack knew he'd get the right mix of people together, with the right amount of talent, and they'd make it big.

And then, halfway through his second year, his father had died, and nothing was ever the same again. Jack had to leave university. They moved to the Isle of Wight and he worked as a plumber's mate for a neighbour who had his own business. Eventually he went to college part-time and got his qualifications. He never really thought about university, or becoming a schoolteacher, after that – none of it seemed relevant to his life any more. But he never stopped trying to get his perfect band together, and it finally happened with the Crazy Snakes. They were good. They were going to get somewhere, he was sure of it. It was the only thing in his life he really cared about – until he met Frankie, anyway. Now he'd left them both behind.

If it wasn't for the fact that he knew he had to get on with it – make a new start and survive, somehow, on his own, he could easily have just sat around, now, feeling sorry for himself and drinking himself into oblivion. It wouldn't have been difficult. When he'd boarded the ship in Southampton it had felt strangely like he'd stepped into a lifestyle he'd never even dreamed of. The ship was huge – there were at least a thousand of them on board, all heading off into the unknown. There was a swimming pool, dining rooms, bars, cinema, library and all sorts of sports facilities like deck quoits, tennis and ping-pong. They weren't going to be allowed to get bored on the journey: the crew organised games, competitions, sports tournaments, dinner dances and even fancy dress evenings. Of course, he'd brought his guitar with him, and for the sake of something to do he'd entered a talent contest early on in the voyage, and won first prize. Since then, he'd often been given the opportunity to play and sing to the guests before the resident band started their set every evening. It didn't make him feel any better about leaving the Crazy Snakes behind, but at least it kept him in practice, and right now it was a relief to have something, anything, to occupy his mind for a while and keep him from the endless thoughts of what he'd left behind.

Sometimes at night when he couldn't sleep, he came up here on deck and looked down into the blackness of the ocean, wondering if there was actually any point going on. The further they sailed – away from Britain, away from Europe – the worse he felt, the more he convinced himself that he'd never come back. If that was the case, he might as well jump into the drink, as sail right round the world to who knows what, who knows where. He was so depressed he couldn't even be bothered to make friends with the three blokes he was sharing a cabin with. They spent their whole time in a state of excitement, talking about the new life ahead of them, and they obviously thought Jack was some kind of weirdo because he just wanted to be left alone with a beer, his guitar, and the memories he was struggling with.

And now he was struggling with more than just memories. He'd been overcome by a ridiculous urge to do something he absolutely shouldn't do. It was madness – he knew he shouldn't even be considering it. But every time he went through the same circle of thoughts about Frankie – round and round in his head: Did she hate him? Did she try to find him? Did she cry – was she still crying? Or had she washed her hands of him and found someone else? – every time, the ridiculous little urge had got stronger. Would it really hurt? If she ever loved him – and she'd told him she did – didn't he owe it to her at the very least to let her know he was still alive? Should he take the risk? What it came down to was: could he trust her?

He kept thinking back to that last weekend when he'd stayed overnight with her. She'd never done it before – never been with anyone – and he hadn't expected her to want to ... but she'd said she loved him, she trusted him, she knew he wasn't going to leave her. Thinking about it again now, he groaned and turned away from the ocean, running back to his cabin to grab his guitar and play himself into oblivion. His cabin-mates were all out, probably in the bar as usual, making the most of the last few days of drinking and carousing before they docked. Before they had to get on with it, start all over again: new homes, new jobs, new lives.

Jack put down the guitar again and took a deep breath. If he didn't do it now, would he ever do it? Would it be too late, the moment lost – would the weeks roll into months, and into years, and the love of his life be forgotten, without him making even this one last attempt to put things right? To at least *apologise*?

Before he could change his mind again, he got out the airmail pad he'd bought from the ship's shop when he'd first started to have these crazy urges. Or maybe not so crazy. Maybe the best thing – the only thing – to do. He found a biro lying on one of the other boys' bunks. He could post the letter as soon as they docked; or better still, he could wait till he'd sorted out a post office box, then he could give her the address in case ... He sighed. Why was he kidding himself? There wasn't the slightest chance she'd ever want to write back to him!

Still, he opened the pad and started to write.
Dear Frankie...

Chapter 5

February 1969 : Dagenham

It was Valentines' day, and Frankie had got a card from a boy at work called Tony – one of the trainees. She knew it was him, because his mate had already told her he fancied her and every time he looked at her he went red. She didn't like him much: he was really immature. But she was thinking maybe she should go out with him just to, well, just to get on with things. Prove she'd got over You Know Who.

Not that she really needed to prove it to anyone. She was over him now, completely, totally, forever. If she was angry before, about the way he'd disappeared, it had been tempered a little by the fact that she was also still anxious that something bad might have happened to him. But now – now she was beyond angry. She was beyond anxiety, beyond forgiveness. She'd got a letter from him. It had been such a shock – of course, she'd recognised the writing straight away, and for a minute her heart had felt like it was doing somersaults. Yes, for a minute she was actually, stupidly, really excited to think he'd finally written to her. And then she realised: it was in one of those blue airmail envelopes – with an Australian stamp.

'AUSTRALIA?' she screamed, dropping the letter onto the carpet in front of her as if it had burnt her. 'Bloody *Australia*?'

Joel went running to his mum, upset about her shouting, and Marianne came out of the kitchen, staring at her.

'Is it from *him*?' she said.

'Yes.'

'Open it, then.'

'No. Put it in the bin. *Australia*, Marianne? Could he *go* any further away? WHY? Why didn't he at least tell me?'

'Open it, Frankie. Or you'll spend the rest of your life wondering. I'll bin it for you afterwards if you want me to. I'll burn it in front of you, if that's what you want. But read it first.'

So she'd picked up the letter, and carried it up to her bedroom, holding it by the corner like it was contaminated. She sat on her bed for at least ten minutes before she finally ripped the envelope open. There was just a single sheet of paper inside, and this is what it said:

Dear Frankie

I know there's nothing I can say to make this easier. If you don't read this letter, if you just throw it away without even reading it I couldn't blame you. I can't even ask you to understand what I've done, because it's not something I can explain. You just have to believe me – I didn't have any choice. I couldn't tell anyone where I was going – and nobody knows. Nobody except you, now. You're the only one I can trust, the only one I'm telling that I'm just about to land in Australia. I'll have a PO box and I'll put its address on the back of this letter before I post it, in case you want to write back. If you don't, I'll understand. Please don't hate me, I honestly didn't have any choice, Frankie, otherwise I'd never have left you. I love you, and I'd never have wanted to hurt you, that's all I can tell you for now. But this is very important – please don't tell anyone, not even the boys in the band – don't tell them I've written to you, or where I am. I know I can trust you – I know you won't let me down. I can't come back, Frankie – that's all I'm saying. What I'd really like is for you to come and join me. Do you think you could do that? If by any chance you still love me, come to Perth and we can be together again. We could get married! All you have to do is go to Australia House, apply for Assisted Passage, get the forms. It only costs ten quid but it takes a bit of time. They want young people out here, you'll get in. In a few months you could be out here with me. Please say you will. At least think about it. I hope you can forgive me.

All my love, for ever – Jack.

The whole letter was in one long paragraph, written on both sides of the sheet. By the time Frankie had finished reading it she was steaming mad. She screwed it up and stuffed it angrily in the bin, then picked it back up, smoothed it out and read it again, hardly able to believe what she was seeing. He *had no choice*? He couldn't explain, but he had no choice? What rubbish was that? And – he couldn't come home? What was he talking about? Perhaps Rob was right after all – Jack was in trouble with the police for something. Well, bugger him, then, if he couldn't even tell Frankie what it was all about! He said he loved her, but he couldn't even ask the one question that should have been bothering him if he really cared about her at all. She presumed it was probably all the emotional upset that had made her period so late, but what if she *had* been pregnant? What would be the use of applying for a bloody Assisted Passage to bloody Australia then? Come to think of it, how did *he* get to Australia so suddenly, if it was supposed to take months to get one of these Assisted Passages? It looked to Frankie like he had this planned ages ago – before he even met her. Before he took her in with all this *rubbish* about loving her. Lou was right – she was a fool. All he wanted was to have sex with her before he went off to Australia. And now it looked like he was playing with her, suggesting she should go out there, all on her own, and that they could get married! What? Did he really think she was stupid enough to fall for that one too?

Well, she might have been a fool for him once, but never again. She was better than that. As far as she was concerned, he could stay in bloody Australia forever, and you wouldn't catch her running after him on some assisted bloody passage.

Don't tell anyone, he said? Well, why would she? Who would care? Nobody, not even the boys from the band – she guessed they'd have got themselves a new lead singer by now and good luck to them! In fact, she had a sudden thought that she might just give Rob a call and see how they were getting on without him. Why not?

She screwed the stupid letter up again and couldn't even be bothered to take it downstairs to burn it. Just to show how little she cared about it, she lobbed it across the room and it landed on top of the wardrobe. Well, it could stay there. And she knew what else could go up there too – a stupid teddy-bear he'd given her – he'd won it for her at the funfair in Dagenham's Central Park, the day after ... the day after *that* night. She'd kept the stupid thing sitting on the end of her bed all this time. At first she'd cried and hugged it every night – pathetic. But now it was just sitting there, reminding her of something stupid she'd done, that she'd prefer to forget about. So, that could get lost as well.

She slung it up on top of the wardrobe too. In fact she threw it so hard, it bounced out of sight behind her suitcase. Out of sight, out of mind.

When she went back downstairs, Marianne just looked at her and said 'Are you OK?'

'Yes,' she said. 'It was just ... a load of rubbish.'

Marianne didn't say any more. But after Frankie made them both a cup of tea, she announced that she might go out with Tony from work. Marianne looked pleased, although the truth was that Frankie wasn't too sure she could really be bothered. She thought she was probably better off on her own.

After dinner, she went down the road to the phone box and tried to phone Rob. She hadn't thought much about the Crazy Snakes since they'd given up trying to find Jack, but now she suddenly really fancied catching up with him. Unfortunately, though, his brother Paul answered and said he was out at a rehearsal.

'I'll tell him you called,' he said. He sounded like he thought it was a huge joke. 'Shall I tell him you said Happy Valentines?'

'No!' she said sharply. Paul was an idiot. He was only about sixteen – Rob himself was quite a bit younger than Jack – and he seemed to be at that stupid stage where he couldn't even talk to a girl without being pathetic. 'You can tell him I just called to say hello, and I was wondering how the band are getting on.'

'They're doing all right,' he said. 'They've got a new bloke, Andy. He's good. Better than your stupid boyfriend.'

'He's not ...'

'He let everyone down. Rob says he was a waste of space after he started going out with you. More interested in getting inside your knick...'

'Oh, *shut up*, Paul!' she said. 'And bloody *grow* up, too! *You're* a waste of space, if anyone is!'

After she hung up, she was annoyed with herself. Losing her temper with Paul was pointless – he was just a stupid kid and it was hardly fair to take out her anger about Jack on him. Anyway, probably Rob wouldn't think much of her when his brother told him she'd shouted at him. So that was that. Maybe it was just as well. If they'd got talking, she might have been tempted to spill the beans about having a letter from Jack. Not that she could care less about his stupid *secret* about being in Australia. As far as she was concerned, Australia was welcome to him.

Chapter 6

Shanklin, Isle of Wight

Rob was surprised at his own reaction when his brother told him he'd missed a call from Frankie. He didn't know what to make of it. Could it be that she'd heard from Jack? Or could it … could it possibly be that she'd just wanted to talk to him? He felt his pulse quicken at the thought of it. She hadn't called since just before Christmas, and she'd been so upset that last time, talking about Jack, saying stuff like she wouldn't care if he never came back. And she didn't fool Rob at all – she was crying her eyes out while she was saying it. He'd thought about her a lot since then – just wondering how she was, of course: whether she's got over him now, the bastard. He'd often wished he could have given her a call, if only she'd been on the phone. He'd always thought she was a nice girl, and he felt sorry for her, the way Jack had treated her. He felt a bit bad, too, that he'd blamed her at first for Jack's disappearance.

Paul had told him she bit his head off on the phone – he suspected his brother had said something stupid to her. He hardly ever said anything that *wasn't* stupid. Well, good for her, it made him laugh to think of her having a go at him. She had spirit, that was what he liked about her. Well, one of the things he liked.

OK, he might as well admit it. He liked her, full stop. Sometimes he wished she'd never met Jack and got hurt by him – but then again, if she hadn't met Jack, *he* wouldn't have met her either. It seemed such a long time ago now – the festival last August. When Jack suddenly walked off to chat up that little blonde who was on her own in the crowd, all his mates had laughed and nudged each other. He'd always been one for the girls – never stayed with them for long. Everyone could see Frankie was a lot younger than him, though. Rob had even had a go at him about it, telling him she was only a kid and he ought to watch his step with her. Jack had laughed and told him to mind his own business. Anyway, that was it: right from the start, he seemed to be hooked. He stopped chasing after other girls. He said she was special. And ... well, maybe Rob thought so too, although he'd never have admitted it.

Rob and Jack were different in many ways, but they'd been good mates. Rob wouldn't have dreamed of going after his girl. He kind of looked up to Jack, really. He had a lot of respect for him as a musician, and the way he looked after his mum – Jack had only come over to the Island because Betty wanted to get away from London and he didn't want her to live on her own. Not many blokes would do that for their mothers. So even though Jack was five years older than him, he reckoned it was fair enough if he wanted to play the field, have a bit of fun instead of settling down with someone. And if it all changed suddenly when he met Frankie, well Rob sure couldn't blame him. He just had to pretend he wasn't jealous.

The problem was, now he knew she'd called, he couldn't stop thinking about her. All day at work, while he was serving giggly teenagers in the record shop in Sandown, he wasn't really concentrating, and when he gave the wrong change to some bloke, the boss had a go at him. He needed to pull himself together. But he couldn't get over the fact that she'd phoned *him.* Was it just to make sure he still hadn't heard from Jack? Was she still hung up on him? Still missing him? He hoped not. Paul had said the message was just to say hello and ask how the band was doing.

By the time he got home that night he'd worked himself up into enough of a state about it to consider sending her a letter – if only he knew her address! He didn't somehow think 'Francesca Kennedy, Dagenham, Essex', would reach her, however much the GPO might pride themselves on being able to deliver anything without a full address. Anyway he still sat down in his room and started doodling a few lines of nonsense ... the things he would have liked to say to her, if only he could. If only he dared! When he looked at what he'd written, later, after he'd had his dinner, he felt pretty stupid. He started to screw up the piece of paper. If Paul were to find it, he'd never live it down, that was for sure – some of the stuff he'd written was excruciating! Even if those were the words of a song, they'd be cheesy ...

And suddenly, Rob knew exactly what it meant when, in kids' comics, they show a picture of someone with a light bulb flashing over their head. He'd never believed before that it actually happens. That flash – that moment when you suddenly realise you've had a brainwave. He didn't get many of those! He unfolded the bit of paper again and had another read. OK, yeah, some of it was so cheesy, he was almost blushing at the thought of Frankie ever reading it. Good job she wouldn't. But for a song ... maybe it could work? If he used *that* line, and maybe changed this bit around ... and used *this* bit for the chorus ... think of a rhyme for this, add another line there, and there ...

He'd got his guitar out now, and he was singing the words to himself as he played a few experimental chords. Well, he was whispering the words actually – Paul was only in the next room. The tune seemed to be inventing itself as he went. This could work. All of a sudden he was getting shivers down his spine. He'd never done this before. He was crazy about music – it was his job and his hobby, his whole life really, but he'd never been a song writer. He couldn't believe he was actually doing this! But he had a strange feeling about it – so strange, that it overcame his embarrassment enough for him to get on the phone to Pete as soon as he'd finished playing about with the words, jotting down the chords and a rough outline of the melody.

'I've written a song,' he said, trying to dampen down his excitement, hoping he didn't sound too ridiculous.

'Yeah?' At least Pete wasn't laughing. 'Cool. Come over, yeah? Let's see it.'

It was gone half past ten but Rob wasn't going to argue. If he left it till the next day he'd probably decide it was rubbish and bin it. If he showed it to someone right now, at least he'd know straight away whether he was kidding himself.

Pete was the only one in the band who rented his own place. He was older than Rob, about Jack's age, and he'd been married. He and Lisa had tied the knot far too young, and within two years she'd left him. So there was no-one else there to worry about. The boys had all their rehearsals at his place, and got together there whenever they wanted. Pete was also the only one who'd done any song writing, in fact they'd performed a couple of his compositions. They were good. That was why Rob had come to him. But he was trying not to look Pete in the eye as he handed him the sheets of paper with his scrawl and his very rough notation on. He felt like he was letting him read his diary.

Pete looked up when he'd finished reading.

'Sing it,' he said.

'Aw, no, it's not really finished, the tune's not right ... I just thought I'd show you ...'

'Come on, sing it.' He handed Rob his guitar. He hadn't brought his own. 'Play some of the chords at least. I really want to hear it.'

Still not looking him in the eye, Rob took back the pages, strummed a couple of chords, coughed a bit with embarrassment, and then thought – to hell with it. And started to sing.

When he'd finished, it was suddenly very, very quiet in the room.

'Bloody hell,' said Pete after a minute.

'A load of rubbish?' Rob said, laughing awkwardly, feeling even more stupid now that he'd not only revealed his feelings about Frankie on paper, he'd also, once he'd got over the timid start, let rip at the top of his voice, screaming out those lyrics to the rooftops. Like he wanted her to hear him, all the way from Dagenham.

'No, mate,' he said. 'You're joking. It's good. Really good. Only ...'

Rob was so amazed that he liked it, he could hardly squawk out a response.

'Only what?'

'Only ... bloody hell, Rob. I never knew you felt like that about her.'

'Nor did I.' He shrugged, the awkwardness coming back. 'Well, I suppose I did, but I couldn't ... you know. Let myself admit it.'

'But now he's gone – Jack – are you thinking ...?'

'No. She's probably still hung up on him. And anyway, she lives bloody miles away. I don't even know her address, she's not on the phone, so ...'

'OK, I get the picture. Well, I tell you what, mate – at least something good's come out of it!' He took the sheets of paper back and looked through them again. 'This could be really great. Can I make a couple of suggestions? I think you should repeat the last refrain, bring it in again even louder, and then just *here*, I think it needs a progression through A minor, D, and then ...'

He took the guitar back and demonstrated, and suddenly Rob was managing to forget the embarrassment of it all and found himself getting enthusiastic – as enthusiastic about the song as Pete seemed to be. Pete got them both a coffee, and they were up most of the night, working on the finer points of the music, twitching a chord here and a lyric there, until he finally punched the air and said they'd got it, it was there, it was perfect and they'd have to show the other guys.

'It's nearly three in the morning,' Rob reminded him, and they both started yawning at the same time, and then laughing with relief when they remembered it was a Sunday. No work to get up for.

'Later, this afternoon, then! I'll call them. I want to try this with the drums. Get the full score written. Get the other boys' vocals sorted.'

'The other ...?' Rob looked at him, puzzled. 'Well, Andy'll be taking the lead.'

'No, I don't think so.' He grinned. 'After the way you belted it out tonight, Rob, I reckon you should lead on this one.'

'Really?' Rob had never sung the lead part with the band before.

'Definitely.' Pete got up and walked him to the front door. 'It's your song, and nobody else is gonna sing it the way you can.'

'Like a strangled cat?'

'No, mate. Like a bloke in love with a bird he can't have.'

Chapter 7

April 1969 : Dagenham

Frankie was at her new evening class when it happened. Her sister turned up at the college, and was brought to her classroom by the principal. Marianne stood there, white-faced at the front of the class, while he explained something to the shorthand teacher in a low, grave voice. Frankie looked up in surprise from practising her thick and thin pencil strokes, through the line, under the line, curved and straight, different angles that represented bafflingly similar sounds – to see Marianne standing next to her.

'It's Mum,' she said, her voice trembling. 'She's in the hospital. They think she's had a stroke.'

The two girls sat on either side of Hilda's bed, holding her hands, staring at each other in shock.

'Why don't you go home and get some rest?' one of the nice nurses told them eventually. 'There's really nothing you can do for the moment. The next twenty-four hours will be critical.'

But Frankie didn't want to leave.

'You go,' she told her sister. Marianne had just found out she was pregnant again and she'd been feeling really sick. 'I'll stay here with her.'

'We'll call you if there's any change,' the nurse said.

'I'm staying,' Frankie insisted. She was on the verge of tears. 'I've done nothing else for her for years, have I.'

'Don't start thinking like that,' Marianne said. 'This isn't your fault. It isn't anybody's.'

But she just shook her head and held on fast to her mother's hands. She'd been a bad daughter, a terrible daughter. And now it was probably too late to make up for it. But the least she could do was try.

The days passed like a long, dark, nightmare. She took leave from the bank, and sat by Hilda's hospital bed every day until she was close to dropping with tiredness. Marianne and Grant took turns to relieve her, and between them they watched as Hilda gradually started to respond. She could move one arm and leg but not the other, and she couldn't talk – when she tried, she got very confused and frustrated. But Frankie discovered she could still read, so she started writing notes to her, telling her little things about Joel, for instance, and her mother would read them, slowly, and try to smile.

After a while Frankie was able to take her out in a wheelchair. She pushed her round the hospital grounds, and Hilda would point at things with her good arm and grunt. Frankie had to respond, like she would to a baby: 'Yes, it's a blackbird. Oh, look at the pretty flowers.' Of course, for a long time she and her mother hadn't been close – but she'd always been a strong, domineering woman and it almost broke Frankie's heart, now, to see her reduced to this.

'Your mum's speech will hopefully come back, to some degree, with regular speech therapy,' the consultant told her at an assessment after a few weeks in hospital. 'But I'm afraid it's likely that she'll always be profoundly disabled.'

'Always?'

'I'm afraid so. Many people wouldn't have survived such a severe stroke. Your mother's lucky to be alive.'

Frankie didn't answer. She wasn't too sure she could agree with him.

'How much longer will she need to stay in hospital?' she asked.

'Strictly speaking, she doesn't need to be here anymore. She can be treated as an outpatient for physiotherapy and speech therapy. But ...' He hesitated. 'I understand she lives on her own.'

'Yes.' She looked down at the floor, feeling the guilt all over again. If she'd been living at home with her mother, could she have done anything to prevent the stroke? Surely she'd at least have found her afterwards, on her living room floor, sooner than the neighbour who'd looked through the window, concerned about the milk left on the doorstep?

'If there's nobody at home to care for her, the family will need to consider moving her into a nursing home. She certainly won't be able to manage on her own.'

'Oh. I see. No, of course she won't.' She swallowed hard. 'Well, I'll need to talk to my sister, and ...'

'Of course you will. It's a very difficult situation for the family.' He smiled at her sympathetically. 'But I'm sure you'll make the right decision for your mother.'

The right decision. All the way home on the bus, after she'd seen Hilda settled down for the night, those words kept running through her head. The right decision. Right for whom? What was the doctor trying to say? *Was* there a right decision – or simply an easier one, a more convenient one? By the time she'd arrived home, she'd made up her mind. She wasn't happy about it, but she was completely resolved.

'I'm going to move back in and look after her,' she told Marianne.

Her sister nearly dropped the teapot. She stared at Frankie in dismay.

'What? You can't ... ! Frankie, listen, you have no idea what you'd be taking on! She isn't going to get better, you know. Or maybe a little bit better, but not – you know – not ever like she was before.'

'I know. The doctor told me.'

'So she's going to need care, Frankie – I mean professional care. You can't ... you'd have to get her in and out of bed, help her to the toilet ... you wouldn't be able to do it, love, not on your own.'

'I know. You can get help, apparently. People who come in every day and help with all those things. If I don't do that, Mari, she'll have to be put in a *home*!' she said, starting to cry. 'Is that what you want?'

'Nursing homes aren't prisons, Frankie. She'd be looked after, cared for properly.'

'Yes, by strangers! She'd hate it, you know she would. She'd want to be in her own home.' She nodded defiantly. 'And I want to be there, looking after her.'

Marianne sat down, sighing.

'This isn't about you leaving home – falling out with her – you know,' she said gently. 'It would have happened anyway. There's no need for you to feel any responsibility. None of us wanted anything like this to happen to her, of course we didn't. But it doesn't change the fact that she gave you a hard time when you were growing up. You don't have to feel guilty for the fact that you wanted to get away from her.'

'I don't. But I'd feel guilty for the rest of my life if I didn't step up to the plate now this has happened. You can't help – you've got Joel, and the new baby coming. It's different for me. I'm single, I haven't got any ties. This is what I have to do. You know it's what's best for Mum.'

'Maybe it is. But what about *you*? You should be going out, enjoying yourself.'

'I'm not bothered about all that,' she said. 'I'm all right as I am.'

Since she'd finished with Tony from work – and in fact that had hardly even got started, she'd only gone out with him for a couple of weeks before she realised they had absolutely nothing in common – she'd decided to concentrate on her career. That was why she'd enrolled for the shorthand classes. She occasionally went out with Lou and the other girls, but she really wasn't that bothered.

'I'm going to tell them tomorrow, at the hospital, that I'm moving back in with Mum,' she said. 'I'll still come and see you and Joel, all the time, and help you when you have the baby.' She stood up and hugged her sister tight. 'I'll miss you. You've been so good to me.'

Marianne held onto her, looking like she was struggling not to cry.

'If your mind's made up,' she said finally, 'Grant and I will do whatever we can to support you. I just hope Mum appreciates what a sacrifice you're making.'

Frankie wasn't quite that deluded. She doubted Hilda would ever appreciate it. She'd never been one to show any gratitude or appreciation, even when the girls had tried to do little things to please her when they were kids. Frankie could remember picking wild flowers for her from hedgerows on the way home from school and giving them to her like they were a wonderful bouquet. They were probably already wilting from being held tight in her sticky little hands – but surely most mums would have put them in a jar and at least pretended to be pleased – not just thrown them straight in the bin? If Frankie had brought home a picture she'd painted of 'Mummy' when she was at infant school it'd be put on the fire instead of being pinned on the wall like she saw other mothers doing. No, Hilda was never a nice cuddly mummy – she was always more concerned with the doctrines of the Church than she was with her children's emotional needs. If Marianne was thinking that Frankie was making some last ditch attempt to win their mother's love, she needn't have worried. Frankie knew perfectly well that she wouldn't ever be capable of giving it – stroke or no stroke.

She moved back into her mother's house early in May. She wanted to get everything ready before Hilda came home from the hospital – clean up the house, air her own old room, put fresh sheets on the beds, get some shopping in. She only had evenings and weekends to do everything, but she didn't mind being busy. They booked a nurse to come in every day to help look after Hilda. And then she had to talk to her supervisor at the bank.

'I'm sorry, but I'm going to need to get away sharply after work in future,' she explained. 'I wondered if I could work through lunchtime and leave earlier?'

The supervisor looked at her dispassionately.

'That's a pity. I thought you had ambitions – that you were hoping to be promoted one day.'

'Yes, well, I'll have to put that idea on hold. I won't be able to carry on with the shorthand course now anyway.'

'OK.' The woman shrugged and turned back to her work. 'I'm disappointed, Francesca, but if that's what you want …'

She didn't even bother telling Lou. They weren't really close friends anymore.

By the middle of May, Hilda was settled back at home, and with the help of her speech therapy, she was to managing to say a few words, although Frankie was the only one who could understand her. Marianne kept saying how much better she was looking, and Frankie did actually start to feel like the sacrifice had been worthwhile. If nothing else, the family had been reunited.

Then, on the morning of the sixth of June, the supervisor told Frankie there was an urgent phone call for her. It was her mother's nurse, to say she'd had another stroke and was back in the hospital. This time, there was nothing they could do. The supervisor actually drove Frankie to the hospital, but by the time she got there it was too late. Marianne arrived soon after and they both just sat there, stunned. Frankie couldn't even cry. She just couldn't believe that after everything they'd done, Hilda had only survived such a short time.

'You'll always be able to look back and know you did your best,' Marianne said.

Frankie knew that was true – but in a really selfish kind of way, she felt like, in the end, it wasn't even worth it.

The funeral was a quiet affair. There were a lot of Hilda's friends from the church, of course, but no-one else apart from Marianne, Grant and Frankie. There was no other family – Hilda had been an only child, and she hadn't stayed in touch with Frankie's father's family after he died. Grant helped her clear out her mother's stuff; it wasn't a nice job but she didn't feel particularly emotional about it. And in a box at the back of her wardrobe, where she'd kept her marriage certificate and loads of other old papers and photos, they found a copy of her will. Frankie was quite surprised – Hilda had never mentioned that she'd made one. It was dated 1953, the year after Frankie's father died, so she guessed his death was what had prompted her to do it.

'I expect it's just standard stuff,' Grant said, unfolding it. 'Your mum never had much money, after all, did she.'

'No. Just her pension, and her share of Dad's. I think she had a savings account, but I don't suppose there was anything much ... What?'

Grant had sat back in surprise, with the will on his lap. He was blinking very fast like he'd had a shock.

'What?' Frankie said again. For a minute she wondered if all these years, her mother had kept a hidden stash of money somewhere – a fortune she'd never told anyone about, all the while she was living off her pension in a council house. She leaned over Grant's shoulder to have a look, but he folded the will over so she couldn't see it.

'We need to show this to a solicitor,' he said. 'I ... don't understand it.'

'What don't you understand? Show me!'

'Frankie,' he said, and she felt suddenly frightened by the tone of his voice. 'Your mum wrote in her will that she wanted everything shared three ways.'

'Three ways?' Frankie frowned, and then laughed, guessing: 'Go on – I bet she wanted to leave most of it to the Church. Right?'

'Wrong.' He took a deep breath. 'I ... don't know if I should tell you ... show you this, without Marianne being here.'

'Well, if it's something bad,' she said, getting worried now, 'for heaven's sake don't spring it on Marianne while she's feeling so poorly with the baby! Tell me first. Come on – what the hell is it?'

He unfolded the paper again and handed it to her. She read through all the legal garbage, wondering what on earth could have made Grant go so white with shock. And then she saw it for herself.

... all my assets to be divided equally between my three daughters ...

'Three ...?' she tried to say, but the word got stuck somewhere. She thought it must have been a mistake. She stared at the text of the will again.

... my three daughters: Susannah Margaret Kennedy, Marianne Rose Kennedy, and Francesca Grace Kennedy.

'Flipping heck,' she said quietly. 'We've got another sister somewhere.'

What the hell had happened to her, and why the *bloody* hell had Hilda never mention her – ever?

Chapter 8

June 1969 : Perth, Western Australia

For the first three months, Jack had been checking the post office box every day on his way home from work. Three months with no reply, not even to the second letter he'd sent, a month after the first, in case it had gone astray. That one came back to the PO box, unopened, with 'RETURN TO SENDER' scrawled on it in angry capitals. The message was clear enough – but still he couldn't stop checking. Just in case.

He kept telling himself he should forget about her. It wasn't like he could find out, from anyone else back in England, whether she was OK, whether she still hated him for what he did to her, even whether she'd met anyone else. Nobody knew where he was – not even his mother. He knew *she* was all right; he'd sent her to live with her cousin in Wales before he left, but he couldn't tell her where he was going. Sometimes he had nightmares that Betty might die before it was safe for him to go back to England, and he'd never know about it. Other times, he had a different nightmare – that Frankie might tell someone she knew where he was. He knew he shouldn't have contacted her; it was stupid, and dangerous – but he'd had this ridiculous hope that she might have agreed to come out to Australia to be with him. It had taken him three months of checking the post before he finally began to understand that it was never going to happen. He must have been crazy to imagine it would. She was only eighteen, and they'd only been going out together for a few months. But that's what Frankie had done to him – sent him a bit crazy.

After three months, he told himself he had to move on. He should have been good at that, after all. He'd already moved halfway round the world, and left everything behind him.

When they'd finally docked in Fremantle, it was early morning and Jack had come up on deck to be half-blinded by the sight of miles and miles of dazzling white sand. The sea was a vivid turquoise blue, the sunlight so intense that everything looked as if it had been bleached. For the first time, he'd felt a slight lifting of his spirits – but then he remembered he hadn't come here for a nice holiday in the sunshine. It was a whole new life – on his own, and possibly forever.

The new immigrants had spent nearly the whole day being checked in at the passenger terminal before being put into a taxi and sent to a hotel in Perth for the first night. By then, he was half dead with sleep, and when he woke up for breakfast the whole thing still seemed quite unreal. But he couldn't afford to sit around feeling sorry for himself – he had to get a job. He'd spent so much money on beer on the ship, all he had left was the fifty dollars he'd been warned he had to keep to show the immigration people. It was a decent sum of money to get him started but it wasn't going to last forever. Ten dollars went straight away on a week's rent in a boarding-house, where he had to share a room as well as helping with the chores. It felt worse than being a student again.

The guy he shared with was luckily almost as morose as Jack, for reasons best known to himself, so he was spared any interrogation about his past life. Within a couple of days he'd been taken on by a kitchen and bathroom fitting company. The pay was good and it didn't take him long to move out of the boarding house and into a rented place of his own. That was the good thing about this new country. If you wanted to work hard, you could get on – and he did want to. He didn't have anything to go home for, after all. The boss seemed pleased with him, and before long he put his wages up again. Jack began to feel a little better. The climate was great – he spent a lot of his spare time at the beach; he'd learned to surf, got a tan, got himself fit. But he was so bloody lonely. He had no friends, and he was living like a monk, playing his guitar on his own in the evenings, always with a couple of beers to cheer him up. He knew he couldn't go on like that indefinitely. He couldn't keep living for the day Frankie might turn up. He had to face it – the whole idea was a fantasy. Of course she wouldn't come. And he needed some company.

There'd been girls on the ship, of course – single girls, lots of them emigrating to Australia with their friends. It was obviously a huge adventure for them, leaving their parents and families behind. The taste of freedom had made some of them throw caution to the wind. They'd drink away their savings in the ship's bars every night, kiss strangers on the deck in broad daylight and take them back to their cabins late at night when their friends were asleep. Jack hadn't had any trouble turning them down – however much they fluttered their eyelashes at him while he was singing and playing his guitar. He told them all he had a girlfriend, he was spoken for, wasn't interested. In time, like his cabin-mates, the girls had left him alone.

And now, there was a girl at work – Shona. She worked as receptionist and typist in the office. She was dark-haired, plump, hardworking and capable, probably a couple of years younger than himself. It definitely helped that there was nothing about her remotely like Frankie – for a start, there was the Aussie accent of course. And where Frankie had been so childlike – sweet and demure one minute but bubbly and sparky the next – Shona was calm and gentle. From day one, it was easy to relax around her. She made him tea when he called into the office, called him with messages when he was out on site, and she was always there, helpful and unflappable, if he needed anything. He'd noticed the flicker of interest in her eyes, noticed how she made a point of asking how his *girlfriend* was settling down, watching his reaction to the question like she'd already guessed the truth, that the girlfriend didn't exist. Shona, with her comforting smiles and cheerful no-nonsense Australian manner, would've been easy to confide in – but he couldn't risk it, couldn't risk sharing his story with her, or with anyone. But after waiting three whole months to hear from Frankie, something gave way inside him.

'The girlfriend and I aren't together anymore,' he told Shona as she handed him the details of his next job.

'Oh.' There was genuine sympathy in her soft hazel eyes. 'Sorry to hear that, Jack.'

He shrugged, and then immediately felt guilty because shrugging seemed to imply that none of it mattered – the time he and Frankie had spent together, the way he'd felt about her, the fact that she'd been so young, a virgin, and he'd had his way with her and then just abandoned her without any explanation. The shrug implied that none of the past three months of waiting and hoping mattered, either. He turned away, picking up his mug of tea, taking a scalding mouthful that hurt his chest to swallow. It helped, taking the edge off the pain already there.

'If there's anything I can do,' Shona was saying quietly, 'Just ask away, won't you? I know how it feels to be ... let down by someone, Jack. It hurts, but sooner or later, we have to move on, right?'

'Yes.' He turned back and nodded at her. 'Thanks.'

He left it a respectful couple of days before he asked Shona to the cinema. And it was another two weeks before they slept together. She wasn't as shy or inhibited as he'd thought she might be. He lost himself, consoled himself, in the soft plumpness of her body, and had to concentrate hard not to call out Frankie's name when he came.

'You'll forget her in time,' she said gently. His face must have given him away.

'I know. Thanks.' He was just grateful that she understood.

He realised he'd struck lucky. Shona didn't seem to ask for anything or expect anything – she just seemed to want to *soothe* him. He didn't love her, but he felt something like real tenderness for her. She was helping him, healing him, and slowly he was starting to feel better. He worked, he got on with his life, he found himself starting to smile more. He'd learned to love his new hometown – its newness and cleanness, the orderly arrangement of its streets. He supposed he'd started to feel like an Australian.

After a while Shona moved in with him. He was aware that it was pretty quick, but there wasn't much point in hanging around. They weren't teenagers. Shona had been spending most of her time staying over at his place anyway, so it made sense for her to bring all her stuff and make it permanent. He wondered how her parents might feel about it, but she laughed and said she wasn't a kid, and hadn't lived at home for years so they weren't going to be bothered.

'Why did you leave home? Did you have a row with them?' Jack asked her as she was unpacking her gear at his place and putting it away. He'd noticed she never talked about them.

She shrugged. 'Let's say we just didn't see eye to eye.'

'But have you told them you're moving in with me? Don't you keep in touch?'

'We're not close.' She sighed, and then turned to him, and he was surprised by the challenge in her eyes. 'What about you, then? Are you ever going to tell me about *your* family? You've never talked about why you came over to Australia. And what about this girlfriend nobody ever met? Did she have a name? Did she even exist? Sorry, Jack,' she added more gently, seeing him flinch and look away. 'But you get my point. We both have stuff in our past we're maybe not ready to share yet.'

She was right, of course. He couldn't talk to her about what had happened back in England, why he'd left. And he couldn't talk to her about Frankie. He didn't know if he'd ever be able to. He and Frankie had been together such a short, precious time, he felt like sharing the memory with anyone might spoil it, kind of dilute it.

Shona had been good to him, and he wouldn't have wanted her to feel second-best. She'd rescued him, in a way, and sometimes he wondered if perhaps he'd done the same for her. Perhaps he was helping her deal with some issues in her own past, just by being with her. He hoped so. It made him feel less of a bastard, because the truth was, he still didn't love her – couldn't love her – even though he said he did.

After Shona moved in, he stopped checking the post office box. It felt disloyal enough to even still be thinking about Frankie, let alone hoping for a letter from her, after all that time. He hadn't got round to cancelling the box yet, but he didn't really need it any more. The only mail he got – mostly bills – came from within Australia, to his own address. There was nobody from back in England to write to him, nobody who knew where he was. So one day when Shona asked him to call at the post office after work to collect a parcel for her from a mail order company, he remembered about giving up the key to the mailbox. Before he did, he had one last quick check to satisfy himself that, as always it would be empty. But when he opened the box ... there was a letter.

Seeing the solitary airmail envelope lying in the box, he actually felt faint for a moment. It was postmarked Dagenham, Essex, on the twenty-first of May. It had been lying there for about a month. Had Frankie finally decided to get in touch? Maybe enough time had passed for her to forgive him? He grabbed the letter, and realised straight away that it wasn't Frankie's writing. Even after so long, he'd have recognised it immediately. Surely, however angry Frankie was with him, she wouldn't have given away his mailbox address to anyone, would she? Not when he'd told her how important it was that nobody found out. Could she really hate him enough to do that? He went cold at the thought of it, wondering again how he could have been stupid enough to confide in her.

He carried the letter back to the car and ripped open the envelope, glancing first at the signature. *Marianne*. Who the bloody hell was Marianne? The name rang a bell but it took him a minute to remember it was Frankie's sister. Then he started reading the letter.

Jack, it began – without any 'dear'. And the writing had been done so forcefully, the biro had gone right through the flimsy paper a couple of times. She was angry with him, that was for sure.

Jack,

I found your letter to my sister. Not because she kept it for sentimental reasons. She'd screwed it up and chucked it out of sight and forgotten it, and I don't blame her, that's all it was worth. Don't worry, I'm sure she hasn't told anyone where you've buggered off to, although perhaps she should have done. Sounds to me like you're in trouble with the police – why else would you do a runner like that? What a coward you must be. I wish Frankie had never got mixed up with you. You've probably put her off men for life, not that you'd care – you obviously only care about yourself.

Well, by now I suppose you've probably found someone else, and forgotten all about Frankie. Did it ever even occur to you to wonder whether you might have got her pregnant before you did your disappearing act? Yes, that's right! I know my sister, she didn't have to tell me you'd slept with her. It couldn't have meant much to you, the speed you took off.

Don't bother trying to reply. Frankie doesn't live here anymore. I hope you never come back.

Marianne.

He sat in the car for about fifteen minutes, holding the letter and staring out of the window. He'd never in all his life been on the receiving end of such vitriol – but he didn't blame Frankie's sister for that. In a way, he respected her for it. He only wished *he'd* been the one to stand up for Frankie and defend her so passionately. She couldn't possibly hate him as much as he hated himself for what he'd done to her sister.

But it wasn't Marianne's anger that shook him most; it was the suggestion that Frankie was pregnant. At the thought of this, he covered his face and groaned, rocking backwards and forwards in his seat like he was in pain. What the hell was wrong with him – why hadn't he even considered this possibility? OK, they'd only made love that once – and Frankie had told him it would be OK – but for God's sake, she was an eighteen year old virgin, as innocent as a schoolgirl, brought up by a strict Catholic mother. Catholic! There's no way she'd have been on the Pill or using any other form of birth control. He was older, experienced, and more to the point, he'd genuinely loved her. Loved her, promised not to hurt her, to look after her – and instead he'd taken advantage of her and assumed she knew what she was talking about when she said it would be OK. Supposing she *was* pregnant! No wonder her sister was as mad as hell. Jack had ruined her life, completely.

By the time he'd stopped shaking enough to start the engine and head home, he'd convinced himself that he'd now got a child on the way, a child he'd taken no interest in, or even taken any steps to find out about. Frankie must have moved out of her sister's home to go and stay somewhere till she'd had the baby. Maybe she was planning to give it up for adoption. Or worse, she might already have gone somewhere in secret to have an abortion – and if she hadn't been able to get a doctor to agree to it, she might have risked an illegal one. Either way, he had to find out. He had to know! And the only way would be to write back to the fearsome Marianne and ask her. He'd offer to pay Frankie's fare, and the child's of course, if there was one – to bring them out to Australia so he could take care of them. He'd never let her down again. He'd make it up to her somehow!

And then he pulled onto his driveway – and remembered about Shona.

'What's wrong, sweetheart?' She put her arms round him and leant her head against his shoulder. 'You look all stressed out!'

'I'm OK. Just a bit tired.'

'Sure. It's warm out there today for this time of year. Why don't you go through and have a shower and get changed. I'll pour you a cold beer. How was work?'

'Busy, as always, you know.' Gratefully, he turned away from her and headed for the bathroom. He could think more clearly under the shower.

'Glad I took the day off, then!' Shona said as he went.

'Yeah. Sorry.' He stopped and turned back. 'Sorry, babe. I should have asked. Did you have a good day?'

'I did.' Her face broke out in a smile. 'I had a very good day, thank you.' She was giving him a look – like she was bursting to say something.

'Oh?' He waited, holding onto the bathroom door handle, anxious only to get under the shower and resume his internal emotional debate about Frankie. 'Anything special happen?'

'Yes. Oh, yes, it did, Jack!' She ran up to him, throwing herself at him and laughing with excitement. 'I was going to tell you when you'd had your shower and got your beer, but ... I just can't wait! Jack, I went to the doctor's – I'm pregnant! Isn't it wonderful! Now we'll *have* to think about getting married!'

Chapter 9

Dagenham

The shock Marianne had felt about her mother's will had been worse, in a way, than the shock of her first stroke – worse than the shock of her dying. She realised how bad that sounded, but the fact was, she and her mother hadn't been close. If anything, their relationship had been worse than her relationship with Frankie. They hadn't even been able to talk to each other without arguing. Marianne hadn't liked Frankie moving back in with her to look after her. Their mother had treated her like a child when she was living with her before, and Marianne had a suspicion that despite everything, Frankie still felt answerable to her. It frustrated Marianne to see her going back there, becoming the dutiful little daughter again, like all the life and colour had been drained out of her.

During the time she lived with Marianne and Grant, they'd watched her blossom. She'd never had many friends – their mother had made sure of that! But she'd started going out, started buying herself trendy clothes and being a proper teenager. The real Frankie was bright, and loud, and funny. The Frankie that caved in and went back to Mum was somehow smaller and quieter. Even when she'd been so badly hurt by bloody Jack Hunter – of course she'd been upset, she'd cried and moped around for a while, but eventually she came up again fighting, angry and resilient. Marianne had been proud of her. She hated seeing her take such a backward step.

And after all that – to find out Hilda had kept such a shocking secret from them both! What the hell were they supposed to make of it? Another daughter they knew nothing about? They could only presume she'd died when she was young, and perhaps their mother couldn't bring herself to talk about it.

'But this will was written in 1953,' Frankie said. 'So she was still alive then, and you would have been ... what, five or six? All right, I was only three. But *you* would have *known* about her!'

They'd searched everywhere for a birth certificate. Marianne's and Frankie's were both in the box where Grant had found the will, but there was nothing anywhere for a Susannah.

'Didn't your mum have any photo albums?' Grant said. But Hilda had never been one for photos. Marianne supposed she'd never had the time, what with the housework and the bloody church. Then, when Grant widened the search to the attic, he came back down holding a large brown envelope, which he put on the table in front of the girls. Marianne opened it very cautiously and found inside a single black and white photo. It was of two little girls, wearing fancy dress. It looked like a professional photograph, and on the back was written: *June 1953*.

'The Queen's coronation – I think there was a street party,' Marianne said. She showed the picture to Frankie and they both stared at it for ages. Eventually, Marianne cleared her throat and said: 'Right: 1953, so the little one in the Bo Peep costume must be you, Frankie. I'm the older one, Red Riding Hood, so ...'

'So ... no other girl. Not at that time, anyway.'

'Maybe she was *younger* than us – a baby when Mum wrote the will. A baby might not have been in the photo.'

'That's true. And that could have been why Mum *wrote* the will. Not just because Dad had died the previous year, but to include the new baby. Maybe she was pregnant when Dad died.'

'But Frankie, like you said before – I would have *known* if there was a baby! Even *you* would have remembered. Look,

Joel's only two and a half, but he knows all about me expecting another baby.'

'But would he forget, in time, if ...' Grant started to say, and then shook his head. Frankie glared at him, but they all knew what he was getting at. It didn't need spelling out, but he had a point. If there had been a baby girl, younger than both Marianne and Frankie, but she hadn't survived for very long, would they have any memory of her?

'I wouldn't have forgotten,' Marianne decided after a moment. 'I've got lots of memories from that time. Starting school, going to church with Mum, playing in the garden. I even remember you being born, Frankie, and I wasn't even quite three then. I was never jealous – I loved you as soon as they brought you home from hospital. I'd definitely remember if there was another baby. There *wasn't*.'

'Don't get upset, Mari,' Frankie said. 'Look, the solicitors are going to find out about her – this Susannah – aren't they. If she's still alive, they must know how to find her.'

'It looks like it'll have to be a mystery until they do,' Grant said.

It's wasn't as if their mother had had much to leave. A bit in her savings account, a few Premium Bonds. It wasn't going to change any of their lives. But having another sister might have done. It was the last thing any of them had expected.

With all this going on, Marianne had completely forgotten about the letter to Jack Hunter. At the time, she'd been worried sick, regretting it almost as soon as she'd posted it. She'd been so angry, at the time she hadn't stopped to think – but straight afterwards she knew it was wrong of her. She shouldn't have interfered. It wasn't her place. And she knew she should tell Frankie what she'd done, but she'd kept putting it off. She'd been worried that Frankie had enough on her plate, moving back into their mother's house, looking after her ... and then, of course, Hilda had her second stroke and the letter went completely out of Marianne's mind.

One morning, a week or so after discovering the will, Grant suddenly started talking, over breakfast, about Australia. The night before, he'd been for a beer with some colleagues after work, and it seemed one of the blokes from his office was emigrating.

'He says the opportunities out there are fantastic. They're so desperate for young people from Britain to boost their population, work in all their industries and services, they're pretty much paying you to go out there. You only have to stump up ten pounds towards the fare.'

'I know. Assisted passage. I've heard about it.' Marianne frowned. 'You're not thinking of *us* going out there, are you?'

'Well, we could do worse, Mari. This country's heading for disaster, if the unions aren't put in their place soon. I can see it coming.'

'But *Australia*, Grant? It's so far!'

'Don't worry.' He smiled at her. 'I'm not serious, not about *us* going – not with two little children. But I can understand why young single people are doing it. People like your sister – she'd have a better life out there.'

'No!' she snapped, getting up and turning away from him. 'She wouldn't!'

'All right!' he said, misinterpreting her panic. 'I know you'd hate the thought of it. I know she'd never leave you, anyway. I was just saying, it'd be good for someone in her situation.'

'But not her. Don't you dare suggest it to her!'

'I wasn't going to!' He laughed. 'Calm down! OK, nobody's going to Australia, forget I mentioned it!'

But now he had, now she'd remembered about the letter, Marianne knew she had to talk to Frankie. And she had to do it today; before she could forget again, or put it off for any longer.

'Are you OK?' Frankie looked at her sister anxiously when she turned up at the house. 'You look a bit worried.'

Frankie had been finishing off the clearing-out of her mother's stuff. She was weary from the exertion of sorting through all the books, crockery, clothes, knick-knacks – a lifetime's worth of clutter – and deciding what was junk and what was worth keeping. Marianne had come round to give her a hand with the final couple of cupboards.

'I'm fine. *You* look exhausted. It'll be a good thing to finish off here today. Then we've just got the furniture to sell and we're done. The council will be wanting to put a new tenant in here.'

'Yes.' Frankie frowned. 'Are you sure it's OK for me to come back, Mari? I mean, aren't you going to need the room for the new baby?'

Marianne brushed this aside. 'I've already told you – the baby will be in our room to start off with, and then it can share with Joel. If it's a girl and she needs a room of her own eventually, we'll worry about it later on.' She paused. 'Shall we have a cup of tea? I'll make it. There's something I need to tell you.'

Frankie waited until they were both sitting down with their tea, before demanding:

'Is it about her – Susannah? Have you found out anything?'

'No. Sorry. It's nothing to do with that. Still waiting for the solicitors to get back to us. Look, Frankie, I should have told you this before. I ... just after you moved out, I decided to give your room a good spring clean.'

'OK.' She laughed. 'So that's good, isn't it? I won't have to do it when I move back in again!'

'Frankie, I cleaned on top of the wardrobe. I got up on a chair and ...'

'Oh – I hope you were careful.'

'Yes, I was! Listen. It was thick with dust up there, where you'd had your suitcase sitting, so I flicked the feather duster over it. And there was something pushed right to the back – I had to stretch to reach it.' Marianne put down her mug, and reached into her shopping bag, pulling out the grubby white teddy-bear.

'Oh. That thing,' Frankie said quietly.

'I wasn't sure what to do with it. I was just going to throw it away. It was covered with dust, and I didn't think you'd want it, anyway. I ... remembered where it came from.'

'The funfair in Central Park,' she said, still gazing at the stupid bear. '*He* won it for me.'

'I know. That's why I thought, in the end, I ought to let you decide. Just say the word, and I'll bin it.'

'No.' Frankie laughed now. 'Take it home, Mari, and when I come back, maybe I'll give it a good wash and give it to Joel to play with.'

'OK,' she said gently. 'I'm glad you're not upset.'

'Gosh, no. I'm over all that.' She paused. 'So was that it – the bear? Was that all you had to tell me about?'

'No. There's something else.'

'Go on, then. What?'

'There was a piece of screwed-up paper that fell down with the bear. Airmail paper.'

'Oh. Bugger.' She covered her mouth and apologised. 'Sorry. His letter. I threw it up there, didn't I. I meant to burn it.' Then, suddenly realising why her sister was being so awkward about it, she added: 'Did you read it?'

'Yes. Sorry, Frankie. I didn't realise what it was at first – I smoothed it out, and then I saw his signature at the bottom. I ... I know I shouldn't have done, but I'd read it before I could stop myself.'

Frankie shrugged. 'Don't worry. It doesn't really matter now, does it.'

'But he was asking you to go out to bloody Australia! And ... asking you to keep it a secret! Not to tell anyone! Why would he do that?'

'Now you can see why I was so upset.'

'Telling you he loved you – but he couldn't tell you why he'd gone off to the other side of the bloody world!'

'I *know*, Mari!'

'I'm sorry, sweetheart.' Marianne took a deep breath. How could she admit what she'd done? 'To be honest, I felt like writing back to him myself. Telling him what I thought of him, buggering off to bloody Australia and not even troubling himself to find out whether you were all right! For all he knew you could have been ...' She patted her stomach meaningfully.

Frankie gave a forced smile. 'Thankfully, not.'

Marianne swallowed hard. 'But did he even bother to *ask*?'

'No, he didn't. Apparently that didn't cross his mind. It obviously wasn't as important as whatever serious emergency made him take off and disappear to Australia.'

'Exactly. Like I say, I felt like writing and giving him a piece of my mind. What ... would you have said if I had?'

'I'd have told you it was a waste of time, Mari. It's done and dusted. Forget it.'

She looked bored by the whole subject. Marianne breathed a sigh of relief. She was pretty sure that if her sister ever did find out that she'd actually done it, actually written back to Jack Hunter tearing him off a strip, she wouldn't even care. And as he hadn't replied, that didn't look likely. Anyway, daft though it had been of her to interfere, she couldn't help feeling some sort of satisfaction from having told him exactly what she thought!

'Shall I burn the letter now, then?' she suggested.

'You might as well. That's what we do with all the other rubbish, isn't it.'

Good! Marianne thought to herself. *So that's the end of that, Jack Hunter. You're out of our lives. Finished. I'll never have to bother Frankie by talking about you – ever again.*

Chapter 10

July 1969 : Perth, Western Australia

It was funny, Jack thought, how he'd never been the kind of bloke who was bothered about getting married, having kids, a family of his own, all that stuff – and yet, here he suddenly was with a pregnant girlfriend and a wedding being planned. And at the same time, he was also lying awake nearly every bloody night, wondering what to do about Frankie's baby. Because by now, he was absolutely sure in his own mind that she was having a baby. He'd kept her sister's letter in the glove-box of his car and read it over and over again, and it was quite obvious that this was the only reason she'd written to him – why she was so furious. He'd worked out that the baby must be due pretty soon, too: nine months from November is August. Unless she'd already got rid of it, but she was pretty sure she wouldn't have done that, not with her Catholic upbringing. She wasn't the type of girl who'd do anything like that, and surely, anyway, her sister wouldn't have let her do it. The closer it got to August, and the more excited Shona was getting about *her* baby, which wasn't due until January for God's sake, the more Jack felt like he was going to explode if he didn't find out soon.

'You *are* excited about getting married, aren't you, Jack?' she said when they were getting ready for work one morning towards the end of July.

'Yeah. Of course.' Despite saying this to reassure her, he felt guilty because in fact the wedding was the last thing on his mind.

'Only – look, I know it wasn't what we planned. Especially when we haven't been together all that long. But you know I couldn't bear for our baby to be *illegitimate.*'

She whispered the word, looking away as she said it – and Jack knew that was fair enough. He wouldn't choose to do that to a kid, either. Not this kid, and not Frankie's kid, God help him.

'Of course not,' he said, putting his arms round Shona. 'And yes, of course I'm excited about it all,' he added, hoping she believed him.

'It's just ... you seem so preoccupied these days. And you look so tired and worried.'

'I'm all right. Just not sleeping well.'

'I know.' She gave him her gentle smile. 'I realise it must all be weighing on your mind – the future, the responsibility – how we're going to manage financially, when I give up work, and with all the things to buy for the baby.'

He hadn't in fact given a thought to any of this.

'Things to buy for the baby? Like what?'

'Oh, Jack, really!' She laughed and shook her head. 'A pram, and a cot! Nappies, and clothes! Babies need lots of things! But don't worry. We can do it on the cheap. I know someone who's selling a cot, second-hand, and, well, we don't have to get the most expensive pram, do we.'

Second-hand, he thought indignantly, *for my baby? A cheap pram? I don't think so!* But just as he was about to protest, he had a sudden vision of Frankie, on her own, an abandoned unmarried mother with no support apart from whatever little help her sister could afford to give her, and he had to swallow back a huge lump in his throat before he could answer.

'It's all right. We can manage. Get whatever we need, for the baby.'

She kissed him. 'Aw, Jack, I just *knew* you were a big softy at heart. Well, look, at least the wedding isn't going to set us back a lot. It's only going to be a quiet one, isn't it.'

'Yes.' He tried to smile at her. She deserved more from him – more interest, more enthusiasm. The wedding was booked for the end of August. She wanted it to be soon, before people started noticing she was pregnant. And as neither of them had family to invite, it was just going to be a select group of her friends and their joint colleagues from work. 'It'll be a special day, though, won't it,' he said, because he wanted to please her. 'Get yourself a nice dress.'

She was smiling to herself as they drove to work, and he was glad he'd said all the right things. But all day, working on the plumbing systems in a new housing estate down the river, he couldn't get that picture out of his head – the image of Frankie pushing an old, battered pram, with the baby in it dressed in rags. It was horrendous. Unthinkable. He couldn't let it happen! And as suddenly as he'd started imagining it, the solution came to him. In his lunch break he jumped in the car, dashed back into town and called in at the bank. In no time at all, it was all set up. And for the first time since he'd read Marianne's letter, he relaxed a little. At least now, Frankie wouldn't have to dress the baby in rags. He still needed to know – was she all right, was the baby all right, was it a girl or a boy? But of course, it was still too early. Perhaps he'd write to her, care of her sister, at the end of August. By then Frankie would definitely have given birth. Perhaps, because of the money, she'd even have started to forgive him. Then perhaps he could start to forgive himself.

In the meantime, he had to make more of an effort about the wedding. Shona had been inviting her best friend Karen round – it seemed like every weekend and several nights after work too, and they sat there for hours talking about dresses, music, menus for the reception buffet. Jack could understand her going a bit overboard with all the girly chat and excitement with Karen, as she didn't have her mum, or any sisters to talk about wedding stuff with. He still knew nothing at all about her parents, and why she'd fallen out with them several years before. He thought it was a shame, for her sake, that she wasn't even prepared to ask them to the wedding. But on another level, he wasn't sorry that she wanted to keep part of her past to herself. It made it easier for him to do the same.

Karen was going to be Shona's bridesmaid and had an opinion on everything, from the colour of Shona's underwear to the way she was supposed to walk down the aisle. Jack found it very wearing listening to them, but he felt it was probably his duty to sit there in the lounge with them, trying to be interested. After a couple of weeks of this, though, it became obvious they didn't want him there. He was only going to be the bridegroom, after all – of no importance whatsoever. Fair enough!

'Shall I get out of your way?' he suggested when Karen turned up again one evening with a pile of wedding dress catalogues.

'Good idea,' said Karen without even looking up.

'Aw, Jack – that's sweet of you,' Shona said. 'You must be getting bored with all this talk about dresses. And I don't want you to see what I'm going to choose, anyway – it's supposed to be a surprise on the day.'

'Sure. I'll go and sit in the bedroom and read the paper, then,' he said, getting up, but she smiled and said:

'Wouldn't you rather pop out to the pub for an hour or two?'

'Sure you don't mind?' he said, surprised.

'No, of course I don't. I know I wanted you to take an interest in the wedding, Jack, but I didn't expect you to sit here listening to us talking about shoes and underwear!'

The two girls giggled together and Jack made his escape, relieved almost to the point of euphoria. There was a pub just a couple of blocks away and he walked there quickly, eagerly anticipating the first pint of Foster's.

Sitting alone at the bar with his beer, he watched the barmaid pulling pints and chatting to the regulars, and found himself intrigued by her – not because he was attracted to her, but because she didn't fit the stereotypical flirty, tarty barmaid in any way at all. She was very butch: muscular, and wiry, with cropped, dyed red hair. She wore jeans, a plain black shirt like a man's, a huge leather belt and a chunky gold watch. She laughed and joked with the drinkers as if she was one of them, and he got the impression she could probably out-drink, out-swear and out-punch a few of them.

'Another pint, please,' he asked her when she came to his end of the bar. 'And get one for yourself.'

'Thanks. Don't mind if I do.' She looked at him curiously as she put his drink in front of him. 'You from round here? Haven't seen you in here before.'

He shrugged. 'Don't get out a lot. But I've just escaped the girlfriend talking weddings with her mate.'

She laughed. 'Can't say I blame you.'

They talked, comfortably enough, for a few minutes about the weather, the recent moon landings, the traffic in town. Someone called her for a drink from the other end of the bar, and she hollered back, laughing, 'Alrighty! I'm coming! No need to shout!'

And as she turned to go to them, she suddenly went into a half-comic rendition of the Lulu hit number from a few years back:

'We..e..e..e..ell, you know you make me wanna SHOUT ...'

As she continued, sashaying down the bar, yelling out the lyrics to the cheers and applause of the punters at the other end, Jack stared after her, his pint glass halfway to his mouth. He felt a shiver go down his spine. She had an amazing voice. And apart from the obvious difference of accent, she sounded exactly like Lulu. She was singing that song with the same raucous energy, the same incredible strength and confidence.

'That Lulu routine – it was fabulous,' he said when she returned to chat to him again. He smiled at her. 'Why the hell haven't you been picked up by somebody and made into a star?'

She laughed. 'A star? I don't think so! Thanks for the compliment though.'

'Seriously! Do you sing? I mean, apart from while you're waltzing down the bar serving customers?'

'Kind-of. Only once a week at a pub down at Freo. They don't pay me a whole lot. I've sometimes thought about starting a band with a mate of mine ... but you know how it is. It's just a dream, really.' She gave him an amused look. 'Why're you so interested?'

'I ... do a bit of singing myself. Or, at least, I used to. Played lead guitar, too. In a band.'

'Really?' She stopped wiping down the bar and looked at him with more interest. 'Were they any good, your band?'

'Yeah. I think we were.'

'So how come you're not still with them?'

'It was back in the UK. Before I came out to Oz.' He shrugged, looked away, not wanting to elaborate.

'One of those ten pound Poms, were you?' She nodded to herself, not waiting for an answer. 'Well, at least you didn't boomerang straight back home like a lot of them.'

'We played at a festival – a big one,' he went on as if she hadn't spoken. 'And we had a manager interested. Before I left.'

'Never thought of taking it up again? Over here?'

'I ... suppose I haven't got around to it. I don't get a lot of chance to play, anymore.'

She narrowed her eyes at him, like she was weighing him up. 'Mind if I hear you play some time?'

He hesitated for only a few seconds. He didn't know where this was leading, but he felt like he shouldn't even be considering it. He was about to become a married man, soon to become a father. He'd have responsibilities. He had a house, a job, a new, grown-up life. He was getting too old to be hanging round pubs with barmaids, playing at being a rock star. Wasn't he?

'OK,' he heard himself say. And, almost as an afterthought: 'Why?'

'If you're any good, maybe we could give it a go together – with my mate. He plays guitar. We could have a go at making that old dream of mine a reality, you know?'

Jack felt a fluttering of excitement in his stomach. He could actually imagine this girl on stage, belting out a rock number. Her voice would be just right for it. And there was something about her he couldn't quite put his finger on ... he just knew, somehow, that she'd have a great stage presence.

'You interested or not?' she said.

'I don't know,' he said, trying to ignore the tingling of his nerve endings just at the thought of it. 'I'd need to make sure Shona – my girlfriend – doesn't mind.'

She laughed. 'She won't mind us spending time together, if that's what you're worried about. I'm not interested in you – only as a musician. I prefer girls.'

'Oh. Right.' He nodded to himself. It should've been obvious. 'But with the baby coming ... and the wedding, and everything ...'

'Don't take this the wrong way. But you know, from what I've seen, most girls don't want their boyfriends getting in the way at times like this. And if ever you're gonna need a bunch of friends, and somewhere to hang out when she's too caught up with the baby and too tired from the sleepless nights to talk to you, let alone bonk you, it'll be when that kid gets born.'

'Right.' He blinked. She was actually making sense. The truth was that Shona was already far more interested in how the baby was growing inside her, and in the wedding of course, than in talking to him. And she hadn't wanted any *bonking*, as this girl so quaintly put it, since she found out about the pregnancy. Said she was too worried it'd hurt the baby – and how could he argue with that? 'Well, I *might* be interested ...'

'OK, we'll have a couple of sessions together, see how we get on.' She grinned. 'You might not like my style. You might think my voice is rubbish. Or I might think yours is!' She gave a snort of laughter at this. 'Then I'll get my mate round. He's got a great voice and he's a good guitarist. If we're all happy, we'll look for a drummer.'

'OK.' He felt his smile stretching until it filled his face. 'OK, then, let's give it a go.'

'Good. Meet me here tomorrow night, I'll try and get off early. Bring your guitar. Oh – just one other thing.'

'What?'

'I don't know your name!'

He laughed. 'It's Jack. What's yours?'

'Ruth,' she said. 'Ruth Cordell.' She shook his hand, and then they both laughed again because hers was wet from the bar cloth.

He finished his beer, gave her a wave and returned home, wondering what the hell he'd just agreed to and how the hell he was going to explain it to Shona. And trying to pretend to himself that he wasn't feeling excited. More excited than he could remember feeling about anything for a long time.

Chapter 11

August 1969 : Dagenham

Frankie was pleased to be back at her sister's place again. It felt more like home to her now than her mother's old house did. Marianne's new baby was due at the end of November and although she was feeling much better than she did early on, Frankie tried to help her as much as possible with Joel, so that she didn't get too tired. She knew she ought to be thinking about moving on, renting a place of her own or maybe sharing with a friend. Marianne kept telling her it was fine, she liked having Frankie around, but when the new baby arrived it was going to be tight for space, whatever she said. The trouble was, she didn't really earn enough, and she'd blown her chances of a promotion at work by giving up the evening classes and refusing to work late when Hilda was ill. Since then, the supervisor had seemed determined to give her all the longest and the most boring jobs, and she wasn't enjoying the work at all. She hadn't really even been all that fussed in the first place about being promoted. It hadn't ever been her lifetime's ambition to be a secretary to a bank manager – she'd only said she was interested because she'd wanted to earn some more money. And if she was totally honest, she'd never even been that fussed about working in a bank at all. It was what her mother had said she should do when she left school, so she did it. She wished now that she'd stood up to her more – but she'd had no idea at the time what she really wanted to do. Come to that, she still had no idea.

'I've been looking in the paper at job adverts,' she told Marianne over dinner. 'I fancy a change.'

'Well, why not?' she said. 'If you find something you think might be interesting – give it a go.'

'Well, yeah – as long as the money's all right, maybe I will.'

'There are plenty of jobs around at the moment.'

'But I don't know what I want to do. And I only got five O-levels. It's not like I'm qualified to do anything really good.'

'Frankie, you're bright and quick and capable, and you work hard. Don't put yourself down. Something will turn up – and when it does, you go for it!'

Maybe she would, if it ever did turn up. But meanwhile there were other things to worry about.

The previous day, they'd finally got a letter from the solicitors about their mystery sister.

'They've found her birth certificate,' Marianne said, holding the letter out to Frankie with one hand while she gripped the back of a chair with the other for support, as if she was about to faint with shock.

'So it's true. She really does exist.' There was a photocopy of a birth certificate stapled to the letter. Frankie stared at it. Up till that moment, she'd tried to convince herself the whole thing was some kind of mistake – but there it was, in black and white:

Tenth June 1945: Oldchurch Hospital, Romford
Name: Susannah Margaret
Sex: Girl
Father: Arnold Kennedy
Mother: Hilda Margaret Ryan
Registered by: H. M. Ryan, Mother, fourteenth June 1945.

'I can't take this in,' Marianne said, taking the letter back from Frankie and fanning herself with it. 'Do you realise what this means? Can you believe it, Frankie?'

'She was illegitimate. Mum and Dad got didn't get married till 1947, did they.'

'February 1947. And I was born in the October. I always assumed – I mean, Mum always led us to *believe* – I was the eldest! I ... just can't believe she had a baby before she was married! How *dared* she take that attitude with *me*!'

Frankie put her arm round her sister. 'I bet that was *why* she was like she was.'

'Yes, and why she was so strict with you! Hardly fair though, was it! When all the time, she'd had some *affair*, some kind of wartime *fling*, and got pregnant ...'

'It was Dad's baby, though!' Frankie reminded her, pointing at his name on the birth certificate. 'Not just some random boyfriend! So why wouldn't he have married her at the time?'

Marianne sat down, slumping in the chair, shaking her head.

'I don't know, Frankie. We can only guess. It's such a shock! I suppose she must have fallen for the baby when he was home on leave – then he went back to the war and she was left to get on with it on her own.'

'And ...' Frankie stopped and looked at her sister anxiously. Marianne was pregnant herself; she didn't want to say anything to upset her, but ... 'What do you think happened to her?' she whispered.

'I don't know.' Marianne's eyes filled with tears and Frankie rushed to hug her again. 'Oh, take no notice of me – I'm just being over-emotional! But it's so sad, to think that we had this sister ... two years older than me, and we never knew about her. All these years ...'

'I know.' They were both silent for a moment, and then Frankie added, looking at the solicitors' letter again: 'But she must still be alive somewhere, Mari! They say couldn't find any record of her death. Or marriage.'

'So what *happened* to her? Would Mum ... do you think she might have given her away?'

Frankie shook her head, pretending to dismiss the idea. But she'd actually had the same thought herself, almost as soon as she'd digested the information on the birth certificate. Illegitimacy must have been even more shameful back in the nineteen-forties than it was now. The so-called Swinging Sixties had brought a bit of enlightenment but even now, nobody wanted to be an unmarried mother. And even though Frankie guessed such wartime pregnancies must have been a pretty common occurrence, she was sure Hilda, with her strict Catholic upbringing, wouldn't have been able to bear the shame.

'I ... just can't imagine what she might have done,' she prevaricated. Not wanting to imagine the possibilities: the handover of a newborn child to a cold, unwelcoming orphanage, or rather more hopefully, into the arms of adoptive parents who might love her as their own but would probably have changed her name, maybe moved away. 'I can't see how we'll ever find her now.'

'The solicitors say they're going to put an advert in the paper, asking her to contact them.'

'Yes. That's true. If she still goes by the same name, maybe she'll see that.'

'I can't bear it, Frankie!' Marianne said, beginning to cry quietly. 'The poor thing – our poor sister! Never knowing she had a family, all this time!'

Frankie did her best to console her. But inside, she was thinking: *Would she really have wanted to know – that she had a mother who would give her up so quickly, and never mention her again for the rest of her life, apart from in her will?* When it came down to it, what was the point of their mother bequeathing Susannah a third of her estate, when nobody knew she existed or how to find her?

And as if that wasn't enough of a shock for one week, something else came in the post the next day. Frankie was on her own at home – it was a Saturday morning and Marianne and Grant were out shopping with little Joel. The letterbox rattled and she went to pick up the post from the mat. A couple of bills, and one airmail envelope. As soon as she saw the Australian stamp, it felt like her breath had all been sucked out of her. She had to sit down. Turning the envelope over, she saw that yes, it was definitely Jack's writing, and it was addressed to her, Miss Francesca Kennedy, 'care of Marianne'. 'PLEASE FORWARD!' had been added in bold capitals beside the address, and underlined twice. Did he think she'd moved? Maybe he did, because she hadn't replied to his other stupid letters; maybe because she'd sent back the second one unopened. She sat on the bottom stair for at least fifteen minutes, turning the envelope over and over, staring at his writing, wondering at the cheek of him – trying again, after all this time! She was torn between wanting to rip it to shreds without even opening it, and the curiosity that demanded she should at least find out what he had to say. Not that anything he said could make any difference, but she was genuinely puzzled as to why he'd want to waste his time writing to her again. What was wrong with him? Couldn't he take a hint, give up, get lost?

In the end, she opened it – quickly, roughly, like she wanted to get it over with before she changed her mind. And inside, there wasn't even a letter. Just a small piece of paper, folded around something that looked a bit like a cheque, but with the words *International Money Order* on it – and it was made out for one hundred and fifty Australian dollars. Frankie might have worked at a bank, but she had nothing to do with foreign currency and no idea how much this represented in pounds, shillings and pence. But anything with the word *hundred* in it seemed like a lot. Her hands were shaking as she unfolded the bit of paper. It had just one line of writing scrawled across it:

Frankie. For the baby. With my love, Jack.

What? *WHAT?* By now it wasn't just her hands that were trembling. All she really wanted to do was shove the money order, and the note, back into the envelope and pretend she hadn't seen them, but she was too shaken – she kept dropping the envelope, the papers kept slipping out of her hands, and eventually she just grabbed them all together, rushed upstairs and stuffed them in her drawer. She couldn't have explained why, but more than anything she didn't want Marianne to see them, and ask about them. She needed time to calm down, think about it, work out what the hell was going on.

The whole time she was dusting and mopping the floors, her mind was whirling with it. How on earth did Jack know Marianne was having a baby? She presumed that was what he meant. And why would he send them money anyway? Just to show off? Perhaps he'd made loads of money out in Australia – people were always saying it was the land of promise, plenty of money to be made out there if you worked hard, and all that. Perhaps he'd made so much money he didn't know what to do with it. Then another thought came to her. What if Rob was right, when Jack first disappeared – that he might have been in trouble with the police? This money might be … flipping heck, it might be money he'd stolen from someone! Money from a robbery! She went hot and cold for a minute, thinking about it. But no – surely that was being over-dramatic. Surely things like that only happened in films! No, he'd probably just sent it because he felt guilty, because he thought that by getting round her with money to help Marianne, he was going to make her change her mind and forgive him, even ship herself off, all the way to bloody Australia to be with him.

Well, he could think again! Flipping cheek – what, did he think she was so cheap he could *buy* her, now? She didn't want his money! But there was this horrible little niggling voice in her head, reminding her that the money wasn't even supposed to be for her – it was supposedly for her sister, for the baby. Perhaps it wasn't her place to refuse it! Was that why he said it was for Marianne? Because he'd guessed that Frankie would have sent it back otherwise? But that just brought her back to the same question she'd started with: *HOW* did he know about the baby?

Suddenly, she realised the answer. Marianne must have written to him. She'd hinted at it, hadn't she – she'd said she'd felt like writing back to him when she found his letter on top of the wardrobe. Frankie had *thought* she looked a bit shifty about it at the time. So she must have done, after all: written to him, and for some unimaginable reason, told him she was having another baby. Why on earth would she have done that? Why did she think it was any of his business? Was she perhaps warning him to leave them all alone – saying they were too busy with the family to be bothered with him?

Frankie needed to ask her about it. But she didn't have a clue what to do about the money. She knew Marianne and Grant could do with some extra cash – everything was so expensive, and Marianne had only been saying recently that although she'd love a little girl this time, in a way she was hoping the new baby was a boy so she could re-use all Joel's baby clothes. The pram was second-hand anyway and Grant said it needed a new wheel, and the cot needed a coat of paint. Wouldn't it be lovely to be able to give them some extra money, right now when they most needed it?

She was just going to have to sit on this for a while, till she'd made up her mind what to do. It was too much to think about – especially coming right on top of the news about Susannah. She picked up the local paper, deciding instead to concentrate on looking for a new job. With any luck she might land herself such a good position, she could send Jack Hunter's money back to him and tell him to stuff it – she didn't need it, she was earning enough to help Marianne herself! Yeah – and pigs might fly!

Chapter 12

Perth

Things had moved on so fast, Jack felt like his brain was whirling. Since that first night when Ruth Cordell had taken him back to her place, sat him down and without further ado proceeded to belt out *Good Golly Miss Molly* like she was on stage in front of a thousand people, he'd known this idea could really work. He'd picked up his guitar to join in, and without missing a beat Ruth went straight into *I Heard it through the Grapevine*. They spent the next hour playing around with numbers like *Mustang Sally, Hey Jude*, and some of the old rock classics from the fifties – Chuck Berry, Little Richard. He lost himself, eyes closed, singing his heart out, imagining himself back with the boys – Pete, Rob and Bernie – thrashing out the numbers in one of their regular rehearsals in Pete's living room. He was so carried away he didn't notice for a minute that she'd suddenly stopped singing.

'You're bloody good,' she told him. 'And I like you. Let's do it.'

He laughed. Some offer! Fortunately he knew she was only after him for his singing – which was just as well, as the only thing about *her* that made *his* knees go weak was her voice, too.

After that it had only taken them five minutes to agree they were definitely going to work together.

'But you haven't met Ken yet,' Ruth said, just as he was looking at his watch and thinking he should be getting home. It was well past midnight and Shona would have gone to bed long before.

'Ken?'

'My mate Ken Warren – the bloke I told you about who sings and plays guitar. You'll like him. I'll get him round.'

'Now?'

'You got something else to do?'

No, he thought. *Just that I'm turning into a middle-aged family man who's normally asleep in bed with his other half at this time of night. Instead of the rock star I always expected to be.*

She was already on the phone.

'Ken?' she shouted. 'Turn the music down, mate – can you hear me? Listen, I've got someone who wants to meet you. Bring your guitar. Yeah, come over now. That OK?' she mouthed at Jack virtually at the same time.

He nodded dumbly. 'Sure.'

He could sleep another time!

Ken arrived ten minutes later.

'How ya going?' he said, shaking Jack's hand as Ruth explained who he was. 'So we got ourselves a band. We got to get ourselves a name now, right, Ruthie?'

'Hold on – we haven't even played anything together yet,' Jack protested. 'You might not want to work with me.'

He shrugged. 'No worries. If Ruth says you're good, you're good.'

'Ken is, like, my protégé,' she said cheerfully, giving him a playful shove. 'I heard him singing in a Karaoke down the pub one time and talked him into getting guitar lessons. He amazed the bloody teacher – turned out to be a natural, practised till his fingers were raw.'

'Kept me out of trouble.' He gave her a quick smile. 'Better than doing time.'

'Doing time?' Jack echoed, giving Ken another look and feeling a frisson of alarm. What was he getting himself into here? But Ruth had already moved on:

'Let's run through a couple of the numbers you've been doing with me, Ken. '*Proud Mary*? And then *Respect?*'

Jack was impressed. More than impressed. He just sat and listened to them – he hadn't learned the chords to *Proud Mary* himself, and the Arethra Franklin number just about blew him away – Ruth's voice was perfect for that song, even more than the Lulu number.

'So we just need a drummer,' he said finally when they'd finished – and they all laughed, like it was a relief to them all that the thing was settled. Jack went home whistling to himself, feeling elated. Ruth and Ken were both brilliant musicians. What a stroke of luck that he'd met her! And so what if Ken had maybe been in trouble once? He seemed like a decent enough bloke now. He was going to be part of a band again! He felt like he'd got his identity back. He couldn't wait to tell Shona about it.

Shona. He stopped whistling at the thought of her. He felt bad about leaving her on her own all evening – and half of the night. And was he really expecting her to be as excited about this as he was? It was all well and good for Ruth to tell him she probably wouldn't want him around after the baby was born – but really, what did Ruth know about it? It was his baby too, after all – and Shona loved him. He felt a pang of guilt, as always, when he thought about her loving him. He should want to be with her, shouldn't he. He shouldn't be planning on spending time apart from her. Not if he loved her the way he should.

But on the other hand ... he'd missed this so much. The fun of being part of a band, the thrill of playing together, the excitement of appearing on stage in front of an audience. The atmosphere – the noise, the heat, the lights, the sweat! He wanted to be part of all that again, wanted it more than anything ... more than *almost* anything else he'd left behind. Shona would understand, wouldn't she? If he explained how much it meant to him. He'd still be there for her, most of the time, but didn't he deserve this too – for himself?

Shona knew Jack had been in a band back in England. He'd sometimes played his guitar to her, sung to her, although she wasn't a huge music fan and had confessed she only really liked the Beatles. But the next day when he told her about the new opportunity, she was happy for him.

'I'll introduce you to the others,' he assured her. 'You'll like them. There's only the three of us at the moment – we need to find ourselves a drummer.'

'OK,' she said, smiling at his enthusiasm. And then she added, laughing: 'Maybe I can stop looking for a band for the wedding reception, then!'

She was joking, of course – the bridegroom couldn't play at his own wedding – but he looked at her thoughtfully and suggested:

'Actually, it might not be such a bad idea to ask Ruth and Ken to play. They're good – and they're already used to playing together.'

'Well, yes – I suppose a duo might be just enough, for a wedding. Do you think?'

'I'll ask them,' he said, suddenly excited. 'And we could go down to the pub at Fremantle where they play on Saturday nights – so you can see what you think of them!'

'OK,' she said, shrugging, smiling.

He hugged her. Why had he been worried? She was easy-going, easy to please. She was a treasure, really. He should consider himself lucky to have her.

He shouldn't ever be thinking about anyone else.

They turned up at the pub in Fremantle that Saturday night without warning Ruth or Ken. He'd already seen them once more that week – they'd met at Ken's place this time for another session – but he hadn't wanted to bring up the subject of playing at the wedding until Shona had met them.

'Don't worry if the music tonight's a bit raucous,' he said as they went into the pub. 'They'll play quieter stuff, if they do the wedding. They can do whatever you want.'

'I think the music's more your department than mine,' she said, smiling at him. 'I only really know the Beatles, remember!'

He laughed. 'In that case I'll make sure they play some Beatles' numbers!'

Ruth and Ken were at one end of the bar, in a corner, sharing a mike. As it happened, as Jack and Shona went in, they were singing *Roll Over Beethoven.* Shona giggled and said 'Oh – that *is* a Beatles' song!'

'Actually it was a Chuck Berry number first – and he wrote it,' Jack corrected her. And then he looked round at her. 'What is it?' he asked in alarm. She was staring at the two singers as if she'd seen a ghost.

'That's the bloke ... the *Ken* ... you've been talking about?' she said.

'Yes. Why? What's wrong?'

'You don't want to get mixed up with him, Jack. He's bad news. Let's get out of here.'

'Wait! Shona, wait – they've seen us now, I'll have to go and say hello. What's the problem? You know him? Where from?'

'Let's just say I *used* to know him. Well. And I *don't* want to know him again.'

She turned her back on him and started to walk back towards the pub door, shaking his hand off her arm as he tried to stop her.

'Wait in the car a minute, then,' he said, pressing the keys into her hand. 'I'll just make some excuse.'

He waited at the bar until they'd finished the number, and apologised quickly for the fact that they weren't staying.

'My girlfriend's feeling sick,' he said, knowing it sounded lame. 'The baby, you know.'

'Shame,' said Ruth.

'I'll ... see you next week.'

'No worries.'

'So what's this all about?' he asked her when he joined her in the car. 'I want to know, Shona. I've just agreed to start a band with this guy, and you're telling me ...'

'I'm telling you he's bad news. He's been in trouble with the police more times than you can count, he's been in fights ...' She swallowed. 'He was a drunk.'

'*Was*?' He waited, and then added, more gently. 'Tell me how you knew him, Shona. Please. I need to know if he's still in trouble, still a drunk – before I sign up to anything with him.'

'Well, *don't*, then!' she began, and then she stopped, sighed, and said, 'Sorry. I know this is important to you. I've never seen you as excited as you've been this last week or so. I don't want to spoil things for you. But I'm not having that ... that ... *person* ... at my wedding.'

'We won't. Of course not.'

He waited. She looked out of the window.

And then she turned back to him, sighed again and said:

'We used to go out together, right? Before I met you. I helped him – got him to AA meetings, got him off the grog. Got him a decent job, somewhere to live. He said I'd got his life back on track. And then he dumped me – just like that. Said he didn't want to be tied down. Needed to be *free*.'

She spat the last word out in disgust, her eyes filling with tears – and he pulled her to him at once, furious with Ken on her behalf. So *this* was who had hurt her before he came along. After all she said she'd done for him! No wonder she was bitter.

Bastard, he muttered to himself. But on the other hand – and here he struggled with his own confused thoughts – if Ken hadn't dumped her, he wouldn't have met her himself. Wouldn't be marrying her, wouldn't be having a baby with her.

'But you've got me, now,' he whispered against her hair. '*I'm* not going to let you down.'

'I know,' she sniffed. 'You're so different from him. I'm sorry I never told you all this before. But I could hardly bear to talk about it. It's been two years since he finished with me, though. I've moved on. I've got someone who really loves me, now.' She smiled at him through her tears.

'Well, I won't see him anymore. I won't have anything to do with this band, if you don't want me to.'

'No. That wouldn't be fair,' she said, straightening up and trying to pull herself together. 'It's up to you, Jack. Just don't bring him home. Don't bring him anywhere near me, will you. And ... well, don't say I didn't warn you. You can't trust him. I should know.'

Jack started the engine, and they drove home in silence. He was stunned. What was he supposed to do now? His dream of a new band – so fresh, so enticing and exciting – might be over before it had even begun. Unless he ignored Shona's advice, to say nothing of her feelings, and carried on, which was bound to make him feel disloyal and uncomfortable.

Only one thing for it. He was going to have to see Ken on his own and have it out with him.

Chapter 13

Dagenham

Frankie threw the paper down with a sigh. She might as well give up looking at the 'Situations Vacant' page. It was depressing. Nearly all the adverts were for office work and she guessed that was all she was qualified for, but she *so* wanted to do something different. She supposed she'd just have to accept that she had a reasonably good job and she should be grateful for it. If only she didn't feel so restless!

As usual she had the radio on – as usual tuned to Radio One, which was the only half-decent thing to listen to since the government had driven the pirate radio ships out of existence two years previously. Tony Blackburn was doing the Breakfast Show and Frankie was only partly paying attention – she was eating her breakfast while Marianne was upstairs getting Joel dressed.

She'd just taken a mouthful of her Cornflakes when she heard her name on the radio. Well, at least, she heard Tony Blackburn say 'Francesca' and she was surprised enough to stop with the spoon not quite to her mouth, because after all it wasn't the most common name in the world. The record started playing, and she smiled to herself. It was quite a nice feeling having a record with her own name on it. There were plenty enough songs about pretty little Susies and Sheilas and Carols. So she turned up the radio a bit as she carried on putting the spoonful of Cornflakes in her mouth. She wanted to hear the lyrics, so that she could have a laugh with her sister or the girls at work about the song. But as she listened, she started to get the shivers all the way down her backbone. Her mouth must have been hanging open because it was a while before she realised she was dribbling Cornflakes and milk down her chin. Marianne came into the kitchen, calling out to Joel about getting his breakfast ready, and Frankie stood up, dropping her spoon, telling her to 'shush', quite loudly and rudely so that Marianne stopped in surprise, staring at her, listening to the song as well.

'What ...?' she started to say as it finished, but Frankie held her hand up, begging her to stay quiet, and turned the volume up even higher as Tony Blackburn came back on, saying in his jaunty, cheerful voice as if it was the most unimportant thing in the world:

'Right, well that was *Francesca* – a debut single for four boys from the Isle of Wight calling themselves the Crazy Snakes. Watch out for that one hitting the charts ...'

Frankie stared at Marianne, speechless, feeling like she'd been struck dumb. She might have still had milk dripping off her chin, she wouldn't have known.

'That ... was *them*, wasn't it,' Marianne said slowly. '*His* band.'

Frankie nodded. Still couldn't speak.

'But not *him*, surely?'

She shook her head. 'But it's the same sound,' she managed to croak eventually. 'I'd have known them anywhere. It's Rob singing.'

'And ... is it just a coincidence? That song? The *name*?'

'Must be,' Frankie said very quickly. She nodded, blinking, suddenly becoming aware again of the time, her breakfast, the paper thrown on the floor, the radio now blaring out *Honky Tonk Woman* at full volume, Joel crying upstairs because he wanted his red T-shirt on instead of his blue one, and the fact that she had to get the bus to work in ten minutes.

'Well.' Marianne was giving her a very meaningful look. 'Quite a coincidence.'

'Yeah.' She turned the radio off, sat down and tried to get on with her breakfast. 'Sorry I shushed you like that ... I just wanted to hear it ... just ... dead chuffed, really, that they've done it ... you know, got a record out ... despite ... you know, Jack ...'

She was shoving mouthfuls of Cornflakes in her mouth and gobbling them up at the same time as saying all this. She hardly even knew what she was saying. Because of course, she knew it couldn't really be a coincidence. Her name ... the words of the song ... the howling, desperate way it was sung. By Rob. Rob, singing it to *her*. Even though it was the most ridiculous, incredible thing ever.

'Well, I'd better go and sort Joel out,' Marianne said. 'Don't make yourself late for work, Frankie.' And Frankie could have sworn she gave her a wink as she went.

She didn't tell anyone at work, after all. She didn't want to share it. Not yet, not till she was sure. But as soon as she got home that evening, she put the radio on again and waited. All the time she was playing with Joel, all the time she was helping Marianne in the kitchen, peeling potatoes and cooking mince for a shepherd's pie, she had one ear tuned into the radio, waiting for that song to come on again. And when it did – when she heard it announced, she didn't have to tell Marianne again to shush – she'd already picked Joel up and taken him straight out into the garden.

'Let's go and pick some beans,' she told him, giving Frankie a smile.

She turned up the radio again, and sat down right next to it, and this time she listened to the words all the way through, until she knew them by heart. She even had a go at writing them down, quickly, using a mixture of handwriting and the little bit of shorthand she'd learnt.

Francesca – oh when I met ya
The world fell apart
You stole my heart.
Francesca – I can't forget ya
But you didn't know

I couldn't let it show.

Forget him, Francesca – he's gone, dry your tears.
Don't save him your love, he won't know, he won't care.
I love you, Francesca, I'm here for you now.
Be my girl, I'll love you, I won't let you down.

Francesca – I'd never let ya
Be sad and blue
If I was with you.
Francesca – I can't forget ya
But he broke your heart
He tore us apart.

And then there was an instrumental bit, with the boys screaming 'Yeah! Wo yeah Francesca!' before the chorus came back – *Forget him, Francesca, he's gone, dry your tears* ...

And that was it. She'd got it all. All the words written down. And the tune pounding in her head. And her heart, racing like she'd been running for hours.

She took a deep breath and told herself it was just a song – after all, who was she kidding? Just because it was her name, just because the words sounded so much like they *fitted* ... just because Rob sounded almost like he was crying as he was singing it ...

Just because it had made her tingle from head to toe ...

After all, it might have been an old song. Just because she'd never heard it before ... just because she was so sure she would have known, if there was a song called *Francesca* ...

It *might* still just have been a coincidence.

Marianne came back in from the garden, with little Joel clutching a handful of runner beans, shouting about cooking them for tea.

'Still think it's just a coincidence?' she asked, like she was reading Frankie's mind.

'I don't know. I can't ... really believe ...'

'Why don't you call him?' she suggested gently. 'You've got his number, haven't you?'

So she did. After dinner, she went down to the phone box and called him. He was still on the same number. He answered the phone himself. And as soon as he heard her voice, as soon as he said 'Hello, Frankie,' she knew.

'I've heard the song,' she said. Her voice was shaking. '*Francesca.*'

'Yes. I hoped you would.' She thought she could hear his voice shaking too. Over the line, over the miles between them, between Dagenham and the Isle of Wight, it was like there was a kind of *quivering* in the air, a buzzing, a feeling that something momentous was about to happen.

'I hoped you'd call, Frankie,' he went on. 'I've been hoping ... for months.'

'I didn't know,' she said. It came out all wobbly.

'No. Well, *I* didn't know how to tell you. You're not on the phone. And I didn't know your address. I did contemplate coming over to Dagenham and just walking up and down all the streets ...'

They both laughed, but then she stopped, abruptly, and said: 'The song. Who wrote it, Rob?'

She held her breath and waited. He cleared his throat, like he was nervous, and then very quietly he admitted: 'I did.'

'The music? Or ... the words?'

'Both. Well, the words, mainly. I had some help from Pete with the music. But the words – I wrote them for you, Frankie. In case you're in any doubt.'

She didn't know what to say. What were you supposed to say to someone who'd just told you they'd written a song for you? Named it for you, and sung it for you – a song to say they loved you?

'I hope it hasn't embarrassed you,' he said.

'No! No, I ... think it's ... fantastic. Absolutely fantastic.'

'You don't mind? That I've ... made it kind of public? The way I feel about you?'

'Rob, I don't know what I think – it's such a surprise. I didn't know. I had no idea!'

'I couldn't say anything, could I. Not while you were with *him*. But now ... ?'

It was a question, left hanging there in the air, waiting for her to answer. The minutes of her call ticked away, and she stood there, not knowing what to say. Not knowing whether she could promise anything.

'You're not still hung up on him, are you?' he asked eventually.

'No! You're joking. I can't even think about him without getting angry.'

'So do I have a chance? Even the slightest, tiniest chance?'

'I don't know, Rob. It's lovely – so lovely, what you've done. But I need time to get over the shock, I think.'

'Can I at least come and see you? Have a drink, have a chat? Would that be OK?'

'Yes. Oh, yes, that would be great. I'd *love* to hear all about what's happened with the band – how you got the recording contract, how all the boys are – who you got to replace Jack ...'

She stopped, realising she was gabbling on about the band, and the other boys, and knowing this wasn't what he wanted to hear, what he wanted to talk to her about. But it felt safer. What he'd said, what he'd declared in that song, was too big, too scary, to discuss on the phone.

'Well, look – we're all moving over to London in a couple of weeks, so ...'

'*Are* you?'

'Yeah, we're taking the plunge, renting a flat together so we can be nearer the action. We'll try to get by with some casual bar work and stuff.'

'Till your record hits the charts! Then you won't need to do that anymore! Oh, it would be good to see you, Rob. I'd really like that.'

'Well our flat's in West Ham – it's much cheaper there than further into the city – so we won't be too far from you. So shall I come down to Dagenham and take you out for a drink at your local?'

'You won't like it!' She laughed. 'It's dead rough!'

'I'm used to slumming it! But if we do ever get a hit record, though, I'll take you to the Ritz. That's a promise!'

'I'll hold you to that!' she said, and then the pips started to go, so they quickly made a date for two weeks later and said goodbye, and she was left standing there, wondering whether she'd dreamt it all.

It was so amazing, so sudden, so unexpected. Of course, she was flattered – thrilled! Who wouldn't be? But she wasn't sure how she felt about *him* – Rob. Of course, she'd always liked him as a friend, as *Jack's* friend. But she hadn't known he was feeling like this about her, and most of all she didn't want to hurt him, lead him on, if she didn't think she'd be able to feel the same. After what happened with Jack, she'd told herself she was giving up on men.

Well, she had two weeks to get used to it, to think about it – and at that moment she simply couldn't *stop* thinking about it! At the very least, she was going to meet him for that drink. And meanwhile – *obviously* – she was going out tomorrow to buy the record!

Chapter 14

Perth

Ken wasn't sure what to make of Jack Hunter. True enough, he and Ruth had been talking about starting a band for a while now, just waiting to find the right person to join them. But Jack? Was he OK? He didn't have a lot to say for himself and Ken wasn't sure he trusted that Pommy accent of his. But the bloke sang like an angel and played the guitar like Jimi Hendrix. Fair dos, he was good, no getting away from that, so he'd agreed straight away to have him in the band. Then he'd come to the pub in Freo the other night with his bird, and ran straight out again with some excuse about her feeling sick. Ken hadn't had a chance to get a look at the girlfriend – he just saw her back view through the crowd as she disappeared out the door. So when Jack turned up the next night at his place, wanting to talk to him about something personal, he wondered what the hell was coming.

And it couldn't have been any bloody worse.

'My girlfriend,' Jack began, without even sitting down. He was looking at Ken like he wanted to thump him. 'She's called Shona. Shona Wilkes. Name ring a bell?'

'Fuck,' said Ken.

'I just want to get some things straight,' Jack went on without missing a beat. 'First, are you still on the booze, are you still getting into trouble, because if you are, you can count me out of this set-up right now.'

'I ... look, not that it's any of your business, but ...'

'Second, from what Shona's told me, you must be a complete bastard. In which case I'm glad she's not still with you. But it makes me want to smash your face in. So we need to have a conversation.'

Ken felt his hands curling into fists. Who the hell did this bloke think he was? With his posh accent and his talk of *needing a conversation* – where did he get off, calling him a bastard? But then he dropped his eyes to the floor, remembering. Perhaps Jack had a point. It was true he'd treated Shona badly.

'I was a boozer, right?' he said, still not looking up at him. 'I'm not any more. And I've been out of trouble since I first met Shona. I could've slipped back afterwards ... but first time I hit a pub, I got talking to Ruth, and when I heard her singing and playing the guitar, I wanted to have a go myself. First time I've ever had something I wanted to do.'

'First time ... ever?' Jack said, curling his lip with disbelief.

'Yeah. Probably hard for you to understand.' He shook his head. No point antagonising the bloke any further. 'Sit down for Christ's sake, if you want this so-called *conversation*. I'll tell you what happened with Shona. Then you can decide if you still want to be in the band with me, or if you'd rather smash my face in.'

Jack hesitated for a minute, and then shrugged and sat down. He'd come here to sort it out, so there wasn't much point in going without hearing what Ken had to say. Even if he had the distinct feeling he wasn't going to like it.

Ken offered him a cigarette and lit one for himself. He'd never quite stopped wanting a drink in difficult situations, but a fag worked almost as well. He wished Ruth was here. She made everything easier. To be fair, although she'd been the one who'd given him the most important thing – his music – she hadn't actually done as much for him as Shona had. But that was another story.

'I met her when I was in the nick,' he began, taking a drag on his cigarette.

And that was how it had started.

He'd had a skinful that day, right enough. He was out of his skull, raging at some bloke who'd refused to serve him another beer, and then raging some more at the cops when they dragged him into the cop station. He remembered the desk sergeant had that bored, resigned look about him. People never seemed pleased to see him in those days.

'You again,' the sergeant said, looking Ken up and down like he was something the cat had dragged in. 'Ken bloody Warren. What is it this time?' he asked the arresting officers. 'Drunk and disorderly again? Public nuisance?'

'Yep. Plus resisting arrest.'

'So, still not learned your lesson, then, Warren? About time you grew up, isn't it, mate – larking around like a teenage yobbo at your age? Still on probation from last time, aren't you?'

Ken scowled. Get on with it, he was thinking. The charges, the cell – just get on with it and let him sleep it off. He was tired. Actually, he'd had enough of it. He was sick of forever struggling to stay inside the law, trying to stop the drink getting the better of him like it always seemed to, so that it didn't take much to aggravate him into losing his temper. He knew he needed to break the cycle, but he just didn't seem to have the strength. Didn't know where to find it.

'Put him in the cell, for God's sake – get him out of my sight,' the desk sergeant said dismissively, turning back to his paperwork. 'Loser,' he added under his breath.

'Fuck off,' Ken shouted. But nobody took any notice of him. They never did. They just shoved him in a cell.

He sprawled on the bunk with his arm across his face, thinking about it. *Loser.* He didn't know why the insult annoyed him so much – after all, that was exactly what he was, there was no denying it. What else would you call a grown man with no job, no permanent abode, no family, no friends apart from the other *losers* on the streets? The cop was dead right – he was too old to be behaving like an out-of-control teenage yobbo. At his age, twenty-four at the time, most blokes were probably settled down with a woman and a mortgage and a couple of kids, or at the very least they probably had a decent job, a foot on some sort of career ladder or else a trade, something to give them a bit of self-respect. Whereas all he had was the drink problem and the anger, the continual bloody anger. It rumbled red-hot in his guts like the core of a volcano, simmering, waiting to burst out of him at the slightest provocation. A threat, an insult, a jostle on the pavement, even the wrong kind of look from someone could make him erupt with a fury he had no idea how to handle.

He slept off the alcohol, till eventually towards morning he sat up, rubbing the back of his neck where he'd slept awkwardly on the hard bunk, and asked himself the question he only ever pondered when he found himself in this situation – in custody, and not drunk. The question was *Why?*

Why was he like this? Whose fault was it? He'd always known it was a weakness; other people seemed to be able to control their drinking, and their anger, so what was wrong with him? Who'd made him like this? Was it his parents? And if so, who the bloody hell were they, anyway, and why did they abandon him? What could he possibly have done, for Christ's sake, as a little kid, that was so bad he wasn't only dumped in a children's home, back in England, but then got sent off to the other side of the world, to be treated like shit, beaten and abused by the bastards who were supposed to be looking after him? He had no idea what it was he'd done, but it sure as hell must have been bad. So maybe he'd been like this from birth – right from a baby, maybe he was born evil, born with this temper, so his parents had sent him away, and here he was, grown up and still just as bad, and probably always would be. And every time he asked himself these questions, he went round in the same circle. There was no answer, and nobody to tell him how to break out of it.

'You've got a visitor.'

There was a new sergeant on duty now, the day shift. He held the cell door open and leered at Ken unpleasantly as he let the young woman in. For a minute Ken just stared at her. She was wearing a blue dress with short sleeves, her dark hair pulled back in a pony-tail and just a suggestion of pink lipstick on her lips. She barely looked old enough to be out of school, never mind visiting drunks in police cells. What the holy crap was she doing here?

'I'll be just outside if you need me,' the officer told her, giving Ken a warning look. 'Watch yerself with this one, miss,' he added to the girl. 'He's a repeat offender. Nasty piece of work.'

'Fuck off,' said Ken.

'You watch your language in front of the lady.' The officer glared at him as he went out, slamming the cell door and staying just outside, watching through the grille as if he expected Ken to leap on the woman or knock her out.

'My name's Shona,' she said, sitting down on the chair opposite him. He carried on staring at her, but she didn't flinch, or look away.

He wasn't was very polite. He muttered something along the lines of not giving a fuck what her fucking name was, and what the fuck did she want anyway?

'I told you to keep your language clean in front of the lady, Warren,' shouted the desk sergeant. 'Just yell if he makes a move on you, all right, miss?'

'It's all right, sergeant,' she yelled back. She gave Ken a grin, like they were on the same side all of a sudden. 'You aren't gonna make a move on me, are you?' Her eyes twinkled at him, like it was a great joke, and he shook his head, too confused to respond. He hadn't had a woman in months, and here was this … bloody gorgeous bit of stuff, turning up in his cell like some kind of mirage, laughing about the possibility of him making a move on her. She had to be out of her tiny mind.

'I don't even know what the bloody hell you're doing here,' he said eventually. 'Am I supposed to know you?'

'Not yet, you don't.'

'You're some kind of bloody do-gooder, is that it? One of these bloody social workers who like hanging around with the yobbos?'

She laughed. 'I'm not a social worker. But they tell me you were the only bloke brought in last night, cursing and swaying and swinging punches. So I reckoned I'd come and have a look at you, now you've cooled off and sobered up. See if you've improved any overnight.'

He wanted to hit her. His face must have said it all, but the funny thing was, it was his hands she looked at straight away. The way he was clenching them.

'Don't do that,' she said calmly. 'You'll end up with arthritis.'

He was lost for words, and that hadn't happened a lot up till then. She was just sitting there smiling at him. It'd been a long time since anyone had actually smiled at him. He was more used to people ignoring him, looking away from him, like he was beneath contempt. But if she thought she was gonna trick him into showing any weakness, she had another thought coming.

'What is it with you?' he said. 'If all you're gonna do is sit there grinning, taking the piss, then you can just fuck off out of it.'

'I'm not taking the piss,' she said calmly. 'And I'll fuck off any time you want me to. I've only come to talk to you, see if there's anything I can do to help you.'

So much for minding his language in front of the lady! She could out-swear him, by the sound of it.

'Yeah,' he said. 'OK, then, you can bring me a car – one of the new Ford Falcons'll do nicely. And a new suit, flash as you like – a bloke needs to look his best when he turns up at the homeless hostel. Talking of which, if you like to grab me a nice little apartment close to the town centre, that'd be bonzer too. And you can get me a job – something where I get a lot of dough without getting my hands dirty. A bank manager, or a schoolteacher – yeah, that's the one, a schoolteacher. Give me a cane and let me thrash the little buggers.' He laughed, but at the same time he could feel his fists clenching again.

'Schoolteachers don't cane the kids these days, Ken,' she said quietly.

He just shook his head. Didn't want to hear all that garbage.

'Is that something that troubles you?' she went on. 'Kids being hit?'

He looked up at her slowly. What was it with this sheila anyway? Coming here, sticking her nose in where it wasn't wanted?

'Get the hell out of here,' he said, getting to his feet.

'Righto.' She got to her feet without complaining. She knocked on the door for the sergeant to unlock it, and walked out without looking round. 'See you later,' she called back.

But she'd unsettled him. Stupid interfering nosy parker. At the end of the day, she was just some bloody do-gooder, whether she was a social worker or not, and none of them had ever done *him* any good, had they.

But the next day she was back again. Like he had any choice in the matter. He'd just been sitting there, waiting for them to let him out on bail.

'OK,' she said, fixing her eyes on him. 'I've got some ideas.'

'Ideas about what?'

'How to get you off with a lighter sentence. Look, when you come up for trial you have to convince everyone you're making an effort, right?'

'And what the hell's it got to do with you?' he said.

'They give us a list – of people we might be able to help.'

'We?'

'A group of us from St Mark's. The church next door to the cop station here, which you could say is fortunate. Or maybe not.'

'Huh! So you're a bloody bible-basher. I should've known.'

'That's right. Your name's on our list. And it's my turn. Lucky old me!'

'So what's the point of all this? You want to save my soul? Forget it, darlin'. You're wasting your time.'

'Nah. I don't think I'd be much good at that side of things anyway. Souls are Reverend Giles's domain.'

'What are you getting out of this, then? Cos I sure as hell don't want you hanging around.'

'Good. Just agree to do two things for me, and I'll be out of your hair. Right?'

It wasn't right. It was bloody ridiculous, this pert little miss sitting here, with her big brown eyes and (today) her fluffy pink jumper with a matching hair slide in her hair – she looked like she should be in a bloody convent school, not a police cell – why didn't she just piss off like he'd already told her? But the mad thing was, he was getting curious. He actually wanted to know what the two things were. Not that he had any intention of doing them, of course.

'OK,' she said, looking him square in the eye, 'Try to get a job. And join the AA, make an effort to get off the grog.'

He snorted in anger. '*Try to get a job*? You don't think I have? Who the hell's gonna employ me, with a criminal record and ...'

'We can get you some interviews,' she said quietly.

'We?'

'People I know.'

'People from the church, right?'

'And so what? You're too proud to accept their help?'

He swallowed back another angry response, looking away from her instead, drumming his fingers on the table.

'Also, I can take you to the AA meetings. Make sure you get there,' she added.

He shook his head again. What the bloody hell did she know about anything? She'd probably never been anywhere near an AA meeting in her sweet little bible-bashing life.

'I know exactly where they're held,' she went on. 'I used to go to meetings myself.'

'You what?'

'I'm an alcoholic, Ken. Haven't had a drink now for three years, though.'

He looked at her in disbelief. 'What – a little bit too much of the communion wine on Sundays, was it?'

He regretted it almost as soon as the words were out of his mouth. She raised her eyes to the ceiling, silent for a moment, before looking back at him and going on:

'No. More like a bottle or two too much of the vodka, *every* day. Vodka, or whatever I could get my hands on. I wasn't going to church at that time. I was in a bad place.' She looked away again. 'Your trouble, I reckon, is that you think you're the only one in the world who's ever had problems.'

Ken sure as hell hadn't seen *that* coming. And she'd hit the nail on the head, fair and square: he probably never did stop to think that other people might have problems. Although maybe not quite like his.

'I bet you've got a family, at least,' he said kind of grudgingly.

'Yes. Although it took me a while to appreciate them. I moved out when I was just seventeen. I'd got in with a rough crowd.'

'But you're all right with them now – yeah? Your parents?'

'Yes. We don't always see eye to eye, but ...'

'You should be bloody grateful you've got them!' he told her, the old anger flaring for a moment.

'I am,' she said gently. 'I am grateful.'

'Right.' He was annoyed with himself for showing his weakness. She was looking at him like she wanted to know more, but wasn't going to ask.

'So are we going to agree on this?' she said finally. 'I'll get you the job interviews, if you'll come to at least one AA meeting?'

He shrugged. 'I don't get it. What's in it for you?'

'I just like helping people. Someone helped me when I was on my uppers. It's ... kind of payback.'

'And if I agree to this ... this *help* you're offering – I suppose you'll start trying to get me into church. Well, you can forget that.'

'I'm not trying to get you into church, OK? The AA meeting is on Wednesday night. I'll meet you outside here at seven o'clock,' she said. 'I'll bring the interview appointments, so if you don't turn up, you won't get those either.'

'Bloody hell. You could drive a man to drink.' He realised what he'd said and actually laughed. 'So who was it?' he said as she got up to leave. 'Who helped *you*, when you were out of luck?'

'Reverend Giles from St Mark's. So think yourself bloody lucky you've got me instead!'

'Good for you. I hope you go to heaven now.'

'That's not why I'm doing this,' she said, smiling. 'But let's hope I do, anyway. It'll sure beat the alternative.'

She got him to the AA meetings. She got him a job. They stayed in touch, and eventually she agreed to go out on a date with him. Gradually, he told her everything – *almost* everything – about his past, and the more he told her, the less he seemed to lose his temper, the less he craved a drink. He had a girlfriend – a decent, proper girlfriend. She never did get him to go anywhere near the church, but she did encourage him to stay out of trouble, stay off the booze, sort himself out.

She paid a heavy price for her involvement with him. Her parents, who'd only recently welcomed her back home after she'd gone off the rails as a teenager, decided Ken was trouble and demanded that she gave him up. When she refused, they chucked her out again and she made up her mind to have nothing further to do with them. He hadn't liked them anyway – but it hadn't been his call to make, and he, of all people, knew how much it hurt to be estranged from your family.

He couldn't really say why he sabotaged their relationship. He supposed she'd been too good for him. Or maybe he just got bored. She started talking about moving in together, getting married – that wasn't for him. Happy bloody families! He wasn't a family man, was he. Hadn't he done enough for her? Got himself sober, got a job, stayed out of bloody trouble.

'What the hell *do* you want?' she'd flung at him during one of their final rows. 'Are you just going to drift on like this, for the rest of your life?'

'I guess so,' he said. Nothing wrong with that, was there?

'So what was the point of all this? You've got a better life now – a job, a bank account, a decent life. What was the point? You've got no *interest* in anything. You've given up the booze, but what's going to take its place? What, if it isn't a wife, and a family?' she added in a very small voice.

'For the last bloody time, I don't want a wife! I don't want a family!' he'd shouted at her. And he'd stormed out and gone straight back to the pub – where, fortunately, while he was still only on his first beer (and the last, as it turned out), he met Ruth in much the same way that Jack had done more recently, and got talking to her about the one thing he *was* interested in: music. He knew he was a good singer; he'd been picked to sing in the school choir. And music was now going to save his life.

He wasn't proud of how he'd finished with Shona. When he thought about her these days, he felt the dull ache of regret he should have felt at the time. He'd sometimes thought about contacting her to apologise – but he realised that was only going to make him feel better, not her.

And now, here was this bloke who *was* in a committed relationship with her, who *was* having babies with her – who wasn't going to be the type (with his posh Pommy accent) to let her down, dump her, break her heart like he'd done. He should feel grateful to him, shouldn't he. He ought to like the bloke, shake him by the hand. But it remained to be seen whether Jack was going to like *him*.

Chapter 15

Dagenham

Rob and the other boys from the band moved into their new place in West Ham on a Friday in the middle of August – and on the Saturday he and Frankie met for a drink. She was worried that it was all a bit rushed, a bit too *keen*. Not that it wasn't nice to see him – in fact, she was thrilled to see him after so long. But all the time she was with him, she couldn't help thinking about the song. It was so *weird*, sitting there in the pub with him, knowing he'd written all that stuff, all those words in the song, for *her*. And meant it all, too, so he said. But as soon as he'd put the first drink on the table in front of her, he coughed awkwardly and proceeded to make a little speech, saying he hoped she didn't feel uncomfortable, and that he wasn't going to embarrass her or try to talk her into going out with him, or anything, unless she decided she wanted to. In one way it was dead embarrassing sitting there listening to him saying all that, but on the other hand she thought it was nice of him, too. Kind of got it out of the way.

Then he just changed the subject, going on to talk to her about the band – and the record. Since its release, it had been played so much on the radio that Frankie could hardly tune in without hearing her name being sung. Of course, it was exciting, but she wasn't sure whether she was most excited about it being *her song*, or about the fact that the Snakes were doing so well.

'It's heading up the charts,' Rob told her with a grin. 'Our manager reckons it'll be in the Top Twenty this week.'

'That's fantastic! But you haven't told me yet what happened – did you get someone new? A replacement for ... Jack?'

'Yeah – we got ourselves a new lead singer – Andy. He's great. But they all wanted me to sing the lead on *Francesca*.' He gave her a little smile, but moved on quickly, to add: 'It's all been going really well. We're going back over for the Isle of Wight Festival again next week. Dave – that's our manager – says if the festival crowds like us as much as they did last year, they'll buy the record. And people who like the record will hopefully buy the next one, and that's how it goes!'

'I'm dead chuffed for you,' she said. 'You all deserve this. Especially after the way *he* let you down.' She pulled a face, and Rob looked like he was going to say something, but he took a gulp of his beer instead.

'So what have *you* been up to?' he asked.

'Oh, nothing much.' She realised she didn't have much to tell him. She'd made absolutely no progress in her life in the months since she'd last spoken to Rob. If anything, she'd taken a step backwards, because of giving up the evening class when she moved in with her mother. 'My mum died a few months ago,' she explained. 'She'd had two strokes, and after the first one I moved back in with her, to look after her.'

'Sorry to hear that,' he said quietly.

'And now I'm back with my sister, but she's expecting another baby and she gets tired, so I help her quite a lot in the house.'

'That's good of you.'

She shook her head. She hadn't meant to make it sound like she was some sort of saint to her family. It was just that apart from this domestic stuff, she couldn't think what else to talk about.

'Are you really all right, Frankie,' he asked as she remained silent. 'Apart from losing your poor mum like that? It must have been rotten for you.'

The unexpected sympathy almost brought tears to her eyes.

'I'm OK. Mum and I weren't really close, but that was why I felt bad – you know? Felt like I had to help her when she was ill.'

And then, because he was looking at her so sympathetically, and because basically he was so nice, and she did like him, even if it wasn't in quite the same way he said he liked her, she decided to tell him about the other thing. At least it was something interesting!

'I've found out I've got another sister.'

'Really?' He stopped with his beer glass halfway to his mouth. 'How come?'

'It was in Mum's will. It was quite a shock.'

'I bet it was!'

'Neither of us – Marianne or I – knew about her. The solicitor has traced her birth certificate. She must have been born before Mum and Dad were married.'

'Wow.' He raised his eyebrows, thinking about it. 'Perhaps she died before you and your sister were born. And perhaps your mum never liked to talk about it?'

'Yeah, that's what we thought must have happened. But there's no record of her death, apparently. It's like she just disappeared after she was born.'

'That's dead sad, isn't it,' he said. 'You must be desperate to find out about her.'

'Our solicitor's still looking into it. Putting adverts out, for her to get in touch, or anyone who knows her whereabouts. Marianne says they're using a private detective.'

'Blimey. What a mystery!'

'Yes. I keep wondering about her – you know, what happened to her, whether she got adopted or something.'

'I hope they find her.' He put his hand over hers. It was a simple enough gesture – friendship, sincerity. But ridiculously, because of the words of the song, Frankie felt herself blushing at his touch, and immediately moved her hand away, picking up her drink as an excuse. Rob pretended not to notice. There was an uncomfortable silence for a minute.

'I'm looking for a new job, too,' she gabbled, out of desperation to say something.

'Are you? Well, good for you. What do you want to do?'

'I don't know,' she said, feeling stupid. She was seriously beginning to wonder why on earth he thought he was in love with her. Even to herself, she seemed to be the most boring person on earth. 'The only thing I can do, really, is typing.'

'OK, but what sort of thing are you *interested* in? I mean, can you imagine yourself working with ... I don't know ... animals, say? Or children? Or sick people?'

She shook her head. 'No – it was one thing looking after Mum, but I couldn't imagine doing nursing or anything like that.' She sighed. 'To be honest, the only thing I'm really dead keen on is music.'

He smiled. 'Nothing wrong with that – I'm exactly the same!'

'No. You're actually *good* at music! You've got a talent – you can sing, and play the guitar! Me, I just like listening to it.'

'Frankie, don't put yourself down,' he said seriously. 'If it wasn't for people like you who love music, people like me and the boys could never get anywhere!'

She laughed, and he added, 'You'll find something that suits you, soon. I'm sure of it. I'll keep a lookout for you, too. You never know what might turn up.'

It was nice of him to offer. But it was hardly going to be much use to her if he came up with a vacancy for a singer or a keyboard player!

He got them both another drink and as he sat down, he suddenly said, all in a rush: 'I take it you've never heard anything from Jack?'

'No.' She thought about his letter from Australia. Thought about the mystery of the money order, still sitting in her underwear drawer, still playing on her mind. If it wasn't for that, she might even have said something to Rob. She had no reason to feel any loyalty to Jack, but he *had* said she was the only one he was trusting with the information about his whereabouts. He'd said other stuff, too – like it would be dangerous for him to come back. Not that Frankie was sure she believed any of it, but since he'd sent that money, she felt like there was a huge question mark hanging over the whole Jack situation – and she wasn't ready to face it yet. 'No, I haven't heard from him,' she went on more firmly, 'And I don't want to, either.'

'I don't blame you. He let us down – the band – but he let you down even more. I can't believe he did that to you. I really thought he …' He broke off abruptly, and then added, 'Anyway, no point going over that now.'

It was a nice evening, even if Frankie felt she was holding out on him a bit, nervous of giving him the wrong idea. But he was the perfect gentleman – just a peck on the cheek to say goodbye.

'Thanks for coming over tonight,' she said. 'And please give my love to the other boys.'

'I can do better than that. Why not come and see us play at the Festival again? We could give you a lift over.'

She hesitated, and he suddenly looked stricken.

'Oh – Frankie, sorry! What an idiot I am. Of course you won't want to go back to the Festival. It was where … it all started, wasn't it. Where you met him.'

'That's all right.' She shrugged, and suddenly made a decision on the spot. 'That doesn't matter anymore. It was just – strange, realising it's been a whole year. But you know what? I'd love to come. Are you sure you'll be able to take me? Otherwise I'll get the train.'

'No you won't! It's no problem. Pete and Bernie will take the van, with all the equipment, and I'm taking Andy and his girlfriend in my car. There'll be plenty of room for another one!'

'Thanks, then – that sounds great!' She smiled, happier now she knew she'd be sharing the ride with a couple of others. 'It'll be so exciting to see you all perform at the Festival again. Although, if your record is in the charts by then I shall feel like I'll have to pay to talk to you all!'

'No you won't. Even if we ever got as big as the Beatles, or the Stones, we'd never forget an old friend,' he said seriously, and then he laughed and added: 'Anyway, how can we forget you when our record is named after you?'

She was glad he was joking about it. It was one thing to know he'd written it for her, and to hold that knowledge in her heart – another thing if he'd kept on being serious about it. It would have made her feel slightly panicky.

'Well, the Beatles and the Stones have had it all their way for a long time now. Maybe the world's waiting for a new band to take their place!'

'Yeah – I like your thinking, Frankie, but we're not getting that big for our boots!'

She went home smiling to herself, looking forward to the festival the following week. Looking forward to seeing the rest of the band, of course, and to hearing them play. That was all. All she wanted – for now, at least. If not for a very long time.

Chapter 16

Perth

Jack drove home slowly from Ken's place. He'd stayed far longer than he intended, and had ended up having a coffee with the bloke and shaking his hand. He didn't really know why he was prepared to forgive him for treating Shona like crap. He guessed he felt sorry for him, up to a point. He'd told him a lot more stuff, over coffee – stuff he said he didn't tell many people.

'From what I hear,' he told Shona when he got home and found her sitting up, waiting for him, 'he had a pretty rough time, growing up.'

'Yes, I know all about that,' she retorted. 'I'm the one who helped him turn his life around, remember?'

'But ... bloody hell, Shona! I was so shocked by what he said! Sent out here from England when he was just a kid, put in one of those boys' homes where the kids got beaten almost every time they opened their mouths. No wonder the poor bugger went off the rails.'

'And you think that excuses everything, do you? *I* went off the rails myself, when I was younger, but I grew up.'

'Look, I can understand why you're bitter, but ...'

'Oh, you can, can you?' She turned to him, and Jack was taken aback by the anger in her eyes. 'Jack, I gave up my life for that man. I gave up my *family*! I gave up my *faith*!'

'I never even knew you were religious. You never go to church.'

'Are you even listening to me? I said – I dropped it, all of it. After Ken and I got together; he kind of talked me out of it. I couldn't see the relevance of the church any more. I'd only gone back in the first place because Reverend Giles had done so much to help me – got me sober, got me back on the straight and narrow. I'd been happy to be back, though, and it pleased my mum, made her think I'd settled down. Helped her agree to take me back home. And then, when they found out about Ken …'

'He told me. They threw you out again.'

'Well, you can see their point, really, can't you? I wouldn't want any daughter of *mine* hanging around with someone like him. But at the time, we had such an almighty row, I've never spoken to them since.'

'You never told me about being an alcoholic, either. I just assumed you didn't drink.'

'I don't,' she said flatly. 'Does it matter why?'

He shook his head, baffled. He was beginning to think he didn't know her at all. She'd always seemed so soft and sweet, so gentle and compliant. He'd never heard her speak so harshly, never seen such a hostile expression on her face before.

'He … Ken … seems really sorry about what he did. The way he finished with you.'

'Right!' she said. 'So that's why he's never called me, not once in two years, to even ask if I'm OK? Get real, Jack. He couldn't give a shit about me. It was my own fault, in a way. I was unbelievably naïve, thinking I was going to take this hardened criminal, this seasoned drunk, under my wing and change him …'

'You did! He's still off the booze, and he's still in employment. That's all thanks to you.'

'And he's still a bastard. People don't change, Jack. I've had to learn that the hard way.'

Jack was beside her in an instant, his arms round her.

'I'm sorry. But why didn't you tell me? Why couldn't you confide in me, Shona?'

But he knew, really, that it was a silly question. She hadn't felt able to tell him about her alcoholism, her involvement with the church, or her relationship with Ken – probably the most significant things in her life – and he hadn't been able to share *his* past history with her either – so what the hell were they doing getting married? Did they really know each other at all? And was this really a good time to be asking that question?

'I'm sorry he hurt you so much,' Jack said, stroking her hair. 'I went round there wanting to smack him in the face.'

'But he talked you round,' she said, 'didn't he.'

'No, he ...'

'He gave you the sob story. Made you feel sorry for him.'

'Shona, love, I *do* feel sorry for him. Of course I'm not saying that makes it all right, the way he finished with you. But in the long run, isn't it better that it *did* finish?'

She sighed. 'Yes, I know that – of course I'm glad I'm with you now. But ... some things you just don't get over that easily.'

'I understand. I've already told you – I won't see him again.'

'No, Jack – I want you to do this. The band. I've seen how much it matters to you. But just don't expect me to speak to him, will you.'

It made it difficult, but not impossible. They normally met up at Ruth's place to practise anyway. Shona tried to take an interest in the band, in much the same way that Jack tried to take an interest in the wedding plans and the books about babies' names. They found a drummer who'd been working with another band, who jumped at the chance of a change, especially when he'd heard the others performing together. His name was Al, and it was only when Ruth once happened to write down their initials – K, R, A, J – that they hit on a name for themselves: *KRASH.*

Despite everything, Jack and Ken quickly developed a rapport. As musicians, they had a lot of respect for each other. Ken openly admired Jack's obvious talent and experience;

Jack was impressed by Ken's natural ability that had enabled him to make so much progress in such a short time. But there was more to it than that. Jack found, as he got to know him better, that he actually liked the guy. He couldn't imagine how, with the start in life that Ken had had, and the way he'd been living up till so recently, he'd managed to retain his sense of humour. He lived on his own in a tiny one-bedroom place and since she'd met him, Ruth had been keeping an eye on him.

'He forgets to pay the bills,' she explained to Jack. 'It gets a bit exasperating, but what can you expect? He's never had the responsibility of a stable adult life before.'

'Good of you to take care of him.'

'Oh, don't get me wrong! I give him what-for sometimes. I went round there one night last week because I'd been trying to get hold of him for days, and he just comes to the door grinning at me, saying *'G'day. What's up?'* – and then giving me his puppy-dog look, the one that might make me want to mother him if I was that kind of girl, and saying the phone had been cut off *again*.' She shook her head. 'I keep telling him to pay the bills as soon as they come in.'

'I can imagine it gets annoying.'

'Well, no point beating him up about it, is there. He's done real good, since he got himself set up in that place and most of the time he's remembered to pay the rent and the bills. He keeps the place clean enough, for a bloke on his own, and so far hasn't managed to wreck anything. And best of all, he's stayed off the grog and stayed out of trouble. Can't say fairer than that, really.'

Ken seemed easy-going enough until something upset him – and then Jack noticed he'd clench his fists and screw up his face, like he was trying to control himself. He saw it happen once when they were leaving Ruth's place together one Saturday, and they saw a father knocking the hell out of his kid in the street for some minor misdemeanour.

'You OK, mate?' Jack said as they walked on.

Ken shook his head and punched his fist into his other hand a couple of times.

'It ain't necessary,' was all he said.

'I guess it's different, though, when it's the kid's own father,' Jack said quietly. 'Not like ... your situation. Total strangers knocking you boys about.'

'I wouldn't know, would I. I never had a dad. Never knew him, anyway.'

'No. Sorry, mate. It must be hard – living with that.'

'Well, look, no good crying about it, is there.' Ken straightened his shoulders and clapped Jack on the back. 'People worse off than me. See you Wednesday, cobber.'

Cobber. Jack smiled to himself as he carried on home. He'd begun by being suspicious of the bloke, had gone through disliking him, to feeling sorry for him, to now having a genuine affection for him. Ruth had told him she was glad Ken finally had a bloke – *'a decent kind of bloke'* – he could talk to, and Jack was glad if he was helping him in some way. But more to the point, Ken was giving *him* something.

Being in the band had helped him to put his other worries to one side. Not that he'd forgotten them – how could he? For a start, he was about to get married, to someone he was very fond of but increasingly felt like he didn't really know well enough. He was going to be a father – when on the other side of the world he might already have a child with Frankie. Every time he thought about this, recalling that he still hadn't had a response from her since sending the money, that he still didn't know whether she'd had the baby yet, he felt the hot panic rising inside him. He didn't know what to do about it, other than sending another letter, begging for information, risking being ignored yet again. He guessed he'd probably do it anyway, but he wished he could discuss it with someone. Wished, desperately, that there was someone he could confide in.

It was too soon. He hadn't known him long enough. But maybe, just maybe, Ken might be the person he could trust.

Already, he was enjoying that warm feeling that came from having a mate he could talk to. Someone he could call *cobber*. The first real friend he'd had, apart from Shona of course, since he'd come to Australia. That had to be worth a lot, didn't it.

Chapter 17

The Isle of Wight and Dagenham

The Isle of Wight Festival was brilliant. Frankie couldn't think, afterwards, why she'd been so worried about going to it again. Well, of course, it brought back memories of the previous year – but only in a good way. It was a lot more fun driving down to the ferry in Rob's car, with Andy and his girlfriend Georgia, than playing gooseberry with Lou and Drippy Terry. Actually that was a bit awkward, as Lou had already asked her if she wanted to go to the Festival with them again, and she'd said no. But it was just too bad. As it happened she didn't even see them over there, in the crowds. Andy was really nice and so was Georgia – they actually *lived* together, in Ilford, not too far really from Frankie, or from where the other boys had their new flat. Frankie didn't think she'd ever met anyone before who'd been daring enough to live together without getting married. Her mother would have been horrified!

She thought the Festival was even better than the previous year. It was held in a different place – closer to the ferry port at Ryde. And it was definitely bigger this time – apparently when Bob Dylan was performing – the highlight of the weekend – there were over a hundred thousand people there. The atmosphere and the music were amazing, again, and considering how many people were there, it was great that there was no trouble, no fighting or anything. Even the police were impressed, and the compere told the crowds that they were the *'blessed generation'*. Frankie wasn't sure whether it was the cider they were drinking, but she actually did feel blessed. Surely no other generation before them had been lucky enough to take part in such a fantastic happening. Everyone there was of the same mind – they were enjoying the freedom, the atmosphere of love and peace and *music*!

'Just like that new festival they've had in the States – Woodstock,' Rob said. 'It's like the whole world is celebrating music, all of a sudden.'

The Crazy Snakes performed on the Saturday evening. Frankie sat with Georgia, and a crowd of the boys' fans from the Island, and felt dead proud to be watching them from right close to the stage. Dead proud to feel like they were *their* band. Dead proud of Rob, especially – although when she caught herself thinking that, she went hot with a kind of panic even though she'd kept the feeling to herself. And when they played *Francesca,* Georgia screamed and put her arms round Frankie, and she could see Rob looking straight at her as he was singing. Afterwards Georgia was still so excited, she turned round and yelled to everyone within earshot: 'This is Francesca! This is who the song's about!' And although Frankie was blushing bright red, she was laughing too, and people all around them were whistling, and cheering, and calling out to her.

'He's crazy about you,' Georgia said when she'd finally calmed down a bit. 'You do know that, don't you?'

'I … do realise he likes me,' she admitted.

'And he's such a lovely bloke. You will give him a chance, won't you?'

She swallowed. 'I'm … not rushing into anything. I want to be sure of how I feel. I don't want to hurt him.'

Georgia hugged her again. 'Groovy. Give it time.' She looked at Frankie carefully. 'Andy says you used to go out with the other lead singer – the one who did a runner?'

'Jack. Yes. But I'm over that.'

'Good!' She laughed and took a swig of her cider. 'Hey, the Snakes are coming back offstage! That was fantastic, boys!' She gave Andy a kiss and the crowds around them whooped and cheered again.

'Do I get one?' Rob asked Frankie quietly, and she gave him a quick peck on the cheek.

She felt so happy and excited, and it had been so fabulous when he was singing *Francesca* – she did actually feel like kissing him properly. But what held her back, of course, was the memory of the same time the previous year – the way she'd kissed Jack Hunter. And remembering how *that* ended up. It would have been so easy to get carried away, in that atmosphere of Free Love, where everyone seemed to be rolling in the grass around them, kissing and cuddling. But she was determined *not* to get carried away like that again. She still felt shaky thinking about how she could so easily have been pregnant. She could have had a baby by now! It didn't bear thinking about.

Rob seemed to accept it; he was the perfect gentleman when he took her back to stay at his parents' place in Shanklin. It was so late, that they were only there for a few hours, and she slept on the sofa – on her own – before they headed back to the Festival again for the Sunday line-up. Bob Dylan didn't appear till eleven o'clock and it was fantastic to see him before they packed up to head back to the ferry. Rob dropped her off right at the door. It was the early hours of the morning and she was shattered. Andy and Georgia were both asleep on the back seat, and Rob just kissed her very gently on the cheek to say goodbye.

She'd carried on with her search for a new job – but the only one she'd bothered to apply for was a sales position at a record shop in Romford. And even if she was offered it, she didn't think she'd be able to accept because the money would probably be even less than she was earning at the bank. She felt like she owed it to her sister to bring in the best wages she could. And eventually, she'd need to be able to afford a place of her own.

The following Friday she arrived home from work to find a letter waiting for her. At first, stupidly, she thought it might be about the job in the shop – but course it wasn't: it was an airmail envelope. It was from *Jack* again. Marianne watched her turning the envelope over and shook her head at her.

'He still writing to you?' she said.

Frankie didn't really blame her sister for sounding so disapproving – and that was without her even knowing about the money order sitting in her bedroom drawer!

'I've got no idea what he wants,' she said, shrugging. 'Maybe I'd better actually send a reply, this time – tell him to get lost.'

'Yeah. Maybe you should.'

She took the letter upstairs to read in her bedroom.

Dear Frankie

I realise you probably haven't had time to reply to my last letter. I can only imagine how hard things have been for you – how busy you must be. But I couldn't wait any longer to ask you about the baby – it must have been born now. Frankie, I really want to help ... but it's difficult. If you give me a chance, I'll explain. But please – at least, please just let me know if the baby is all right, and whether it's a boy or a girl. Be fair, whatever you think of me, I need to know that, at least! I know you probably still hate me, and I understand why, but I really do want to help with the baby. I'm just sorry that it will have to be done in secret. Did you get the money? I'm wondering if these letters are reaching you, as I'm not sure where you're living now so I'm writing c/o your sister. I can send you some more money next month. Please just tell me you and the baby are all right. And if by any chance you've started to forgive me, even just a bit, would you think about sending me a photo?

I still think about you, every day, and only wish things could have been different. But it's so complicated now.

Love from Jack

Frankie put the letter down, shaking her head. She didn't have a clue what to think about this. It was going from bad to worse! What on earth was he talking about? She seriously wondered whether he'd lost his marbles. Maybe the heat in Australia had melted his brains. Why in God's name would he be so obsessed with finding out about Marianne's baby, and why would he think it had already been born? In the end, she decided enough was enough. She had to find out. She charged back downstairs and confronted Marianne.

'Did you write to Jack? You know – when you told me you'd found his first letter and you said you *felt* like writing to him ...'

Marianne sighed and sat down, looking at Frankie apologetically.

'Yes, I did. I'm really sorry, love. It was a spur of the minute thing – I was just so angry with him, at the time – the way he treated you. Now I'm starting to realise I've probably made things worse, haven't I. I told him not to try to contact you any more – but he still has.'

Frankie brushed this aside. 'I don't care about that. I can throw his letters away. But I'm just so confused by what he's been saying. Did you tell him about the baby?'

Marianne put her hand on her tummy. 'About *my* baby? Why would I do that?'

'Well, that's what I thought. But he keeps on asking about the baby – he's asking now whether it's been born yet, and whether it's a girl or a boy, and even asking for a photo!'

'*WHAT?*'

'Yes. And ... oh, sis, I should have told you, but I didn't know what to make of it. He sent me a money order, about a month ago – a lot of money. He said it was for the baby!'

'He sent *money?*' Marianne said, looking horrified. 'What did you do with it?'

'Nothing. It's still in my drawer. I'd have to pay it into my account, but I didn't want to. And I didn't want to write to him, so ... I've just ignored it. Now he's asking if I got it, and saying he'll send more! What on earth's he doing? You don't ...' She swallowed hard. 'You don't think he's trying to get rid of money he shouldn't have, do you? Like, money he's *stolen* or something?'

For a minute, Marianne just stared back at her. Then she shook her head and looked away.

'No. I think I can actually guess why he's sent it. I ... think he's got the wrong end of the stick, Frankie. Something I said in my letter ...' She went a bit red. 'I'm sorry. It's my fault.'

'Why? What did you say?'

'That he didn't even bother to find out whether he'd made you pregnant.'

'Oh.' She sat down opposite her. 'So it's nothing to do with *your* baby! He thinks ... oh blimey!' She started to laugh. 'He thinks *I've* had a baby!'

'I'm really sorry ... I was just so angry ...'

'Good!' She was still laughing. 'Ha! It serves him right, Mari! Let him bloody think it! Let him feel guilty! Serves him *bloody* right!'

'You can't ...', Marianne said, looking at her nervously. 'You can't take his money, Frankie. Whatever he's done, that wouldn't be right.'

'I won't. I'm not going to spend it, or even pay it in. I'll send it back eventually. But not yet. I'll just let him sweat for a bit longer. Serves him *bloody* right!' She laughed again.

Marianne looked at her anxiously. She was slightly worried her sister had gone a bit loopy. But Frankie was actually feeling better about Jack Hunter than she had in a long time! She went back upstairs and looked at the letter again, chuckling to herself. It all made sense now – and it was a relief to know what he was talking about. He must be like a cat on hot bricks, wondering whether she'd had a baby and what it was. Wondering whether he was a father! She chortled to herself. It was really was quite funny! Well, she deserved a bit of amusement at his expense, just for a little while longer – didn't she?

That Saturday night, the Crazy Snakes were playing at the Up Beat club. Frankie had already said she'd go. She sat with Georgia again while the boys were playing. This time they kept more of a low profile – even when Rob sang *Francesca*, Georgia didn't start hugging her and showing her off to the crowd. The atmosphere in the club was different from at the festival, obviously. The Snakes went down a storm again – everyone was cheering and clapping – but the girls were sitting on their own in a corner near the stage, and didn't want to get mobbed by people who realised they were with the band.

After their performance, they all headed off to the pub just down the street. It wasn't too busy in there – most people were in the club – so they were able to sit down and have a proper chat together. The boys were all in a great mood – singing and joking and buying beers all round to celebrate their success. Since their appearance at the festival the previous week, their record was now at number nine in the Top Twenty and their manager was talking about making a second recording as soon as possible, together with an album, and organising a UK concert tour.

While the other boys were talking amongst themselves, Rob was asking Frankie about her job-hunting.

'No luck yet,' she said, and told him about the job in the record shop.

'That's what I used to do!' he said. 'It's actually a great job if you like music. Except … for the pay.'

'I know. That's the trouble. I know my job at the bank's boring, but it's better money than working in a shop. And if only I could bring myself to stick at it, and do the evening classes again, I could earn even better money one day.' She sighed. 'I think I'd better just stay where I am, after all.'

Rob listened sympathetically. 'I wish I knew what to suggest,' he said. They both fell silent for a minute, and became conscious of the others talking.

'It's really mounting up,' Pete was saying. 'I managed to sort through one boxful the other day, but there are about another half dozen boxes waiting to be read and replied to.'

'I know. I did a whole lot of replies last week,' Andy said. 'I had terrible writer's cramp – I didn't think I'd be able to play the guitar afterwards!'

'They're talking about the fan mail,' Rob explained to Frankie. 'Not that we don't appreciate it – it's amazing that so many people are writing to us! But I reckon we need a full-time secretary just to deal with all the …' He broke off, stared at Frankie for a minute and burst out laughing.

'What's funny, Rob?' Pete called across to him.

'You got an idea about the fan mail, mate?' Bernie said. 'Have you learned to type, or something?'

'No!' Rob was smiling broadly. 'But I know a girl who can!'

Over another round of drinks, plans were quickly discussed, and to Frankie's amazement, by the time they said goodnight, just like that, she'd been given a new job. For a better salary than she was being paid by the bank, she'd work from her own home, with a typewriter and all the stationery provided. She was not only going to respond to all the fan mail, but at her own suggestion, she was also going to set up and run the Crazy Snakes' Fan Club, producing a mailing list, membership cards and quarterly newsletters with photos of the band.

'That's assuming we last longer than a quarter!' Rob joked.

'Well, if you get too famous, I might need an assistant!' she joked back, excitement making her feel light-headed and slightly hysterical.

'If that happens, we'll give you as many assistants as you like,' Bernie assured her.

Georgia looked just as excited about it as Frankie was. She was a teacher – far too busy with her own career to be involved in running anything for the group. But Frankie had gathered she was also keen to marry Andy, the sooner the better.

'You make sure you warn those girls, Andy's spoken for!' she said, only half joking.

'That'd be a bad move, actually,' Andy said, putting his arm round her. 'Remember what happened when John Lennon finally admitted he was married? Some of the Beatles' fans went mad, crying and threatening to kill themselves. It'd be a mistake to ruin their little fantasies about getting one of us for themselves one day!'

'Huh!' Georgia said. 'As long as it's only fantasies!'

'Don't worry.' Frankie smiled at her. 'I'll find a way to keep them interested without letting them get too close. Although – take a look at this bunch! Do you really think the girls are all going to be screaming over them the way the Beatles' fans did?'

'We're not that bad, are we, lads?' Rob protested.

They were all laughing together as they got up to leave the pub. But they'd only got halfway out of the door before a couple of girls approached the boys, their eyes wide with excitement.

'It *is* you, isn't it!' one of them squealed. 'We've been looking at you ever since you came in, wondering if it was really you! I said I thought it was you, but my mate said …'

'I couldn't believe it was really you!' said the second girl. 'I mean – the Crazy Snakes, actually here in Stratford! Can we have your autographs?'

'We've been playing at the Up Beat club – don't miss us next time we're there, girls!' Pete joked.

Frankie nudged Rob. 'We should tell them about the Fan Club!' she whispered.

Within minutes she had her first two signed-up members. It looked like she needed to get cracking on her new job as soon as possible! She decided there and then that she'd hand in her notice at the bank on the Monday.

'I'm sorry to say this, Frankie,' Bernie told her as they said goodnight, 'but I really hope old Jack, wherever he is, knows about us getting into the charts. I'm not bitter – no point, now – but I'd like him to know we've done it without him.'

'In spite of him running out on us,' Pete agreed. 'Yeah. Me too. I hope he's pig sick, to be honest.'

Rob didn't say anything. He just looked at Frankie, his eyes full of apology.

'It's OK,' she whispered. 'They're right – I agree with them. I hope he *does* know about it.'

But there was only one way of making sure Jack found out about the boys' success: someone had to tell him about it. And as she was the only person who knew where he was, that someone was going to have to be her. She'd write back to him, that's what she'd do – maybe just for a laugh she'd string him along a bit about the non-existent baby – and she'd take great pleasure in telling him that the band he *deserted* had got a hit record out.

Sorry, Jack Hunter, she thought to herself as she sat down later with her pen and notepad. *But I'm afraid you deserve this.*

Chapter 18

September 1969 – Perth

The band – Krash – were rehearsing at least twice a week now and were getting a decent repertoire of numbers they were confident of performing together. Jack thought they couldn't be too far off approaching some venues in the city about doing their first gig. It was pretty exciting when they were together, running through the numbers. The boys worked well together, but it was Ruth's voice that really added the special touch. Jack knew they could do well. But if he thought about it when he was on his own, when he could be entirely honest with himself inside his own head, he knew they'd never be as good as the Crazy Snakes were. And he felt guilty for even wishing they could be.

One night, early in September, they were at Ruth's place as usual and had been rehearsing for about an hour when they stopped for a coffee. And as they were drinking it, she suddenly asked:

'Has anyone heard that new Brit group they're all raving about?'

'Which one?' Jack said.

'They're called the Crazy Snakes. Came out of nowhere, apparently – the story is they all lived on some island in England and they've made this phenomenal hit record, tipped to be number one next week in the UK charts.'

Jack's coffee slopped all over his jeans and dripped onto the floor.

'You OK, Jack?' Ruth asked as she went to get a cloth. 'Was it something I said?'

'I ... yeah.' He opened and shut his mouth a couple of times like a fish. 'Sorry. Sorry about the coffee.'

'It's OK. You want another one?' When she came back with a replacement coffee she was looking at him curiously. 'What's up? You look like you've seen a ghost.'

He swallowed hard. He bloody *felt* like he'd seen one.

'I ... used to know those guys. The Crazy Snakes ... if it's the same band.'

'Oh, right. From when you lived in England? Wow. Were they mates of yours?'

He shrugged awkwardly, realising he might have been about to give too much away. He couldn't have anyone linking him back to his old band; it'd make him too easy to trace, especially if they were ... bloody *hell*! ... especially if they were about to have a number one hit record!

'Nah, not really,' he backtracked quickly. 'I just kind of knew who they were, that's all.'

'Wow, cool. Were they good, back then?'

'Yes. They were.'

'So listen out for their record!' she said. She was nodding at him enthusiastically. 'It's fantastic. I reckon it'll go to the top of the Aussie charts too. You other guys heard it?'

They were shaking their heads. 'What's it called?' Ken asked.

'*Francesca.*'

Spilling one cup of coffee over someone's floor could be put down to carelessness. Spilling the second one – and practically falling off his own chair at the same time – was definitely going to be classified as peculiar. Suspicious. He was swearing, and apologising, and running for the damp cloth again, and all the time he had a buzzing in his head, a ringing in his ears like he was going to pass out.

'I think I'd better head home,' he told Ruth after apologising for about the fifth time. 'I'm really sorry. I don't feel too good.'

'What – you think you might be coming down with the flu?' she asked, looking him up and down. 'You OK to drive?'

'Yeah. I'll be OK. Just want to get home, you know, before I start feeling any worse.'

'I'll give you a lift, mate – don't drive if you're feeling crook,' Ken offered. But Jack didn't want company.

'No – honest, I'll be fine. I'll go straight home and get myself to bed.'

But of course, he didn't. He drove a couple of blocks away and then stopped, and turned on the radio. He ended up sitting there until nearly midnight, but he was determined not to move until he'd heard it. And eventually, he did. And then he wasn't sure whether he *would* be able to drive home. He was shaking like a leaf.

What he'd just heard was the best fucking record of the century. And it couldn't be a coincidence, could it. Somebody, one of his so called mates from the Snakes – probably Rob Marchant, as he was the one singing his bloody heart out – had written a fucking love song to *his girl*. Not only was it a love song, it was a song to tell her to forget Jack – that he was gone, that he didn't care! No, it was no bloody coincidence, that was for sure, and it was a good job he was in Australia or someone would be on the receiving end of a right-hander!

Needless to say, at that moment Jack wasn't thinking terribly logically or sensibly. Frankie, of course, *wasn't* his girl, hadn't been his girl for very long in the first place, and certainly not since he disappeared out of her life back in December. Which meant that no other man alive, even the best friends he'd abandoned in a very similar fashion at the same time, could be blamed for writing her a love song, going out with her, making love to her, marrying her and having babies with her, if they felt so inclined. But Jack wasn't in the frame of mind to see it that way. Probably *because* of the very fact that they'd been together such a short time – because it was a courtship that had never got beyond the first stage of romantic obsession, never gone on to endure the normal setbacks of arguments, doubts, irritations, taking each other for granted – his mind had played the trick of remembering her as his one perfect love. He knew, in reality, that she'd almost certainly never be *his* Francesca again. But he also knew he couldn't bear the thought of her being anyone else's – and certainly not Rob Marchant's. Rob, who was young – almost as young as Frankie – and was fresh-faced, blond and blue-eyed, good-humoured, easy-going and naturally charming. Jack was jealous – jealous beyond all reason.

Shona was asleep when he got home. He helped himself to a beer from the fridge and sat downstairs for a long time before going to bed, quietly, making sure he didn't wake her. He'd have had a hard job explaining what he was so worked up about. He couldn't sleep anyway, and in the morning felt so rough he actually thought he *might* have the flu. Shona took him aspirins and hot lemon juice and made him feel even more guilty than he already did.

'I'll tell the boss. We'll send the new guy out to your bathroom job.'

'Thanks.' She was so good to him, he felt ten times worse.

'You stay in bed, now, OK?'

He gave it half an hour after she'd gone, then got up, got dressed, got himself some breakfast. Once he was pretty sure the boss wouldn't phone, he got in the car and nipped into town to the record shop.

'Fastest-selling disc this week!' the pimply kid in the shop told him excitedly when he asked for *Francesca*. Saying the title out loud made him feel shaky. He was reading the record's label before he'd even left the premises. The song was written by *R. Marchant*. He knew it. Fucking *knew* it! He stormed back to the car, threw the record on the back seat and sat there, desperately trying to cast his mind back – trying to remember if there had been any signs, back then, a year ago … any signs that Rob had fancied his girl. Was he giving her the eye, even while Jack was going out with her? Sneaking crafty looks at her, maybe even trying to get off with her behind his back? He was hot with rage at the thought of it.

'When I met ya – the world fell apart – you stole my heart.' So he was lusting after her even then, was he, probably chuffed to bits when Jack departed – couldn't wait to tell her to forget him! Couldn't wait to have her for himself – and all this time Jack had been imagining the boys were *missing* him! What a complete idiot he'd been! They hadn't missed him for a minute; they'd been getting on with things, writing new songs about *his girlfriend*, making hit bloody records, probably saying to themselves that they were glad he'd gone, things had been better for them ever since – well *fuck them all*! He slammed his hand against the dashboard, trying to put the images out of his mind: images of Rob with Frankie. Talking to her, telling her he'd always loved her and had only been waiting for him, Jack, to be out of the way before he made his move. *Kissing* her – oh, *Christ*! He couldn't bear this!

And then he remembered: what about the baby? A cold shiver ran down his spine. She *must* have had the baby by now. Why hadn't she told him? Even if she really hated him, you'd think she'd have told him about it herself, but no – he'd only found out about her pregnancy through her sister. You'd think she'd write and tell him what a bastard he was, and demand money from him to support the child. But no, she hadn't even replied to say she'd got the money he'd sent. Why would that be? Surely ... surely *he's* not ...

Taking on my child. Jack couldn't finish the sentence, not even inside his own head. He wanted to scream to block out the thought. Instead, he started up the engine and drove, fast, heading back out of town, not sure where he was going. And then suddenly he changed his mind, did a U-turn in the middle of the road, ignoring the blare of horns from other motorists, and roared back into the city centre again, pulling up with a screech in front of the post office. He still had the damned PO box – and in spite of himself, he still checked the damned thing, from time to time, hoping … hoping against hope …

And – bloody hell. There was a letter.

This time he didn't even wait to get back to the car before reading it. He ripped open the envelope and stood right where he was, blocking the way for other people trying to get to their mailboxes. His money order fluttered out of the envelope as he unfolded the paper.

Jack, she said – no *dear*.

I'm sending back your money. Please don't send any more. I don't need it. Things are going really well for me. You might not hear it, as you have gone to the other side of the world, but the Crazy Snakes have made a brilliant record which is in the charts here. They're going to make another single and an LP and then they are going on tour. And Rob has come up with a fantastic idea, which should guarantee me a better future.

Don't write again – there isn't any point.

Frankie.

He was going to marry her. Jack had to hold onto the post office wall, and was nearly sick. People were looking at him strangely. Well, it was quite obvious from that – Rob had offered to marry her, to *guarantee her a better future* – that was his *fantastic idea*. And she had obviously accepted, she was obviously chuffed to bits about it. Mrs Francesca Marchant. It was … just unbelievable.

He shuddered, fighting against the disloyal thoughts crowding his brain. OK, OK, he knew he was getting married to Shona, but only because she was having a baby. Ouch. He didn't mean that, did he? He was just too upset to think straight. Of course he didn't mean it. He was sorry, sorry to be thinking like this – it wasn't fair on Shona, but it wasn't his fault. It was Rob's bloody fault!

The shock of this letter was ten times, a hundred times, worse than finding out about the baby from her sister's letter. Frankie's tone was so dismissive; it hurt far more than

Marianne's anger. So, things were going really well for her, were they? So much for all his concern and worry about her, about the baby! And as for the baby – she still hadn't even had the decency to tell him what it was, when it was born, whether it was all right, whether it *looked like him*! And it was easy to see why. Oh yes, he knew what was going on here ... bloody Rob Marchant was not only marrying her, he was planning to bring up *Jack's child* as his own!

Why had she written to him? Why bother, when she wasn't even going to tell him about the baby? It seemed she'd only written for one reason – to hurt him, make him mad with jealousy. Well, she'd bloody well succeeded!

He staggered back to the car like a drunk, got in and stuffed the letter, for what it was worth, into the glove box together with the money order, and slammed it shut. He ought to just throw it away. He doubted he'd ever want to read it again.

When he got home, he stood at the front door for a moment, leaning against the porch, trying to calm down – before he suddenly realised the phone was ringing inside. He let himself in quickly and ran to grab it in case it was the boss. But it was Shona, asking how he was feeling. .

'You sound out of breath,' she said. 'I hope it hasn't gone to your chest?'

'No. I'm OK. I was ... asleep, and I woke up with a start and ran to the phone.'

'Sorry, sweetheart. Go back to bed. Take it easy. I'll bring you home some cough linctus.'

'No, honest – I'm OK. I think it was just, you know, one of those twenty-four hour viruses. Tell them I'll be back tomorrow.'

He hung up, feeling like a complete heel. She loved him, she cared about him. She'd probably been worrying about him all morning, while all he'd done was fantasise about beating up the bloke who'd written a song about Frankie. He had to sort himself out. His head was in a mess – *he* was a mess!

He'd been keeping things to himself for too long, that was the trouble. Maybe he needed a shrink!

Or maybe ... maybe he just needed a mate to talk to. It was Friday afternoon – he couldn't do anything now. He'd have to wait till tomorrow, in the afternoon when Shona went out shopping with Karen. That's what he'd do. The only thing he *could* do. He'd go and talk to his mate.

Chapter 19

Perth

The doorbell was ringing so furiously, so insistently, that Ken nearly tripped over his own feet in his haste to get to the door.

'All right, mate. Where's the fire?' he said, seeing Jack standing on the step. And then, looking at Jack's face, he led him into the kitchen and put the kettle on. 'What's up?'

'Nothing ... sorry, nothing really, just ...' Jack shrugged, looking uncomfortable. 'Thought I'd call round.'

'Righto. Saturday arvo, I've got the footy on the telly, you just want to sit and watch it with me? That why you were ringing the bell like you wanted to wake the dead?'

'No,' he admitted. 'Not really.'

'You'll have a cuppa, anyway? Or a Coke? Sorry, I don't keep beer in the house, obviously.'

'Cup of tea will do fine. Thanks.'

'OK.' Ken made two mugs of tea and carried them through to the lounge. He gave the TV a regretful look and turned the sound down. 'Come on then. There's obviously something up. Spill.'

Jack was quiet for a moment, sitting on the sofa, holding his mug, looking down at the floor.

'Just want to chat?' Ken prompted him. 'Work worries? Financial? The wedding?'

Jack's head jerked up at the mention of the wedding, and Ken knew he was getting somewhere.

'It's not Shona's fault. Nothing to do with her.'

Another silence.

Ken took a deep breath. Bloody hell. He hoped this wasn't what it sounded like.

'You've met someone else?'

'Christ, no!' Jack said, sounding appalled. And then, dropping his eyes again, 'Well, in a way, I suppose – yes.'

'You're not making a lot of sense, cobber.'

'I met her back in England. Before I ... emigrated. Before I met Shona.'

'OK. And ... what? You're still in touch with her? Regretting leaving her, is that it? Think you've made a mistake with Shona?'

'I've regretted leaving her all along. And ... oh, God!' Jack groaned, leaning back on the sofa. His tea slopped about in his mug and Ken leant over and took it out of his hand. He didn't want Jack spilling another drink – he'd get himself banned from everyone's house before long. 'Her sister wrote to me. She was pregnant. I got her pregnant,' he said, in a rush. 'I ... asked her to come out here and be with me, marry me, but she didn't reply. So I sent her money, for the baby, but ...'

'Whoa, slow down, slow down!' Ken looked at his new friend anxiously. 'You're *sure* she was pregnant?'

'Well, her sister said so.'

'But you sent her money ... mate, have you thought about this? You're sure she wasn't just trying to get some cash out of you? Oldest trick in the book.'

'No! She's not that kind of girl!' Jack snapped, so fiercely that Ken actually recoiled.

'OK, I hear you, she's a nice girl, but she got pregnant. So – she didn't reply, so you met Shona and now *she's* pregnant.'

Jack flinched. 'It sounds bad, put like that. But I really do like Shona. She was good to me. She helped me get over ...'

'The bird in England.'

'Yes.'

'So what's the problem, now? You don't really want to marry her?'

'I thought I did ... no, I do, of course I do!' He ran his fingers through his hair. Ken didn't know whether to feel sorry for Jack or irritated by him. He didn't seem to know his own mind. 'I wouldn't want the baby to be illegitimate,' he said.

'If that's the only reason ...'

'No! It's not. I do love her. More than you did, that's for sure.' He glared at Ken. 'So don't start getting all sanctimonious.'

'Relax! I'm not getting sancti – what you said.' Ken grinned. He had no idea what the word meant. 'Just trying to help.'

'Sorry. Look, the thing is, I do want to marry her. But we haven't been together all that long, and sometimes I feel like we don't really know each other. For instance, I didn't know anything about *you* – all the stuff about why she fell out with her parents. And there's a lot she doesn't know about me.'

'Like the girl in England.'

'Yes. And ... oh, Jesus. It's so complicated.'

'Go on.'

'I've just had a letter from her.'

'The English one?'

'Yes. All this time, no letters, nothing – I've *asked* her to let me know about the baby – she must have had it by now. But nothing. And now, suddenly, she's written to me saying ...' He hesitated. 'Well, *implying* that she's going to marry someone else. A friend of mine.'

'Well.' Ken wasn't one to beat about the bush. 'You can't blame her, can you, mate? From what you've said – you got her in the family way, left her and came out to Oz, and now you're marrying someone else yourself!'

'She doesn't know that! I *offered* to marry her. I didn't know about the baby when I left England!'

Ken slapped him on the back and told him to drink his tea. The poor bloke looked shattered – like he hadn't slept all night. His own opinion was that he needed to shape up and get over it – but Jack had obviously come round for some advice, or at least some sympathy. Ken was flattered. He wasn't used to being sought out as a confidant.

Jack took a gulp of his tea and sighed.

'I guess the truth is, I feel a fool. That's part of it, anyway. All these months I've been worried about her – the girl in England. Especially after I found out about the baby. I imagined her still being upset about me leaving her. I ... suppose I've hung onto this thought that one day, somehow, we might get back together.'

'Even now you're marrying Shona?' Ken laughed and shook his head! 'And you thought *I* treated her bad!'

'I know. Sorry. Perhaps that was why I was so mad at you. It was bad enough knowing I was being kind-of lukewarm about my own wedding – finding out she'd already been dumped by you ... I suppose it just made me feel even more guilty.'

'You don't have to apologise to me, mate. I feel guilty enough about her myself.'

'I won't let her down. I can't do that to her. She's having my kid, and I'm not about to ruin her life. But ...'

'But you're mad as hell about the other one marrying your mate.'

'Yes. I guess that's about the size of it. I feel like she couldn't wait to jump into his arms – and he was obviously eyeing her up all the time I was going out with her.'

'You don't know that.'

'Well, why the hell else would he write her a love song?'

Ken looked up at him in surprise. *Love song*? Where did that come from?

'What love song?' he started to ask, but Jack was already stumbling over his words in his haste to take it back.

'I mean, I bet that's what he did. To get her to go out with him. To have his way with her. That's just the sort of thing he *would* do. I bet ...'

'Yeah. All right, mate.' He looked at him curiously. He was a strange bloke. Ken admired him, what he knew about him, but there was a hell of a lot he was keeping to himself.

Well, fair enough, he supposed we all had stuff in our past we didn't want to share.

'I used to really like the bloke,' Jack was saying now, more quietly. 'But the thought that she might be having *sex* with him makes me feel sick. I only ... she was a virgin, and we only did it the once.'

'Right.'

'And the thought that he might be taking on *my baby* – wanting to bring it up as his own ...' He shook his head.

'You need to let it go, cobber,' Ken told him gently. 'Seriously. It's gonna eat you up, otherwise. Just don't send her any more money.'

'Don't worry. She sent it back. Says she doesn't want it anyway.'

'Well, it looks like she's telling you straight, doesn't it? She's moving on. And so are you.'

'Yeah.' He swallowed the last mouthful of his tea and got up, taking the mug out to the kitchen. 'You're right. I know you're right. Thanks for listening, man.' He grasped Ken's hand. 'I appreciate it.'

'Oh, any time, right?'

'I guess I just needed to get it off my chest. I'll be OK now.' Ken thought Jack was starting to look a little sheepish. 'I'm sorry for interrupting your afternoon – and for being such a big wuss. I know my ... problems ... aren't anything really, not compared to the stuff you've been through.'

Ken shook his head, brushing this aside. He'd only told Jack a little about his childhood.

'That's in the past,' he said. It was his standard response to anyone showing him sympathy, even though he knew the past was still with him, and always would be.

To his surprise, Jack reached out and took him in a clumsy hug. Never having had a close male friend, Ken wasn't used to such things, and wasn't quite sure how to react. He'd grown up as a typical macho Aussie bloke – hugs were for girls. But in the brief moment of the embrace, he caught the whiff of alcohol on Jack's breath. So he'd needed a drink – or two – to give him the courage to come round and pour out his heart. No wonder he was so emotional. Ken was pretty sure there were times, when he himself used to drink, that he'd got soppy and miserable and possibly even wept like a woman.

'You'll be all right, mate,' he told Jack. 'Take it easy.'

'Yeah.' Jack turned towards the front door, and then looked back over his shoulder and added, 'You're a good bloke. I ... guess I've just realised I needed a friend. How about you being my best man?'

Ken's eyes widened. Truth be told, he wasn't sorry, himself, to have a friend, although he might not be the type to say it in so many words. But – best man? At his wedding to *Shona*? Wasn't that a stretch too far?

'You'd better check with Shona,' he said. 'I doubt she'd like that.'

'Ah, she'll be all right with it. Come on, I haven't got anyone else. I was going to ask my boss, and I don't even like him that much.'

'Check with Shona first,' Ken insisted. 'If she's all right with it, then yeah, it'd be bonzer.'

He grinned. For someone who'd lived so much of his life on the edge of decent society, never getting invited to anything so respectable as a party, never mind a wedding, this was certainly a first. He hoped it wasn't just the drink talking, because he was flattered and proud that Jack had asked him. If only *Shona* wasn't the bride. He'd have a hard job keeping his feelings to himself, standing in church next to the man who was going to marry her.

Because ... well, the fact was, it should have been him. If only he hadn't been such a daft drongo and given her the flick.

Chapter 20
Dagenham

There was a lot of fan mail to catch up on, as well as the job of organising the fan club and starting to compose the first newsletter. Frankie was loving the work. At last she was doing something she enjoyed, something she was really interested and excited about – and the bonus was being able to work at home. There wasn't room anywhere in Marianne's house for a desk, so she was starting off by working at the dining room table, her shiny new electric typewriter treated with such respect by her sister that Joel wasn't even allowed to venture anywhere near it.

'Auntie Frankie's working,' she'd tell him, and Joel, bless him, would look suitably impressed and tiptoe past her – as if the slightest noise or whisper might put her off the serious business of responding to the pleas of desperate teenage girls for photos and information about the band.

Despite her sister's encouragement and pride, she knew it wasn't fair to expect the family to make long-term concessions to her work. Her new salary – paid by the band's manager Dave into her bank account every week – was such an improvement on her pay from the bank that she was already able to contemplate moving into a place of her own as soon as she'd saved up a deposit. She wasn't going to rent – she'd buy her own place. Everyone, including her brother-in-law Grant, was saying it was the way to go. Bricks and mortar, he told Frankie, would never let you down – it was the best investment possible. She knew this was probably true, and saw the sense of it, but she couldn't help feeling a little nervous of the prospect of taking on a mortgage. She'd seen how much of a struggle it was for Marianne and Grant, paying the mortgage on their little house and managing the bills as well. Still, she only had herself to worry about – no family – and with the little bit of money she'd inherited from her mother to add to what she was squirreling away already from her new wages, she thought she might be able to get herself a little one-bedroom maisonette.

'And you know what the solicitor says,' Marianne pointed out as Frankie talked to her about these plans. 'If they can't find ... our other sister ...'

'I know. But I don't want to think like that.'

The solicitor had explained that if it proved impossible to find Susannah despite the newspaper adverts and all the efforts of the private detective, the third share of Hilda's estate would eventually be divided between Marianne and Frankie. Needless to say it wouldn't amount to a fortune, and Frankie preferred to think that Susannah would be found, somehow. That she should inherit her rightful share of her mother's small estate was the least of it – she just wanted the mystery solved, and their missing sister found.

It was good to be busy. It kept her mind off other things. Well, OK, it was difficult to keep her mind off *one* thing – the question of Rob, and his obvious interest in her, and her own somewhat reluctant realisation that she did actually like him too. Hard to keep that to the back of her mind when she was confronted on a daily basis with a pile of photographs of him, and reading letters from girls who insisted they were dying of broken hearts because of him. But the other thing – the question of Jack, and the letter she'd sent ... that was something she desperately wanted to bury away in her subconscious.

When she'd sent the letter, she'd imagined it was going to make her feel better – that by doing something to get back at him for the hurt he'd caused her, she'd finally be able to lay the ghost of her brief relationship with Jack Hunter. She'd told herself he was out of her mind for good now, just as definitely as he was out of her life. She was too busy with her new job to even think about him. Besides – she wasn't a silly kid any more. She was nineteen, nearly an adult, and moving on from silly teenage relationships was part of adult life.

But sending the letter had, in fact, left a bitter taste in her mouth. She wasn't normally a vindictive person. She couldn't remember ever before in her life saying, or writing, anything with the express purpose of hurting someone. She knew well enough how Jack would have felt, reading about the Crazy Snakes' chart success – and reading the mean little hint she'd given that she was involved with Rob. He probably did deserve it – but two wrongs didn't make a right, and Frankie was, most of all, ashamed of the fact that she'd said nothing to refute his belief that she was pregnant. She guessed she ought to write again, put that straight, draw a line under it – and she would; she'd get around to it, when she had a moment, when she'd caught up with the fan mail and finished the newsletter. She would.

Of course, she still *wasn't* involved with Rob at all. Although he had asked her – more than once.

'We could just go out as friends,' he'd tried to persuade her recently. 'To the pictures or just for a drink occasionally. Couldn't we?'

'We *are* going out as friends,' she reminded him gently.

'You know what I mean, Frankie,' he chided her. 'Going out on our own a bit more – without the other boys. Nothing heavy. Just … well, to keep each other company. We're both single, aren't we.'

She wondered if that was probably the point. The other three boys currently had girlfriends. Andy and Georgia were getting married the following year, and although Pete's and Bernie's relationships didn't seem to be so serious, she guessed Rob must be feeling a bit left out.

'You're going to have all those fans screaming for you when you go on tour,' she teased him. 'Throwing their knickers at you, desperate just to touch you. I bet you'll be glad you're still single, then!'

'I'm not like that, Frankie,' he said, looking pained. 'I'd rather spend my time with someone ... special.'

'Then I hope you find her soon,' she said, putting her hand over his. He was such a nice bloke, and if she was honest, the simple gesture of touching his hand made her long for something more. A hug, a kiss ... it had been a long time, and she didn't want to turn into a nun. But she was afraid. Afraid of the fact that he'd declared his love for her, and she wasn't sure if she could return it. She liked him too much to use him as a casual boyfriend when he so obviously wanted more.

'I understand,' he said, looking at her sadly. 'As long as it's not because of what happened with Jack.'

'Of course not!' she retorted. 'That was all dead and buried long ago.'

'Good. Because I'm about as different from Jack as you could get.'

'I know. I do realise that.' He was gorgeous, of course, in his own slim, fair, perfect way. She hadn't been joking about girls being desperate for him – they'd already started yelling out his name when the band appeared at local clubs and dance-halls, and the music on the forthcoming tour was likely to be drowned out by the screaming fans. But could she ever love someone who was so different from Jack? However nice Rob was, however good-looking, however sure she was that he'd never mess her around or let her down – he didn't have whatever it was about Jack that had made her fall so desperately in love with him. And when Rob looked at her with his soft, puppy-dog eyes and eager smile, she didn't see how it could be fair to give him any false hope.

As it was, she had to endure the looks she got from Marianne whenever *Francesca* was played on the radio (almost all the time), and the smiles – virtually nods of encouragement – whenever Rob came round.

'He's here about *work*. About the fan club!' Frankie whispered crossly at her, one evening when the meaningful looks were making her feel particularly embarrassed. Rob had gone out to his car to get another box of stationery supplies for Frankie, and Marianne was behaving with such lack of subtlety, she might almost have been nudging and winking like a old-time music hall comedian.

'Oh. Right. Sorry. Is that why he's gazing at you like you're a three course meal and he hasn't eaten for years, then?' Marianne giggled and Frankie sighed with exasperation. She felt like telling her older sister to grow up!

'He's going on tour next week,' she said. 'And probably, some teenage fan will throw herself at him and he'll get off with her, and forget all about me.'

Marianne was silenced for a moment. She looked at Frankie sadly.

'And that's what you want, is it?' she said.

Frankie tutted and got back to sorting out batches of letters for the post. She had no idea what she wanted! Why did Marianne think she'd thrown herself into her work? She didn't even want to *think* about what she wanted!

'Just leave me alone and stop interfering,' she said irritably. 'You're getting on my nerves. The sooner I can move out, the better.'

Frankie was appalled at herself. She and Marianne had always been so close, had never bickered the way other siblings often did – and she'd done so much for Frankie, taking her into her home, always there with support, encouragement or sympathy, whatever was needed at the time. She didn't understand why she'd become cross enough to speak to her the way she had – she regretted it as soon as the words were out of her mouth. But not nearly as much as she did when, in the early hours of the next morning, Marianne suddenly went into labour three weeks prematurely.

'Stay here,' Grant insisted, as Frankie, in her pyjamas, jumped from foot to foot at the front door, almost hysterical with alarm while she watched him help her white-faced sister into the car. 'Please, Frankie – try to calm down. We need you to look after Joel when he wakes up.'

'Mari – I'm sorry!' she shouted. 'I didn't mean ...'

'Not now, Frankie,' Grant said tersely, shutting the passenger door of the car, a barrier of steel and glass between them. Marianne held up a hand to Frankie as they drove off – a feeble kind of wave – and Frankie tried to convince herself by that, that everything was going to be OK. That her sister wasn't mad at her, that they were still friends. And, more to the point, that the baby was going to be all right.

It was late in the afternoon before Grant arrived home. Heavy-eyed, unshaven, the clothes he'd thrown on at two o'clock that morning mismatched and rumpled, he fell into an armchair and gazed at Frankie through red-rimmed eyes.

'They're in intensive care,' he said.

'They?' Frankie's heart was pounding so hard, it was hurting her chest. 'Mari ... is she ...?'

'Mari's fine. Exhausted but fine.' He managed a small, tired smile as he added, almost as if it was an irrelevance: 'We've got twins. Two girls. Two beautiful little girls, Frankie!'

With which he burst into tears, and Frankie promptly joined him.

It turned out the babies had been lying so closely one behind the other, that neither the doctor nor the midwife had been able to detect the presence of an extra one. Despite their early arrival into the world, the twins turned out to be little fighters and within a week had been moved from intensive care to be beside their mum in the maternity ward, where Frankie was able to take their excited big brother to meet them.

'They're so gorgeous,' she said, leaning over to kiss the soft downy little head of each twin. 'Just like their mum!'

Marianne laughed. 'I don't feel too gorgeous at the moment! I think I'm still in shock!' She looked up at Frankie. 'You won't move out *just* yet, will you? I'd really appreciate a bit of help for a few weeks!'

Frankie sat down on the bed and hugged her sister carefully. 'Of course I won't. I didn't mean what I said – I don't know why I flew off the handle like that.'

'Well, I do. I was winding you up, and I thought it was funny, but you were right – it wasn't. Shall we forget about it?'

'Yes please.' Frankie smiled. 'So, tell me – what names have you decided on for these two little beauties?'

'Oh, didn't I say?' Marianne smiled back. 'This one – ' She held up the slightly smaller twin, whose tiny fragile legs hung from her hospital-issue smock like two wobbly thin sticks of rhubarb – 'we're calling Frances Grace. After her Auntie Francesca.'

'Oh!' Frankie said, her eyes widening with delight. And 'Oh!' again. It was all she seemed to be able to say.

'And *this* one,' her sister went on, demonstrating the bigger of the two, 'is Susan Margaret.'

'After Susannah,' Frankie said, her voice breaking slightly. 'That's lovely, Mari.'

Marianne stroked little Susan's head gently, her eyes filling with tears. 'I just wish we could let her know. Wouldn't that just be perfect? If, some time, somehow, we could introduce them to each other.'

'It still might happen,' Frankie tried to reassure her. 'Who knows? *Anything* might happen.'

She didn't say so to her sister, of course – but in actual fact, Frankie doubted it very much. Wherever Susannah was, whatever had happened to her, she was pretty sure the private investigators would have found her by now if they were ever going to.

Chapter 21

September 1969 : Melbourne, Australia

In a coffee-shop in a suburb of Melbourne, Sue was being interrogated by an older woman with steel grey hair and piercing blue eyes who stared at her over her glasses. Maureen Pringle was sceptical about this tiny slip of a girl – she didn't look much more than a teenager, and appeared as frightened as a rabbit. What the hell use was a kid like this going to be? What were the agency thinking of? She'd asked them to send her someone experienced.

'How old are you, girl?' she demanded. If she'd come fresh from school, or worse still college, thinking she knew it all, she could take a running jump.

'I'm twenty-four,' Sue said, trying to sound more confident than she felt.

'Really.' The woman looked her up and down again. Well, they were certainly breeding them skinny and feeble-looking these days. 'And apparently you've got catering experience?'

'Yes, Ma'am. Back in WA, I worked on a farm, in the kitchen. I had to cook all the family's meals.'

'Worked for a family, did you? In WA, you say?' She levelled her steely gaze at Sue again. 'Why d'you leave?'

'I ... um ...' Sue stammered, a blush rushing up her neck to her cheeks – a process she could never control once it had started. 'Personal reasons, Ma'am,' she finished, lifting her chin. If this old cow didn't like it, she wouldn't hire her. She'd have to look elsewhere, that was all. Stuff it.

'I see.'

Maureen was a woman of the world. And she hadn't got to the age of fifty-two, and succeeded in business without ever having acquired the dubious and, in her mind, overrated benefit of a husband, without learning a little bit about people – how they behaved, and why. The answer to the *why*, she'd discovered long ago, was nearly always concerned with the opposite sex. She nodded to herself as she regarded the twig-thin blonde-haired young woman in front of her, who was trying her best to look defiant but being let down by the flush of embarrassment – or was it shame? – consuming her. Whatever she'd got up to in WA, her decision to travel halfway across Australia had something to do with a man, and the need to put a hell of a lot of distance between herself and him, that was for sure. Despite her misgivings about the girl, Maureen had to admit she kind of liked that about her.

'All right,' she said eventually. 'I'll take you on a month's trial. If you're no good, you're out –right? You'll be working six days a week, starting when we open for breakfast at eight, finishing after we've served teas, about six-thirty. You'll get two tea breaks, mid-morning and mid-afternoon, and you'll get your lunch on the house. You'll help out back in the kitchen. If we're busy, I might need you to wait tables. Any problems?'

'No. That'll suit me fine.' Sue grinned with relief. She hadn't expected to get the first job she'd gone after since she arrived in Melbourne. The coffee shop was in a good position too, close to a busy suburban shopping centre and not far from a high school. She wanted to be busy. She didn't want time to think. 'I'll take the job. Thank you, Mrs Pringle.'

'*Miss*,' Maureen corrected her sharply. 'When can you start?'

'Tomorrow?'

'Good. I'll see you at eight o'clock.'

Sue strolled back to her digs, enjoying the late afternoon sunshine. It wasn't as hot here as it had been out in the outback of Western Australia. She'd only been here two days, but already she was feeling better. She'd always known she'd have to get away from the farm, from the only life she'd known since leaving the orphanage in Perth at the age of fifteen. But until she'd finally saved enough for the fare, and done it – walked away from that bloody farm in the back of beyond, away from the Andersons without a backward glance or a word of explanation, walked all the way to the nearest town where she got a bus into Perth and boarded a flight east – she hadn't realised how free she was going to feel. How could she have realised it, when she'd never actually tasted freedom before, in her entire life, as far back as she could remember?

She thought she was probably about eight or nine when she'd arrived in Australia. She had vague memories of being on a ship with a lot of other children, and in particular of a boy called Christopher who had been taken off somewhere, together with all the other boys, in a lorry. She couldn't remember who he was, exactly, or why she'd cried for him for weeks when she first arrived at the orphanage with the other girls. Eventually she'd stopped crying because the nuns had no patience with it, any more than they had patience with bed-wetting or talk of running away. The girls were expected to be grateful for their luck, having been brought to such a wonderful country, given a place to live, a cold bare bed to sleep on and meagre rations of food to eat. And to be fair, Sue might have been grateful, if only she could remember exactly where she'd come from, and what she'd done to deserve being sent away.

'Your parents are all dead,' the girls at the orphanage were told repeatedly by the nuns. 'You had no future back in England. You'd been abandoned. You'd have been homeless, living on the streets, starving. You're very fortunate that the Australian government has agreed to take you in. So stop snivelling and get on with your work.'

There had been lessons, but the girls were also expected to help with the running of the orphanage. As she grew up, Sue had developed a preference for working in the kitchens rather than the laundry or the gardens – so at first, she was excited about being sent to the farm to work for the Anderson family.

She had to work hard, but at least she had her own room and a reasonably comfortable bed. And enough to eat. Mr Anderson and his older two sons were out working on the farm all day, coming home at nightfall expecting a substantial meal ready and waiting for them and the farmhands. There were often seven or eight men to feed. There was no Mrs Anderson – apparently she'd died giving birth to Michael, the youngest son. By the time Sue had been at the farm for a couple of years, Michael was in his last year at school, and more often than not, he arrived home while the men were still out in the fields. He was supposed to have some chores to do in the yard, but mostly he hung around the house, being obnoxious.

Michael was two years younger than Sue, but tall and brawny with huge thick arms and hands like shovels. She was no match for him, and he terrified her with his leering, his insults and eventually his furtive sexual assaults. When he realised she couldn't fight him off, he became more brazen, moving on finally from groping her in corners to dragging her into his room and forcing himself on her. The first time, screaming in terror, fighting and sobbing as he held her down and ripped her virginity from her, she threatened to tell his father.

'Tell him what, orphan girl?' he'd sneered. 'You think he'd believe you – a dirty, lying little orphanage girl? He'd send you packing, that's what he'd do, and where d'you think you'd go, eh? Nobody wants you! If anybody had wanted you, why d'you think you got sent to the orphanage?'

To Sue, who for as long as she could remember had been told she was nothing, who believed she was a nobody, from nowhere, this rang completely true. Michael seemed to be his father's favourite – he was indulged and excused at every turn. Mr Anderson never exchanged more than a few words with Sue and she was sure Michael was right – if she could even pluck up the courage to tell him what his son was doing to her, he wouldn't believe her. He'd be furious. He'd throw her out on her ear, and at seventeen, with no family, no friends and no-one she could turn to for help, she'd have nowhere to go.

If she'd had any shred of self-worth at all, if the nuns had been able to give her and the other girls at the orphanage even the tiniest bit of care beyond providing the basic necessities of life and instilling the fear of God into them, she'd never have endured Michael's abuse for nearly four years before formulating the plan for her getaway. It then took another three years of saving her meagre wages, and systematically raiding the pot in Michael's drawer where he kept his savings, a few cents at a time so that it wouldn't be noticed, before she had enough for a ticket to Melbourne – the furthest she could afford to go, the furthest she could get from Michael Anderson and the life she had hated for as long as she could remember.

And now she was ready to start afresh. She had a room in a boarding house. She had a job. She was free. Sue was *somebody,* at last. It felt good – in fact it felt great! But it was never going to stop the empty ache inside her when she lay alone in her bed at night. It was the ache of loss – for the family she'd never had and couldn't even imagine having.

Chapter 22
Perth

'You've got to be joking. Tell me you're flipping joking?'

Jack looked away from Shona's indignant stare. He'd been putting off telling her for over a week, but now the wedding was only days away and he'd run out of time. He'd already pretended, to Ken, that she'd given the OK – but seeing the look on her face now, he wondered how the hell he'd ever convinced himself it was going to be all right.

'I can't *believe* you'd ask him to be your best man?' she went on, her voice rising and beginning to tremble. 'How long ago did you decide this, for crying out loud? I've asked you so many times who you were going to choose, and you kept saying it'd probably be Frank.'

'I didn't even ask him,' he admitted. 'I didn't want it to be him. He's a good boss, but I don't even really like him much as a bloke. We could hardly say we were friends.'

'Fine, so ask someone else! God! Why have you left it so late?'

'Because I wanted Ken. And I wasn't sure what you'd say.'

'Well, now you know, don't you. I'd have thought it was obvious – for heaven's sake, Jack, you *know* what I think of the bloke!'

'But he's going to be *my* best man,' he said, suddenly obstinate, suddenly determined. 'Not yours. You've got Karen.'

'You're being childish. Of course I've got Karen – she's my best friend. But ...'

'Exactly! Your best friend, Shona – do you realise how lucky you are to have one?'

She looked away, silenced, then replied more calmly:

'Yes. I do. I'm sorry, but I don't know how you found yourself in this position – no friends, no family, no existence whatsoever, as far as *I* know, before I met you! You don't talk to me about your life in England at all, Jack – I know something bad must have happened to you, and I understand it might be difficult to talk about but we *are* getting married!'

'I know. I'm sorry.' He took a deep breath. It was no good. Telling Shona his story would be unthinkable. It would open up his past, make his old life collide with the new one he'd so carefully fabricated. It just couldn't happen. 'I've said before, there's nothing in particular to tell you – I just don't really talk about my past life. There's nothing worth sharing with you.'

'Nothing you *want* to share.'

'Well, it took *you* long enough to spill the beans about Ken, about your parents, and being an alcoholic, didn't it!' He stopped, shook his head. They'd been down this route, round in this circle, so many times, and it was never going to get them anywhere. 'This is stupid, Shona. I don't want to quarrel with you.'

'I don't want to quarrel either. Just tell me you'll pick someone else. Not Ken.'

'There *isn't* anyone else. That's what I'm trying to tell you. Ken is the first real friend I've had, apart from you, since I've been out here.'

She softened a little then – he could see it in her eyes, in her mouth.

'You said you didn't mind me seeing him,' he pressed on.

'As long as *I* didn't have to!'

'He's sorry, Shona – he's genuinely sorry for the way he treated you. Wouldn't the wedding be a good time for you and him to shake hands ... put the past behind you?'

'Oh, right, just like that! He's sorry, is he, so we can all get together and be friends, and say no more about it? I turned my back on my *parents* because of him, Jack!'

'I know.' He paused. 'It's not too late, though, is it? Look, you could *still* invite them to the wedding, if you wanted to – make the peace, tell them about their grandchild?'

He patted her slightly rounded stomach gently, and although she responded with a fleeting half-smile, she still shook her head firmly.

'No. Too much was said, at the time. Too much to forgive. It *is* too late.'

He hugged her. 'I'm sorry,' he said again. 'I was just hoping ... for my sake ... you might be prepared, just for one day, to make an allowance.'

She laid her head against his shoulder. 'He'll ruin the wedding.'

'No he won't. He's changed. You know that – it was because of you. You *helped* him change. He's a nice guy, Shona. He knows he hurt you and I can understand why you don't want to forgive him. But he's my friend and I'd really, really, like him as my best man.'

'And what if I say no?'

He shrugged. 'I'll have to be my own best man,' he joked. 'I really don't want anyone else.'

There was a silence. He waited, still holding her close to him. He could hear her breathing, he could smell the sweet, floral fragrance of her hair beneath his nose, feel her arms tightening around him. And he'd never loved her more than when she finally sighed, and said in little more than a whisper:

'All right, then. For you. I don't like it, but I don't want you to be your own best man. You might lose the ring before you give it to yourself.'

He kissed her. She was an angel! He truly was a lucky man.

The wedding was on the last Saturday of September. It was a stinking hot day, and to Jack, who still hadn't completely adjusted to the climate of Western Australia and who during the slightly cooler weather of the preceding couple of months had actually forgotten how intense the heat could be, the wedding service seemed interminably long. He was sweating like a pig in his suit and tie.

Ken, standing next to him as they waited for the bride, fiddled with his collar and coughed nervously. Jack glanced at him quickly and gave him a reassuring smile. Perhaps it should have been the other way round, but Jack knew his friend was anxious about the day – anxious to get everything right, not to let Jack down, and most of all, anxious not to upset the bride all over again.

Unlike the two men, Shona looked cool and composed in her sleeveless white dress when she joined him at the front of the church, her cheeks only slightly pink, probably from excitement as much as from the heat.

'You look beautiful,' he whispered, and he meant it – she really did look lovely, she *was* lovely, and he was determined to play his part and make it a good day, a special day for her.

But as the hymns and prayers went on, and on, he had to struggle with a feeling of desperation for it to be over, so he could take off his jacket, loosen his tie, and get hold of a cold beer. After the service there were the photos, and what seemed like hours standing around outside being congratulated by people he'd never heard of, let alone met – people who seemed to want to tell him how long they'd been friends with Shona, and in the case of some of them who'd known her from school, relate funny stories about when she was a little kid.

'Shame there's no-one here from her family,' one woman whispered to him. 'I *do* think it's sad when families fall out, don't you?' She looked around, something obviously having only just struck her. 'What about your own folks, Jack? I suppose they couldn't make it out from the old country for your wedding?'

'No.' He looked around him for Shona, desperate to move away, change the subject, leave, or preferably all three.

'Sorry to hear that,' the woman went on, touching his arm sympathetically. 'That's a real shame for you. I'll bet they'd liked to have been here, though, see their son marry a lovely girl like Shona – proudest day of a father's life, seeing his son married, isn't it. Still, you say they couldn't make it? Too far to travel, I suppose?' She peered at him accusingly, as if she suspected it was Jack's own fault for not sending them the money to fly out for the wedding.

'Actually my parents are both dead,' he said in a rush, trying to move away. It was what he'd told Shona – what she still believed. It made it easier to explain his lack of ties to the UK. But saying it now, out loud to this stranger on his wedding day, when his mother should by rights have been there with him – not halfway across the world, unaware that it was even happening, unaware, in fact, of where he was living, never mind who with – made him suddenly wince with a spasm of sick pain, as if he'd been kicked in the stomach, and his eyes filled up with tears.

'Aw, cripes, Jack – I'm sorry.' The woman was beside herself now, hugging him awkwardly and looking around her as if for help. 'I didn't know – gees, nobody told me that. That's real bad luck – your mum and your dad, both of them? Crikey, look, I didn't mean to upset you, on your wedding day for crying out loud.'

'It's all right – I'm OK – just got something in my eye. Excuse me, I need to, um, go and talk to somebody ...'

He could feel her eyes on him as he walked away, heard her muttering to another woman about the bridegroom's '*bloody bad luck*' – did she realise both his parents had '*kicked the bucket*'? He caught up with Ken, near the entrance to the churchyard, and leaned close to mutter in his ear, 'Can we get out of here?'

Ken took one look at his face and said, calmly, 'OK. Wait here, I'll go and get Shona.'

Within minutes he was back, bringing Shona with him, announcing loudly to everyone that it was time for the bride and groom to leave for the reception. Shona, who so far had avoided looking at Ken at all, was now glancing from him to

Jack with ill-concealed concern. Jack grabbed her hand and as they headed towards the wedding car a cheer went up, people followed them, throwing more confetti and shouting for more photographs, but they were out of the churchyard, into the car, thank God, and on their way to the reception before she'd even had time to ask him what was wrong.

'He ... Ken said you were feeling a bit poorly.'

'Sorry, love. I guess it was the heat.'

'Poor you.' She squeezed his hand. 'Isn't it mad that you're expected to wear a jacket – for God's sake take it off, Jack! And the tie!'

'Are you sure? I didn't want to look ... wrong, scruffy or anything, for any of the photos. I don't want to spoil ...'

'Aw, stuff it – who cares? I don't want you flaking out on me, do I?' She laughed. 'Well, we've done it, Jack – we're man and wife! Are you happy?'

'Course I am,' he said, kissing her quickly as he peeled off his jacket. 'You're gorgeous. And thanks for giving in, about Ken. I appreciate it.'

'Well. I have to admit, he's been very proper. So far.'

'He was more nervous than me. Honestly, he's desperate for it all to go well. He wants to make it up to you.'

She nodded, but looked away, and he knew that hadn't been the right thing to say. It'd take more than getting her bridegroom to the church on time, and remembering the ring, for Shona to forgive him.

The reception was a relatively small affair in a local restaurant, and while Shona excused herself to go to the ladies' room, Ken cornered Jack before the rest of the guests arrived.

'You all right now?'

'Yes. Sorry, mate. The heat ...'

'Makes you cry, does it, the heat?' Ken said quietly.

'Well – that and, you know, a bit of ...'

'Emotion?'

Jack nodded, embarrassed.

'Well, fair enough, cobber, it's your wedding day, probably normal to feel a bit emotional, so they say.'

'Maybe.' Perhaps it *was* the fact of his wedding making him feel uncharacteristically weepy. Making him miss home, and everyone he'd known back in England, making him wish they were with him. 'But – it's ...

'Thinking about the other girl? Back in England?' Ken said very quietly, looking straight ahead.

Jack closed his eyes. He didn't feel proud of the fact that thoughts of Frankie, Frankie with Rob, were never far from his mind – but so far he'd managed to keep them to the background today.

'No, not her. Not her in particular. I suppose I just feel kind of *lonely,* you know? I really wish my Mum could've been here.'

'Aw, mate, yeah, it must be hard knowing your folk didn't live to see you married.'

A shadow passed over Ken's face. Jack knew his own situation was even more painful but he couldn't stop now. He just had to say it, finally, to someone:

'My mum's actually still alive.'

'No kidding! Right. I thought ...' Ken swallowed, obviously confused. 'I thought you said they'd both passed away?'

'My dad has. But Mum ... she's still back home. And she doesn't even know where I am, or anything about me getting married, or the baby, or anything,' he added in a fierce rush. 'I can't tell her. Or anyone back home.'

'Blimey. That's a tough one.'

The typical Aussie understatement, together with the sudden relief of confiding in someone, almost made Jack laugh.

'Yeah,' he said. 'It's tough, all right. Specially today.'

'Sure. I can imagine. Does Shona know about this?'

He shook his head. 'I'm not burdening her with it – the reason I had to come out here. I tell everyone what I told you – I just emigrated, like all the others, for a better life.'

'But there's more to it.'

Jack nodded.

For a moment, they were both silent. Then Jack caught sight of Shona and Karen coming out of the ladies' room, and at the same time the restaurant door burst open and the first group of guests came in, chatting and laughing excitedly and heading for the bar.

Ken laid a hand on Jack's arm. 'I get that it's something you want to keep quiet,' he said. 'And I don't care why. But if you ever do need to talk about it, well, I'm good at keeping things to myself.'

'Thanks, mate.' Jack nodded. 'I'll remember that. And thanks again for today.'

'No worries.' He turned away, and then added quietly, 'I was chuffed to be asked.'

Jack watched his bride sip her orange juice, radiant and happy as she mingled with the guests. It was probably unusual that neither of them had a single member of family present at their wedding, but looking around him now, he realised that apart from Ken, some work mates and the few of Shona's friends that he'd met, he knew absolutely nobody here. The realisation increased his loneliness even more, and for a minute he felt peeved that no consideration had been given by Shona or Karen to his empty side of the church while they were drawing up the guest list, sending out the invitations and ordering the champagne and the bloody vol-au-vents. Then again, when it came down to it, it was all about her, the bride, wasn't it. He couldn't really have cared less if they'd carried on living in sin, but he had to do the right thing by her, and make his child legitimate – so he straightened his shoulders, put the smile back on his face and went to stand by his wife's side while she introduced him to yet another old friend from way back when.

He'd have liked, at least, to have sent his mother a wedding photo, but he knew he couldn't risk it. She was never going to know he was married, or that she was going to be a grandma, and that was just the way it was.

Chapter 23

October 1969 : Dagenham

The twins, Susan and Frances, were feeding voraciously and gaining weight at an almost alarming rate. All through the night Frankie could hear one or the other of them waking and squealing for a feed. They'd been so tiny at birth that they both fitted into the same crib next to Marianne and Grant's bed, and for the first couple of weeks Marianne had attempted to feed them herself. But the visiting midwife had put a stop to it.

'You're wearing yourself out, love,' she said cheerfully. 'These are two hungry little souls, and you'll be better off putting them straight on the bottle so your husband can help out with the feeds.'

She added, as was the thinking of the time, that the twins would probably thrive better and be more satisfied on formula milk anyway – so Marianne didn't feel bad about following her advice.

'It's a good thing,' Frankie agreed. 'I can help out too, now. Give me a shout during the night, if they both want feeding at the same time. Then Grant can get his sleep – he has to get up for work, after all.'

'So do you!' Marianne reminded her.

'Ah, but it's different for me. I can take breaks whenever I like, as long as I keep the work up to date.' Frankie smiled. She knew how lucky she was to be working for the Crazy Snakes. It was as if her prayers had been answered, and her perfect job had dropped out of heaven specially for her. But it *was* getting busier already. Dave, the manager, had been round to see her just the other day.

'What you really need is a proper filing cabinet,' he'd said, looking round Marianne's living room thoughtfully. Frankie was using shoe boxes, stacked on top of each other in the corner of the room, to file letters and copies of fan club mailings.

'I know. But there's no room for one.'

'Hmm. We ought to be thinking about setting you up in a proper office.'

Frankie was silent. She knew Dave was right, but she wanted to work here for a little longer yet so that she could help Marianne – and it wouldn't exactly be professional to say so!

Just at that moment, Frances woke up and started yelling for her bottle – while Frankie knew her sister was changing Susan's nappy.

'Do you want to go and see to that?' Dave said, without even looking up from the paperwork he was checking.

Frankie blushed. 'But I'm supposed to be working.'

Dave looked up at her, smiling widely. 'Frankie – I've got three kids myself. The youngest is five months old and the oldest is only three. It's like a war zone in my house. The boundaries between family and work have never been so blurred. Trust me, I wouldn't be saying this if I didn't know how conscientious you are, and how hard you've been working. But as long as nothing gets overlooked that needs to be done – I'm not going to dock your wages for stopping occasionally to give one of your nieces a bottle.'

'Thanks.' She ran out of the room and returned with Frances tucked under one arm and a feeding bottle in her hand. 'I really appreciate this.'

'It'll get easier,' he said. 'And when it does – we'll move you into an office. OK?'

'Thank you,' she said again. 'That'd be great.'

The band had been on tour for the past week – they'd been up to Colchester, Ipswich, Norwich, and Birmingham. They were playing at Manchester that night, Liverpool the next, and then going up to Scotland before flying back down south to do another week of venues, finishing in London. Dave had got a phone line installed at the house specially for Frankie's use – and she'd been keeping in touch with the band because part of her job was going to be describing the concerts in the newsletter, for those fans not lucky enough to have tickets for any of the venues. Quotes from 'the boys' about their performances and experiences on the road helped to liven up her prose, and were best reported (taken down in Frankie's shaky basic shorthand) before anything could be forgotten. And anyway, she liked talking to Rob. She was slightly perturbed by how much she was missing him while he was away. She and the other boys' girlfriends had free tickets to the final night of the tour, at Hammersmith, and she was literally counting the days till then.

One day, towards the end of the tour, Frankie realised she hadn't had her usual call from Rob to update her on the previous night's shows. She knew they were travelling from the west country back up to Surrey, and assumed they simply hadn't had time to stop and make the call. But later, just as she was preparing the evening meal, the phone rang – and this time it was Pete.

'Hello.' She couldn't help feeling surprised. 'Is everything OK?'

'Of course.' Pete sounded defensive. 'Why shouldn't it be?'

'Oh – no reason.' She shrugged. She shouldn't expect it always to be Rob who called her, should she. 'So – how did it go last night?'

Pete gave her the run-down of the sell-out concert at Exeter, and they exchanged pleasantries before saying goodbye. She had the distinct feeling Pete sounded a bit odd – that he was holding something back. But she told herself she must be imagining it. He was probably tired, that was all.

But the next day, when it was Pete again who called about the Guildford concert, she couldn't help asking, 'Is Rob all right?'

'Course. He's fine.'

'Just ... busy, I suppose?'

'Yeah. He's fine,' he said again. But there was definitely a wary edge to his voice, and he was quick to change the subject and move on to talking about which songs they'd performed the previous night.

The following day, Andy called, and the day after that, Bernie – and then it was Pete again. By now, Frankie knew there was something up. Either Rob had broken both legs and been taken to hospital and nobody wanted to tell her ... or he was avoiding talking to her.

The day of the Hammersmith concert finally came round. Frankie and Georgia travelled across London together on the tube.

'I've missed Andy so much!' Georgia said. 'I'm glad we're getting married. If he's going to be doing this every year – off on tour, all those girls lusting after him – it'll be a good job to get a ring on his finger, whether he likes it or not! Don't you think so, Frankie?'

'Mm.'

'Frankie? You all right?' Georgia laughed. 'Penny for your thoughts!'

'Sorry. Miles away.' She smiled at the other girl. 'Yes. It's good you're getting married. The two of you are brilliant together – and you've been together for ages. It's time he made an honest woman of you!'

Georgia chuckled happily. 'How about you?' she said a moment later. 'Have you missed Rob?'

'Come on, you know we're not a couple.'

'I know. But ... oh, never mind. Hey – we're there, Frankie! Hammersmith! Come on – let's go and see how much *they've* missed *us*!'

They, and the other two girlfriends, had arranged to meet the boys backstage before the show. And they'd been booked into the same hotel as the band for the night – Frankie, of course, booking a single room.

As soon as they were let into the dressing room, Georgia flew into Andy's arms. Pete and Bernie were both already hooked up with their own girls. Rob was sitting on his own, studying the play list for the evening.

'Hi.' Frankie pulled up a chair next to him. 'Nice to see you!'

'Hi,' he said, without looking up.

Some welcome, after two and a half weeks! She felt a surge of irritation. What was the matter with him?

'Was it something I said?'

'Sorry. Just ... concentrating on this.'

'OK. So I'll just sit here and wait, shall I?'

'If you like,' he said, still not looking up.

'Right.' Humiliated, she got up and walked to the door. 'I'll see you later, then.'

'Frankie, wait!' Pete called after her.

'Don't go!' Georgia, turning from Andy's embrace, looked at her in surprise. 'Wait – I'll come with you.'

'It's all right. I'll just go and get some air.'

Bernie and Andy were both looking from her to Rob and back again, mouths opening and closing as they searched for something to say. It was quite pointed that Rob was the only one saying nothing.

She slammed the dressing room door behind her and walked, quickly, out of the stage door of the cinema and into the street. Tears stinging her eyes, she shoved through the queue of waiting fans, already extending round the side of the building, and strode down the road until she came to a pub. She'd never been in one on her own before – and certainly never ordered a drink at the bar herself.

'Bacardi and Coke, please. A large one. With ice.'

She sat, defiantly alone, ignoring the stares and several interested comments, and drank her drink in greedy gulps, allowing the alcohol to calm her and steady her resolve. So! He was annoyed with her, for whatever reason she couldn't imagine. Well, if he couldn't even have the decency to talk to her, to explain what she was supposed to have done – if he couldn't even bring himself to *look* at her, but preferred to make her look a fool in front of all the others – well, bugger him, then! So much for his so-called *love*! So much for writing her a song and all the ... nice things he'd said, all the gentle, caring, nice things he'd done.

Right! She swallowed the last mouthful of her drink and stood up, straightening her skirt and pulling on her jacket. Well, at least now she knew where she stood. She'd go to the concert, and applaud like everyone else, and then she'd go home and get on with her work for the band, and from now on she'd know there was no favouritism, no special treatment. It was just a job, and Rob was just a member of the band.

The other girls were in their seats in the front row by the time she returned to the cinema.

'Where have you been?' Georgia whispered. 'Are you all right?'

She nodded. She didn't want to open her mouth and betray her lone drinking by the Bacardi fumes. The girls looked at each other anxiously, shaking their heads, but fortunately the show was just about to start – the lights went down, a drum roll sounded, the crowds started to squeal with excitement as the curtains opened and there were the Crazy Snakes, launching into one of the numbers on their new LP. Frankie sang and clapped and cheered along with everyone else – and it was only when, halfway through the show, Rob sang the words of *Francesca* with every appearance of the same husky, desperate yearning as ever, that Frankie was glad nobody could see, in the darkness, the tears streaming down her face.

Because it was the last night of the tour, there was the traditional party afterwards – but Frankie had never felt less like partying. She made her apologies to the other girls, pretending a headache, and slipped back to the hotel on her own. She was in bed, trying in vain to get to sleep, when just after one o'clock there was a tap on the door.

'Who is it?' She sat up and pulled on her dressing gown. Georgia, perhaps, coming to offer sympathy and persuade her to go back to the party?

'It's me. Rob.'

She took a deep breath. The cheek of him! Slighting her so horribly, and then turning up like this, at this time of night!

'Go away. I'm asleep.'

'No you're not. Please, Frankie – let me in. I just want to say sorry.'

'You've said it.'

'I want to *explain*. Please.'

This was ridiculous – shouting across the room at this hour – they'd have the rest of the hotel clientele complaining. She got up and opened the door a fraction.

'Not much point explaining, Rob,' she said coldly, without meeting his eyes. 'You made it quite obvious you don't want me around, so I'm going to sleep now, and going straight home in the morning, and ...'

'But I do. I do!'

'You do what?'

'Want you around! Oh, for God's sake, Frankie, let me just come in and tell you – please! I'm sorry – really sorry. I need to just tell you ... and then you'll understand.'

Sighing heavily, she held the door open and let him walk past her. He went to sit on the bed, apparently thought better of it and stayed on his feet, facing her.

'This is so hard for me to say.' He was almost whispering. 'I couldn't speak to you on the phone; and I couldn't tell you in front of everyone.'

'What is it? Why couldn't you?' She was still angry with him, but now she was worried too. He was speaking fast, and his voice was shaking slightly. 'What's happened?'

'I've been ... seeing ... somebody.'

For a minute she just blinked at him, uncomprehending. 'Somebody ... what? A girlfriend?'

He gave a curt nod. 'I suppose you could call her that.'

'Why, what else would you call her?' This suddenly felt completely surreal. What the hell? He couldn't speak to her, couldn't even look at her, had to come here in the dead of night and act like he had some dreadful secret to tell her ...

A girlfriend.

Frankie felt her heart thud. She looked at him now – properly, for the first time – his slender frame, his soft floppy fair hair, his kind blue eyes. He'd been her friend for more than a year, but she'd held him at arm's length, and now ... he had a girlfriend. She couldn't blame him, could she? It was inevitable. She'd even told her sister that was what would happen. He'd meet all these girls on the tour, she'd said, and ...

'What do you mean – you *suppose* you could call her a girlfriend?' she repeated, staring at him.

'She's just a fan,' he said, dropping his eyes from hers. 'She's followed the band everywhere. She comes to the stage door, begging to see us. Begging to see *me*.'

'And? You asked her out?'

'Not exactly.'

'Rob, you're talking in riddles, and I don't know what this has got to do with me. I'm tired, and if you want to know the truth, I'm upset about the way you ignored me earlier. And I don't particularly want to hear about this girl you did, or didn't, ask out.'

'I didn't ask her out,' he said, meeting her eyes again and holding them. 'I shagged her.'

'Sorry?' She gasped. 'You *what*?'

'You heard. I screwed her. Fucked her.'

'*Rob!*' The language shocked her almost as much as the fact of what he'd done. 'You took advantage of a fan ... a girl you hardly even know?'

'Oh, grow up, Frankie! It's what happens! These girls don't get taken advantage of – they're begging for it! It's well known – all the bands have these girls ...'

'And do the other boys do it? *Shag* these girls? *Screw* these girls? Do you all do it?'

'No.' He looked away again. 'No, they don't, because they've got girlfriends at home who they love. Who love them. Who they don't want to hurt.'

'Whereas you ...' she said, and began to choke on her words. So he was saying it was *her* fault, was he? Because she wouldn't be his girlfriend, wouldn't say she loved him, he was reduced to ... to ... *doing it* with some fan who *begged* for it?

'Frankie, for God's sake, try to understand how I feel, can you? Do you think I *like* myself for what I've been doing?'

'Doing?' she retorted. 'So it wasn't just the once?'

'No! Did I say it was? No – it was twice the first night, twice the next night, plus again the next morning, then ...'

'With the same girl?'

'Yes! For crying out loud, yes! She wants to be my bloody girlfriend! She thinks we're going steady, because I've sh – because I've *done it* with her half a dozen times. She wanted to come back to my room with me tonight. And Frankie, believe me, I had a hard job saying no! You hear me? I *wanted* to sleep with her again. She's sexy! She's good-looking! She's bloody crazy about me! Why would I *not* want to go to bed with a girl like that?'

'You tell me,' she said quietly, miserably. 'Why wouldn't you?'

'Because, you stupid girl – why do you think?' He was shouting now. Grabbing hold of her arms, holding her, almost shaking her, shouting at her. 'Because she's not *you*, for Christ's sake! Because I don't love her, it's just sex, and it makes me feel ashamed. Because I love *you*!'

With which he kissed her, at first so forcefully that, taken by surprise, she didn't even struggle. And then, stopping for a moment to look into her eyes, seeing the glint of tears there, with a groan of apology he began to kiss her more tenderly, more gently, more wonderfully than she'd ever been kissed before. Even by bloody Jack Hunter. Even in her dreams, those dreams of Rob that she never told anyone about, hardly even liked to admit to herself.

'Don't let her be your girlfriend,' she muttered eventually, when they'd somehow found themselves on the bed and it had become obvious he was staying there until the morning. 'Don't sleep with her any more – please. I couldn't bear it. I'm sorry if it was my fault you ... had to ...'

'Don't be daft. It wasn't your fault, it was mine. I gave into the temptation. Why do you think I couldn't talk to you? I felt too ashamed of myself. It won't happen again. I promise.'

'You do? Promise?'

'Absolutely. I'd promise you anything you wanted. You know that. You must do!'

'I think ... if it's all right with you ... I just want *you*. Please.'

They ended up keeping the hotel room for another night, and stayed in bed the whole time. The poor besotted fan waited outside Rob's unoccupied single room until she fell asleep on the corridor floor and, on being evicted by the management, went home alone to cry over her fan club photographs. She'd learnt a hard lesson that night.

And she wasn't the only one.

Chapter 24

December 1969: Perth

Shona had left work at the beginning of November. The baby wasn't due until the middle of January and although she was keeping well, she'd got pretty big and felt tired in the heat. Jack agreed it was best for her to be at home, resting as much as possible in the cool of their house where they'd had the latest air-conditioning installed.

In the office, there was a new girl to take her place, a school-leaver who forgot phone messages and didn't make him cups of tea. And at home, the baby preparations had stepped up a gear. When Shona wasn't shopping for the mountains of things a baby seemed to need, she was busy knitting shawls and cardigans. He had no idea why. Temperatures in January often reached ninety degrees and rarely dropped below sixty.

'Why does a baby need all this woolly gear?' he asked in exasperation, moving yet another pile of knitting, another bag of wool, from his favourite chair.

She laughed. 'Babies can't regulate their temperature like us. By April or May it might be getting cold at night, don't forget – and by then I'll be too busy to knit.'

'Won't the baby be tucked up asleep in bed at night-time?'

'Ha ha!' This was apparently the silliest comment even a mere male could make. 'Babies don't sleep through the night, you know! Sometimes not for years!' she added, almost gleefully.

He was actually beginning to feel redundant already. The painting and decorating was done – she'd wanted him to do up the lounge room, and then their bedroom, after he'd finished the nursery.

'We won't have time after the baby comes,' she kept saying, giving an excited little giggle every time she mentioned it.

Jack couldn't quite see why she wasn't going to have all the time in the world after the baby came – she wouldn't be going out to work, and surely one little baby didn't need someone running around it all day every day?

He'd put up the cot and fixed shelves for the baby's myriad pots of cream, piles of nappies, cotton wool, bibs, and all the other things it was apparently going to need. He felt uncomfortably aware that the baby seemed to have taken over their lives already, before it was even born. It felt like it had taken over his wife, almost as soon as he'd married her. And he had a suspicion it was only going to get worse.

Fortunately, Shona was still quite happy for him to get together with the band in the evenings, which was just as well, because they were now playing regularly at the same pub in Fremantle where he'd first heard Ruth singing, and they had other bookings lined up too.

'What we need,' Ruth said one night after rehearsals, as they sat in the backyard of her apartment drinking iced Coke to cool them down, 'is some promotion. Get ourselves known a bit further afield.'

Jack put down his glass. The hairs had suddenly stood up on the back of his neck. Get themselves known? Further afield? How far afield? And why the hell hadn't he thought this through? Of course, this was the inevitable next step; the band was doing OK, but they needed to get themselves known. And he *couldn't* – couldn't chance it. Had he been so desperate to be in a band again, he'd just closed his mind to the risk he was taking?

'If we do that,' he blurted out before he'd thought any further, 'I want to change my name.'

The others looked at him in surprise.

'Why?' Ruth demanded. 'Got yourself in trouble with the tax office or something?'

'Not a problem, is it, Ruthie?' Ken intervened. He glanced at Jack, gave him a brief nod of understanding, and went on: 'If a bloke wants to change his name, it sure doesn't matter to me and I don't much care why, personally.'

'Same here. No worries, mate,' agreed Al.

Ruth kept her gaze steady for a moment, then shook her head and shrugged. 'Just don't make it Ringo or anything kooky like that, then.'

'What's it gonna be, then?' Ken asked him afterwards. Since the nights had been so warm, they'd got into the habit of walking back to their respective homes instead of driving, and for part of the way they walked together, close to the river. 'Elvis Hunter? Jack Jagger?'

'I don't know. I've only just decided to do it.'

'This is because of what you told me, isn't it. Nobody back in England knowing where you are.'

'Yeah.' He shrugged. 'Best not to take any chances.' Even though he knew he already had. He'd taken the biggest risk of all with that very first letter to Frankie.

'Jack, mate, if someone wants to track you down badly enough, they'll do it. You know that, don't you?'

He shivered, despite the heat. 'I can't think about that. If I did, I'd never have joined the band. I'd never have got a car, or a job, or a house out here. I ... maybe I should have changed my name straight away.'

'Wouldn't mean a thing. You needed your real ID, didn't you, to get married, buy your house – all that stuff. You'd still be traceable. Nobody ever just vanishes, without a trace.'

'You did!' Jack retorted. And then, because Ken was silent for so long, he added: 'Sorry. But you did, didn't you? I mean, I don't want to rub it in or anything, but you were sent out here from England, God knows why, and nobody's ever managed to trace you, have they?'

'There's nobody to try,' Ken said quietly. 'My parents are both dead.'

'No brothers or sisters? No aunts or uncles?'

Silence.

Jack stopped walking and took hold of his friend's arm. 'Sorry,' he said again. 'I don't mean to upset you, mate. I'm just trying to say – look. It happens. People disappear to the other side of the world, and nobody seems to manage to find them.'

'OK, OK, I get your point!' Ken snapped. He shook off Jack's hand and started to walk again, fast, so that Jack had to run to catch him up. This time, he grabbed Ken's arm with both hands and pulled him to a stop. 'A few years back,' Ken said, breathing heavily in the darkness, 'anyone who did that to me would've been lying in the gutter with a bloody nose by now.'

'Sorry,' Jack said again. 'I was just ...'

'Making a point, yes, and you're right. You're dead right, and that's what hurts. Jack, mate, I don't *know* if I had any brothers or sisters. I think I did. I think I remember being in a house with other kids, but you know, I might just be confusing my early memories of the Barnardo's home. I think I remember my dad – but not my mum. They told me I'd been in the home since I was three. It was all I knew. Do *you* remember anything before that age? Nobody does, do they?'

'No.' Jack was sorry he'd started this. He hadn't meant to upset his friend. But now Ken was on a roll, and he didn't like to stop him – it was unusual enough for him to talk about his childhood.

'I was eleven when I was sent out here,' he went on, staring out at the lights across the river. Nineteen fifty-four. We thought we were going off on an adventure.'

'You came out with some friends?'

'Not friends exactly. Just other kids the same as me, all of us from children's homes. Some of them a lot younger than me – just little kids, not much more than babies.'

'All boys?'

'No … no there were girls too. But they split us up when we got here. Boys one way, girls the other … even if they were from the same family.' He paused, a look of surprise in his eyes. 'Holy shit, I'd almost forgotten about that. It was bloody awful. One of the girls …' He covered his eyes, as if he were trying to avoid seeing something, and shook his head. 'Never mind.'

'You poor kids.' Jack sighed. 'All of you. Poor bloody kids. I can't believe they did this – to a whole shipload of you!'

'Blimey, Jack, I don't think we were the only shipload. Not from talking to other kids at the boys' home here. It seemed pretty much the norm – so we all kind of accepted it. We just thought it was what happened to kids nobody wanted.'

Kids nobody wanted! Jack shook own his head. He felt ashamed for thinking *he'd* had a hard time.

'I'm sorry I brought it up,' he said, touching Ken's shoulder.

'Look, don't worry about it. I was one of the lucky ones, in a way – at least I know who I am – I was old enough at eleven to remember that, at least. Some of the younger boys didn't know a bloody thing about themselves. One little kid at the boys' home here – he was only three when he was brought over. Three! He couldn't say what his name was, so they called him Tommy and made up a birth date for him. He had no idea in the world who he really was.'

'Jesus, no. That's terrible.'

'Yeah.' Ken gave his characteristic shrug. 'But I just do wonder sometimes … about some of the others from the ship. What happened to them all.'

'They'll be grown up by now, mate, like yourself. Probably all turned out fine.'

'Yeah.' He didn't sound convinced. Jack wondered what the chances were, in fact, of any of these *kids nobody wanted* actually turning out fine, and who could be surprised about it? They started walking again, in silence, Jack now unable to get the pictures out of his head – the heart-rending image of an eleven-year old Ken, amongst a horde of even younger children, arriving in a strange country with the bewildering prospect of never going home – brothers and sisters perhaps being separated for the rest of their lives.

'Where were you from originally, anyway?' he asked as casually as he could, trying to normalise the situation somehow – bring it back down to earth, back to basics. 'Whereabouts in England was your children's home?'

Funny that he'd never asked him. Ken's accent and his mannerisms were Australian through-and-through, so it had been difficult to think of him as coming from England.

'Oh, kind of London way,' Ken said with his characteristic shrug. 'Never think about it too much now, to be honest. How about you?'

'Me? Yeah, I was from London originally, too, mate.' Despite himself, Jack's thoughts immediately began to stray back to his life in London – his old life before his father had died. And the two friends strolled on home in silence, each lost in his own tormented memories.

Chapter 25

January 1970

All over Christmas, Shona complained that she felt like she was about to burst. She was uncomfortable no matter how she sat, or lay, and was finding the heat unbearable.

'If the baby doesn't come soon, I think I'll go mad,' she said on New Year's Day, sitting next to a fan and panting like a dog. 'I can't possibly get any bigger!'

In fact, it was only a couple more days before baby Steven made his entrance, bang on his due date on the third of January, and when he was brought home from hospital, a week later, the night-time temperatures had dipped to a temporary and very unseasonable low, causing Jack to eat his words straight away about the need for knitted shawls. In fact by the time the baby had been home for a couple of days and Jack had witnessed the speed at which he soaked his clothes with vomit, excrement and dribble, not necessarily in that order, he was beginning to wonder whether Shona should have knitted half a dozen more of everything. He felt completely overwhelmed by the responsibility of this kid – *his* kid – who was so tiny, so helpless and fragile, but with whom he had no idea how to interact. If he picked Steven up, Shona told him to put him back down. Whenever he did hold him, he was apparently doing it all wrong. He made him cry. He made him sick. He was too nervous, too awkward, too loud, too heavy-handed – whatever he did, it was never the right way, or the right time for it. Shona needed to feed him, or change him, or put him down to sleep. Basically, Jack felt in the way.

After he'd been at home with Shona for three days, her friend Karen visited. She dived into the room, hugged Shona and swooped Steven into her arms virtually at the same time, rocking him and cooing over him and asking what she could do to help. Jack, who'd retreated to the kitchen to make coffee, couldn't help feeling resentful that the baby wasn't crying or vomiting over *her*.

'I've got some time off. I can come round every day if you like – whenever Jack has to go back to work. Just till you get back on your feet,' Karen was offering as he brought in the coffee.

Shona gave Jack a questioning look. 'When do you have to go back to work?'

It was as if both women were holding their breath, looking at him with hope in their eyes – and suddenly he saw it clearly. She didn't want him there. He was more trouble than he was worth. She'd rather have Karen, who knew how to pick up the baby, who didn't do everything wrong and make Steven scream.

'Well,' he said, trying to sound regretful about it, 'I probably should go back on Monday, really, but …'

'I can come on Monday,' Karen said at once. 'I'll stay over, if it helps.'

Shona practically jumped at it. So Jack went back to work, went back to spending his evenings with the band, and when the band weren't actually practising he just hung out with Ken. By the time he went home at night, both Shona and the baby were usually asleep.

'You oughta be at home with her,' Ken warned him once or twice during the first few weeks. 'It's not right, you know that, don't you – she's just had the kid.'

'She doesn't want me there, mate. She's so wrapped up with the baby, it's like I'm out on a limb. She doesn't even notice whether I'm there or not.'

'Yeah, well, they say women go kind of crazy just after they've given birth. You married her, didn't you – it's your kid …'

Jack turned on him, exasperated. 'You're not exactly the one to talk, are you? At least I was *prepared* to marry her, and have a family with her!'

'So don't stuff it up! Christ! What's wrong with you? Don't you think I still regret ...' He tailed off, shaking his head, looking embarrassed.

Jack stared at his friend. 'You do, don't you,' he said with sudden realisation. 'You regret it – finishing with her. You still fancy her? You fancy my fucking wife?'

'Calm down, I never said I fancied her, did I? I regret hurting her, that's all I said. And I don't like seeing you doing the same thing all over again.' He shook his head. 'I'm on my own – probably always will be. It's my own fault, just the way I am. Whereas *you* – you're so bloody sorry for yourself about the girl you left behind back in England, who doesn't even want you any more – face it! – but you've got it all, here in Oz, the perfect life: job, house, wife, kid – and you're going the right way to fuck it all up.' He stopped, slapped Jack on the back, and added, 'I'm only telling you because you're my mate.'

'Wouldn't like to hear the way you talk to your enemies,' Jack grumbled.

But he knew Ken was right. And he also knew he'd been right himself – Ken was definitely sorry he'd let Shona go. He still liked her, fancied her, no matter what he said. Probably wished he was in Jack's shoes – no wonder he thought Jack should be more appreciative. They'd only been married a few months and if he wasn't careful, someone else who fancied her like Ken did would come along one day and ... well, then he'd only have himself to blame.

'You're right,' he said eventually. 'I'll spend a bit more time at home. If she wants me there.'

'It'll come good,' Ken said. 'Give her time.'

'And what do you know about it?'

'Absolutely fuck all,' he said with a grin, and they both laughed.

Part of his trouble, of course, was that Ken was right about the other thing too. The *girl back in England.* Jack had tried his best to put Frankie firmly out of his mind. He'd had plenty to think about instead – first Christmas, then the baby being born. And music – the band. He kept telling himself to concentrate on that. It was exciting, it was the future. He wouldn't think about the past. Wouldn't think about *her.*

But of course, it was all he *could* think about. When he closed his eyes, he could picture her house – where she lived with her sister. He could still remember walking down her road, looking up at the windows of her house, his heart racing with excitement at the thought of seeing her … *the girl who didn't even want him anymore.*

It was true – he knew that now, clearer than ever. She was with Rob. There was no point whatsoever wasting any more time thinking about her, wondering about her, or the baby. His life was here, now, with Shona and Steven. *Get over it.*

The conversation with Ken about his transportation to Australia had played on Jack's mind ever since. He felt so sad, and so angry, on behalf of his mate and all the other children who had been sent away, he would have loved to be able to do something – anything – to help them find some answers. Whatever Ken said, surely he must want to know *why* he was uprooted from the home in England, why he was chosen to be sent to Australia? Jack felt sorry for him, not knowing, living with this huge question mark hanging over him. He wished there was a way he could help him – someone in England, perhaps, who could look into it all, delve into the mystery of why the kids were sent out here.

But the only contact he had back in England, of course, was Frankie. And that brought him back round in the same old tired circle; he had to forget about Frankie, get on with his life here, not try to contact her again, concentrate on his music, concentrate on Shona and the baby, be a proper husband like Ken said he should; stop looking back, start looking forwards.

No, he couldn't do it. He wouldn't weaken; he wouldn't write to Frankie again. Not even to help his mate.

Chapter 26

<u>Shenfield, Essex : April 1970</u>

Sometimes Frankie would wake up in the night, stare round the room, stare at the man sleeping next to her in the big double bed, and feel like she had to pinch herself. How had her life changed so dramatically in such a short time?

The Crazy Snakes had gone from strength to strength; their tour had been a runaway success, their first LP had gone to number one in the album charts, they'd now had a second number one single and were about to release their third record. Rob was looking for a house of his own, even before he sprung his surprise on Frankie at Christmas.

She'd invited him for Christmas dinner.

'Is that OK?' she checked with Marianne anxiously. 'I mean, I don't want to give you any extra work – you know I'll cook the dinner, or look after the twins, or whatever ...'

'Frankie, love,' Marianne said, giving her sister a tender smile, 'I'd be upset if you *didn't* invite Rob for Christmas! You can't imagine how happy I am that you two have finally got together. I always knew he was the right one for you.'

'How? How come you knew, and I didn't?'

'Just put it down to sisterly intuition!'

Over drinks before dinner, Rob had produced a small wrapped box from his pocket and handed it to Frankie. He was flushed with nerves.

'Happy Christmas, baby,' he said, his voice shaking slightly. 'I ... hope it's all right.'

It was a diamond engagement ring – simple but elegant, the diamond set within a ring of tiny sapphires. Frankie could only stare at it and gasp 'Oh!'

'Will you marry me, Frankie?' Rob asked, almost hoarse now with his anxiety. 'I mean ... there's no rush ... if you want to think about it for a while, or a few months, or ... well, forever, really, it's fine, but please wear the ring anyway, and we'll talk about it ... maybe some time ...'

'Shush!' Frankie, laughing with happiness, had launched herself at him and kissed him, much to the hilarity of little Joel who'd danced around them squealing and giggling – and much to the excitement of Marianne and Grant, she'd added eventually: 'Of course I'll marry you! How quickly can we set a date?'

The house was a solid, four bedroom detached in Shenfield, a very upmarket town further out in Essex, from where there was a fast train connection to London. Frankie had walked around the house and garden, open-mouthed in wonder. She'd never been inside such a lovely house in her life.

'Are you sure we can afford it?' she'd whispered to Rob, out of earshot of the estate agent who was showing them around.

'Absolutely!' He laughed and caught her hand. 'It's like a dream come true, isn't it?'

It *was* like a dream, for both of them – but this was a new decade, the age of majority had been brought down to eighteen, and young people were taking control of their own lives now instead of being treated like children until they were twenty-one. Rob was twenty-three anyway, although Frankie wouldn't be twenty until the summer – but anything was possible now, and Rob and Frankie were going to enjoy their success and grab life's pleasures with both hands while they could.

One of the bedrooms in the new house was converted into an office, with a proper desk, filing cabinets, and even one of the newest and most efficient photocopying machines, finally freeing Frankie from the need to produce multiple carbon copies or type a stencil for use on the Gestetner machine in Dave's office. When she loaded all her files and boxes of stationery into Rob's car to move them to Shenfield, she felt nothing but relief, to be giving her sister back the use of her dining room. But when it came to packing up her own clothes and possessions the day before her wedding in March, she was torn between excitement and regret.

'Will you manage all right?' she asked her sister. 'I mean – I know it's just as well I'm going, in one way – you need the room, for the babies, but ...'

'But you've been the most fantastic help,' Marianne finished for her, enveloping her in a bear hug. 'And of course, I'm going to miss you like crazy. But I'm so happy for you, darling! And anyway ... Grant and I have got our own plans.'

'You have?'

'Well, we thought it was time we joined the exodus from Dagenham.'

'You're moving?' Frankie gasped in surprise.

'We're hoping to. Not far, you know ... we've found a house we like in Brentwood. We went and looked at it last week when you were out with Rob, and we've had an offer accepted.'

'Oh, Mari! That would be *perfect*! You wouldn't be far from us – I could still see you and the children!'

'Well, it isn't quite definite yet. That's why we haven't told you – we didn't want you getting too excited about it. But it's all happened so fast – it's the first house we've looked at, and already there's a young couple interested in our house, and they could complete really quickly, so ...'

'Oh, that's fantastic! What's the house like?'

'Quite a lot bigger. We really needed the space, and with Grant's salary increase, and the little bit extra, you know, from Mum ...'

The solicitor had finally been granted an order from the court, allowing them to distribute their mother's entire estate including the share allocated to Susannah, who still hadn't been found. Marianne and Frankie had mixed feelings about this. It was difficult to draw a line under the situation, when somewhere in the world they still might have an older sister alive, who should properly have been entitled to her share.

'We'll pay her back,' Frankie insisted. 'If she ever turns up, we'll pay her back her share. No matter what.'

'Of course,' Marianne agreed. 'But meanwhile, Frankie, we have to face facts. Susannah might never be traced. The solicitor can't hold onto the money for ever.'

Frankie and Rob were married on the fourteenth of March – in the local C of E church where her sister had been married, and all the children had been christened. The irony of her mother's feelings about this church wasn't lost on Frankie, but she had no desire to be married in the Catholic church, and Rob was simply happy for the service to happen wherever she wanted.

Straight after the wedding reception, a small affair in a local pub, they took a taxi to Southend airport from where they flew off for a honeymoon to Jersey. It was the first time either of them, or anyone in either of their families, had been on a plane. Frankie was terrified, clinging to Rob as the plane taxied down the runway, and then gasping with surprise as it lifted smoothly into the air. By the time they landed in Jersey she was over her fear and pronounced the whole thing unbelievably fantastic. But she had to phone Marianne from the hotel in St Helier, to reassure her sister that she'd survived the experience!

And now they'd been in their lovely new home for a month, and Frankie was working almost full-time in the office upstairs, dealing with fan mail from all over the world, composing fan club newsletters and sending out membership packs.

'If you need an assistant,' Rob said one morning, looking at the piles of letters waiting to be answered, 'just say the word. Dave has already hinted that you might need one.'

'I can manage at the moment.' She smiled at him. 'I enjoy it. But if you become any more global, I might have to take you up on it.'

There had been a lot of fan mail coming in from America, from all over Europe, from as far afield as New Zealand and Australia. Since her marriage, Frankie had been able to look at letters bearing Australian stamps without the slightest flicker of emotion. She'd more or less forgotten about Jack. Even Rob hardly ever mentioned him now.

There were phone calls, too – Dave had had a dedicated fan club phone line put into the house, the calls coming straight through to an answerphone in Frankie's office. Most of them were requests for membership of the fan club – the number was given on all the fan club literature. Frankie would simply listen to the messages once a day, take down the addresses and send out the membership packs. Some of them were different, though – fans asking questions about their favourite band member, wanting to know when their birthdays were, what their favourite colours were, where they were born, or whether they were married. That was a tough one, of course, as it wasn't unusual for girls to burst into tears on hearing that their idol had a girlfriend or a wife, so Frankie tried her best to avoid answering directly.

The number of phone messages and letters from overseas was rising constantly, and this was why Dave and Rob had both been suggesting Frankie might need an assistant. As it happened, it was in fact just as she'd given in and asked Dave to look for someone part-time to come in to help her, that she received the letter that changed everything.

Chapter 27

May 1970: Melbourne, Australia

Sue had been working for Maureen Pringle in the coffee shop for more than six months now, and she couldn't imagine being any happier. The hours were long, the work could be quite hard, but for the first time in her life, she had some self-respect. She felt like a real adult, a proper member of society. She had money to spend – tips on top of her wages – and places to spend it. She loved looking round the shops on her day off, staring at the vast array of goods on offer. She'd never seen anything like it before. Closeted as she'd been in the children's home, and then stuck out on the Andersons' farm in the back of beyond, she didn't have any idea of life in a city, or the freedom to wander the streets and parks at will. Not that she was being wasteful with her money. She'd opened a bank account and was saving for the day when she might be able to afford a place of her own. She loved Melbourne with a kind of fierce loyalty. Melbourne had rescued her. She wanted to spend the rest of her life here, working hard and being a good citizen. After the start in life she'd endured, Sue wanted nothing more than to blend in and be normal.

It hadn't taken Maureen long to realise that there was something unusual about her new recruit. Most girls in their twenties (and Maureen had employed dozens of them over the years) were flighty, chatty, spent too long in the cloakroom fiddling with their hair and make-up, wore their skirts too short and flirted too ostentatiously with the men. Sue, on the other hand, seemed to have been dropped here from another planet. She was young for her age, and so naive it was ridiculous. She'd stared at the money in her first wage packet in awe, like she'd never seen so much in her life. She wore her blonde hair in a simple pony-tail, with no make-up, no mini-skirts, platform shoes or any of the other fashion trappings sported by the other young waitresses. She was quiet, polite, worked hard and never flirted with the male customers – in fact, she seemed nervous around them, blushing madly and looking quite panicky if anyone tried to chat her up.

One day when Sue was waiting at tables, a particularly lecherous regular customer, known to the other girls as Gary the Groper, grabbed her hand as she gave him his bill, and laughed nastily when she struggled to free herself.

'Come on, darlin', don't be shy!' he teased her. 'Give Gary a little bit of fun to earn your tip, there's a good girl.'

'Let me go, please,' she said, her voice breaking.

'Just a little kiss, come on! Sit on Gary's knee for a minute and I'll show you a nice surprise.'

Maureen strode up behind him and grabbed his arm. 'Leave her alone!' she ordered coldly. 'Let her go, *now*!'

'All right, all right, keep your hair on, woman,' he grumbled. 'Only trying to have a little bit of fun with her.'

'My waitresses are here to work, not to pander to your dirty little fantasies. Now, pay your bill, please, and leave.'

He rounded on her in furious disbelief. 'You talk to me like that? I come in here nearly every day – I expect a little more respect from you!'

'Why? You don't show any respect to my girls. If you don't like it, don't bother coming back.'

'Don't worry, missus, I won't!' He threw some money on the table and got to his feet, hoisting up his trousers. 'Jumped up little tart,' he hissed at Sue as he pushed past her. 'Think you're better than all the rest, do you? Look at you, skinny little bitch! Should be grateful anyone *wants* to have a feel of you.'

'Get out – now!' Maureen said. 'Or I'll call the police, I'm warning you!'

The whole place had fallen silent. But as the door swung shut behind a scowling Gary, a cheer went up from the other customers.

'Well done, love,' one woman called out. 'He was a nasty bit of garbage, that one.'

'Too right! Good riddance!' echoed another. 'He was trying to get a look down my top – I moved tables to get away from him.'

The other waitress on duty nodded her head in agreement. 'We all hated it when he started getting fresh with us. Dirty old man.'

Maureen found Sue in the cloakroom, trembling as she washed her face at the sink.

'I'm sorry,' she stammered. 'I've lost you a good customer.'

'Stuff and nonsense! I don't expect you to put up with being mauled by the likes of him. I'm glad to see the back of him – he was upsetting the other customers.' She took a good look at Sue, and added more gently, 'You all right, now? He's a nasty bit of work, but I doubt he'd have hurt you, you know.'

'I know.' Sue was trying hard to stop her teeth chattering. 'I'm sorry. I just ... can't ... I don't like ...'

'Hey, no need for tears, now! Come and sit in the kitchen for a minute and drink a cup of tea. Can't have you crying on the job!'

Sue did as she was told, and, grateful for her boss's no-nonsense sympathy, felt the need to apologise again afterwards.

'I'm sorry I got so upset. I'll get straight back to work again now.'

'Sure you're all right?'

'Yes.' Sue straightened her shoulders. 'Thank you for being so nice about it.'

'No worries.' She nodded at the girl, and watched her return to her usual calm efficiency. But she kept an eye on her after that, and made a point of showing her a little extra kindness. She had a feeling the kid hadn't been shown an awful lot, before.

Within a couple of months, Sue was promoted to full-time waitressing. She'd worked hard, taking her job seriously and was naturally courteous and careful. She was also aware that Maureen had taken a special interest in her and was watching over her like a rather severe mother hen. Sometimes at closing time they'd be the only two left in the place, and on these occasions Maureen began to probe gently into the mystery of her favourite employee's background.

'Your family still back in WA, are they?' she asked one day. And 'How come you're all on your own over here in Victoria?'

And slowly, with a studied patience born out of genuine concern, she retrieved Sue's whole story, in bite-sized chunks manageable to the teller – a little more each day, until with the final episode, the tale of her rape and abuse at the hands of Michael Anderson, Sue broke down and sobbed into the arms of the older woman, who had to swallow back her own tears of outrage. And from then on the two became firm friends.

Sometimes during the heat of the summer they'd sit together outside the coffee shop after they'd closed up, enjoying the cooler evening air, and Maureen, understanding that Sue had never before had anyone to confide in, would encourage her to talk some more about her experiences.

'It wasn't like I was particularly badly treated by the nuns at the home,' she explained. 'They were strict, and we had to work hard, but it could have been worse. But look, I just felt so *lost*. I knew I didn't have anyone else to look after me – no family – I'd been in an orphanage somewhere in England before they brought me out here. But somehow I still kept thinking that somebody *might* turn up one day and take me back again. Maybe an aunt or an uncle or a friend of ... whoever my parents were ... *somebody*. But that was daft, wasn't it. Nobody would know where I was.'

'And they never told you *why* you'd been sent out here?' Maureen asked quietly.

'No,' Sue said. 'I've never understood. Nobody ever seemed to talk about it. So ... I didn't, either. I had enough to worry about, just staying out of trouble and getting all my work done. As we got older we had to help in the kitchens or the gardens after classes. I was exhausted most of the time. Probably just as well. Stopped me thinking about ... well, hoping for ... I don't know.' She sighed. 'Someone to say we could go home again.'

'And were there many others? Other kids who were sent out here like you were, for no apparent reason?'

'Oh yes. Nearly all the girls at the home had been sent out from England. They kept telling us to be grateful.'

Maureen hugged her. She still couldn't quite believe what she was hearing. Why was this allowed to go on? Was it *still* going on? Why didn't anyone seem to know about it? She guessed it must have just been the one orphanage in Perth that had taken these kids in – otherwise people across Australia would surely be up in arms about it – wouldn't they?

Over the following few months, she was pleased to see her young friend beginning to come out of her shell. While she might never be loud and exuberant like the other girls, she was slowly gaining confidence, trying out some of the new fashions from the shops and getting into pop music. Maureen enjoyed watching the metamorphosis. It seemed to her that Sue had a lot of catching up to do – she'd completely missed out on a normal adolescence, going straight from a deprived childhood to a unnaturally serious maturity.

'What's your favourite pop group?' she asked her one evening, smiling as she watched Sue toying with the new portable transistor radio she'd bought herself.

'Oh, the Crazy Snakes! Have you heard of them? They're a British group, they've had two number one hit singles. They're fantastic!'

'I'll have to listen out for them,' said Maureen, who in fact never listened to anything other than trad jazz. But she didn't forget the conversation, and on Sue's next day off she happened to find a copy of a music magazine, abandoned on one of the tables she was clearing – with the front page headline screaming:

SNAKES' NEW SINGLE RELEASED. WILL THEY PLAN OZ TOUR NEXT?

– and a half-page colour picture of the band.

She kept the magazine and gave it to Sue the next day.

'Thought you might like the picture!' she said.

'Thanks, Maureen!' Sue glanced at the front page quickly and put the paper in her bag to take home with her. She didn't really have much of a clue how things like record releases and tours worked – it was all new to her, but she loved pop music and she was keen to learn.

And so it was that when she arrived home that evening and spread out the music magazine on her little kitchen table to read while the kettle was boiling, she noticed the small print at the bottom of the article about her favourite band:

To find out more about the Crazy Snakes or to join their fan club, contact:

Mrs Francesca Marchant, Fan Club Secretary, 16 Oak Drive, Shenfield, Essex, England.

Sue had hardly ever written a letter in her life. Who would she write to? But if nothing else, the nuns at the girls' home had given their charges a good basic education in the three R's. She tore a page from the notebook she used for shopping lists, and began to write.

Dear Mrs Marchant

I have found your address in an article about the Crazy Snakes in the Australian Music Now! *magazine, and I am writing to say that I hope their new record will be released quickly in Australia and also that I would be very happy if they decide to do a tour of Australia.*

Yours sincerely
(Miss) Susannah M. Kennedy
PS: I notice your address is in Essex. I think I came from Essex originally.

As soon as she'd written the PS, she felt silly and embarrassed at herself. When she'd seen the word *Essex* she'd been struck, momentarily, by a memory – or perhaps only a half-memory – that this was once part of her own address. She couldn't be sure; she'd forgotten, within a short time of being in the orphanage in Perth, where she'd come from, what the town was called or the name of her school. She'd been so young, and the shock of her transportation so great, almost every detail of her life in England seemed to have been wiped from her mind, and if she asked the nuns, they told her it didn't matter anymore. But on seeing that name – *Essex* – she didn't even know whether it was a town, a city or a state – she'd felt such a sense of familiarity, she had an urgent impulse to tell someone.

Maybe she'd have been better, she thought ruefully as she sealed up the envelope, to wait and share it with Maureen tomorrow, instead of blurting out such a stupid PS to the fan club secretary just because she lived in Essex! And now, because she felt such a fool, she hadn't even checked through her letter before folding and sealing it. She couldn't remember whether she'd written her own address on the top, the way she'd been taught in English lessons. But then again – it didn't really matter, did it. She wasn't expecting a reply.

She put the letter in her bag to take to the post office during her break the next day. And didn't think any more about it.

Chapter 28

May-June 1970 : Perth

With the start of the rain, the worst of the heat that year was over and Jack was glad to see the back of it. The baby was sleeping better at night, so Shona too was getting more sleep and seemed more settled, less exhausted. Ever since the conversation with Ken, back in January, Jack had been making a concerted effort with his wife and child, and as far as he could tell, it was only inside his own heart that he felt it still wasn't enough – that she still didn't seem too bothered whether he was there or not. He must be imagining it; after all, there hadn't been any arguments, she was as calm and pleasant as always – but there was a distance between them; even within the same room they were talking to each other like polite strangers. If he tried to put his arms around her, kiss her or make any affectionate overtures to her, it always seemed that Steven suddenly needed attention. He told himself to be patient; after all, she'd had a baby – she was probably still recovering. He had no idea how long the recovery was supposed to take, but he did know he needed to be kind and understanding, and to give his wife whatever time she needed to get back to her old self. He owed her that, at the very least.

    Meanwhile he kept himself busy with his work, with his rehearsals, and with the bookings that were coming in more often now for the band. Ken, Ruth and Al had all become his close friends – but it was always with Ken that he felt most able to open up. They'd confided stuff to each other than neither had talked about to anyone else, and this had given them an understanding of each other that would normally have taken many more months, or even years, of acquaintance to build up to.

It was a month or so back that Ken had told him quietly one evening while they were packing up from a gig:

'I've been thinking a lot about what I told you. How I got sent out here as a kid. *Why* the hell we all got sent out here. I've been wondering whether it's about time I tried to find some answers.'

'I can understand that. Where are you going to start?'

Ken laughed. 'I haven't got the faintest idea.'

'I've thought about it myself. Wondering if I could help. What you really need is a contact back in England who could maybe ask some questions in the right places.'

'Yeah. And contacts in England are what we're both short of.'

Jack remained silent. Ken looked at him and smiled. 'Oh, I get it. Your other girlfriend. Stop right there, Jack – you're not gonna get back in touch with her, are you.'

Jack frowned to himself. It was true. He'd promised himself he wasn't going to write to Frankie again, not even to help Ken. But ...

'Look, I could ... just to see if she knows anything – or if she knows any government body, any address you can write to, anything like that.'

'As an excuse to get in touch with her again, you mean.' Ken had stopped smiling now. His tone was sharp. 'Seriously, mate, I don't want to find out about this badly enough for you to risk your marriage.'

'It's not gonna risk anything. I'm just saying ...'

'You've been telling me how it is at home, with you and Shona. I know how these things work, Jack. One little spark between you and this girl in England, and before you know it ...'

'She doesn't want me anyway! You told me that yourself, and you're right. She doesn't – she's with another bloke, probably married by now. If you want to know the truth, I thought about getting in touch with her when you talked to me about this before. I liked the idea of seeing if I could find out anything for you – why you got sent over here. But I talked myself out of it, because of what you'd been saying to me about putting it all behind me, concentrating on Shona and Steven.'

'Well? I was right, wasn't I?'

'Course you were. That's what I've *been* doing. But look, if you're serious about finding some answers to your situation, how the hell else are you going to do it? Where else are you going to start?'

'I dunno. Maybe ask the Australian government what the hell they were playing at back in the 1950s.'

'Good luck with *that*, then.'

Ken didn't answer. But Jack had already made up his mind. He'd write to Frankie anyway. He'd promised himself he wouldn't, and he hadn't had any intention of breaking that promise. But this was different. It wasn't for himself.

His letter was short and to the point. He purposely kept the tone businesslike, ignoring the fluttering of his heart as he imagined her opening the envelope, telling himself over and again that he was married to Shona, that *she* was probably married to Rob, that he wasn't going to get upset or angry about it anymore, that he was over it, that his life had moved on, that this was purely an attempt to get some information for Ken.

He sent the letter care of Frankie's sister again, posting it on the last day of May and telling himself that he'd check the post office box after a couple of weeks. He felt sure that this time Frankie would reply – he'd explained briefly why he needed her help, to help his friend. She was already aware, after all, that he couldn't write to anyone else in England for help. He hadn't said anything personal that she could take offence at. The Frankie he'd known and fallen in love with was too kind-hearted to ignore such a request, he was sure of it. And after he'd had her reply, he was going to let the post office box go. He wouldn't need it any more. This time, he really meant it!

After the two weeks had passed, he checked the post office box nearly every day, but there was nothing for a full month. And then he found his own letter in there; it had come back with *Return to sender: addressee gone away* written on it. Jack knew when he was beaten. As soon as he'd got over the disappointment, he handed back the key to his post office box. No point hanging onto it any longer. Frankie had gone, presumably her sister had moved too – he should have known better than to hope for help from that quarter. He'd never hear from her again, and never find out about the reason for Ken's childhood transportation. He was just sorry he hadn't been able to help his friend. When he finally admitted that he'd written to Frankie about it, but that the letter had been returned, Ken merely swallowed hard and thanked him for trying.

'I doubt your bird in England would have known anything about kids being abandoned and shipped out to Oz anyway,' he said. 'Nobody else in the bloody world seems to know anything about it, so why the hell should she?'

Chapter 29

June 1970 : Shenfield

Frankie's new assistant, Lesley, was a nice enough girl but not the fastest typist in the world, and Frankie was beginning to wonder how much help she was going to be. The pile of unanswered fan mail seemed to be growing higher instead of diminishing. Frankie sighed as she grabbed another batch of letters from Lesley's desk. She was supposed to be opening them and passing them to Frankie as they arrived, but she didn't yet seem to be capable of keeping up with the flow. For a while Frankie worked in silence, opening letters, reading them and marking each one clearly with instructions for Lesley: *Send fan club pack*; *Send standard thank-you letter*; *Send information sheet plus photo*. Those letters needing a more personal response, she slid into her own in-tray. The one halfway down the pile bearing the Australian stamp, she gave no particular attention to as she slit open the envelope. There was more and more mail coming through from overseas now. She skimmed the short, neatly written page quickly and was just about to scrawl: *Send information sheet* on the bottom of it when she noticed the signature.

'What's the matter?' Lesley was staring at Frankie anxiously. She'd jumped to her feet as if she'd been shot, clutching the letter, stammering something about someone called Susannah. 'Are you all right?'

'Sorry. Sorry, Lesley.' Frankie was flushed and flustered. 'Can you just carry on with those for a minute? I ... need to talk to someone.'

She rushed out of the room, leaving the surprised Lesley shrugging to herself and looking for her magazine and nail file. Frankie ran straight downstairs to the kitchen and used the personal phone line to call her sister.

'Mari? I've got a letter ... and ... well, it's from Australia, and she says she came from Essex, and the name is the same, but ...'

'What? Frankie, calm down, I haven't got the faintest idea what you're talking about! Are you all right?'

'Yes, yes, of course I am,' Frankie said impatiently. 'It might be *her*, Marianne! I mean, I know it might be a coincidence, but ...'

'*Her*? Who?'

'Susannah! Our *sister*.' There was silence at the other end of the line. 'Mari? Are you still there?'

'Yes. Yes, I've just had to sit down, Frankie. How on earth ... I mean, I didn't even know you were still trying to find her.'

'I wasn't! This is just ... oh, I know it's almost too much of a coincidence. It's a letter to the fan club. From a *Susannah M. Kennedy.*'

'From *Australia*?'

'Yes!'

'Frankie, come on. This is just a coincidence. There must be thousands of Susannah Kennedys in the world.'

'Susannah *M.* Kennedy, *M* for Margaret – that makes it more unusual, surely?'

'Well, maybe, but I still think ... sorry, love, I think you're getting carried away. I mean, what are the chances of her ending up in Australia? It's not very likely, is it.'

Frankie sighed. 'I suppose you're right. It's just ... I saw the name, and she's put this PS at the end of the letter about Essex.'

'Did she actually say she came from Essex? Did she say whereabouts?'

'No. That's the weird thing. She just says ...' Frankie picked up the letter again and read it out: '*I notice your address is in Essex. I think I came from Essex originally.*'

'She *thinks* she came from Essex? That's a funny thing to say, isn't it? Doesn't she *know*?'

'You're right, it is a strange thing to say, but if she does come from Essex, don't you think she *could* be our Susannah?'

'I don't know, Frankie. It ... seems like too much of a long shot. And why would she be writing to the Crazy Snakes' fan club, anyway? Think about it: our Susannah would be ... twenty-four or twenty-five by now. Not a teenager!'

'So? *I* still like their music! So do you, and you're not a teenager either!'

'Yes, but I wouldn't ...' She stopped and sighed. 'Oh, I don't know. I suppose what I'm saying is, don't you think joining a fan club would be a kind of immature thing for someone of that age to do?'

'Not really, no! But anyway she hasn't asked to join the fan club – she's just ...' Frankie glanced at the letter again. 'Basically, she's just saying she hopes the new record's going to be released in Australia, and that the boys will do a tour out there.'

'And will they?'

'Nothing decided yet. Dave's been looking into them doing some foreign tours – but it'll probably be America first. Maybe Australia next year, who knows.'

'So write back and tell her that, and ask whereabouts in Essex she comes from.'

'Shall I ... Mari, do you think I should say anything? About whether she might be our Susannah?'

Marianne hesitated. 'No, I wouldn't,' she said, and then added: 'Maybe you could just say what a coincidence it is – that your maiden name was Kennedy too. Maybe just ask if by any chance she came from Dagenham. If you just make it kind of friendly and casual ...'

'Mari – '

'You could suggest she writes back to you again ...'

'But Mari – '

'No, listen, Frankie! I'm telling you, if you start asking her if she's your sister, you'll freak the poor girl out. Just get her to write again so you can discuss the surname and where she came from in Essex, and go from there.'

'But I can't, Mari. I've just noticed something. I can't write back to her at all. There's no address.'

'What? Oh, for crying out loud! What's the point in writing to you if she can't even give you an address to write back to? Are you sure? Nothing on the back of the envelope?'

'No. Nothing. Oh, what a disappointment! I can't believe it! I was so excited ... so *sure*.'

Marianne said nothing for a minute. Frankie wondered whether she was trying to hide her own disappointment. She might not have sounded as excited as Frankie, but surely she must have agreed it was an amazing coincidence, and *might* have been the right Susannah!

'Read me the whole letter, Frankie,' she said eventually.

'OK. It's not very long.' Frankie started to read, but she hadn't got beyond the first paragraph when Marianne stopped her.

'*Music Now*! magazine,' she repeated.

'What about it?'

'Well, it's obvious, isn't it. She saw the article about the band in *Music Now*! so she's probably a regular reader. Write to the magazine and see if they'll put an advert in, asking Susannah Kennedy who recently wrote to the Snakes' fan club to get in touch with you again.'

'Oh! Good idea! Yes, I'll ...' She stopped. 'But how am I going to get the address of *Music Now*!? It's an Australian magazine.'

Marianne laughed. 'Well, I'll have to leave that to you, sis. You're the one in the music business! Listen, I've got to go – Frances is crying and I need to pick up Joel from playgroup. Let me know how it goes, but – Frankie, please don't get your hopes up too much. I know it's a coincidence, but ... well, coincidences do happen. And if it *was* our sister, I don't see why she would have ended up in Australia.'

Frankie didn't comment. She knew only too well that people could, and did, end up in Australia for all sorts of unknown reasons, and if Marianne hadn't had half her mind on her children she probably would have remembered that, too. But it had given Frankie an idea. There was one very obvious way of solving the problem of the Australian magazine's address. She'd had no communication with Jack now since writing to him the previous September and hinting that she and Rob had got together. Although she'd felt bad about it afterwards and intended to write again to reassure him that there wasn't a baby, she'd never actually got around to it and of course, soon after that she really had got together with Rob. She'd been relieved that the whole thing was over, and anyway now she'd moved, he wouldn't have been able to get in touch with her even if he'd wanted to. But maybe now, he could help her. He owed her that, at least, didn't he? She still had his mailbox address somewhere – she'd nearly thrown it away so many times, but now she was glad she hadn't.

She wrote the letter on the Fan Club headed notepaper, and kept it brief – explaining the favour she needed, without going into too much detail. But she did just add a PS, as an afterthought: *By the way, I ought to let you know – Rob and I are married now and we live in Shenfield. And I'm sorry if I misled you somehow. But there never was any baby.*

She waited for a response. And when it never came, she wondered whether the PS had been the problem.

Chapter 30

July 1970 : Geraldton, Western Australia

In the office of a girls' home about six hours north of Perth, Sister Bernadette sighed as she regarded the young man glaring at her across her desk.

'I'm sorry, but as I keep telling you, every time you come back here asking me the same questions ...'

'I only *keep* coming because you won't give me any bloody answers!'

'As I've told you before,' she continued, keeping her voice level, 'it's impossible for me to give you any information about children who may, or may not, have been in our care in the past. I'm sorry.'

'Can't you at least look in your records?' he insisted, breathing heavily with suppressed annoyance. 'All I want to know is whether you had a girl called Susie here – from about 1954. She'd probably have been about nine when she arrived.'

'I'm afraid we don't keep records about children who have left our care. And even if we did, I wouldn't be at liberty to divulge ...'

'That's bloody ridiculous! How am I supposed to go about finding her, if there aren't any records?'

'Well, for a start do you have a surname?' Sister looked at him calmly. 'You can't expect anyone to be able to help you trace a person with just a Christian name. *Susie*. Would that properly be a *Susan*, or ...'

'I don't bloody know, do I?' he exploded, his frustration obviously getting the better of him. 'Why do you think I'm trying to get some help here?'

'Calm down,' she warned him quietly, as she was joined by Sister Marie-Theresa, who was looking at him as if she was prepared to throw them out.

He shrugged a grudging gesture of apology.

'I'm sorry, but can't you understand why I'm upset?'

Actually, Sister Bernadette *could* understand – which was the only reason she was even entertaining the presence of this very angry person in her office at all, never mind for the third or fourth time in as many months. She felt sorry for him. He'd explained, the first time he turned up out of the blue, that he'd been brought up in an orphanage himself, and shipped out from England as a boy. Apparently this Susie was the only friend he'd had with him at the time. He'd told her he'd become tormented recently by a need to find out what had happened to her.

'She was just a little kid – scared as shit, she was, on the boat with all these other kids,' he'd told her on that first visit, adding in not much more than a whisper, almost to himself: 'I ... promised to look after her. But in the end, I didn't – I couldn't.'

'And it seems you were only a child yourself,' she'd responded. That first time, he'd been more polite, more hopeful of help, probably, and she'd been struck by his sincerity – the depth of his anguish about having lost touch with his friend. 'Come now, you weren't responsible ...'

'They took her away,' he'd said. She was surprised by how keen he seemed to be to confide in her – a complete stranger. It could only have been because he was so desperate for her to help him with his search. 'When we docked at Freo, they herded us, like bloody cattle ... separated the girls from the boys. She – Susie – she went hysterical; she was scared, right? I was as mad as a cut snake – fought with the bloke in charge, trying to get him to let us stay together, but he just slung me across the dock, into the boys' line ...'

'*Slung* you?' At this point she'd begun to think he was exaggerating.

'Yeah. And when I argued, I got hit.' He gave a short laugh. 'That was my introduction to Australia.'

She hadn't quite known what to say to this, but exaggeration or not, it had still evoked her sympathy.

'You know what?' he'd gone on. 'I cried for her for months.' His voice had dropped, almost to a whisper. 'Not for myself, you know? Not cos I needed her or wanted her with me – she was only a little girl, just a baby. I cried cos I'd broken my promise. I couldn't forget seeing them take her away. She was screaming for me. It was ... it was fucking awful.'

She'd reprimanded him gently for his language and expressed regret at not being able to assist him – but he'd come back a few weeks later, asking if she'd found anything out. She wished she could help him, but it was becoming tiresome having to keep repeating that she couldn't.

'I take it you've tried other orphanages, like I suggested last time?' she said now.

'Yeah, yeah, I went to the other place out in the bush near Bridgetown. They gave me the same bloody run-around as you lot.'

'Well, maybe you need to understand ...' began Marie-Theresa. Bernadette held up her hand, warning her to be a little less unsympathetic, but it was too late.

'No, *you* need to understand!' he retorted. 'I just need to know if she was here, for God's sake! I suppose you do take kids from England, do you? Kids who get sent out here from orphanages in England?'

'We have had them here, right enough – although not in the last couple of years,' Bernadette replied, trying to keep her tone light. 'Seems like they've stopped sending them. Maybe they've cleared the streets now.'

'Cleared the streets?' He stared at her. 'What's that supposed to mean?'

'Well, you do know that was why you were all sent over? Too many poor kids in England, apparently, living rough on the streets, no hope of a decent life over there, so ...'

'Tell me you're joking? Kids living rough on the streets? Are you out of your mind?'

Bernadette was a little more concerned now. This bloke looked like he had steam coming out of his ears. Marie-Theresa had taken a step forward as if to be ready to evict him. 'Take it easy, now,' she warned him. 'I'm sorry, but that was what we were told.'

'Well, let *me* tell you, I have *no idea* why I got sent out here from England, or why Susie any of the other kids were sent here. But it sure as hell wasn't because we were living on the streets. We *had* a decent life there! We might have been orphans, but we were looked after properly, housed and fed and schooled and we *weren't* beaten or abused like ...' To Bernadette's horror, at this point the young man choked over his words and nearly broke down.

'Well, I'm sorry,' Marie-Theresa repeated firmly, 'but Sister Bernadette has already explained that we can't help you. She folded her arms across her chest. 'Good afternoon. I hope you find your friend.'

'So do I, you useless bloody *penguins*, you!' he spat at them as he turned to leave. 'And when I find her, if it turns out she was badly treated here, I'll be back!'

At which point Marie-Theresa threatened to call the police, and the young man retaliated by threatening to report *them* to the police for '*stealing children and beating them*'.

'What an unpleasant individual,' Marie-Theresa commented as the door slammed behind him. 'I really think we should let the police know he's been bothering you, Sister Bernadette. I should imagine he could quite easily become dangerous.'

'Oh, leave the poor soul alone, Sister,' replied Bernadette wearily. 'Can you not see how tormented he is, God love him?'

In truth, she was terribly disturbed herself by some of the things he'd told her. They'd certainly cared for a great many girls from England over the years – poor homeless orphan girls, they'd been told, who'd been lucky to be given the opportunity of a new life in Australia. It had always seemed a little inhumane to her, the way they'd been brought all this way up country, fresh from the long voyage from England, crammed into buses or even trucks, but God knew she'd done her best for them all, treating them decently and sending them all off eventually into some kind of employment. She couldn't have done a lot more, could she?

'It troubles me, Sister, to be honest,' she said thoughtfully to Marie-Theresa, 'to hear that young man talk of beatings and abuse. And he claims he never was on the streets back in England. Do you think there's any truth in that, at all?'

'I think he's a liar and a troublemaker, Sister Bernadette, and you should take no notice of a word he says. Why in God's name would children be sent out from England if it wasn't that they were living in dire poverty and needed the good care we could give them?'

'I can't imagine,' Bernadette responded quietly. 'Unless it was for some underhand purposes of our two countries' governments. The British population needing trimming of burdensome responsibilities, perhaps, and the Australian one needing boosting with young blood.'

Marie-Theresa laughed and shook her head.

'Fantasies, Sister Bernadette! But it would make a very good movie, right enough!'

They never saw the angry young man again. But Sister Bernadette often wondered about him over the years. And wondered whether her uncomfortable feeling about the children from England had any basis in the truth.

Chapter 31

August 1970 : Perth

One Saturday afternoon in the middle of August, Jack had been minding the baby while Shona went shopping in town. He was feeling pretty proud of himself for keeping Steven happy all afternoon, thinking that his son was finally getting used to him, when Shona burst in through the front door, throwing down bags of shopping and slamming the door shut again in an almost theatrical display of temper. It was so unlike her, he watched transfixed from the kitchen doorway for a few minutes, before asking somewhat nervously what was wrong.

'Wrong?' she repeated shrilly, turning a furious face to him. 'You want to know what's *wrong*?'

'Well, it would help!' he retorted, feeling aggrieved. What the hell was she mad at *him* for? 'I can't exactly do anything if you don't tell me, can I?'

'OK,' she said, shoving past him and slamming a shopping bag full of cans down on the worktop. The noise startled Steven, who was sitting in his highchair banging a spoon on the tray, and he began to scream. She completely ignored him. 'I had an accident in the car today.'

'Oh, God – are you all right?' he asked in alarm.

'Yes, of course I'm all right – don't I look it?' she snapped.

'Well, don't get upset. It's only a bloody car – we can get it fixed.'

'Stuff the car! It's only the rear bumper. The other bloke drove into the back of me in the car park.' She turned to look at the baby, irritation all over her face. 'Can't you keep him quiet? Are you completely bloody useless as well as being a total bloody *bastard*?'

Stunned into silence now, Jack shushed Steven quietly and gave him his soother, stroking his soft little head to comfort him as he waited for Shona to explain herself. He had no idea what had happened. The car accident didn't sound serious, but had it upset Shona beyond all reason? Or was she actually having some kind of breakdown? He'd never seen her like this before and didn't know how the hell to handle it.

'I don't know what I'm supposed to have done,' he said eventually, trying to speak calmly. 'Steven's been absolutely fine all afternoon – he's only upset because you're frightening him.'

'Oh, right, so it's all *my* fault now, is it?' she raged.

'Shona, calm down, for God's sake! What's got into you? Was it the accident? Has it shaken you up?'

She shook her head at him, sighing as if he were unbelievably stupid.

'I don't care about the frigging accident, Jack. You really don't know, do you? It's what I found when I got the bloody *insurance papers* out of the glove-box. Yes, that's right!' She picked up a handful of papers and envelopes from under one of the bags she'd slung on the worktop. 'Recognise these? Of course you do! Were you ever going to tell me about this, Jack, or were you just going to walk out on me one day and go back to her?'

At the sight of the letters, Jack had gone cold from head to toe. He closed his eyes, all the breath leaving him for a minute. Why the hell had he left them in the glove-box? It was a wonder Shona had never found them before. There was nothing incriminating about them, though, was there? He tried quickly to remember, while Shona was angrily smoothing out the sheets of letter paper on the worktop and jabbing furiously at them with her finger – but all he could think was that this was all so very open to misinterpretation.

'Look,' he said, running his hand through his hair. 'There's nothing untoward about this, OK? This was a girl I went out with for a while, back in England, long before I met you, and I've never seen her since.'

'You've been writing to her, though – haven't you! Don't deny it – I've read these letters. You've been ... for Pete's sake, Jack, you've been *pestering* this girl – her sister even had to tell you to stop! And sending her *money*! I can't believe you've actually been sending her money out of our bloody account. Don't look at me like that – it's there, look, on the bloody table in front of you – a money order for a hundred and fifty bucks! At least she sent it back – bloody hell, *we* need that money, Jack! We need it for food, and baby clothes – we haven't got money coming out of our ears to splash around on your *bloody* ex-girlfriends, in case you haven't noticed!'

'I know ... I'm sorry ... it was a mistake ... I thought ...' Jack was floundering. But Shona wasn't going to let up.

'And *why* were you sending her money, as if it wasn't flaming bloody obvious? You got her pregnant, didn't you. I couldn't believe what I was reading in this letter!' She waved Marianne's note in front of Jack's face, her eyes filling with angry tears. 'You got that poor girl pregnant and *ran out on her*. Not good enough to leave town, oh no, you had to leave the bloody *country*! No wonder her sister was flaming mad – and what's all this about being in trouble with the police?' She screeched to a halt, sat down in a chair and shook her head again. 'I don't know you any more, Jack Hunter. I don't know who the hell you *are*!'

Jack had been trying without success to protest his innocence all through this diatribe, but now she'd run out of steam he pulled up another chair and sat down in front of her.

'I know how it looks,' he began – and waited while she snorted with derision. 'But I'm *not* in trouble with the police, and I *didn't* run out on Frankie. I didn't know she was pregnant until I got this letter.'

'Jack, you can make all the excuses under the sun, but if there was nothing to hide, why didn't you tell me about any of this? Why did you keep these letters hidden in the car?'

'I don't know! I just thought ... well, I didn't want to upset you ...'

'You didn't think it'd upset me when I finally found out that you're still *writing* to this girl! Even now – don't deny it! You're sending her letters even though they're getting returned to you!' She picked up the envelope marked 'Gone Away' and waved this in his face now. 'She's gone away, Jack – get it? Probably sick of you harassing her! What is it – are you obsessed with her, or something? Sorry you walked out on her? Why didn't you go back to bloody England and marry *her* – she's already had your baby!'

Shona started to cry – noisy, furious sobs and gulps that sounded like they were going to tear her apart. Steven spat out his soother and let out a wail of distress, and Jack jumped up to lift him out of the highchair.

'Please don't cry!' he begged her. 'Look – you're upsetting Steven.'

'*I'm* not upsetting him! *I'm* not the one carrying on a secret affair!'

'Shona, there *is* no affair! Look, I'm being honest with you now – yes, I wrote to her, as soon as I arrived in Australia, before I even met you; I didn't know she was pregnant! And yes, when I found out, I felt terrible, I wanted to help, so I sent some money ...'

'So why didn't you *tell* me? That was *our* money, Jack – you had no right! No right to send it to your *ex-girlfriend* without talking to me about it! What ... were you going to keep on sending it? Every month, were you? Even though we're struggling to make ends meet ourselves now I'm not at work?'

He hung his head. 'I don't know. I hadn't thought it through. I guess I'd have told you ...'

'Don't lie to me!' she snapped, wiping her eyes crossly. 'If she hadn't sent that money back, you'd have kept on – keeping it a secret, sending her money for her *kid* – and anyway!' she added suddenly, picking up Frankie's letter and looking at it again. 'What's all this about the Crazy Snakes? They're that group everyone's talking about, aren't they – they keep making hit records! Why did you think she needed *our* money, if she's involved with *them*? She must be loaded!'

'I didn't know she was *involved* with one of them,' he said wearily. 'And I didn't know, till I got this letter, that they were doing so well.' He paused, shrugged. There wasn't any point keeping anything from her any more. 'They were my band. I was their lead singer and guitarist, all right?'

'Oh, sure!' She snorted again. 'Jack, I seriously believe you've lost touch with reality. Writing to pester someone who doesn't want you, sending her money she doesn't need, claiming to be a bloody pop star ...'

'I'm not claiming to be ... they weren't famous when I left them! Oh, look, it doesn't matter. I'm just trying to explain, all right?'

'Well, you're not making a very good job of it! And I'm not listening to any more of your stupid lies.' She picked up the 'return to sender' envelope again and threw it down in front of him. 'Whatever you say, you've still been writing to her. I suppose you're going to say that isn't your writing on the envelope?'

'Of course it is. But this wasn't anything personal!' He opened the envelope and pulled out the sheet of paper inside. 'Read it! Go on, read it if you don't believe me! I didn't *want* to write to her again ...'

'Oh, no, of course you didn't!'

'I was trying to help Ken, for crying out loud! That's all! He wanted to find out why the kids from England were all sent out here, and she – Frankie – is the only person I'm still in touch with back home, so I thought she might be able to ask someone some questions ...' He sighed at Shona's sceptical expression. '*Read* it!'

He pushed the letter towards her but instead of looking at it, she screwed it up fiercely and threw it across the room.

'I don't *care* what you're writing to her about – it's obvious you're still trying to stay in touch with her, Jack, and if it was so bloody innocent, you wouldn't have kept it secret. You know what? I'm sick of you – I wish I'd never met you!'

'You don't mean that, Shona. You're just upset. The accident ...'

'Will you shut up about the flipping accident? I'm *glad* I had the accident! If I hadn't had it, I'd never have found out about all this, would I? What a fool you must have taken me for! I felt sorry for you, didn't I, when we first met! Thought you'd had an unhappy break-up with someone, thought I could make you feel better! What an idiot! All this time, you've still been in love with her!'

'No!'

'*Yes*, Jack! I should have realised, shouldn't I. You were never too enthusiastic about getting married, were you? You weren't even excited about our own child – you don't even care about him now! You'd rather be out with your mates, playing with your *band*.'

'That's not true!' he said, clutching Steven to his chest. 'I love him! I've *tried* to be a good father, but you wouldn't let me do anything for him!'

'Oh, shut up, Jack,' she said, suddenly looking tired. She got to her feet, lifted the child out of his arms and began to carry him upstairs. 'I'll go and stay with Karen until we sort this out.'

'I'd rather sort it out now!' he protested, following her. 'Look, I'm sorry – I'm really sorry for not telling you about Frankie. But honestly ...'

'*Honestly?*' she retorted, stopping at the top of the stairs and looking back down at him. 'Don't make me laugh. Your whole life here has been a sham, hasn't it. Even your *ex-girlfriend* didn't seem to know why you came out here. Well, why don't you sling your hook back to bloody England – she's welcome to you, not that she seems to want you anyway, even if she has had your baby. And I don't blame her. *I* don't want you either.'

With which she took Steven into the bedroom and slammed the door behind her.

Jack stood at the bottom of the stairs, breathless from the shock of the confrontation. He thought about following Shona upstairs, but he guessed it wasn't going to help – it would only prolong the row. If he left her to calm down on her own for a while, perhaps she'd be ready to make up later. Or would she just be even angrier? Jack had absolutely no idea. He'd never had a row with Shona before, in fact he didn't think he'd ever had a row with any woman before, full stop. Most of his previous relationships, before he met Frankie, had just fizzled out – there had never been fireworks or blame on either side. He was pretty sure, once she cooled off, she'd see that she was overreacting. OK, he knew it had been a mistake not to tell her about Frankie, and ... well, OK, he guessed it was true that he'd still felt ... *something* for Frankie – but he was telling the truth now, that it was all over, that his latest letter had been completely innocent! She'd see that, wouldn't she, when she calmed down. Perhaps the best thing he could do would be to get out of her way for a couple of hours. He suddenly needed, desperately, to go and talk to Ken about it. Ken would tell him what to do. He was his best mate – and he still cared about Shona, too. He'd help him sort it out. He might even agree to come round and talk to Shona for him.

He went upstairs, tapped gently on the bedroom door.

'I'll give you some space,' he called gently. 'OK? We'll talk about it again later.'

There was no response. She was probably sulking now – but that was better than the shouting and the crying. She'd come round, he was sure of it.

He let himself out of the house and, feeling absolutely shattered, drove slowly to Ken's place. By the time he came back a couple of hours later, Shona and Steven had gone.

Chapter 32

September 1970 : Perth

Ken was finding it difficult to face Jack. Apart from at the band sessions and bookings, he was trying to avoid him. At first Jack was phoning him all the time, turning up at Ken's place looking drawn and tired and wanting to talk – going over it all again and again, until Ken felt like shaking him. Couldn't he see it was all his own bloody fault? He'd mooned over this girl back in England, kept her bloody *letters* for Christ's sake – what the hell had possessed him? – and hadn't spent enough time with Shona or the baby. What did he expect? At first he'd offered him sympathy and even hope, telling him she just needed to cool off, and she'd get over it. But now, he couldn't do that anymore. He didn't want to see him.

Well, OK, it was Jack's fault, but Ken knew he was behaving badly himself, too. He was taking advantage of the situation. It wasn't what you were supposed to do when a mate was in trouble. But holy Dooley, who could blame him? He'd messed things up with Shona back when they were together, and regretted it ever since. If Jack couldn't learn from that, but had to make his own stupid mistakes and mess up too, well he had to accept that things were going to move on, that life wasn't going to stand still and wait for him to catch on.

He had to admit, he was shocked when Jack had turned up at his door that Saturday arvo. He looked half demented and could hardly get his words out.

'She found some letters,' he spluttered after Ken had sat him down and turned off the TV. 'And she's just jumped to completely the wrong conclusion.'

Oh, really? Ken had thought, but he kept his mouth shut.

'I told you I wrote to her, to Frankie, to try and help you, didn't I?' Jack went on, looking at Ken almost beseechingly.

'That's all it was! I'd got over ... all the other stuff. There was nothing personal in the letter, I was just asking her if she knew how to find out about it for you – why you were all sent over from the children's homes.'

'And you didn't get an answer.'

'No – it came back, unopened, return to sender.'

'So why did you keep it?'

Jack shrugged miserably. 'I don't know. No reason! I just shoved it in the glove-box, I wasn't hiding it.'

'Have you shown it to Shona – shown her what it was about?'

'She wouldn't read it! Threw it across the room!'

'Why?'

He looked away. 'Because she was already mad about the other letters.'

'Ah, right. You kept some other letters.'

'Yeah – only one from her, for God's sake, and one from her sister! And only because I forgot they were there!'

'Right. And what was in them, that made her mad?'

'Something about the money I sent her. For the baby.'

Ken sighed and shook his head. 'Well, sorry, mate, but I can understand why she spat the dummy about that!'

'I know, I know. I should have told her, it was stupid of me ... but it's not like Frankie even accepted the money – she sent it back, told me not to send any more.'

'Mate, can you hear yourself? So she didn't accept it – and you want Shona to feel happy about that?'

'OK, I was an idiot. I know that. So what am I supposed to do now? To make it up to her?'

'You're asking *me*?' Ken had felt a bitter taste in his mouth. 'I'm the one who messed her life up before, remember? I was kind of hoping you wouldn't do it too.'

'I haven't messed up her life. She's just angry at me. Really angry. I've never seen her like it! I said I'd give her some space while she calms down.'

'What – you want to kip here? You can have the sofa, mate, feel free.'

'No! No, I meant just a couple of hours. I'm hoping she'll have come round by then.'

For a couple of hours, they'd drunk coffee and smoked cigarettes while Ken did his best to sympathise with Jack and not lose his patience. The truth was, much as he liked the bloke, he was acting like a big baby. Instead of running away he should have fronted up and accepted Shona's anger – he sure as hell deserved it!

And then, ten minutes after he'd eventually gone home, he was on the phone almost in tears.

'She's gone! Taken the baby, and the suitcases, and all her clothes!'

'Did she leave a note?'

'No. But she'll be with Karen – Karen must have picked her up, or else she called a cab.'

'Have you called her? Karen?'

'Tried. She won't pick up. Bloody hell – I never thought she'd actually walk out! Over *nothing*!'

'It's obviously *not* nothing to her, though, is it. Look, mate, if she wanted to talk to you she'd pick up the phone, or her friend would.'

'So you don't think I should go round there?'

What was he – a bloody marriage guidance counsellor now? Ken sighed. He was getting irritated. 'Give it a while,' he said. 'By the sound of things, she'll probably slam the door in your face right now.'

And so it had gone on. From what Ken could see, Jack didn't seem to be able to think for himself anymore. Almost every day he was calling on Ken, or phoning him, asking what he should do. And the more he asked, the less patient Ken became with him, and the more sorry he felt for Shona. She deserved better than this bumbling bloody idiot. Jack hadn't appreciated his luck right from the start and now he had no idea what to do. He seemed more concerned about his own feelings than hers! And eventually there came the day when, in the middle of a long diatribe from Jack about how he missed her, and wanted her back, and had never meant it to come to this, Ken suddenly snapped.

'For Christ's sake. Do you want me to go and talk to her? Is that what you want?'

There was silence for a moment. Then: 'Do you really think she'd listen to you?'

Ken had to swallow hard. He knew what the implication was. He wasn't stupid. He was pretty sure Shona hadn't wanted him to be best man at their wedding, and that she'd told Jack she hadn't wanted to see him again, ever. But Ken knew he'd been her first love. She'd changed her whole life for him – given up everything. He had a feeling that the reason she didn't want to see him wasn't so much because she hated him. However entitled she was to hate him, he suspected there might still be a part of her that could be tempted to take him back. Especially now.

'I think I might be able to get her to listen,' he said. 'If I could just get her to agree to see me.'

'Would you give it a try, mate – please?'

Ken shook his head. What was wrong with the bloke? He must be mad to send her ex-boyfriend round there – her ex-boyfriend who'd always made it clear he regretted finishing with her!

'You sure that's what you want?' he said, giving Jack one last chance to change his mind.

'I'm desperate, Ken. I gave her space, gave her time, but she's refusing to see me or even speak to me. You're my last hope.'

Well, that made him feel a whole lot nicer about it.

So Jack only had himself to blame, really, didn't he?

He guessed he had the surprise factor on his side. He'd be the last person she was expecting to see. As luck would have it,

Karen was out when he called round there, and when Shona looked through the window to see who'd rung the bell, he could almost see her eyebrows go up.

'What do *you* want?' she demanded when she opened the door. 'I suppose Jack sent you round to do his dirty work for him – well, you can tell him it's too late.'

Ken didn't even hesitate. His mate had no chance anyway.

'Jack didn't ask me to come,' he lied. He looked her straight in the eyes. 'This is nothing to do with him.'

'Oh?'

He wasn't imagining it. There was a definite spark of interest behind the surprise.

'I just thought you might need cheering up,' he ploughed on. Paused, held her gaze. 'Can I come in?'

He told Jack later that she'd refused to see him. It only served to postpone the inevitable punch-up for a little while, of course. *Once a bastard*, he thought without much regret – *always a bastard*. At least he knew that much about himself – even if not much else.

Chapter 33

Shenfield : September – October 1970

With no response from Jack to her letter about the music magazine, Frankie broached the subject with Rob when the band returned from a short tour of Europe.

'You really think this could be your sister?' he asked when she showed him Susannah Kennedy's letter.

'Marianne keeps telling me not to get carried away. But it's the same name, and even the same middle initial.'

'But *your* Susannah might not even be a Kennedy now, any more than you or Marianne are: she might be married too.'

'I know. *And* she's living in Australia. But look, she says she originally came from Essex. And ...' She smiled at him. 'She obviously has the same taste in music as me!'

'That's no guarantee she's your sibling!' he said, laughing and kissing her. 'My brother's got terrible taste in music!'

'OK. I know it's a long shot, Rob, but I just wish there was some way I could check it out.' She turned away, hating herself for still keeping something from him – especially now they were married – but she was convinced it would do more harm than good now for him to find out that she knew where Jack was. What would be the point in mentioning that she'd tried to contact him – especially since he hadn't even replied? 'Do you think there's any way we can get an address for this magazine she mentions – the Australian *Music Now!*'

'Of course – I'm sure we can. But how's that going to help?'

'Marianne suggested we could have an advert put in it. As it's where she read the article about the Snakes, maybe she reads it regularly.'

'Fine.' He frowned, and then added gently, 'As long as you're not going to be upset if this all comes to nothing. She might *not* read the magazine regularly, and even if she does, she might not notice the advert. And ...'

'And she might not be the right Susannah anyway. I know. I just feel like we have to try.'

'OK. I'll get Dave to talk to the press office. They'll know about the article anyway.'

'I reckon it could have been quite a big feature. That'd explain why there have been a lot of applications for membership from Australia recently.'

'All good news then! Especially as it looks like the Aussie tour has been confirmed for next year.'

'Ooh! That's good.' Then her face fell. 'But you'll be away for ages.'

'You could always come too.'

'I could,' she agreed, 'As long as I'm not pregnant by then.'

He nodded, giving her a hug, and Frankie responded with a little smile to show she wasn't worried. They had hoped it was going to happen straight away; but ... well, they'd only been married for six months – it was too soon to be concerned about it.

A few days later, Dave came back with the news that the feature about the Snakes had been in an issue of *Music Now!* from two months back. It was a weekly magazine, so Susannah, whoever she was, must have picked up an old copy from somewhere.

'So she probably *isn't* a regular reader,' Frankie said.

'No. But it doesn't make a lot of difference anyway. You can't advertise in that magazine. It folded after the last issue of August. Too much competition apparently; their sales had fallen off.'

'Never mind,' Marianne said when Frankie told her. 'You know, even if you *had* been able to do the advert ...'

'She might not have seen it, and she might not be the right Susannah Kennedy anyway. I know! Rob must have told me that fifty times.'

'Sorry.'

'No – Mari, *I'm* sorry. I didn't mean to bite your head off. I'm just disappointed. I had such a strong feeling about this girl – and even if I'm wrong, I just wish we could have checked her out. Now, I feel like I'm always going to wonder.'

Marianne was quiet for a few minutes.

'I know she didn't put an address on her letter,' she said. 'But where was it postmarked?'

'Australia – that's the whole point!'

'I know. But *where* in Australia?'

'Oh. Melbourne, I think. Hang on.' Frankie found the letter, safely stowed back in its envelope in her desk drawer. 'Yes. Melbourne. Why?'

'I just wondered if it was worth contacting one of the newspapers out there. Australia's such a huge country, there's no point putting it in a national paper, if they have such a thing. But if they have Melbourne papers – maybe you could get something put in one of them? Or all of them?' she added.

'Yes! Mari, that's brilliant – why didn't I think of it?' They both laughed, and then Frankie added cautiously: 'But do you think we ought to be going through our solicitor with all this?'

'No. Come on, Frankie – it'll take ages – even if they agree to do it. They might just say we're wasting our time. If we get anywhere – *if* she responds, and *if* it's the right person ... that's the time to tell them.'

'Yes, you're right. OK, I'll ask Dave to talk to the PR people again – they seem to have ways and means of finding out these things. Hopefully within a week or two we can have every Melbourne paper carrying a big bold message asking Susannah Kennedy to get in touch with us.'

'I imagine Melbourne's probably quite a big city,' Marianne warned her. 'With a big population, and maybe suburbs of its own.'

'Yes, but even if she doesn't read it herself, surely someone who knows her will read it.'

'Let's hope so. At least we will have tried.'

In fact it took a little longer than they expected for the PR people to come up with the names and addresses of the Melbourne papers – all two of them – and to contact them regarding advertising rates and conditions, while Frankie virtually fidgeted with impatience every day as she worked on the latest fan club newsletter. It was well into October by the time they were finally told the adverts were going in.

'Now keep your fingers crossed,' Rob told her. 'But don't hold your breath. I'd hate for you to be disappointed.'

But Frankie couldn't help it. She *was* virtually holding her breath – every day when she opened the mail. As the weeks passed, she stopped crossing her fingers for luck and started to shrug off the disappointment, but didn't give up hope altogether. They'd asked for the advert to go in the papers every week for a month – so there was still a chance.

Australia was on everyone's minds anyway, with the Crazy Snakes' tour there now only months away. One day Rob brought home some copies of Australian music magazines to read.

'Dave's been getting them sent over. He wants the PR boys to keep abreast of the sort of stories they all run, so we can start feeding them promotion in advance of the tour.'

Frankie thumbed through them that evening.

'It's ironic, isn't it,' she said, as she flipped the pages. 'The one magazine we can't read now is the one Susannah Kennedy got in touch with us through.' She stopped, looking at Rob thoughtfully. 'Actually, do you think she might be reading one of *these* mags now instead? We could always ...'

'Frankie, love – I think you need to give it up,' he told her gently. 'Don't get obsessed over it. It's probably not even her.'

'No, I suppose you're right.'

'If she's in Melbourne, she'll see the ad in one of the papers for sure. We've done all we can.'

'Yes. I guess so.'

Nodding to herself, she turned another page, scanning the pictures of various Australian groups and singers she'd never heard of – and barely paying any attention to a small paragraph at the bottom of one of the middle pages. It referred to a little-known band from Perth in Western Australia who had split up, apparently very acrimoniously, because of a love triangle situation amongst their members.

They were called KRASH, and the band members' names were Ken Warren, Ruth Cordell, Al Page and Jet Harnuck. And while the last one was certainly an unusual name, it wouldn't have crossed Frankie's mind – or anyone else's, come to that – that it was an anagram.

Chapter 34

October 1970 : Melbourne, Australia

Sue picked up the *Melbourne Gazette* along with her grocery shopping. It was her day off and she fully intended to get started on the serious business of house-hunting today. Maureen had been paying her generously and she'd been banking all her tips and cutting back on the frivolous spending. She was ready to get out of bedsit land and become a fully-fledged adult at last – a house-owner. Everyone said the property pages in the local paper were the best place to start.

She'd only been home for five minutes and was just unpacking her shopping in her tiny kitchen area when her landlady hammered on the door.

'Phone call for you!'

Sue traipsed back downstairs and picked up the phone in the hall.

'G'day, how are you?' It was Maureen. 'Look, I've been wanting to have a word with you, and it'll be quiet here in the shop now till lunchtime – Janet can handle it. Can I call round?'

'Sure, I'll get the kettle on.' Sue ran back upstairs and quickly finished her unpacking while the kettle was boiling. Waiting for her boss to turn up, she picked up the *Gazette* and started looking for the property pages – swiftly flicking past a page of small ads where one particularly large advert in bold type in a display box took up nearly a quarter of the page – but before she could read anything, Maureen was knocking at the door.

'I've got a proposition for you,' she said as soon as they were both sitting down with mugs of tea in front of them. 'And I'll come straight to the point.'

'OK,' Sue said, cautiously.

'It's this. You know I've been pleased with you. You're far and away the best member of staff I've had for as long as I can remember. No – don't go all coy on me, it's true and that's a fact. So I want you to move to Sydney with me.'

Sue nearly dropped her tea. '*What?*'

'You heard. I've kept this to myself, not because I didn't trust *you* but because some of the other girls couldn't keep anything quiet if their lives depended on it. I'm selling up the coffee-shop and buying a restaurant in Sydney.' She smiled, and Sue saw the excitement in her eyes. 'It's bang slap in the city centre, overlooking the harbour. It's the real deal – a successful business, making big money from the tourists. The owner's retiring; they've got a good chef who's staying on, together with some of the staff ...'

'But ... but ...' Sue was squawking, blinking, hardly able to make sense of what Maureen was telling her. 'Why do you want *me* to come to Sydney?'

'To help me run the place, of course! I'll help you find somewhere to live – don't worry, you won't be on the street, you can stay with me to start with.'

'With you? But you live here in Melbourne!'

'I've got a place in Sydney lined up already. My brother lives there – he's been sorting it out for me.' She grinned. 'Like I said, this is a decision I made quite a while back. So: are you coming with me or not?'

Sue hesitated. She'd only lived in Melbourne for a little over a year, and loved the place. She was reluctant to up-sticks and move to another state all over again. But on the other hand, how much of her enjoyment of this area was due to her work – to the coffee-shop, and to Maureen Pringle in particular? Nearly all her friends here, with the exception of a couple of neighbours who'd been quite pleasant, were staff at the coffee-shop. But it was Maureen who'd made her feel the most welcome, who'd been the most sympathetic, the most helpful – who she'd miss the most, if she moved and Sue didn't go with her. She'd been more than a friend to her, in fact. She'd been, in some ways, Sue's idea of a mum. She'd kept an eye on Sue, helped her grow up, the way her mum might have done if she'd had one. Sue didn't want to be without her. And anyway, she wanted to help her make a success of her new venture.

'No rush to decide,' Maureen said, draining her tea. 'Tomorrow will do!' she added, winking.

'It's OK. I've decided.' Susie looked up and smiled. 'I'll do it. I'll come to Sydney. Thank you so much for asking me!'

'I'm glad,' the older woman said. 'And as for asking you – who else would I ask? I know you're going to be an asset to the new business. And I'll make it worth your while.'

After Maureen had gone, Sue looked around her little rented room, noticed the local paper she'd thrown down in such a hurry, and laughed to herself. She wouldn't be needing to look at the property pages after all, then! She felt a sudden frisson of excitement. Perhaps it would be good, after all, for her first real home, the first place she was going to actually buy herself, to be in a different city again. Sydney! She pictured the city centre as she'd seen it in countless photos – the harbour with its magnificent bridge, and the new opera house, controversial because of its ambitious design and architecture, still not completed after more than a decade of financial wrangling. She couldn't wait to see all the sights. And Maureen had hinted that the new restaurant was sited right in the most auspicious tourist area, at Circular Quay.

She picked up the Melbourne Herald and without giving it another glance dropped it in the wastepaper bin. No point buying *that* again! And while she was at it, she'd have a clear-out of some of her other old papers. She turned to the pile of music magazines next to the sofa. Among them was the issue of *Music Now!* Maureen had given her, months ago. She smiled to herself, thinking about the letter she'd rushed off to the fan club of the Crazy Snakes. It had seemed so important at the time – she'd just begun to enjoy living her life here as a normal single girl, buying clothes and make-up and pop records. But now, only six months later, it seemed incredibly immature. She was going to move to Sydney, buy her own home, and work as the assistant manager of a restaurant! She was *really* an adult now!

She picked up the pile of magazines, and before dumping them in the bin, had a quick look at one she'd only recently purchased. It was called *Beat*, and according to its front cover there was a *hot news item* about the Snakes inside. Aw, no point chucking it out without reading it, was there. She sat down and turned to page eleven, where under another picture of the band it was confirmed that they were definitely touring Australia early in the new year. *Sydney: Friday 19th and Saturday 20th March 1971! Tickets available soon!*

Sue chuckled to herself. Well, all right – even if she *was* becoming a fully-fledged member of the adult population, it would be ridiculous to miss the opportunity of seeing her favourite band performing live, wouldn't it! She'd look out for the tickets as soon as she moved to Sydney, and she'd have to book a night off from the restaurant before she'd even started! She knew Maureen would understand.

Happy and excited about all the decisions she'd made, she snapped the magazine shut and added it to the others being consigned to the bin. Too many other things to think about, to waste time reading the rest of it.

Which was ironic really. Because if she'd only turned over a few pages, she might have noticed a quite amusing story about a band from Perth who had barely got themselves started before they'd split up, after a massive row between two of the members. Apparently one had shacked up with another one's wife, even though they'd supposedly been best buddies.

They were called KRASH, and the band members' names were Ken Warren, Ruth Cordell, Al Page and Jet Harnuck. And although none of the names would have meant anything to Sue, she'd have been surprised to know exactly how much she had in common with one of them.

Chapter 35

March 1971 : Sydney

Rob was beginning to understand why so many members of the big rock bands took drugs. Not that he'd been tempted, but he sure as hell would have liked something a bit stronger than Coca-Cola to keep him going on these punishing overseas tours. None of the boys had got much rest on the long flight from Heathrow, and the stinking hot weather in Perth, their first destination, had sapped their energy. They'd made the mistake of trying to cool down with copious amounts of cold beer – and quickly realised this just made matters worse. Before each performance they were wired up – nervous but excited, ready to rock. The screams and wild applause from the audience gave them all the energy they needed, and they'd feel like they could go on forever. The high lasted for the rest of the night, after they came off stage drenched in sweat, hugging each other amid congratulations from everyone backstage. There'd be more drinks back at their hotel and then they'd sleep until midway through the morning. And wake up exhausted, looking and feeling like zombies.

'It's dehydration,' Dave warned them. 'Cut down on the booze or you won't last the tour.'

Adelaide had been almost as hot as Perth; Melbourne fortunately a little cooler. But now, in Sydney, the heat had returned and Rob was sick of it. How did people live in this climate? It was a sticky heat, punctuated by heavy downpours of rain that didn't cool anything off. People walked around in shorts and sandals with umbrellas up. He'd have liked to see the sights – he'd heard a lot about the Harbour Bridge and the new Opera House – but they were all too exhausted to set foot out of their hotel, and knew they'd be mobbed if they attempted it anyway.

'I don't want to do this anymore,' he told Andy.

They were lying on the bed in Rob's room with their eyes closed, the air conditioning on, lazily enjoying a cigarette while discussing the running order for that night's show.

'Give up, then. I'm gonna try, when we get back. They say it causes cancer.'

'Not talking about the fags. I might try, though – you're right. Frankie keeps telling me I should.'

Saying Frankie's name aloud, he wanted to groan with the pain of missing her. Now nearly four months pregnant, she'd been feeling too sick at the time the flights were booked to even contemplate the idea of travelling to Australia, and anyway he wouldn't have wanted to put her through all this travelling, the heat, the late hours. The pregnancy, their unborn baby, was too precious to them both to take any chances. And Andy was in the same position – Georgia's baby was due a few weeks before Frankie's, so he and Rob had both travelled alone while the other boys had brought their girlfriends with them. Hence they were spending a lot of their time together. At least they knew the two girls had each other for company at home: they were so excited to be pregnant at the same time.

'So what, then?' Andy persisted. 'What don't you want to do anymore?'

'This. The touring. Being away for so long. Especially after the baby's born.'

'I know, mate. It sucks. But it's part of the life, isn't it. The fans expect it. Look, maybe we can have a break for a while after this, but ...'

'But Dave's talking about us going back to the States later this year.' They'd done a couple of shows in New York just before Christmas, and had gone down a storm. Now there were calls for them to do a tour. 'It's gonna be a killer. We'll be away for a month, at least.'

'Maybe by then the girls could come with us. Bring the kids!'

Rob shook his head. 'Maybe by then I'll have had enough.'

'What else are you gonna do, man?' Andy said softly. 'Music's in your blood, same as me. This is what we worked for, prayed for, all those years – sitting at home making our fingers bleed learning our guitar chords when we were kids ...'

'I know.'

'We've *made* it now. This is it – we've arrived. It can't get any better than this.'

'So maybe it's best to quit while we're on top.'

'You don't mean that!' Andy sat up, looking shocked.

'Well, where do you go from the top, if not down? What happens, when bands carry on once they've made it? They either start bickering and split up, like the Beatles, or they get into drugs and go weird.'

'You're just depressed, man, because you're missing Frankie. You'll feel different when we get home. You'll feel different tonight when we're on stage!'

'I know. You're right, I'm just on a downer. Ignore me.'

But even during that night's performance, despite the roar of the crowd, he couldn't quite shake the feeling. And when he launched into *Francesca* – still the fans' favourite song, the one that always had them going wild – he felt like the words were being wrenched from his very soul. He missed her so much – he wanted to be home with her! Perhaps, even now, he really did want it more than he wanted to be with the band.

And then, when the lights came up, he thought he must be hallucinating. She was there – in the second row from the front! Half hidden from his view by a taller girl in front, she'd jumped to her feet and was waving her arms and clapping, calling out for more, along with everyone else. He felt himself rooted to the spot with shock. What was she doing here? It was a good few minutes before he realised it wasn't Frankie after all. This girl's hair was longer, and she had it in a different style – no fringe. She was small like Frankie, but even slimmer

– actually quite skinny. Definitely no baby bump. But apart from that, she could have almost passed for her double.

'You all right?' Pete mouthed at him, and he realised with a start that he'd missed the opening chord of the encore number.

He nodded and they started again, but throughout the song he couldn't take his eyes off the girl who looked so like Frankie. Was he going mad? This was the second time during this tour that he thought he'd seen someone! During the first show at Perth, he'd caught sight of someone at the end of a row halfway back who he could've sworn was Jack Hunter. This guy hadn't been clapping or waving his arms – he was sitting stock still in his seat, staring intently at the stage. At *him*. Rob had been so unnerved, he'd actually planned to run round to the front of the theatre after the show and look out for him in the crowd as they left – but the Jack lookalike had got up and walked out before the end of the show.

'Are you mad? You'd have been mobbed!' Pete had said when he admitted, afterwards, what he'd intended to do.

'I know. It was a dumb idea. And anyway, I'd never have found him in the crowd. But you didn't see this bloke – honestly, Pete, he was the spitting image of Jack. If it wasn't him, he must have an identical twin living in Australia.'

'Or a doppelganger. A double. They say everyone has one, somewhere in the world.' Pete laughed. 'Calm down, mate. It might've looked like him, but honestly, what are the chances?'

'I guess you're right.'

'In that light, with so many people, you couldn't possibly have seen the bloke that clearly. There was obviously just something about him that reminded you of Jack.'

'Yeah. Sorry – it just freaked me a bit.'

Pete had slapped him on the back and told him to have a drink and forget it. But the weird feeling had stayed with Rob all through the next couple of shows. He'd found himself scanning the audiences, whenever the lights allowed, half expecting his mind to trick him into thinking he'd seen the bloke again. And now he was imagining his own wife in the audience! It was no good – he was definitely losing the plot. Perhaps it was one of the symptoms of exhaustion. Or dehydration. Or the heat was getting to him. Or he was just missing Frankie too much. One thing was for sure – this time he wasn't going to tell any of the others about it. They'd think he'd finally succumbed to the LSD!

The normal bunch of determined fans and autograph hunters were thronged outside the stage door. Rob could hear them shouting, screaming, singing lines from their songs and banging on the door as the boys made their way back to their dressing room.

'First half dozen only,' he heard their road manager saying firmly to the security guards. 'Two at a time. Give the lads ten minutes, OK? Try and get rid of the rest of them.'

The first few girls were very young, very shrill and excited, with very little conversation apart from repetitions of 'Oh my God I can't believe I'm actually talking to you!' and 'Oh my God I can't wait to tell the girls at school!' The boys went through the usual motions, autographing books, record covers, programmes and posing for photographs. Making the day, or possibly the lifetime, of the lucky few. And then the door was opened to the last pair. A young lad learning the guitar, who wanted to quiz the band on how they got started. And ... it was her. The short, skinny blonde girl, who at close sight looked even more like Frankie. Too much like her to be ignored. All the boys actually did a double-take as she went in, and looked at each other in astonishment.

'She's the image of Frankie!' Andy exclaimed.

'Sorry for staring at you,' Rob said. 'But you look just like my wife.'

'*Just* like her!' Pete agreed, sounding stunned.

'She could be her bloody twin sister,' said Bernie.

The girl blinked in surprise, looking taken aback and a little uncomfortable.

'Sorry,' Rob said again, still staring at her. 'Obviously just a coincidence, but ...'

'I only came round to try and get your autographs,' she said, looking from one of them to the other doubtfully. 'I didn't expect to get picked. I'm not even in the fan club, although I did write to them once. I thought I was a bit too old for that kind of thing ...'

She tailed off, shrugged, looked at the other fan, a wannabe rock guitarist who'd been stopped mid-flow in his list of questions.

'Sorry,' she said. 'If you could just ...' She held out an autograph book. It looked brand new. Obviously not a seasoned hunter! 'It's to show a couple of the girls at work,' she explained, suddenly blushing, and causing Rob to gasp out loud, as this made her resemble Frankie even more. 'A couple of the young waitresses at the restaurant – they're huge fans, but they couldn't afford to come.'

'Sure.' Pete was the first to pull himself together, but even he continued to look at the girl in amazement. Rob took the autograph book from her and, trying to ignore the spooky sensation that he was looking into his wife's eyes, smiled shakily and asked her name for the autograph.

'Oh, just put *To Sue*,' she said shyly. 'Thank you!'

To Sue, Rob wrote on the first page of the book. *Thanks for coming to the show! Rob Marchant (Crazy Snakes) 20 March 1971 x*

He passed the book to the others to sign, still finding it difficult to stop staring at the girl.

'Thanks,' she said again, closing the book and turning to go.

'You're welcome. Hang on, I'll get the door for you.' As he held open the heavy dressing-room door, he took a last, puzzled look at her face. The resemblance wasn't just surprising – it was absolutely uncanny. Bernie had made that comment about her looking like Frankie's twin sister, but this girl was actually more like Frankie than Marianne was! Maybe she actually was a relative! Perhaps Frankie had a branch of the family out here in Australia, that she hadn't even told him about. Genes were funny things ... distant cousins could actually look very similar to each other, couldn't they? And then ... he remembered.

Afterwards, he wondered what the hell had taken him so long. Probably because they were in Sydney, not Melbourne where the letter to the fan club had come from – the one that had convinced Frankie she might have found her other sister. She'd even asked him, before he came away on the tour, if he had time while he was in Melbourne to try again, somehow, to find her – like it was going to be possible, with only two days in the city, both of them taken up with performances! He had to admit, he hadn't even given it a thought. But now ...

'Sue,' he said, still holding onto the door, his voice suddenly coming out croaky. 'Is that ... by any chance ... short for Susannah?'

'Yes,' she said. She gave a bemused half-smile. 'Why?'

'What's your surname, Sue?' he whispered.

There was a complete hush in the dressing-room. The other boys were all staring, mouths open, waiting.

'Kennedy.' She was looking worried now. 'Why?' she said again.

Rob had to sit down. He felt the room spin. This was just too much.

'I have to tell you,' he said, trying to smile at her but feeling tears welling up in his eyes at the thought of how excited Frankie was going to be. 'Sorry to spring this on you. But I think you're probably my sister-in-law.'

There was another moment of stunned silence, with Sue herself now holding onto the door for support, before they all started talking at once. And in the middle of the boys' exclamations, Sue's shocked demands for explanations and Rob's garbled and emotional attempts to provide them, there was a lone voice suddenly interrupting them all:

'Can I carry on with my list of questions now? I want to know whether I need to learn how to read music.'

'Sorry mate,' Bernie told the would-be guitarist quietly. 'Can you come back tomorrow?'

Chapter 36

Perth

Why had he bothered to go? Two weeks after the Crazy Snakes' concert in Perth, Jack was still kicking himself for making everything even worse. If that were possible. He'd never felt so low, so alone, in his life. Even when he was sailing away from his old life in England, heading out into the unknown, completely on his own, at least he'd assumed he had some kind of a future. It had been scary, and lonely, and full of sadness and regret – but he'd known, back then, that it was up to him to build something new for himself. Now, all that was gone, and it was worse than being back where he started because now he'd known what it was like to have a wife and child, to be a member of a new band, and have a friend.

A friend! What a joke. Some friend Ken had turned out to be. Why had he trusted him? He should have known he'd never miss an opportunity to wheedle his way back into Shona's affections. Unbelievable! After dumping her the way he had – so callously – and supposedly breaking her heart! He must have been chuffed to bits to see the cracks appearing in her marriage to Jack. Pretending to be his mate, just biding his time so that he could get in there again.

And as for Shona – so much for her hatred of Ken, her determination never to give him the time of day again! One word from him – when he was *supposed* to be pleading Jack's case but obviously had other ideas – and she was jumping back into his arms. And his bed. Jack still couldn't believe how quickly, how easily, it had happened. And over – what? Nothing! Over a couple of letters he'd stupidly, carelessly, left lying around in the car. Letters that didn't even mean anything! If they *had*, if he'd actually been carrying on some kind of illicit correspondence with Frankie, he'd have destroyed the evidence, wouldn't he!

He wasn't about to admit to himself that, for much of the short time he'd been with Shona, he'd actually been hoping for exactly that kind of scenario. As far as he was concerned, he was the innocent party, the injured party – betrayed by both his wife and his so-called best friend. Not just betrayed, but ostracised too, as if everything was *his* fault. He'd barely seen Shona since the split, apart from the rare occasions when she agreed to let him visit Steven. She and the baby had moved in with Ken, and it wasn't a particularly enjoyable experience for Jack to visit his son. Ken always made sure he was out, but Shona insisted on staying in the room, without speaking a word to Jack, watching him like a hawk as though he couldn't be trusted with the baby. Jack was aware that he hadn't bonded particularly well with Steven anyway, and the visits were so awkward that he was already feeling less inclined to make them.

Since the almighty bust-up that had taken place when Jack found out about the affair, he and Ken had never spoken. Jack had phoned Ruth to tell her he was leaving the band.

'Can't you put personal issues to one side, for the sake of Krash?' she'd asked calmly.

'Personal issues?' he'd retorted. 'Are you joking? This man is sleeping with my fucking wife! He's moved her and my kid into his place like it's all OK and hunky-dory! No, I do *not* think I can put that to one side, Ruth, and quite honestly I don't give a shit what happens to Krash anymore. Sorry. My life's gone down the toilet and I don't exactly feel like singing rock music, especially not with *him*.'

Following which, he'd gone round to Ken's place when Shona was out and given him a black eye. Not that it had made him feel any better, because Ken had immediately retaliated with two swift punches, one to his guts and the other almost breaking his nose. *Once a thug*, he thought as he sat doubled over at home with a cold flannel on his nose, *always a bloody thug*.

And then, just to really twist the knife, fate had presented him with the fact of the Crazy Snakes appearing in Perth. He'd toyed, for weeks, with the idea of going to see them. Would it be risky? Would they be able to see him – recognise him? Surely not, from the stage, with all those lights. He was torn between curiosity – seeing the boys again, hearing them perform with the new lead singer, finding out what had made them so successful since he left – and the bitter realisation that it wasn't going to do anything to cheer him up.

In the end, the curiosity won and he bought a ticket, being careful not to be seated too near the front. As soon as they came on stage, he knew it had been a mistake. He couldn't stop looking at Rob Marchant and imagining him with Frankie – and his baby! What was it about him that his two so-called friends had both ended up taking both his girl and his child? How could history repeat itself so cruelly? It was bad enough having to listen to the band performing all those songs he'd loved to sing when he was with them. Songs from his own life – his other life – the one he'd had to give up and which had never stopped haunting him. It was bad enough hearing them perform the old Beatles' number *Ticket to Ride* – the lyrics about someone going away, leaving the person they loved, were enough to make him cry his heart out. Bad enough watching them perform in front of this wildly enthusiastic audience, being globally successful – without the added insult, the sheer *pain*, of seeing Rob belting out the lyrics of *Francesca*. He'd had to go, halfway through the song. He'd been shaking with rage.

Who was he actually angry with? Rob? Frankie? Shona? Ken, obviously. But perhaps himself, too. He wished he'd never come to Australia. Sometimes he wondered what he was still doing here. Would it be safe to go home? He began to long for a return to England, convinced it was the only thing he had left to look forward to, the only way his life would ever be happy again.

One day at the beginning of April, a card was delivered along with his mail, asking him to call at the post office in town to collect a letter. Intrigued, he presented himself there the same afternoon.

'It was in your old mailbox,' the clerk told him, handing over an airmail envelope. 'Looks like it's been there some time. The bloke who took over the box from you obviously just left it there, but the box has just changed hands again and the new bloke brought your letter in straight away. We don't deliver, in these circumstances – sometimes people move away, you understand? That's why we just sent a card.'

'That's OK,' Jack said. He turned the envelope over in his hands, and his heart skipped a beat. Frankie's writing. 'Thanks.' He signed for the letter and took it straight out to his car to read. The letter was dated 30th June the previous year. It had lain there for over nine months, addressed to him but obviously arriving after he'd given up the mailbox. He cursed the bloke who'd taken over his box. What was the matter with him? Would it have hurt him to take the damned thing into the post office?

And what was it all about anyway? He scanned the page, puzzled and perturbed. It was a sheet of headed notepaper, bearing a logo of a drum set and guitars, and the words *CRAZY SNAKES FAN CLUB*. And the letter, signed by Frankie, was asking him if he could possibly let her know the address of a magazine called *Music Now!*

What the hell? So was she running their bloody fan club now, then? He supposed she might as well, what with going out with the lead singer and having their number one hit written for her. He had no idea why she'd needed an address for some magazine – presumably something to do with organising the band's tour.

And then he read the final paragraph.

By the way, I ought to let you know – Rob and I are married now and we live in Shenfield. And I'm sorry if I misled you somehow. But there never was any baby.

He got drunk that night, and listened to his copy of the *Francesca* record over and over at full volume until he fell asleep with the needle of the record player stuck and jumping in its groove. He couldn't think, in the morning, why he'd wanted to listen to it. *There never was any baby.* So it had all been for nothing – the risk he'd taken, sending her money – Shona finding out, the row, the end of his marriage. She'd *misled* him? How? Why? He couldn't believe she would have done such a thing deliberately.

There was an address for the fan club at the top of the letter. He wrote straight away, venting his frustration with an outburst of anger, his pen going right through the flimsy airmail paper several times, calling her names, calling Rob names, telling them both they'd ruined his life. At the bottom of the page he ran out of steam, threw down his pen and screwed up the letter. Whatever had happened, it was too late, it wasn't their fault, and it wasn't going to make him feel any better.

And then, while he was preparing breakfast, his morning paper was delivered. And letting his toast burn and his coffee go cold, Jack finally read the headline he'd been waiting for. He leant back in his chair and tried not to cry.

He was free to go home. At last, he could leave this life behind and go back to the UK. He'd go to his mum – find her at her cousin's place in Wales and live quietly with her on their own. After everything that had happened out here, the thought of a quiet life in Wales beckoned to him like the glimpse of a promised land.

He handed in his notice at work the same day, put his house on the market and started to sell his furniture. He didn't even tell Shona he was going – but he did set up a bank account for his son. Within a month, he'd bought his ticket to ride. His ticket home.

Chapter 37

October 1971 : Sydney

Even now, nobody seemed to have been able to explain it to Sue. She was a mess of conflicting emotions – on the one hand, overjoyed, thrilled beyond her wildest dreams to have discovered her family. On the other hand, frustrated that she still didn't understand. Oh, she got the picture about her mum, all right. She even felt sorry for her – finding herself pregnant while her boyfriend, fiancé, whatever, was overseas, fighting for his country. In those days what else could she have done? Especially as Hilda, and her family, had been strict Catholics – thank goodness, from Sue's own point of view, even the very idea of an illegal abortion would have been completely out of the question. Yes, she understood perfectly well why she'd been put into the children's home. The shame must have been absolutely mortifying for her mother – her family would have pushed her into getting rid of her, the child, the *bastard*, as quickly as possible and pretending she'd never been born.

But ... after they were married, hadn't her mother *ever* been able to tell her father about her? Was he perhaps such an old-fashioned tyrant of a man that she was afraid to tell him, to explain about the baby that he, too, had been responsible for bringing into the world? If she'd told him, wouldn't he have wanted to rescue his first-born daughter from the orphanage and bring her up in the family, where she belonged? Or had they both decided they just didn't want her – they'd gone on to have two other daughters, and perhaps they agreed that their unfortunately-conceived first one was better off forgotten about?

At the time of Rob's shock announcement after the concert in March, Sue had been desperate to get to know her family, as quickly as possible. Rob had invited her back to the hotel where they were staying in Sydney, the following morning, and had spent a couple of hours just talking to her about Frankie and Marianne, about Marianne's children and especially the twin who was named after her. Sue couldn't stop crying – she'd spent the whole of her life, or what she remembered of it, telling herself that she had no family, and adjusting herself to cope with that.

'My parents?' she'd asked shakily.

'Sorry.' He just shook his head. 'Although ... your mum only died two years ago. That was when we found out about you. She'd split her estate between her three daughters. The other two hadn't had a clue that you existed.'

'I want to meet them,' she said. 'Soon! I don't want to waste any more time!'

'Of course. I've phoned Frankie already. She and Marianne are both desperate to meet you too!' He wrote down a phone number for her. 'Call Frankie as soon as you're ready to talk to them. Do it from the hotel here – the call will go on the band's account.'

He'd had to leave soon afterwards, with the rest of the band, flying up to Brisbane for the next leg of their tour. She'd clung to him, choking back tears, thanking him for realising who she was and promising to meet up with him again in England. It had felt so odd: when she'd met him the previous night he'd been someone she'd admired from afar – a member of her favourite band, and yet here she was, parting from him as a member of his family. She'd phoned Frankie straight away, her heart pounding in her chest while she dialled the number.

'*Susannah*,' Frankie had said. 'We've found you.'

My sister! thought Sue, unable to speak for a moment.

But once they'd started to chat, they found it hard to stop. Eventually Frankie had passed her over to Marianne, and it had started all over again – the excitement, the tears, the questions about her life and theirs – until finally, Marianne had demanded:

'It's no good doing this on the phone. We need to meet you.'

'I know. I've already decided. I'm coming to England. I just have to talk to my boss. I've ... only recently started a new job. It might be difficult.'

'Talk to her now! Today!'

Sue laughed. 'I will. And I'll call you again. As soon as I can!'

Maureen had been amazing. As soon as Sue explained what had happened, she'd enveloped her in a hug and cried tears of joy for her.

'I take it you're going to England to meet them?'

'Well ... of course, I'd like to. But can you spare me for a couple of weeks?'

'A couple of weeks? Don't be ridiculous, girl! You'll go for a month, at least – it'll take you a week to get over the jet lag!' She'd stopped and looked at Sue with affection and regret. 'I'd come with you if I could. Give you some moral support. But I can't leave the business, so soon, with both of us gone ...'

'Of course you can't. And I'll be fine on my own. They'll meet me at the airport and ...' She'd grinned with excitement. 'I'll be with my family.'

She'd flown out at the beginning of May, and had stayed with Frankie and Rob – they had more room in their house. But she'd spent just as much time getting to know Marianne, Grant and the children. Meeting her namesake, little Susan, had been one of the most emotional moments. Frankie had been nearly six months pregnant by then – her own daughter Rebecca was born in August – but she was still running the Crazy Snakes' fan club, with the help of her assistant, Lesley, whose work had thankfully improved now that she knew she was going to take over from Frankie after the baby was born.

Seeing Marianne with her children, and Frankie so excited about having a baby of her own, it was even harder for Sue to understand why their mother had never taken her back out of the orphanage. Hadn't Hilda felt any love for her at all? Or had the whole experience of being pregnant before her marriage frightened her so much that she'd never properly faced up to the fact that she was her daughter? If so, wasn't it odd that she'd provided for her in her will – without telling a single soul about it?

'We'll never know all the answers,' Frankie told her gently. She'd put her arms round her new sister. 'But at least you've got *us*, now.'

But of course, if the questions about her mother hadn't been tormenting enough, the real thousand-dollar one was why she'd been sent to Australia.

'I don't even remember which children's home I came from,' she said. 'I was only eight or nine – all I remember is being told we were going on trip. I'd never even heard of Australia. I don't think I was given any choice in the matter.'

'That's ridiculous!' Frankie said. Privately, she was sure there must have been more to it. Sue must have forgotten some of the details. Surely she'd been consulted about it properly – or as much as it was possible to do with a child of that age? And surely their mother would have been consulted, too? Wouldn't she have had to sign papers? They couldn't have just carted a child off to the other side of the world without anyone giving their permission! 'Well, there's only one children's home around here. It's a Barnardo's home. Let's pay them a visit and see if it brings back any memories.'

'OK,' Sue said, somewhat doubtfully.

'If you were living there, they're bound to have some record of you. We can see who signed permission for you to go to Australia. They'll be able to tell us more about it.'

'OK. Yes, that would be good.'

But the visit to the Barnardo's home had simply added to the frustration. It had brought back memories all right – as soon as they drove through the gates, Sue was gasping as they all came flooding back. The iron railings, the big old red-brick walls. The tiled floors, the painted interior walls, the conflicting smells of polish and cabbage. Seventeen years, and hardly anything had changed.

'It's the right one?' Frankie said, squeezing her hand, and she'd just nodded. She didn't remember being unhappy there. But she didn't remember being particularly naughty, either – so why had she been chosen for what amounted to deportation?

'I'm afraid, back then, it wasn't usual to keep records of children who left us,' the manager of the home told them. 'I'm sorry I can't help.'

'But ...' Frankie sighed. 'My sister didn't *leave*. She was sent away – to Australia! We just want to find out why. And who authorised it.'

'Australia?' He looked surprised. 'Well, I can only presume a parent or guardian must have requested it. Perhaps there was a relative in Australia who'd agreed to take you in?' he added to Sue.

'No. I was just sent to another children's home,' she said abruptly. 'It was exactly the same, but hotter. And thousands of miles from everything I'd ever known. And I got smacked for being homesick.'

Frankie's eyes filled up with tears and she gripped Sue's hand harder.

'That sounds most unlikely ... are you sure it's what happened?' the manager said.

'Of course she's sure!' Frankie retorted. 'She lived through it! Can't you *try* to find out anything for us?'

'I wish I could help. I'm sorry,' he said, not sounding it.

'Let's go,' whispered Sue – and because Frankie could see how upset she was, she agreed.

That evening, Sue told her everything: the whole story about her life on the Andersons' farm, about the years of abuse she endured from Michael Anderson, how she'd saved up slowly for her escape and got away to a new life in Melbourne.

'I never looked back,' she said simply.

'My God,' was all Frankie could say. She wondered if her mother was turning in her grave.

'I just put everything behind me, and started again. I hit lucky – got the job in the coffee shop like I told you, and Maureen Pringle just took me under her wing. I ... guess I'd never been a teenager, up till then, so I started going wild for pop music and clothes and so on. I was a late developer!'

'You should have reported him to the police. That Michael. You still could!'

She shook her head. 'I don't want to revisit it, Frankie. It's part of my past that I've dealt with and closed the lid on.'

'You're amazing.'

'No. I've just found a way to survive. I ... just hope the other kids have, too.'

'What other kids?'

Sue looked at her in surprise. 'Well, there were others, obviously. The ship going out there was full of kids like me.'

'From that same home?'

'No – from all over the country, I think. Although there was one boy from the same home. His name was Christopher – he was older than me, but I remember he looked after me on the journey.'

'So ... there were at least two of you, taken from that home? And they're saying they don't know anything about it!'

'Maybe we were both troublemakers. That's all I can think of.'

'Sue, they *couldn't* have sent you to Australia as a punishment! You were only eight!'

'Well, all I do know is that in the home in Perth, the nuns told us all that our parents were dead and nobody in England wanted us.'

'That's terrible! Your parents *weren't* even dead. Why did they tell you that?'

Sue shrugged. 'I have no idea. We all used to imagine someone would turn up one day and take us back to England. Then ... I guess we just grew up.'

'This Christopher – was he taken to the same home as you?'

'No. It was just a girls' home. They split us up when we arrived.' She swallowed hard. 'It's quite a vivid memory, actually. The boys got taken off in lorries. He wanted to stay with me. They hit him and dragged him away.'

'Bloody hell.'

'I can still remember crying for him to come back. He was in the back of this lorry, being driven away – and he was crying too. Presumably he went to one of the boys' homes. I never saw him again.'

'But there were *lots* of other kids? *Lorries* full of boys?'

'Yes. And busloads full of girls.' She looked at Frankie solemnly. 'I'm telling you – it was a whole shipment of kids. None of us knew why we were going.' She paused. 'I've always presumed we were the only ones – my shipload, I mean. But thinking about it now, there were plenty of older girls at the home who'd come from England too.'

'You think there was *more* than one shipment? *More* kids who'd been sent to Australia?'

'Well, I suppose there must have been.'

Frankie and Sue stared at each other in silence.

'Why?' Frankie whispered eventually. 'Why doesn't anyone seem to know about this?'

'I suppose,' Sue said, 'because we were just orphanage kids that nobody wanted.'

'*We'd* have wanted you! If only we'd known about you!'

'So let's make up for lost time,' Sue said, hugging her sister. 'And let's not waste any more of my visit, looking back and regretting stuff we can't change.'

'You're amazing,' Frankie said again. And because she could see it was what Sue wanted, she changed the subject, and concentrated on trying to give her the best visit to England that anyone had ever had. And when Sue had finally had to leave, to return to Australia, she made both her sisters promise that they'd visit her there one day.

She'd picked up her life in Sydney again and worked hard to help Maureen with the new restaurant. At the beginning of September, one of the regular customers, a quietly-spoken kindly young schoolteacher called Tom, had asked her out on a date. She hadn't been out with anyone before – the memory of Michael had stopped her even wanting to – but she liked Tom and told him she'd think about it.

'I'm nervous,' she admitted to Maureen.

'You'll be fine. He's a good one.'

He was. But after Maureen had had a private word with him about how she looked upon Sue as the daughter she'd never had, and how she'd swing for any man who hurt her, because she'd been hurt too much already in her life, he treated Sue with such tenderness and respect that she felt as if she was half in love with him after just the first date.

It had lasted a couple of months, and had only ended because Sue had now discovered that the opposite sex weren't all like Michael Anderson, in fact she now realised there were probably other men out there in the world who might be just as nice as Tom. She didn't want to hurt him – and in fact they remained good friends. But she wanted – *needed* – to have a little more fun before she settled down!

Chapter 38

November 1971 : Llangenith, South Wales

Jack had been home for three months – home, but not really home. He'd moved straight in with his mother and her cousin Peg in the remote cottage they now shared in a tiny hamlet in rural south Wales. He'd been relieved and delighted to find Betty still alive and relatively well, and had wanted to spend as much time as possible with her, but by now the smallness and mind-numbing tedious sameness of life in Llangenith was getting to him. It was great to be back in Britain, but now he was free to go where he wanted, he was itching to get his life back again. He knew it couldn't be his old life, but it could at least be a new one that resembled it as far as possible.

'I don't want to go back to Shanklin, love,' Betty had told him during the first week he was there. 'I like it here, and Peg and I look after each other. We're company for each other. It's lovely having you back, but I can't expect you to hang around with me all the time – you've got to get a new job, haven't you, and probably you'll want to get back with that band of yours.'

Jack didn't tell her that the band had moved on without him, that they'd actually become a household name and she was possibly one of the few people in the country who didn't know about them. News, and fashions, were slow to reach Llangenith.

One day during September he'd got the bus from the village into Swansea, where he'd bought himself a car and spent the rest of the day investigating the employment possibilities in the area. There wasn't much work around, but he didn't have his heart in it anyway.

'I'm thinking of moving back to London,' he'd told Betty over dinner that night. 'Would you mind?'

'Not as long as you visit me from time to time,' she said. She smiled at him. 'I've been a long time without you, love. But you need to live your own life, and I know there's nothing around here for young people. Only farming, and the pub.'

So he'd spent a few weeks travelling back and forth to London, looking for work, looking for accommodation, and finally finding his dream job – managing the bathroom and plumbing department of a new DIY superstore in Stratford, East London. He could work civilised hours, wear a suit and never again have to lie on his back on someone's floor looking for leaks in their toilet.

It was when he was studying flats to rent, in an estate agency window on Stratford Broadway, that something caught his eye – a description of a property in Dagenham. It was the wrong area, and the wrong type of property for him. But it made him think about Frankie again, and when he returned to the cottage in Llengenith for the weekend, he looked among his things for the letter he'd carried with him on the long journey home. Reading it again, he was suddenly overcome with a need to contact her.

He told himself he just needed to set things right – explain, at last, why he'd left her. It couldn't do any harm, could it? He wouldn't ask to see her – she was married to Rob, he understood now that her life had moved on, and of course, he couldn't blame her, or Rob, for that. Just one letter, apologising for letting her down – then he'd really try, at last, to forget her.

The letter wasn't easy to write. He was careful to make it clear that he wished only the best for both Frankie and Rob and that he wasn't going to get in touch any more. He told them, briefly, what had happened to make him leave the country. He hoped they'd understand. That was all he could ask for. He sealed the envelope and addressed it to Frankie at the fan club office address on the top of her letter. There was no post office in Llangenith – the nearest one was in another village fifteen minutes' drive away – so he put the letter in his jacket pocket, resolving to post it the next day.

In fact it stayed in his jacket pocket until a few days later when Jack went back to London to continue his search for a flat. He was walking down Stratford Broadway again – it was a cold, bright, autumn afternoon, the type of day that just never happened in Perth, and he was feeling light and free in the bustling street, heading for the estate agents to enquire about a property that had just come on the market, when he felt in his pocket and remembered the letter. There was a post-box on the other side of the street. Whistling to himself at the thought of clearing things up with Frankie, pleased to be doing the right thing, he paused at the kerb and waited to cross.

The car with blacked-out windows came hurtling round the corner out of nowhere. People turned, startled, moving away from the kerb as it veered towards the pavement. Jack took a step back. In the split second that it took for him to see the passenger window slide down, to notice the gun being raised, he tried to duck – but the bullet had already been fired, and by ducking he simply allowed it to hit his head instead of his heart. There was a second shot, but he didn't feel it even although it was the one that did the most damage. As he crumpled to the ground, the sounds of the car screeching away and the people around him screaming seemed to fade into the distance.

'So this is how it feels,' he thought, and found it strange that he had no desire to fight it. Wasn't that supposed to be instinctive?

People were surrounding him now. Someone was touching his hand, telling him to hold on, that an ambulance was coming. A woman was crying. He thought of his mother, and made an effort to speak, to ask someone to look after her, but the words seemed to drown in a gurgling mass in his throat.

'What did he say?' the woman cried.

The man holding Jack's hand was feeling for his pulse. 'I don't know, love,' he said gravely. The ambulance was approaching, its siren blaring, its lights flashing, and people were moving aside ready for the paramedics. 'But it's too late. He's gone.' He sat back on his heels, looking sadly at the body of the poor chap lying on the pavement. 'Whoever he was, somebody mustn't half have hated him.'

Chapter 39

Shenfield

It was all over the papers the next day. Frankie and Rob, who'd already seen the story reported on the TV news the previous night, had read the headlines and almost the whole account – about an unidentified male who had been shot down in broad daylight on a major thoroughfare in East London – before coming to the small paragraph, added at the foot of the page before the paper went to press:

The dead man was identified last night as ..

'*Oh, God!*' Rob exclaimed, his face suddenly turning white. 'It's Jack.'

'What? No – it can't be. He's in ...' Frankie shook her head and grabbed the paper out of his hands.

... identified last night as Jack Hunter, 30, former lead singer of the popular rock group Crazy Snakes. Mr Hunter had only recently returned from abroad. Police are treating his death as a possible gangland killing.

'I'm going to be sick,' Frankie said.

They stayed at home all day, almost too shaken to talk to each other. Dave called to advise them not to speak to the press.

'I don't know how they picked up the connection with the band so quickly. But you can bet we're all going to get hounded.'

He was right, of course, and after the first few calls Rob took the fan club office phone off the hook. Marianne called Frankie on their private line but even to her sister, Frankie was barely able to string together a coherent sentence.

'*Gangland killing?*' Marianne said. 'What the hell ...?'

Someone had been after him. Frankie had no idea who, or why, but he'd gone to Australia to escape them. She'd thought he was exaggerating when he'd told her it would be dangerous for him to come back. So why had he?

'We knew where he was, didn't we,' she whispered.

All that time, she'd known he was in Perth, and she'd never told anyone apart from Marianne. Not even Rob. And after trusting her to keep his secret all that time, he'd suddenly given up and come home anyway. It didn't make sense.

The police wanted to talk to Rob. Still half frozen with shock, he had to describe how Jack had disappeared without telling anyone why.

'His mother went too,' he remembered.

'We've got his mother. She's been living with a relative in Wales. She's helping us with our enquiries.'

'*Helping you* ...' Rob ran his fingers through his hair. 'I can't believe this. I mean – you're telling me Jack was mixed up with something ... surely his *mother* wasn't involved?'

'I'm afraid I can't tell you any more at this stage, sir. Fortunately we have witnesses to the shooting, we have a description and registration for the car and there are officers on the trail of the killers as we speak. We hope to have the suspects in custody as soon as possible.'

'The suspects. You know who they are?'

'We have a good idea, sir.' The officer paused, and then took something out of his pocket. It was an envelope, contained in a plastic bag. 'This was in Mr Hunter's pocket when he died. It's a letter, addressed to your wife. I think perhaps we should speak to her too, please.'

'Right. OK, I'll get her.' Rob got to his feet. He hesitated. Frankie had already told him that she'd known all along that Jack was in Australia. If he was hurt that she hadn't confided in him, he was pushing this to one side, trying to understand how conflicting Frankie's feelings must have been. 'She ...

was his girlfriend. Briefly, before he – Jack – went missing. She's pretty upset.'

'We'll bear that in mind, sir.'

Frankie faced the police officer across the table.

'I knew where he was,' she said straight away. It came out as a strangled half-whisper. 'He wrote to me.'

'Did he?' The officer wrote something down. 'Did you tell anyone else?'

'Only my sister. Well – she found out. Nobody else. He warned me, told me not to – that it would be dangerous for him. He said he couldn't come back. So why did he?'

'We think he may have misinterpreted certain information in the newspapers, that led him to believe it would be safe. I can't tell you any more at the present time. Our officers are working towards ...'

Frankie swallowed, trying not to cry again. 'Please – just tell me he wasn't mixed up in anything ... I can't believe he would have been involved in anything criminal!'

'He never told you anything?'

'About what? I mean, we weren't together very long.'

'Did you know why he and his mother moved out of London?'

She frowned. What did that have to do with anything?

'His father died. His mum wanted a complete change, so they moved to the Isle of Wight. Why? Was there more to it, then? Are you saying he lied to me? Was he involved in some ... *gangland* stuff, like the papers are saying?'

The officer tapped the letter, still in its plastic bag, with his fingers.

'This might give you some answers, Mrs Marchant. It was found in Mr Hunter's pocket – it's addressed to you and we think he was on his way to post it.'

Frankie frowned in surprise. Jack had written to her again? She reached out to take the letter, but the officer shook his head and instead handed her two folded sheets of paper.

'This is a photocopy for you. I'm afraid we had to open the original letter and read it. We need to keep it. It's evidence.'

'Evidence,' she repeated.

'Yes, vital evidence, in the event of any trial. Which brings me back to the previous letter you mentioned. Do you still have it?'

'No. There was another one, too, but I burnt them both.' She hung her head. 'I ... was upset with him. I didn't know why he left me. I was furious that he'd gone off to Australia without even telling me why. And then I was annoyed that after all that, he was writing to me.'

'Of course. I understand.' The officer got up to go. 'If you think of anything else – anything at all that might be relevant – please get in touch with us straight away.' He glanced out of the window at the throng of reporters gathered on the pavement outside the house. 'If I were you, I'd stay in the house and ignore the doorbell. Or go away somewhere quiet – until the fuss dies down. Just be sure to let us know where you are.'

'We're not under any kind of suspicion, are we?' she said, alarmed.

'No, not at all.' He smiled at her.

'Or in any danger? Only I've got a three month old baby.'

'You're not in any danger, Mrs Marchant. Only from that mob out there,' he added, nodding at the crowd of journalists again. 'Take it easy.'

She read the copy of Jack's letter on her own, in the bedroom. It was hard to take in. She had to read it twice before it even began to make sense.

Dear Frankie

I'm writing to let you know I'm back from Australia. Everything is OK, there's no need for me to hide any more. I've been living with my mum and her cousin in Wales – I had her sent there for her own protection when I went away. She didn't know where I'd gone, but I didn't want anyone to hurt her, trying to find out.

I'm coming back to London soon – I've got a new job in Stratford and I'm looking at flats. But don't worry, I'm not going to interfere in your life. I've caused you enough trouble already. I'll never be able to apologise enough for leaving you the way I did – or to Rob and the other boys for leaving the band in the lurch. Believe me, I've lived with the regrets every day of my life since I went. I can only hope it will help you forgive me if I try to explain, now that I can.

I told you, didn't I, that my mum and I moved to the Isle of Wight after my dad died. What I didn't tell you was that many years ago, Dad had got involved with some crooks in the East End. Mum and Dad were hard up – he got tempted by the pay-offs. His role was pretty minor, handling stolen goods, keeping his mouth shut – I don't think he even appreciated how dangerous these blokes were – although he found that out eventually.

Dad had got tired of it all – dodging the police, hiding money from robberies in his house, living in fear of the knock on the door. He wanted to get out of it, but they wouldn't let him – he knew too much. It turned out the small time crooks he was working for were under the protection of the Kray twins and their gang. This was about ten years ago. Ronnie Kray had been in jail for 18 months for running a protection racket and when he came out he wasn't taking any prisoners. They suspected my dad of 'squealing' to the police. One day he was walking home down our road and a car mounted the pavement and knocked him down. He didn't live long enough to tell the police anything. Everyone said it was a random hit and run – but I knew it was deliberate. I'd been on our front doorstep at the time, looking out for Dad because he was late home. I used to worry about him, knowing who he was mixed up with.

I'd got the registration of the car, and the police caught the bloke who did it. Needless to say, he was just the hit man – the tip of the iceberg. I was in danger as soon as I went to the police. They told me and Mum to get out of the area and change our names. So I didn't actually become Jack Hunter until we moved to the Isle of Wight. That's why none of my mates over there knew anything about my past – my life in London, where I went to school ...

    That was the first time I had to leave everything behind. I'd had to give up university – I needed a job anyway then, to support Mum and myself. But we settled down, I got work, and eventually I started the band. At first I was too scared to come back over to London, but after a while I got more complacent. I needed to go to London sometimes with the band, and of course, eventually to meet up with you. I stopped thinking about the risk I was taking, of someone recognising me. As you know, the Krays and a dozen or so of their gang were arrested in 1968, and put away for life, so I reckoned I was safe. But my dad's murder was mentioned during the trial, along with all the others – and needless to say, there were still other gang members and hangers-on in town who were desperate for reprisal.

    Well, eventually someone obviously did recognise me, and when I went home to Shanklin after that last weekend I spent with you, they had me followed. When I saw the car tailing me, the faces watching me, the memory of Dad's murder came back to me and I panicked. I slipped down alleyways and footpaths to lose them, but I knew it was only going to be a matter of time now before they tracked me down. I couldn't put my mum at risk. I'd already decided Australia would be my bolthole if ever it came to it – and I'd been accepted for assisted passage, but hoped never to have to take up the offer. But I made a few phone calls and was lucky enough to get a cancellation on a sailing to Fremantle the same week. I phoned Mum's cousin in Wales and arranged for her to move there – arranged everything for the removal and told her not to answer the phone or the door to anyone. And then I just disappeared. I stayed in a hostel in Southampton until the day the ship left, and by then Mum was safely in Wales.

So now you know. I wasn't joking when I said it was dangerous for me to come back. It's been a long wait, but finally I read the news that the blokes who were after me have been caught and put away. I knew who they were – so did the police. It was just a question of waiting for them to get too cocky, do something the police couldn't ignore and they'd be banged up for a good long time. They're all inside now – that's the last of them. The whole gang culture in the East End has been wiped out, and good riddance.

I realise all this will come as a shock to you but I'm glad I can finally explain, to you and to Rob. I'll admit I was upset when I first found out you two had got together. But now I'm glad you're both happy and part of the reason for this letter is to tell you I won't be writing again, or phoning, or bothering you in any way. If we happen to bump into each other one of these days let's just smile and say hello like old friends. No hard feelings? I hope not.

I really loved you, Frankie. I never wanted to hurt you.

With love – Jack

'Are you OK?' Rob asked her, finding her sitting in the dark in their bedroom a little later, the copy of Jack's letter on the bed beside her.

She nodded. She was all cried out.

'I wonder why he thought it was safe to come back?' she said, after Rob had read the letter. 'He seemed so sure all the gang members had been jailed.'

'I don't know.' He sat down next to her on the bed. 'It seems pretty naive of him not to realise there'd always be *someone* left who wanted revenge, or someone who'd been paid by the guys in prison.'

'Do you think ...' She hesitated. 'Perhaps he was so unhappy, he didn't care anymore.'

'He might have just been sick of hiding, in the end, and was prepared to risk it.'

'We'll never know, will we?'

'I suppose not.' He put his arm round her and she laid her head on his shoulder. 'But if he wanted to come home so badly – wanted to see his mum again, and live his own life again – well, at least he got that, for a few months anyway.'

Frankie nodded. 'I suppose that's the best way to look at it.'

Rob looked at her thoughtfully for a minute. 'There's something else,' he said quietly.

'Go on?'

'You told me he wrote to you a couple of times.'

'Yes ... Rob, I'm so sorry I didn't tell you – it was just that I was so cross at the time ...'

He shook his head. 'It doesn't matter. But did he mention that he was married?'

'What! Married? No!' She stared at him in surprise. 'What makes you think that?'

'It was in today's paper – something to the effect of it having been revealed that he'd left a wife and baby in Perth.'

'A wife and *baby*?' Frankie echoed. She shook her head, stunned. He'd been writing to her, saying he hoped she'd go out and live in Australia with him – sending her money because he thought *she'd* had his baby! – and somehow, all along, giving her the impression he was still in love with her. So much for that! 'So why the hell did he leave them behind?'

'I don't know, Frankie.' Rob stroked her arm gently. 'Maybe there was someone in England he cared about, more than he cared about them.'

Frankie swallowed hard. 'I can't think who,' she said quietly. And then: 'His mother, I suppose.'

Chapter 40

The next day : Perth

Shona was feeding Steven his bedtime bottle while she was watching the television news, and she came so close to dropping both the child and his milk on the floor that Steven yelled out in fright – and so did she.

'What the hell's going on?' Ken shouted, running into the room just in time to see Jack's face on the screen. 'Fucking hell! It's fucking Jack Hunter!'

'Don't swear in front of the baby!' Shona said automatically, even though she was still gasping with shock and trying to calm the child at the same time.

'What's he done?' Ken said, turning the TV up louder. 'What are you yelling about?'

'They're saying he's dead, Ken! Shot! In London! I didn't even know he'd left the bloody country for God's sake!'

'*Shot?*' Ken sat down abruptly, his legs shaking. 'What the ...?'

'Ssh! *Listen*! Maybe they've got it wrong. It can't be him, can it? Shall I phone him and see if he's ...'

'No.' Ken was concentrating on the news item now that his son had stopped crying. 'No, Shona – I know what this is. I heard it earlier, on the radio, but they didn't give out his name then. It's a gangland killing – something to do with reprisals.'

'But how can Jack have been mixed up in anything like that? He's been living over here for ... for years ...' Unexpectedly, she began to cry. 'Oh God. He never talked about his life in England. He just kind of let me assume he emigrated like all the other Poms – I always wondered why he never wanted to talk about it. What, was he some sort of *crook*, then? He must have been, if he got shot like that! Oh, no – I was married to him, Ken, and I never knew ... he might have had a gun ... he might have turned violent ...'

'He didn't, though, did he,' Ken said abruptly. 'Don't be stupid. You were only married to him for five minutes, and he treated you decently, didn't he. *You* left *him* over some stupid argument, remember?'

Shona stared at him. 'Stupid argument, was it? Well, I didn't notice you thinking it was so stupid at the time! You couldn't wait to jump into his shoes, if I remember rightly. I don't know what gives you the right to talk about *decency*. Supposed to be his best mate, weren't you?'

'And *you* were supposed to be his wife!' Ken flung back.

The row had escalated within minutes, both of them too shocked and upset by the news to think what they were saying. The baby, frightened by their raised voices, began to cry again and Shona picked him up.

'I'm putting him to bed,' she said without looking back at Ken. She cried all the way through changing her son's nappy and rocking him to sleep. When she finally came back to the lounge room, Ken had turned off the TV and was drinking a Coke.

'They said he was a witness to his father's killing ten years ago,' he told her, more quietly now. 'He went to the police and got some big names put away, so he was always going to be at risk. He'd already changed his name once. When they found him again he just bottled it and came out to Australia. Can't say I blame him.'

'So he *wasn't* mixed up in anything himself.'

'No.' He looked at her, put down his drink and held out his arms. 'And it's pretty bloody silly for us to start bawling each other out, isn't it. It's not going to bring him back.'

'No.' She sat down next to him. 'It's just such a shock. I still can't believe it. And ... well, I reckon we both feel kind of ...'

'Guilty,' Ken said at once, staring straight ahead.

Shona started to cry again. 'You're right. He was always decent to me. I didn't give it a chance. I shut him out after I had Steven.'

'And I did the dirty on him. My best mate.'

'But only because it was what I wanted too.' She shook her head. 'I should never have married him.' She sighed, regret flooding her again. She'd married Jack knowing that she'd never got over Ken, despite everything she said about hating him and never wanting to see him again. Oh, she'd tried to stay away from him. But in a way, by becoming his friend and insisting on having him as his best man, Jack had pretty much pushed them back together.

'None of this is helping now,' Ken reminded her. 'Whatever else we both did to hurt him, it wasn't our fault he decided to go back to England.'

'So why *did* he? I don't understand – if he was at risk, why?'

'They were saying on the TV that he'd probably heard reports about a couple of the gang who'd still been at large, being jailed. He must have thought it would be safe to go back. But there was a police spokesman on there, saying he should never have just taken himself off to live over here in the first place – he should have applied to them for police protection and been given a new identity again.'

'All very well for them to say that!'

'Yeah. I guess he felt like he couldn't go through life changing his identity every few years – better to disappear and lie low for as long as he needed to.'

They were both silent. Ken picked up his Coke and took another swig.

'So he only left her ... that girl in England ... because he had to,' Shona said after a few minutes.

'No point thinking about that.'

'But I suppose he went back to England to be with her. How must *she* feel now? Apparently she had his baby!'

'So did you, Shona.'

'Yes. You know what, Ken? I feel really bad now about applying for a divorce! And for talking about you adopting Steven.'

Ken didn't reply. He felt bad too, but there was one indisputable fact: there wouldn't be any need for a divorce any more, and adopting Steven wasn't likely to be a problem either. And then he felt even worse for thinking along those lines when he'd only just found out Jack was dead.

'He was a good bloke,' he said eventually, half to himself. 'We got pretty close at one time. I never had a close mate before.'

Shona looked at him suspiciously. 'Did he *tell* you? All this stuff – about why he came out to Oz – did he confide in you? He did, didn't he! Crikey – he never breathed a word of it to me, and I was his flipping *wife*!'

'Calm down. No, he didn't tell me. He just dropped a few hints – about having to come out here without telling anyone. Leaving everyone behind. Including his mum.'

'His mum's dead!'

'No. He just found it easier to pretend she was. That was why he got upset on your wedding day.'

'Flipping heck. I think you knew him better than I did,' she said regretfully. 'I wish he could've trusted me with the truth.'

'I guess he couldn't risk telling *anyone*. He used a different name in the band, didn't he – when we started getting better known.'

'Yes, and it's obvious why, now, isn't it. Did you hear what it said on the news? He used to be the lead singer with the Crazy Snakes! Did you know that?'

'Of course I didn't! I'm as shocked as you are!'

'Well.' She sighed. 'Maybe I'm not completely shocked. He tried to tell me – when we had that big bust-up. I thought he was lying. I mean, they're *famous*! How could he have been their lead singer without us knowing about it?'

'He must have been so nervous the whole time that someone would track him down. I remember telling him once that anyone could be traced, if someone wanted to find them badly enough. That must have really spooked him.'

'It turned out to be true though, didn't it,' Shona pointed out, wiping away a tear. 'Poor Jack.'

Ken nodded agreement. He was so shaken about poor bloody Jack he could hardly think straight. And so worried that it had been partly his fault he'd died. By taking Shona and the baby away from him, had he driven him back to England to find that bloody girl he'd never got over? Well, Ken supposed he'd just have to live with the guilt. And fair enough, it was no less than he deserved.

Chapter 41

October 1987 : Shenfield

A hurricane. That's what they were saying on the news. Frankie stared out at the garden, at the fence lying flat on the lawn, the branches flung from the trees, dumped across each other as if some giant in the sky had been playing Pick-up-Sticks. The wind had kept her and Rob awake most of the night, but they'd been shocked to the core to see the extent of the damage.

'Yay – we've got the day off!' Rebecca shouted from the kitchen, where she'd been glued to the school closure reports on Essex Radio.

'No school?' her brother Martin echoed. 'Excellent! Can I go and knock for Duncan, Mum?'

'Change out of your uniform first, then.' Frankie smiled at him. At thirteen, Martin's life still revolved around his mates – playing football in the park, larking about at the swimming pool, anything rather than knuckling down to anything serious. She'd insisted on both kids dressing for school this morning despite the reports of national catastrophe, of roads being blocked by fallen trees, homes damaged and power lines down – but she wasn't really surprised to hear now that their school couldn't open. She'd have liked her son to sound a little less thrilled about missing his lessons but she couldn't blame him, and this *was* an exceptional situation.

It was slightly different for Rebecca. At sixteen, and one of the youngest in her school year, she'd recently started in the sixth form, and although she'd done really well with her GCSEs, the transition to A-level work was proving a challenge to her. She really couldn't afford to have time off. Frankie hoped school was going to be back to normal tomorrow.

'Have you got any homework to catch up on?' she asked her daughter.

'Nope. Done it all.'

'Maybe spend a bit of time going over that French you were struggling with the other night, then?'

'Oh, *Mum*! It's a day off!' She looked at her mother slyly. 'If I help you with some of the chores first, can I go round Gavin's later?'

Gavin. Her first proper boyfriend. Frankie looked at her daughter with a mixture of pride and regret. She'd grown up so fast. Was sixteen really old enough to be forming such a steady relationship – with a boy in the same class? She thought back to her own teenage years and smiled to herself. Maybe it was better this way. At least Becky wasn't going off to rock festivals and ending up with someone nearly ten years older than herself.

'What's the matter, Mum?' Rebecca was looking at her anxiously. 'You OK? Is that cool, then – if I go to Gavin's?'

'Yes, love.' Frankie gave her a hug. 'No problem.'

She was lucky. Her daughter talked to her. Frankie and Rob gave her some freedom, appropriate to her age. They agreed that she should have boyfriends, that she should have some independence, some fun, as long as they always knew where she was. She hoped their relationship was always going to be completely different from hers with her own mother. History was not going to repeat itself in this family.

With both the children out, and Rob occupied in his study with some song-writing, which was the direction he'd taken more and more since the band had stopped touring, Frankie took a cup of tea up to her sister's room. Sue was barely awake, having arrived from Sydney only the previous day and suffering from jet-lag. No matter how many times she came to the UK to visit her family – and it was usually at least once or twice every year – she'd never got used to it.

'Thanks.' She sat up in bed and blinked at Frankie sleepily. 'Sorry – didn't realise the time. I had a bad night. It was windy, wasn't it?'

'That's an understatement!' Frankie laughed. 'It was a hurricane.'

'Really? I didn't know you got those in England!'

'Me neither. It's the first one I've ever known. You wait till you look outside. The news is awful – lots of houses damaged. I think we've been lucky. Rob's been checking the roof for missing tiles, but the only damage seems to be the small window in the downstairs loo – a branch of the big oak out the front smashed into it.'

'Wow. Glad my flight got in yesterday morning, then, and not today!'

'Good point. Drink your tea, and I'll make you some breakfast when you're ready. No rush.'

She went back downstairs just as the phone in the office started to ring.

'Can you get that, Frankie?' Rob called out. 'I'm on the other line.'

She put her head round the office door. The call was coming through on the fan club line – not such a common occurrence these days, although with the UK revival tour being planned for the Snakes, they were aware that it could start to get busy again. Luckily they'd invested in one of the new cordless phones, enabling Frankie to pick it up and walk out to the kitchen, so as not to disturb Rob's conversation.

'Hello – Crazy Snakes Fan Club. Can I help you?'

There was silence. Frankie repeated, slightly louder: 'Hello – Crazy Snakes ...'

'Um – hi.' The accent was Australian; the tone very cautious. 'I ... look, I'm sorry to disturb you. Is that ... Frankie, by any chance?'

'Who is this?'

'Sorry. Look, you don't know me. My name's Shona and I ...' The caller gave a kind of nervous gulp and then went on in little more than a whisper, 'I was married to Jack Hunter. For a while. I ... just ...'

'Oh my God.' Frankie sat down with a bump. 'Shona. Yes. I remember seeing your name in the news,' she said faintly. 'How on earth did you get hold of this number?'

'I didn't. I mean – look, sorry, this is complicated. It was my ex – Ken, he's in London at the moment and he phoned me. We keep in touch, right? I've been supporting him while he tried to trace his family in the UK, and ...'

'Sorry, I don't know what this has got to do with me.'

'I know. I know it sounds muddled. But I'm trying to explain. He picked up some leaflet or other about the Crazy Snakes doing a tour again, and the fan club number was on there, and obviously we heard, you know, when he died? – that Jack used to be the lead singer. We never knew before – I didn't know anything about his past life, obviously he had to keep it all under wraps, as it were ...'

Frankie, still trying to recover from the shock of hearing from this woman – from the woman Jack *married*, for God's sake! – was struggling to keep up with what she was talking about.

'Ken said your name was on the leaflet,' Shona went on. 'And ... straight away I knew it had to be *you*. The girl he was in love with. You were the reason we broke up. The reason I went back to Ken.'

'*What?*'

'I found some letters, letters he'd hidden from me. Her name ... sorry, *your* name ... was Frankie. It was ... look, it's all a long time ago, now. It was mostly my own fault. Sorry,' she said again. 'I won't go into it all now, not on the phone. I expect you're wondering why the hell I've called you.'

'To be honest, yes. You've completely thrown me. It's been – what? – sixteen years since Jack died!'

'I know,' Shona said quietly. 'I've got a seventeen-year old son.'

Jack's son. Despite herself, Frankie's heart skipped a beat. He'd be not much older than her Rebecca. What would he look like? Would he be like his father?

'Why *have* you called me?' she asked, trying to keep her voice steady. 'Just curiosity? Because you happened to find this number?'

'Like I say, Ken found it. He's in London to meet his family.' Frankie actually heard her take a deep breath before she went on. 'His birth family. He … he's just found them.'

'*Birth family?*' Frankie looked up to see Sue come into the kitchen, rubbing her eyes and heading for the toaster.

'Yes. I don't suppose you've heard anything about this, but there's been a huge fuss out here about the children who were shipped out to Australia from the UK – the child migrants, they're calling them – there were thousands of them, it went on for decades. Well, anyway, Ken was one of them. He never knew where he came from, who his parents were. He was told they were dead …'

'Oh my *God.*'

Sue stopped in the act of putting two slices of bread in the toaster, whirling round to look at Frankie in concern.

'I know, it's unbelievable, isn't it,' Shona was going on. 'There's an organisation been set up now, they call themselves the Child Migrant Trust – they put out an advert in the papers out here, asking people to get in touch if they'd been affected.'

'Yes. I know.'

'You've heard about it? It's going to cause a huge scandal out here, I can tell you …'

'I know. My sister … I have a sister …' Frankie couldn't go on. Sue dropped the bread and came over to her side, mouthing '*Are you OK?'* at her.

'Look, what I wanted to ask you,' Shona was ploughing on, 'was whether Ken – my ex – can come and see you while he's over there? Would that be OK? Would you mind? He wouldn't call you himself. He's … look, he's a bit emotional at the moment, what with just being reunited with his father and meeting the stepsisters he never knew about – can you imagine? So I thought I'd take a chance and call you for him. I know it's raking up the past, and if you'd rather not, well you'd better just say – we'd understand. But it'd mean quite a lot to him, to meet you and shake your hand and …' Frankie heard her sigh. 'It'd mean quite a lot to both of us, to feel we'd done that. For Jack's sake.'

'Right,' Frankie whispered.

'So can I tell him it'd be OK? He's only in London for another couple of weeks, so …'

'Yes, sure. Tell him to call me and fix a day. I'll give him directions and …' She swallowed hard. 'Yes, I'll be happy to meet up with him.'

She hung up and sat staring at Sue, blinking fast, shaking her head.

'What's up?' Sue asked. 'Who was it?'

'Jack's wife. His *widow.*'

'Jack – the guy who was murdered – the one who used to be in the Snakes?'

Frankie nodded. 'And her … I don't know – her *ex*, she called him … he's over here. He wants to come and meet me.' She looked up at her sister, shaking her head in amazement. 'He was another child migrant, Sue – he's over here to meet up with his family. Can you believe that? Talk about coincidence.'

Sue's eyes widened. 'And he's only just found his family?'

'Apparently.'

'Well, at least I know exactly how he's feeling – maybe I can have a talk to him when he comes.'

'Sure. The two of you can compare memories.'

'What's his name? Did she say?'

'Ken, I think.'

'Ken. OK. Well, it'll be good to talk to someone else who went through the same stuff.'

Frankie looked up. Her sister was staring into the distance.

'What?' she said.

'Nothing.' Sue shook her head. She didn't want her sister to know how much it unsettled her, even after all this time, to have to think about the past all over again. She'd moved on, she was happy, it didn't always serve any purpose to look back. But if it was going to help this Ken to have a chat, that was fine – of course. She smiled at Frankie. 'Let me know when he's coming.'

Chapter 42

Four days later

Ken stood on the doorstep, feeling awkward and uncomfortable. He'd had no trouble finding the house, but he was surprised at its size, and the location – obviously a really upmarket area. Then again, if this Frankie and her husband had been involved with the Crazy Snakes, they must have made a lot of money back then. He straightened his shoulders as the front door was opened.

'Hi. Um … Frankie?'

'Yes. You must be Ken? Come in. Good journey?'

He smiled, despite himself. He couldn't get used to the way these Poms seemed to think it was a journey if you'd only come from half an hour away.

'Good thanks. Although it was quite a shock to see so many trees down.' From the train window, the devastation of the countryside had been plain to see. He'd sat up, the night of the hurricane, watching from the window of his father's retirement flat where he'd been sleeping on the sofa since he arrived in England two weeks before, but the effects of the storm were a lot more noticeable outside of London. 'I didn't realise you got hurricanes here in England.'

Frankie laughed. 'My sister said the same thing.' She led him into the lounge where she offered him a seat and added, 'She's from Australia too. I'll get her to come and say hello in a while. But first I'll get you a cup of tea – or coffee?'

He sat down, his hands nervously on his knees, looking around the comfortably furnished room and wondering again about the woman he'd come here to meet. Unlike himself, she seemed completely at ease with the situation, despite the fact that Shona had described her as having sounded shocked and quite distressed when she'd called her. He could understand that. He hadn't been too sure about this – intruding on her, bringing up the subject of Jack after all these years – but at the same time he had a feeling it would help, in some way. Help him, and Shona, to live a bit more easily with Jack's memory, perhaps.

'Here you are.' She'd come back into the room with a tray of tea and a plate of biscuits. *Very English*, he thought to himself. *Afternoon tea and bikkies*. His British heritage was still sufficiently new to him to be a constant source of interest and intrigue. Frankie settled herself on the sofa opposite him and took a deep breath. 'I have to tell you, I was so completely shaken by the phone call from your … from Shona, I nearly bottled out of this meeting a couple of times.'

'But you didn't.'

'No. I've had time to calm down now. But I don't really know how it's going to help – either of us – to dig up the past now.'

'I don't want to dig up the past. Or cause you any … hurt. I just wanted to meet you, to let you know …' He hesitated.

'Go on.'

'I was Jack's best friend out in Perth. But I did him wrong. Shona and I – we both did.' He hung his head, the old familiar guilt enveloping him again like a black shroud. 'If it hadn't been for that, I don't know whether he would have come back to England.'

'And you blame yourselves, do you? For what happened to him?' she said, sharply, her eyes flashing at him. 'You want me to say something to make you feel better?'

'Of course not.' He looked up and met her eyes. 'You couldn't. Nothing could. It weighed so heavily on both of us, it's why we're not together any more. We're still friends, though, me and Shona. She's been the best mate – the most amazing support to me in this other business, this search for my family. But the whole thing with Jack's murder – it was too much of a strain on our relationship. We were going to get married, I was going to adopt Steven, but …'

'Steven,' Frankie repeated, staring at him. 'Is that his name? Jack's son?'

'Yes.' He smiled and took out his wallet, passing her a couple of photos. 'I guessed you might want to see these. He's a great kid. And it looks like he's inherited his dad's talent. He's into music in a big way.'

'He looks just like him.'

Ken noticed Frankie wiping away a tear. 'You can keep those if you like,' he said lightly. 'I've got plenty more. I still see a lot of Steven.'

'No.' She handed the pictures back to him and sat up straight. 'Thank you for showing them to me. I'm pleased the boy's … turned out well. But he's nothing to do with me. I've got two teenagers of my own. *None* of this has anything to do with me now.'

'I understand.' Ken took a sip of his tea, and then added, 'But you know, Jack never stopped thinking about you. Even though … he tried to make a go of it, you know, his marriage to Shona. He was a good bloke, a good husband. But he was torn. He told me about you – how bad he felt for leaving you the way he did. I'm sure he'd never have left you if it hadn't been for the threat to his life.'

'I know,' she said simply. 'He wrote me a letter – when he came back. He was on his way to post it when … it happened. The police gave it to me. I've come to terms with it all – long ago.'

'And now I've turned up and brought it all back again. I'm sorry.'

'Well, I could have said no, couldn't I.' She put down her cup and fiddled with the sleeves of her cardigan for a minute. 'We could probably go over and over this for hours, but I'm not sure it would help either of us.'

'Perhaps you're right.'

'If you want me to say that I don't blame you, or Shona, then – I don't. Jack would probably have come home eventually, one way or another, and those guys were never going to let it go. They'd have found him. They might even have found him in Australia.'

'I suppose so.'

'And if Shona walked out on him because of something to do with me, because she believed he was still ... thinking about me ... well, perhaps the marriage was never going to last.'

Ken nodded. He knew Jack had only married Shona because of the baby. But he was beginning to agree with Frankie. There wasn't any point raking through any of this now, even though he wasn't sorry he'd come to meet her. Even now she was a mature woman in her thirties, a wife and mother, he could see why Jack had fallen for her. She was small, slim, and stunning-looking. He could just imagine how she'd looked at seventeen.

'I'll go,' he said, finishing his tea and standing up. 'It was really good of you to agree to meet up with me, Frankie – but I won't take up any more of your time. You're right – we shouldn't be dragging up the past.'

'No – don't go just yet,' she insisted, jumping to her feet and heading for the door. 'I wanted you to meet my sister.'

The sister from Australia. He sat down again. *Oh well, probably should be polite and show some interest.* He waited, looking at his watch, wondering about the times of the trains back to London. He was here in England for a month – he'd taken extended leave from his job, everyone, including his boss, being understanding about the fact that, thanks to the Child Migrant Trust, he'd finally found his father. But already, the time seemed to be flying past. In just over two weeks, he'd be on his way back to Perth, and bearing in mind his father's advancing years, he couldn't say when, or whether, he'd be able to see him again.

He was deep in contemplation of this when the lounge door opened again and Frankie ushered in her sister. She was small and slender like Frankie – almost frail looking – but with a warm smile and, when she said hello, it was with a WA accent that made him feel at home.

'My name's Sue,' she said. 'Good to meet you.'

'Likewise.' They looked at each other awkwardly for a moment. 'Your sister tells me you went out to Oz as a child migrant too?' he added as she sat down.

'Yes. It was actually quite bizarre how my family – my sisters here – found me. I was at a Crazy Snakes concert in Sydney, back in seventy-one. Rob recognised the likeness between us.' She nodded towards Frankie. 'I've been coming over here regularly ever since. I ... guess I'm really lucky – to have been reunited with my family like this. Although ...'

'It doesn't take away the hurt, does it,' Ken finished for her quietly.

'Not completely. I ... I've accepted why my mum put me in the orphanage. I understand that she would have been too ashamed to keep a baby born out of wedlock. Frankie and Marianne – my other sister – have explained she was a very strict Catholic. It would have been hard for her.' She paused. 'But I guess I'll never know why she didn't take me back after she married our father. Or why I got sent out to Australia.'

'I guess there are some things we might never understand. Have you been in touch with the Child Migrant Trust?'

'No. I've only just heard about that. It's great that someone's finally doing something to help people like us find our families. Up till now, nobody I spoke to about it even seemed to believe me – they couldn't believe that it was going on at all. Frankie says they've put you in touch with your father?'

'Yes, they have. It's ... just amazing.' He shook his head. 'Talk about an emotional roller-coaster – I'm still pinching myself. You know what I've found out? My dad only put me into care as a short term measure when my mum died. I was only three, he was working long shifts at the docks and had no-one else to look after me. He told them he'd come back for me as soon as he'd sorted something out. He says he was desperately trying to get hold of an aunt, or cousin, or someone who could come and stay with him to take care of me. But nobody came forward, and the time went on, and what with his work, and his grief over my mum, he didn't get to visit me as much as he should have.' Ken swallowed hard, looked down at the floor and eventually managed to go on, 'The years kind of drifted past, and in the end he'd stopped coming at all. When I got to the age of eleven, apparently the director of the orphanage took it upon himself to decide I'd been abandoned, and that I was a good candidate for the Child Migrants Programme. We were sent to Australia to help boost the population out there – the British government needed to offload some of the disadvantaged kids they were having to look after, and Australia needed *good white stock.*'

Frankie gasped. *'Good white ... ?'*

'Yes. It was seen as a benefit for both countries. I was told my parents were both dead now, that nobody in England wanted me, so I'd be better off somewhere else.'

'Me too,' Sue said quietly. 'I was told the same thing.'

Ken's fists were clenched. He bit his lip, trying to stop himself from reverting to his old habit of punching one hand into the other.

'I was told I'd be given a good education out there, that I'd have a good life, better than I could have had here,' he went on. 'But in fact I was beaten and abused. The only education I got was in slave labour. Back here, I'd passed the scholarship for grammar school. I was going to ...' He took a deep breath. 'I wanted to be a doctor.'

He saw Sue's eyes fill up with tears, and he tried to smile, to reassure her that he was OK now, that it didn't matter, that his life hadn't been so very bad after all – but he couldn't quite seem to manage it.

'Instead,' he finished gruffly, 'I became a drunk and a dropout.'

'That's so sad – so awful,' Frankie said softly.

'I'm not a drunk anymore,' he added quickly. 'Thanks to Shona. She got me off the booze. And out of jail – literally. I owe her a lot. She gave up her family for me.'

'I'm sorry you broke up, then,' Frankie put in. 'I hope it wasn't just because of ... you know. Jack. Me.'

'No – not just. I guess I never really deserved Shona. I'm ... still a bit of a mess. Probably always will be. Hard for anyone to take that on board. But at least she's made her peace with her mum and dad again now. And she's found someone new, apparently – someone who might treat her better.'

There was a silence. He coughed, looked back up at Sue.

'Sorry. Enough about me. How about you – I hope the girls weren't treated as badly as we were?'

'Probably not. We got hit if we played up – you know, if we wet the bed or cried too much. But ...' She ducked her head. 'My worst ordeal came after I left the girls' home.'

'Sue got sent to work on a farm,' Frankie went on when her sister couldn't manage to continue. 'She was only fifteen. She had to cook for the farmer and his men. And the youngest son raped her repeatedly.'

'Jesus fucking *Christ!*' Ken swore under his breath.

'I got away in the end,' Sue said, holding her head up and meeting his eyes again. 'Saved up my money – stole some of it from *him* – and got myself a new life in Melbourne – and now Sydney. I've done OK,' she added firmly, 'I've been lucky.' Ken could tell from her voice that this was what she'd schooled herself to believe, but he nodded slowly. He was impressed by her courage.

'How old were you when they sent you out?'

'Eight,' she said. 'Nineteen-fifty-four. I don't remember much about it.'

'Same year as me,' he said. Sue looked back at him sharply, staring at him now. He shrugged and laughed. 'It'd be funny if we were on the same ship.'

'Where were you living?' she said in a very quiet voice. 'Before – where was the orphanage you came from?'

'Not far from here, actually. Dagenham.'

Sue gasped. 'Really? Me too.' She looked down, taking a quick breath, and then back at him, going on quickly: 'There was a boy called Christopher – on my ship. He was from my orphanage. In Dagenham. He looked after me.' She didn't seem to be able to manage more than a few words at a time. They stared at each other again. 'He was dragged away from me. When we landed at Fremantle.'

'*Susie?*' he said, saying the name as if it had been forced from the very depths of his being. Suddenly he was on his feet, gasping, holding out his hands to her, dropping them by his side again, tears springing to his eyes. 'You're not ... are you telling me you're *her*? Holy shit, I can see it, too! It's you, isn't it – you were that little kid – I can see you now, skinny little thing with pigtails, always crying. Bloody hell, I never imagined I'd find you. I'm so sorry! So sorry!'

'You're *him*? You're Christopher?' She was trying to hold back the tears. 'I wondered, you know – you looked a little familiar, but I thought – because Frankie said your name was Ken, I thought it was ridiculous to even imagine ... '

'Kenneth's my middle name,' he said. 'They made me use it when I arrived at the boys' home, because there was already a Christopher in my dorm. And I never bothered to change back.'

'It's ...' Sue was open-mouthed with shock. 'It's just incredible! I never dared to hope! There must be thousands of kids who went out to Australia – *hundreds* of thousands apparently who got sent out there the same way we did!'

'And ... I promised I'd find you. I remember – still remember it so clearly ...'

'You being carried off on that lorry. They hit you, didn't they – because you tried to stay with me.'

'You were standing watching me on the quayside, left behind, crying, calling out to me. It tore me to shreds. I swore I'd find you again one day. But ... life at that boys' home – it was so tough. So bloody brutal. Eventually I gave up begging and pleading and getting smacked across the face and told to shut up every time I asked about you. It got so that ... well ...' He swallowed hard and looked away. '... there wasn't really room in my head to think about anything other than my own survival. I'm sorry ... it became ...'

'Just a distant memory. I know.'

'But I did try later!' he insisted. 'Years later – I remembered about you, got myself into a right state wishing I hadn't let you down. It was when Jack and I were mates, actually – but I didn't even tell him what I was doing. I kept going to the girls' homes around Perth, annoying the life out of the nuns, demanding to know whether you'd been there! They were no bloody help, though. I think they thought I was a dangerous nutter.'

Sue smiled. She got to her feet, walked towards him, holding out her arms, and as they hugged each other, both giving way to the tears they'd been storing up for each other for over thirty years, Frankie quietly got up and headed for the door.

'I think this calls for more tea and coffee,' she said, wiping her own eyes, 'at the very least.'

But neither of them heard her. They had thirty years to catch up on. Thirty years of memories, thirty years of hurt, thirty years that had, finally, led them back together.

EPILOGUE

Two weeks later : Heathrow Airport

He held her hand as they walked together towards the departure gate: a stocky, good-looking man with closely cropped brown hair and a small, slim woman whose blonde shoulder-length hair was clipped neatly off her face. They turned one last time to wave to their families: her sisters, so alike, with their arms entwined so that their blonde heads were almost touching each other – his elderly father, leaning on the arm of one of his two daughters by his second marriage.

'See you again soon!' one of her sisters shouted just before they went out of sight round the corner.

'Yes!' she called back. They looked at each other and smiled. 'We'll come back together next time!'

They fell into step with each other as they headed for the gate, dropping each other's hands, both suddenly shy now that they were on their own, away from the constant presence of family members.

'Let me take your bag,' he said.

'It's OK. It's light.'

'Are you …?'

'Will you …?'

They laughed, and she began again. 'You first.'

'I was just going to say – will you be staying long? In Perth?'

'Only a few days. I promised Maureen – my boss – I'd go and see one of our suppliers en route home. To be honest I don't relish the thought. I've never been back to WA since … back then.'

He took her hand again. 'You'll be OK.'

'I know.'

'And we'll get together for dinner? Before you fly out again?'

She smiled. 'Of course we will.'

'And I'll be over to Sydney for the weekend in a couple of weeks' time. I expect the best table at your restaurant!'

'Done!' She hesitated. 'And … did you mean what you said yesterday?'

'About moving out of Perth? Abso-bloody-lutely. I should've done it years ago. Meeting you, hearing how you moved away, got yourself together, changed your life – it's made me realise where I've gone wrong – hanging onto the past, feeling sorry for myself.'

'That's not …'

'It's true! And now I've got nothing to stay there for, nobody apart from Shona and Steven. Shona's been a good friend but she needs to live her own life now, and as long as I'm hanging around, it's not easy for her. And Steven …' He shrugged. 'He's not my son. I love him, you know – but if we can't maintain a relationship interstate, it doesn't say much for either of us.'

'Well, as long as you're not going to rush into anything.'

'What?' He stopped and turned her towards him, gently. 'What, like rushing into something with someone I've known since I was eleven?'

'Someone you've only just met up with again after thirty-odd years,' she corrected him. But she was grinning back at him. 'I think both our families were worried that we *are* rushing things, you know.'

'I think they're just happy for us, actually. Anyway – we're not moving in together, are we. Not straight away,' he added.

'Not until you move to Sydney permanently,' she agreed. 'It could be difficult until you do!' They both laughed.

And they continued on to their departure gate, joining the queue of travellers showing their passports and boarding cards, waiting for their flight to start boarding, waiting to leave the country of their birth all over again.

But this time there was no-one shouting at them, no-one blowing a whistle and telling them to hurry up. No-one calling him a troublemaker for wanting to stay with Susie, pushing him and hitting him because he wanted to protect her. This time there was no need for tears, no need for the terror of the unknown, the horror of being parted from the one person in the world they could call a friend.

This time they were going back to Australia voluntarily, because it was their home. This time they weren't being parted – they were coming back together.

'Don't worry, Susie,' he said, gripping her hand tighter as the crowd of passengers finally surged towards the walkway to the plane. He grinned at her, and suddenly it seemed like only yesterday – that fateful day in nineteen-fifty-four. The day he'd lost her. 'Stay close to me,' he said, and this time he knew it was true: 'You'll be all right.'

'We both will,' she said, squeezing his hand back. 'Finally, Christopher –' She hesitated, looking at him a little shyly, 'Are you sure you don't mind if I call you that?'

'I think I prefer it. Especially from you.'

She smiled. 'Then, finally, Christopher, I think we're both going to be all right. Let's go home.'

Author's Note:

The transportation of child migrants to Australia and other Commonwealth countries actually happened on a large scale from the late 19th century until the 1960s. My story and characters are entirely fictional, but in writing this book I was inspired and helped by reading the true account in the book EMPTY CRADLES by Margaret Humphreys, which was made into a film called ORANGES AND SUNSHINE.

Printed in Great Britain
by Amazon